THE ACCELERATES
FORTY DAYS TO DUST

TAK SALMASTYAN

www.TakSalmastyan.com

First Printing

Praise for *The Accelerates: Forty Days to Dust*

"A hauntingly lyrical descent into a fractured world where memory and survival collide." — ***The Literary Reporter***

"A riveting post-apocalyptic tale with a memorable cast." — ***Kirkus Reviews***

"The writing is intense, sometimes brutal, but always meant to push you deeper into the emotional core of the story." — ***Literary Titan***

"A well-written dystopian novel about a world ravaged by a dangerous virus outbreak." — ***Readers' Favorite***

*For the ones we love,
and for those in memory.*

"A friend loves at all times, and a brother is born for adversity."—Proverbs 17:17

Introduction

In a world torn apart by a viral apocalypse, fifteen-year-old Ethan Mercer lives for one purpose: to protect his brother, Leo. A one-year-old trapped in a body aging at an unspeakable rate, Leo embodies both the horror of humanity's tampering and the last thread of hope for redemption. Unlike the savage Accelerates, twisted children of the virus, Leo clings to the fragments of his humanity, his innocence a fragile spark in a world bent on erasure.

With Mia and Clara, now infected and transformed by the company that unleashed this nightmare, Ethan embarks on a harrowing journey through the ruins of their former life. They cross a landscape decimated by GeneCorp's creations, but it is Leo's unyielding grip on his humanity that drives them forward. Through fire and blood, they face the painful truth that Leo, the source of their hope, may also become the harbinger of the world's final downfall.

In a final act of self-sacrifice, Leo accepts his fate, altering the course of their fractured world in a way no one could have foreseen. His transformation becomes a force of reckoning, a desperate attempt to salvage what remains of humanity, to restore something more than GeneCorp's monstrous legacy. In the aftermath, the earth bears the weight of the loss, and the survivors must learn to rebuild.

Years later, amidst the ruins, the last of the living plant sunflowers in a place they name Leoland, where the ground holds the whispers of those lost and the promise of rebirth. It becomes a sanctuary where love endures long after the ashes have settled, a testament to hope's enduring light when everything else has turned to dust.

Part I

Chapter 1. Prologue: The Birth of the Collapse

1.1: Leo

The air was thick with the acrid taste of ash, stinging Ethan's lungs as he clutched his brother's hand. Their grip was unyielding, palms slick with sweat and soot, the residue of a dying world. Each breath scraped against their insides, like inhaling the very essence of death itself. The wind howled, dragging ash through the air, coating everything in a blanket of gray, as if the earth had exhaled its last breath, leaving only decay.

Ethan glanced down at Leo, barely one yet walking like a child five times his age. His legs wobbled beneath him, as if the rapid growth had aged his frame, burdening him with limbs not yet his own. His tiny hand clung to Ethan's with innocent determination, aware, or perhaps disturbed, by the devastation that surrounded them.

Leo's angelic face bore a weight no child should carry. His cobalt-blue eyes, too sharp, too knowing, looked up at Ethan with a gaze that spoke of loss, of understanding far beyond his age. It was a look no child should wear. A quiet recognition of something irreparably broken. The world that had once promised him a future was slipping through his fingers like sand, leaving him stranded in the nightmare of a violent virus that was forcing him to grow by the minute.

***

Ethan had always wanted a brother. Whether older or younger, it didn't matter, he just longed for someone to share adventures with. He dreamed of a companion to climb the treehouse with, play baseball under the golden sun, and whisper secrets beneath a blanket of stars. A sister wouldn't have been so bad either, but the idea of a brother had firmly anchored itself in his heart.

That wish came true when Leo was born.

Ethan was thirteen then, already dreaming, imagining the memories they'd make. The world, still intact and ordinary, held nothing but promise.

He had watched protectively as his parents brought Leo home, marveling at the tiny, wriggling bundle in their arms. Every gurgle and coo ignited Ethan's imagination. He pictured the two of them racing through the backyard, building forts on rainy days, sneaking extra marshmallows into their cocoa on winter nights. Leo would trail him everywhere, eyes wide with awe. Ethan would finally know what it meant to be a big brother.

He cherished the sound of Leo's laughter filling the house, a bright, bubbling joy that could turn even the dullest afternoon into something magical. Every milestone, his first grasp, his wobbly steps, babble morphing into words, was met with Ethan's cheers. He loved the weight of Leo's chubby arms around his neck, the way his giggles floated through the air like wind chimes.

But those dreams shattered before they even began.

When Leo was nine months old, the first signs of illness appeared, a slight fever, a pale complexion. Ethan noticed how his brother's laughter weakened, how the light in his eyes began to dim. He asked his parents what was wrong, but they only spoke in hushed voices, faces tight with worry.

Days passed. Then weeks.

Leo stopped crawling. His cries thinned to night whispers.

Doctors came and went, murmuring complicated words Ethan couldn't understand. He hated the lingering smell of antiseptic and the muffled sobs he heard from behind closed doors.

But what he hated most was helplessness.

He could do nothing but watch as Leo began to fade.

***

When the first injection from GeneCorp arrived, it brought cautious relief. Leo's fever broke. Color returned to his cheeks. He even laughed, a fragile, breathless laugh that lit Ethan's world again.

For a moment, it felt like the nightmare was over. But it wasn't. The real nightmare had only just begun.

On Leo's first birthday, April twenty-first, the unimaginable began. His limbs stretched. His skin thickened. His eyes shifted to a brilliant, unnatural cobalt blue. His face took on an angelic, almost ethereal quality.

Each day, he grew, in size, in strength, in knowledge. By the end of forty days, Leo had the body of a five-year-old and the eyes of someone who had lived lifetimes. Ethan could no longer lift him. And the warmth, the laughter, gone. In its place: chilling silence. A calculating stare that unsettled Ethan in ways he couldn't name.

And then the world began to crumble.

Whispers of other children, just like Leo, spread through the news. They were called Accelerates. Biological miracles. Or abominations, depending on whom you asked.

Cities locked down. Schools shuttered. Fear spread like fire.

Ethan clung to the brother he had once prayed for. But Leo was no longer just a brother. He became a warning. The world, once filled with promises, now teetered on the edge of something dark. Something irreversible.

1.2: The First Cry

The fluorescent lights above Clara's head buzzed, their harsh glare leaching warmth from her skin. Each contraction carved her breath into jagged gasps, serrated, vicious, unrelenting. She wasn't breathing anymore, not really. She was surviving each second one scream at a time. The sterile scent of the vinyl mattress beneath her clung to the air, mingling with the musk of sweat pooling at her back. Somewhere, a faucet dripped, synchronizing with the fetal monitor's beeps, a metronome ticking toward something unnamed.

"One more push, Clara," Dr. Varma urged. Her voice stayed steady, but her eyes flicked to the clock, then Clara's bloodied claws. The second hand jerked forward as if time itself were splintering.

Clara's mind flitted back to the sunflower fields just weeks ago. She had laughed, her belly swollen with the life she was about to bring into the world. The promise of Ava. But now, as the hours stretched on, that laughter felt like a distant echo, a cruel joke.

The air stung her throat, lemon and bleach pretending to be clean and behind her eyes, the image of Mark, his wedding band cold against her palm, began to blur. He had been there at the start, but now his absence clung like a shadow she couldn't outrun.

***

Her forehead met the glass. Cold bit into her skin like teeth. Her breath fogged the surface, forming a trembling halo: saint, ghost, mother. All of it blurred by fingerprints.

Inside the isolation, her baby girl lay under harsh UV light. Wires and tubes coiled around her, feeding fluids into her veins. The pulse of crimson veins across her chest: lub-dub, lub-dub, was a haunting lullaby.

"What is that?" Clara whispered, pressing her palm to the glass.

Dr. Varma appeared beside her, her voice clipped. "Her telomeres are regenerating forty times faster than normal."

"English, Priya."

"She's aging," Dr. Varma said, the words blunt and cold. "By tomorrow, her bones will rival those of a three-month-old."

Clara's stomach churned. "Is it contagious?"

The silence felt like betrayal.

The baby's eyes snapped open, too aware, pupils dilated wide like a cat's. Her tiny fist clenched the IV, yanking it taut. Alarms blared. One foot twitched. Her mouth opened, not to cry, but to mimic breath, like she was trying to speak before she had ever wept.

"She shouldn't be able to do that," Clara breathed.

A nurse rushed in, trembling. The infant tracked the nurse, her lips curling into a rictus: part smile, part threat.

Clara slammed her palms against the glass, her breath ragged, her heart pounding. "You're taking her to research. No!"

Dr. Varma's voice softened as she gripped Clara's shoulder. The grip was maternal, clinical, apologetic. All of them at once, and not enough. "We need to move her. CDC protocols."

Clara's knees buckled. The scent of Mark's abandoned coffee still lingered as a cruel reminder. He had brewed it that morning, humming, promising to come back. It was his ritual: coffee, then their morning walk. Coffee, then life. That smell lingered: his last gift, rising like smoke from the ashes of everything they'd built. She tried to steady herself, but her body betrayed her. The pain of helplessness surged.

1.3: Forty Days to Dust

Clara jolted awake as the alarms blared, a shrill, grinding and sound that scraped against her bones. The lights flickered. Jagged shadows slithered across the walls. Her ribs ached, sharp and raw, a raw reminder of the hollow where her baby had been. The call button slipped from her sweat-slick fingers, clattering to the floor just as the door burst open.

Nurses flooded the hallway, their blue scrubs blending into a panicked wave, faces masked, anonymous, interchangeable.

Clara staggered to her feet, her legs trembling as though the marrow had been drained from her bones. The cold metal of the IV pole pressed against her palm, its wheels squeaking like tortured mice as she lurched into the corridor. The air was thick with the smell of antiseptic, tainted by something darker, perhaps burning insulation or the acrid tang of ozone that precedes a lightning strike. With each step, her bare feet stuck to the linoleum, and the foot that peeled from the tile seemed to synchronize with the intercom's monotone announcement: "Code Blue, NICU. Code Blue..."

No. No, no, no...

The observation window loomed ahead, its glass smeared with the greasy residue of countless desperate palms. Through it, Clara saw her.

Her baby girl.

Not her baby.

The isolate was too small now. Her body grotesquely distended, six-month-old proportions achieved in seven days. Limbs rippled with muscle, their ropy contours stretching the skin so thin it seemed translucent. Crimson veins spiraled across her chest, fractal patterns pulsing like bioluminescent fungi. Her eyes glowed cobalt under the UV lamps, slitting pupils widening as a nurse adjusted her oxygen tube.

"Shh, sweetheart," the nurse cooed, her gloved hand trembling.

The baby's gurgle turned into a laugh, wet and guttural, a sound no infant's throat should make. Tiny fingers clamped around the nurse's wrist with a crack that shattered the latex. The nurse yelped, jerking back as the monitors erupted in a cacophony of noise: not just alarms, but a dissonant chime, like a funeral dirge.

"Stop!" Clara slammed her fists against the glass. The impact rattled her bones. "You're scaring her! Let me in...!"

Dr. Varma appeared, her presence marked by the sharp scent of iodine and stale coffee. Her gloves were streaked with black fluid, faint smoke curling from her hands.

"Clara, don't,"

"What did you do to her?" Clara suddenly turned, her hand gripping the IV pole so hard that the needles scattered like silverfish when it crashed to the floor. She lunged forward, fingernails carving crescents into the doctor's arms. "You turned her into, into this..."

This was her fault. She had asked for medicine. She had begged God for a miracle to save her baby. And He had delivered a star-devouring angel instead.

Dr. Varma grasped Clara's shoulders, pulling her back with surprising strength. Her mask slipped, revealing chapped lips and shadowed eyes.

"We're moving her to containment. It's the CDC's orders."

"She's mine..."

Inside the isolation room, the baby went unnervingly still. Her head turned, joints popping, until those cobalt eyes locked onto Clara's. The rash beneath her skin flared, revealing a network of luminous veins converging at her fingertips, pulsing in time with the intercom's announcement:

"Containment protocol Alpha initiated…"

Clara's knees buckled. Dr. Varma caught her, lowering her gently to the floor as hazmat teams rushed past, their suits rustling like the shells of insects. The baby's laughter echoed through the speakers, a twisted lullaby, sweet yet sharp.

"Her telomeres are… unraveling," Dr. Varma murmured, her voice a hollow echo as she directed her words more toward the shadows than to Clara. "GeneCorp Virus-40-DZX. Forty times faster. Forty days to…"

Clara didn't hear the rest. The world seemed to blur. Her baby's lips parted, gums glowing raw and swollen, and a single word slipped out:

"Mama."

It resonated low, vibrating the glass until her fillings hummed, in perfect harmony with the shrieking alarms.

Dr. Varma yanked Clara upright.

"Go home. Rest. I'm afraid this is going to take time."

1.4: Day Forty

The power went out at 3:17 a.m., severing the city's mechanical heartbeat. Silence descended like a suffocating blanket, so profound Clara could hear the drip of her sweat hitting the mattress. Moonlight carved the bedroom in silver and black, a monochrome prison. The air felt heavy, saturated with a cloying sweetness, like fruit left to rot in the dark.

Clara was alone in their bed. Mark had left after her labor, for fresh air, forty days ago. He had fled, or perhaps vanished. The shadows had swallowed him without protest. Coward. She could still trace the hollow imprint of his absence in the dented pillow beside her. The mattress still held the ghost of his weight, but the cold sheets offered no comfort.

Her throat burned from days screaming her daughter's name into the void.

"Ava."

The name escaped her cracked lips like a prayer, but the walls remained silent. No answering cry. No soft gurgle. Just the rhythmic drip from a leaking faucet, like a mocking taunt.

Ava. Ava. Ava. She repeated it, not as a name, but a command. As if calling back a goddess she once dared name. It echoed, distorting in the air around her.

The nursery pulsed with unnatural gravity, as if time itself avoided it. She hadn't entered it since Mark left. The door, just a sliver of darkness, remained ajar, daring her to step inside. The mobile above the crib must be frozen now, paper stars caught mid-twirl. The pastel walls, so lovingly painted, would be bare and accusatory.

But worse than the silence was the smell.

Sickly sweet, it crept through the air vents, growing stronger each night. It resembled spoiled milk, like something left to rot. She had searched desperately under the floorboards and behind the walls. Nothing. Yet the smell lingered, clinging to her skin and hair. She could taste it when she swallowed.

Outside, the city remained dark. No hum of refrigerators. No distant wail of sirens. Even the streetlights had surrendered. The sky, stripped of its artificial glow, pulsed with a thousand unfamiliar stars, staring down at her unblinkingly.

The basement generator refused to start. Mark had promised to fix it, one of his many unfinished tasks. Clara had long since stopped trying. Each attempt left her hands slick with oil and her heart heavier with frustration. The lanterns were useless now, drained of fuel. Only the pale moonlight remained to illuminate the room.

She shifted beneath the sheets, the damp fabric clinging to her skin. The air tasted of copper. Somewhere, a clock ticked, though she hadn't set one. Its presence unnerved her; she didn't own a clock that ticked.

"Ava."

The name trembled in the air, but it no longer sounded like her own voice. It echoed, distorted as if someone else had whispered it from the far corner of the room.

The shadows thickened. Movement teased the edges of her vision, a slight, swaying shape, like a child on unsteady legs.

The crib was empty, she reminded herself. She hadn't set foot in the nursery.

Hadn't she? The door had been closed. She remembered that. Didn't she?

The clock continued to tick. The air grew heavier. And still, the power did not return.

"Ava."

The name repeated relentlessly, until Clara could no longer tell who was calling whom.

Then, a rustle from the corner.

Clara's breath hitched.

On the windowsill, backlit by the bloated moon, perched a silhouette. Limbs elongated. Joints bent at impossible angles. Skin mottled with a lattice of crimson veins, now necrotic at the edges, blackened, charred, as if she'd clawed through hell itself. The hospital gown hung in tatters, revealing muscle fibers that writhed like worms beneath translucent skin.

Her face, though, still round, still angelic, twisted into a smile that split her cheeks too broad, too wrong.

"Mommy." The voice didn't plead, it summoned.

The voice, gravel and honey, innocence, and decay, sank talons into Clara's spine. She recoiled, her back slamming against the bed's metal rails.

"Ava...?"

The figure shifted. A bone cracked as her limbs adjusted, the sound reverberating in the oppressive stillness. Moonlight pooled in her wide, gleaming eyes, too cobalt, too bright, too knowing. Ava's head tilted, strands of hair clinging to her gaunt face.

"Missed you, Mommy," she said, her voice crawling under Clara's skin. "Come closer. Say my name again. Let me in."

Clara's stomach lurched. The words crawled from the child's mouth like maggots from carrion. She tried to move, but her body betrayed her, paralyzed by fear.

"You're not supposed to be here," Clara hissed, narrowing her eyes as she took a step forward instead of back.

Ava's high-pitched, choked laughter filled the room, a warped echo of bedtime giggles. The air thickened, reeking of copper and something sickly sweet. Clara's fingers clutched the sheets, her knuckles whitening.

"You watched, didn't you?" Ava said. "You watched them take me and did nothing. That's why I come back, to remind you what apathy tastes like."

"No," Clara choked out. "I tried. I tried to save you."

But Ava crept closer. Each step oozed malice, the floorboards beneath her bare feet groaning. Bruised veins pulsed as if something dark and ancient slithered beneath her skin.

They said I was broken. But look at me now, Mommy. I'm the prototype. I'm the first wave."

Her smile widened, an unnatural maw gleaming with crimson-stained teeth. Shadows twisted, bending unnaturally around her form. The air pulsed with a low hum, like a distant heartbeat.

And now you can hear them too," Ava said. "They're not whispers anymore. They're orders. I'm not haunting you. I'm recruiting you."

Clara stumbled from the bed, her pulse roaring in her ears. She clawed at the door, fingers slipping against the handle. Locked. The walls pulsed, synchronizing to Ava's voice. A distant wail echoed through the dark, a thousand voices whispering in unison.

Ava loomed, her eyes glowing with the light of the gibbous moon. Her arms reached out, impossibly long, veins writhing beneath her flesh.

"Stay," Ava hissed, her voice layered and fractured.

Clara's scream tore through the night, swallowed by shadows slithering across the floor. The whispers grew louder, the walls shuddering under their weight. The door rattled as unseen forces pressed from the other side.

Then, silence.

Ava's smile lingered, a twisted echo of what once was.

"Soon."

She tilted her head like a spider assessing prey. Moonlight caught her eyes, slit pupils dilating, reflective as a cat's.

"They'll call me Patient Zero," she crooned, swinging a leg over the windowsill. "But I'm just the first note."

Clara's hand flailed for the phone, fingers brushing cold plastic.

"Don't," Ava giggled, the sound like shattered glass. "They're sleeping. Even Priya." She licked her lips. "She tasted like almonds. Bitter. Sweet."

Clara's stomach convulsed. Dr. Varma's perfume, always almond oil. "What did you do?"

Ava dropped to the floor, limbs unfolding with liquid precision. Her feet left steaming prints, the air thick with scorched ozone. She crouched beside the bed, her breath reeking of copper and burnt sugar, the scent of candied apples at a funeral.

"Fixed things," she whispered, tracing a finger along her wrist. Veins pulsed beneath the paper-thin skin, dark tendrils twisting like roots.

"Where is Daddy? Is he scared?" she asked in a singsong voice, mocking. A laugh spilled from her lips, wild, untamed. It reverberated through the room, twisting Clara's insides.

The memories struck without warning.

***

The ultrasound room hummed softly. Mark squeezed Clara's hand, anticipation shining in his eyes. Dr. Varma's gentle chuckle broke the tension. "Ten fingers, ten toes. Perfect." The image on the screen flickered, revealing a tiny heartbeat, steady and strong. Ava. Her name had come so easily, as if it were always meant to be.

But there had been a shadow too. A faint smudge along the edge of the scan.

"Just an artifact," Dr. Varma had assured her, her voice calm and soothing.

Now that echo mocked Clara.

Lub-dub. Lub-dub.

***

"Do you remember, Mommy?" Ava's voice jolted Clara back to the present. The girl's fingers twitched, and the air filled with an electric hum. Shadows along the wall seemed to pulse with her movements.

Clara's throat tightened. "This isn't you. You're sick. We can fix this."

Ava's smile widened, splitting pale lips too far. "Fix?" She trailed her fingers along the bedpost, her nails scraping against the wood. "They tried, remember? The tubes, the needles. But I fixed myself. I'm better now."

A gust of wind rattled the windowpane, and distant sirens howled in the background. The city beyond the walls was no longer a refuge. Reports of GeneCorp Virus-40-DZX had spread like wildfire, fueling panic and triggering quarantine measures.

Ava traced the veins on her wrist once more, narrowing her eyes. "Daddy ran, didn't he? He left us. Just like they all will."

Clara's heart twisted at the thought. She wanted to deny it, but the empty side of the bed spoke louder than words. Mark's absence pulsed like a wound.

"But it's okay, Mommy," Ava said, stepping closer, her voice a low purr. "We don't need him." Her fingertips hovered just above Clara's cheek. "We have each other."

Day Forty.

Forty days since birth.

Forty days since the old world died screaming.

1.5: Ethan

Wilson Middle School exhaled its last breath of innocence. The power flickered off at 9:07 a.m., and though the basement generator kicked in, it sputtered out just moments later.

Only a handful of students had shown up for class.

The hallways, once alive with the sounds of squeaking sneakers and carefree laughter, now echoed with a silence so thick it pressed against Ethan's eardrums. The classroom felt frozen, time preserved in crayon and glue. Construction-paper galaxies curled, crayon dinosaurs mid-roar, stick-figure families grinning beneath a sun. Fluorescent lights buzzed like dying wasps, their flickers casting twitching shadows over the drawings.

One by one, the few students who had shown up left.

Mrs. Naltakian, her face as pale as chalk, muttered about her granddaughter's backpack. Mr. Carter refused to look at anyone as he yanked his daughter's arm hard enough to leave bruises. Last was Lila Morales, her mother's gold crucifix swinging wildly as she hissed, "This is not a school anymore."

The intercom crackled, emitting static that tasted metallic on Ethan's tongue.

Principal Alvarez, her voice fraying, said, "Shelter in place. Police are responding to..." A wet gurgle abruptly cut her off. New voices slithered through the speakers, children's voices, giggling and breathing into the mic.

Ethan rushed to the window.

He thought they were mannequins, until they held hands. Until they sang.

Across the street, the Sunshine Daycare was engulfed in flames, its pastel sign melting into distorted letters. Fire trucks stood idle, their hoses limp like dead snakes. Firefighter Ramirez, Ethan recognized him by the Cubs cap he wore, stepped forward, his voice cracking: "C'mon kids, let's..."

"Ring around the Rosie..."

The song floated up, harmonized by a dozen voices. But it didn't come from the street; it came from the school's charred playground.

Ethan's breath fogged the glass. There they were, first graders, maybe second, moving in lockstep through the smoke. Maria Torres led them, her pink unicorn backpack charred, her eyes reflecting flames like twin supernovas.

"Pocket full of posies..."

Firefighter Ramirez stumbled back. "What the..."

They surged forward.

Maria was the first to reach firefighter Ramirez. Her small hands, still adorned with glittery nail polish, gripped his turnout coat. The others rushed in, a blur of denim and teeth that seemed too sharp. A wet crunch echoed in the chaos as the hose twisted, spraying water that was a deep red, resembling blood.

Ethan's knees buckled beneath him, and the floor felt like it was tilting.

"Ashes... ashes..."

The intercom hissed, and lockers rattled. Down the hall, something scraped, was it nails on a chalkboard? No, it was nails on lockers.

His phone shook. Mom. Dad. Leo. The line rang once, twice...

The window. The fire escape. He needed to move.

As he wrenched the window open, freezing air slapped his face, carrying the stench of burning plastic and vanilla. Maybe it was from the daycare's snack cupboard.

Below, the playground stood empty. Maria's backpack lay abandoned, crayons and a class photos spilling from it, smiles now a cruel reminder.

His phone buzzed with a text from his mother:

Mom: Leo won't stop humming that song. I can't pick you up. Neither can Dad. You have to walk home.

The message ended.

Somewhere, glass shattered, and the tapping grew louder.

Ethan climbed down the fire escape, which shivered under his feet. Above him, the classroom lights went out with a final pop. In the dark, the dinosaur drawings glowed faintly, their teeth elongated in the shadows.

1.6: Mia

Mia Davtian was twelve years old last year when her sister Clara married her high school sweetheart, Mark. Clara had always been Mia's compass, her rock, her inspiration. With a heart full of joy, Mia eagerly anticipated the arrival of her niece, Ava. She dreamed of sunny afternoons in the sunflower fields, where laughter would echo through the breeze as Clara and Ava held hands with her, the golden petals swaying around them. Their family farm was her sanctuary, a place of warmth, resilience, and endless summers.

But that night, her dreams shattered.

Mia jolted awake to the sound of her mother's screams, which tore through the darkness, raw and frantic. Her father's voice roared back, his urgent commands lost in chaos. Heart pounding, Mia stumbled from her bed. The walls of her room pulsed with an ominous glow; shadows writhed and twisted like specters, and fear clutched at her chest as she staggered to the window. Outside, the night was ablaze.

Flames devoured the barn, a monstrous inferno crackling with savage hunger. Smoke choked the stars, curling skyward like ink spilled on velvet. Embers danced, spiraling upward before vanishing into the void. Through the acrid haze, she saw her parents struggling against the raging blaze.

Mia watched, her hands pressed against the glass, as her mother wrestled with the stubborn barn door, barefoot in the dirt, her arms trembling. Her father, his face streaked with soot, called to the terrified horses inside. The animals' screams mixed with the roar of the flames, their eyes wide with primal fear. Outside, the fire lashed at the sky like furious serpents.

"No," she whispered, her voice drowned out by the raging storm of fire.

The horses reared and kicked, their sleek bodies illuminated by bursts of orange and gold. Her father pulled desperately at the ropes, but the flames rose, consuming the broken wood. The roof groaned as beams twisted and snapped beneath the heat.

Then came the collapse.

A thunderous roar. A blast of sparks. The barn buckled inward, swallowed whole.

Mia's scream snagged in her throat as she clawed at the window, her nails scraping against the cold glass. The twisted shadows of the fire danced across her tear-streaked face. For a brief moment, the night seemed to hold its breath, then it was gone. The barn lay in ruins, a skeletal husk glowing with embers.

There were no voices. No movement. Only the hiss of smoldering ash and the faint echoes of giggles and singing: "Ring around the Rosie..."

Mia's knees buckled as she collapsed to the floor, sobs wracking her small frame. The world outside blurred through the fog of her tears. Clara's wedding, Ava's first smile, the sunflower fields, now distant and unreachable. Only smoke and the bitter sting of loss remained.

She curled inward as sirens wailed in the distance. The stars had vanished behind the thick smoke, and Mia knew that nothing would ever be the same again. She sat on the floor of her bedroom, knees tucked to her chest, trembling under the weight of the night. The echoes of her mother's screams and her father's desperate shouts still rang in her ears. From the window, the remnants of flames crackled in the distance, their dying embers casting eerie shadows that danced along her walls. The barn was gone. Her parents, swallowed by the blaze. The grief throbbed through her, thick and unbearable.

She clutched her phone, its screen smeared with trembling fingerprints. Call logs and messages remained unanswered.

"Clara, please," she whispered, her voice quivering as tears spilled down her face. She had called repeatedly, left voicemails, and sent texts, but there was still no response. Her sister's silence was a void, threatening to consume her. The thought that Clara might also be gone twisted her heart until it ached.

Her sobs broke free, raw, and unrelenting. She cried for her parents, for the life that had been shattered in an instant, and for the fear that gnawed at her every thought. Yet amidst the sorrow, a flicker of determination sparked within her. Clara was still out there. Ava was still out there. They had to be. And Mia was no longer a child who could wait for someone else to save them.

She wiped her face with the sleeve of her shirt, restraining herself. She wouldn't let fear hold her captive. Her hands trembled as she emptied her school backpack, letting the textbooks and notebooks tumble to the floor. In their place, she packed with purpose: a flashlight, bottles of water, a first-aid kit, and granola bars. She also included a Swiss Army knife that her father had given her last Christmas. From the closet, she pulled out her thick cargo pants and sturdy hiking boots. The hoodie that Clara had once borrowed still had a faint scent of her sister's perfume. She slipped it on, feeling its warmth, both physical and emotional.

Downstairs, the silence of the farmhouse was unbearable. Every creak of the floorboards made her flinch, but she pressed on. At the back door, her father's old toolbox sat rusted and worn. She pried it open, and the metallic scent mingled with memories of his steady hands. A crowbar gleamed beneath the clutter, and she gripped it firmly.

Above the toolbox, her slingshot hung on the wall, the same one she used to scare off rats. She pulled it from its hook, feeling its familiar weight settle into her palm. Without hesitation, she slid it into the side pocket of her cargo pants, a small sense of reassurance flickering through her. Then, she opened the cabinet drawer, rummaging through its contents until she found all the available glass slingshot ammunition. She tucked one pack into her left pocket and carefully placed the rest in her backpack, ensuring they were secure.

One last glance around the house, the very place that had once been filled with laughter and warmth, revealed it as a hollow shell. The walls seemed to hum with the remnants of the fire's rage. Mia's tears welled up again, but she didn't let them fall. Taking a shaky breath, she squared her shoulders and stepped through the door.

The night air was sharp and bitter, and smoke lingered, curling through the skeletal remains of the barn. She averted her gaze, unwilling to see what lay beneath the ashes. The moon hung low, casting a pale silver light that barely illuminated the winding road ahead.

"I'll find you, Clara," Mia whispered into the darkness. Her voice trembled, but her resolve remained strong.

She adjusted the backpack on her shoulders, tightening her grip on the crowbar. With one last look at the farmhouse, she turned away. Each step through the embers felt like crossing from her old life into the shadowed unknown. But no matter what lay ahead, Mia's path was clear.

She was determined to find her big sister, her North Star. Her inspiration.

1.7: The World Stopped Breathing

Three years earlier, during a nationally televised presidential debate, candidate Gabriel Dion promised that, if elected, he would usher the country into a new Golden Era. He vowed sweeping reforms across education, healthcare, and housing, an ambitious plan that, he claimed, would empower the next generation: the so-called Genius Generation.

When pressed by his opponent on how exactly he intended to achieve such monumental change, and particularly how he planned to "boost the Genius Generation," Dion offered a single, confident answer:

"By science."

At the time, Dion was a junior senator and the former CEO of GeneCorp.

Following his election, taxpayer-funded research grants began flowing directly into GeneCorp's R&D department. Initially, the company's public focus was a revolutionary cancer treatment, based on the research of world-renowned geneticist Dr. Anya Voss.

But soon, GeneCorp shifted course.

The cancer cure faded quietly into the background as the company began channeling resources into developing a controversial line of hormone-based infertility drugs. These treatments, administered during pregnancy under tightly controlled conditions, allowed prospective parents to design their children in utero. Through DNA manipulation, parents could select desired traits, eye color, hair color, skin tone, and even gender, sexual orientation, and projected profession.

What had begun as a promise of progress had transformed into something else entirely: the commodification of human life, masked behind the glowing façade of scientific innovation.

Today in Washington D.C., now President Gabriel Dion was preparing to address a nation on the brink. A crisis had erupted just a day earlier: swift, chaotic, and still unraveling. Now, he stood ready to speak.

The Oval Office burned beneath the harsh glare of camera lights, its polished surfaces sparkling under studio brightness that turned the air hard with heat and tension.

Dion clutched the mahogany podium, his knuckles pale with strain. The scent of lemon polish and hairspray clung to the room, mixing with the subtle musk of his cologne as a thin disguise against the sharp, metallic tang of fear.

Behind him, the presidential seal flashed: the polished emblem of authority in a world coming undone.

The camera zoomed in, catching the glisten of sweat on his upper lip. Off-screen, a silent TV ticker scrolled:

>>> BEGIN NATIONAL BROADCAST <<<

PRESIDENT GABRIEL DION:

"My fellow Americans, let me be clear: these incidents are isolated. There is no cause for alarm."

Camera zooms in. Sweat visible on the upper lip. Teleprompter scrolls: 'RIOTS IN MILWAUKEE HOSPITAL — INFANT QUARANTINE FAILED.'

PRESIDENT GABRIEL DION:

"Our scientists assure us this is a rare genetic anomaly," Dion continued.

He lingered on the word 'anomaly,' tasting it like something spoiled.

"It is treatable. Containable."

TV screens flicker. Emergency sirens activate across major cities.

The world wasn't listening anymore.

First in D.C. Then New York. Then Chicago, Los Angeles.

And within hours, the howling swept from coast to coast; from the northern reaches to the southern border, from east to west, a deafening symphony of panic that drowned every city, every home.

In less than twenty-four hours, the world was screaming.

And seventy-two hours later the entire planet was in silence.

Dark and absolute.

The kind that falls only when the world itself stops breathing.

Chapter 2: Only Memories and Each Other

2.1: The End is a Child

The oversized hoodie hung loosely on Leo's growing frame like a ghost, swallowing him whole. The fabric, which may have once offered a comforting embrace, felt like a shroud, a grim reminder of life before the virus ravaged the world. It showed how quickly everything had changed and how little time had passed between the promise of tomorrow and the desolate wasteland they now walked through. The hoodie's worn edges fluttered like flags of surrender, as if it, too, had given up the battle against the inevitable.

Around them, the city sprawled in grotesque disarray. What was once a thriving metropolis had become a broken carcass. The skeletal remains of towering skyscrapers pierced the smog-choked sky like broken ribs, their bony fingers reaching desperately for something they would never grasp. These buildings stood as silent witnesses to the end of an era, their jagged windows splintered like broken glass, leaving only hollow shells behind. The city, once teeming with life, purpose, and hope, had turned into a barren wasteland, a monument to human hubris and the unforgiving hand of nature.

Every step they took felt heavier, as though the very ground beneath them had absorbed the pain of its people and now refused to let them go unscathed. The crumbling streets were littered with debris, burned-out cars, discarded belongings, and remnants of lives abruptly cut short. Graffiti slashed the walls in violent strokes, urgent words spray-painted in stark letters:

THE END IS A CHILD.

It was as if the very walls were crying out for a final reckoning, expressing truths no one had dared voice before the world collapsed. The message was haunting, an omen etched into the bones of a civilization that had long since forgotten how to care. It was more than a warning, it was a confession. The virus, a twisted, uncontrollable force that had changed everything, was born of humanity's own arrogance. Their need to play God had birthed a catastrophe that unraveled everything.

The end had arrived in the form of a child, innocent, yet destructive. The virus had stolen that innocence and replaced it with something darker, something terrifyingly powerful. The last fragile vestiges of humanity now lay in the hands of those too young to understand the enormity of the world they were inheriting. Yet Leo, though part of this new generation, was also something else. He stood between two worlds, the final flicker of what once was and the inevitable collapse of what would come.

"Ethan, my legs hurt," Leo whined, his voice wavering between childish complaint and something deeper, something raw. The sound gnawed at Ethan's heart, no child should have to speak like that. And yet, there it was, spilling from his little brother's mouth with unsettling clarity. Ethan could hear the strain beneath the words; there was exhaustion, yes, but something else, something too old for Leo's small frame. It was as if his body, already fighting to keep pace with the virus, was beginning to rebel. The creeping edge of pain, something neither of them could fully understand, cut through Leo's voice, as if the child inside him was being buried under the weight of transformation.

Ethan glanced down at Leo's feet, and his heart sank. The sneakers, once bright and clean, were now barely holding together. The fabric split at the seams, threads unraveling with each step as if they, too, were exhausted from the journey. The soles, once sturdy, peeled away like tired skin, leaving behind only a thin, fragile layer of rubber and cloth that barely shielded

Leo's feet from the harsh world. Ethan had tried to patch them up, hoping to make them last a little longer, but the truth was undeniable, they were beyond repair.

Leo's ankles were swollen and the too-tight socks dug into his skin, pinching the delicate flesh. They were the ankles of a child who had grown too quickly, too violently, and whose body couldn't keep up.

Ethan's stomach clenched watching his baby brother stumble forward, each awkward, uneven step a painful reminder of the toll the virus was taking on him. It wasn't just exhaustion, even though Ethan knew that was part of it. No, it was the relentless pace of it all. The virus was pushing Leo's body to change faster than it was meant to. Every day, every hour, Leo's muscles and bones were struggling to keep up with the virus's demands, and it was too much. Too much for a one-year-old. Too much for any child. But the virus didn't care. It was an unstoppable force, forcing Leo to grow at a pace no human body should ever have to endure.

"Just a little further," Ethan said, his voice steady, even though he didn't believe the words himself. It was a lie, smooth and automatic, the kind you tell someone you love when you lack answers and have no plan other than to keep moving. Ethan wasn't sure where "further" would lead them. He had no destination, no map, and no safe place to point to. The world around them was nothing but rubble, with cities reduced to piles of ash and crumbled buildings. He didn't even know where they could go next. The last safe place he had known, the home they shared with their parents, was gone, destroyed in a gas line explosion that had taken everything away from them. Their apartment, once a cramped but warm refuge, was now just a memory, a fading image of family dinners and soft laughter, now consumed by the inferno.

Ethan clung to memories, hoping they might rebuild something resembling normal. But now, as he walked through the desolate wasteland of a once-thriving city, he realized how futile those thoughts had been. The home they had known was gone, and there would be no return to it. There was only the endless stretch of a broken world and the weight of responsibility pressing down on his fourteen-year-old shoulders.

His eyes flicked to Leo again, and he saw the pain in his baby brother's eyes, pain that had nothing to do with his swollen ankles or the exhaustion from their journey. It was the quiet, unspoken realization that Ethan's world, the world his big brother had known, was lost forever. As much as Ethan wanted to protect Leo, to shelter him from the horror of it all, Leo understood that there was nothing left to protect him from. The world was gone, and all Leo had left was Ethan, his big brother.

2.2: Ashes of What Was

Their neighborhood had become unrecognizable. The once-familiar grid of brownstones and corner cafés that Ethan had walked past every day, where the smell of fresh bread from the bakery mingled with the inviting aroma of coffee from Mr. Patel's shop, was now twisted into a maze of ruin and shadow. The roads that had once bustled with life and conversation were empty. What had been a place filled with the sounds of children playing, cars honking in traffic, and occasional laughter from the open windows of apartments above had been reduced to silence. There was no hustle, no chatter, no warmth. The vibrant heart of the neighborhood had withered and died, leaving only the remnants of a broken world.

The air, which had once carried the comforting scents of pastries and warm coffee, was now thick with something else, ash, metal, and the sickly-sweet rot of things that had once been alive. It was the smell of decay, of a world in its death throes, struggling to hold onto the last vestiges of what it used to be. Ethan's breath came shallow, the taste of soot lingering in the back of his throat, and each inhale felt like a drag of poison. The city around them had become an open grave, and all that remained was the echo of what had been.

As they walked through the empty streets, their footsteps muffled by the fine layer of soot that had settled over everything, Ethan tried not to look at the destruction. He tried to block out the haunting images that would linger with him for the rest of his life. But they were there, inescapable, like ghosts in the corners of his vision.

Ethan had seen them. The bodies.

There was Mrs. Alvarez, his old math tutor, whose kind smile had once greeted him every afternoon after school. She lay half-buried beneath the shattered remains of a storefront awning, her outstretched fingers coated in dust. It was as though she had been frozen in time, a part of the ruin, her death a silent testament to the world that had ended. Her face, once so full of life and knowledge, was now just a mask of decay. Then there was Mr. Kim from the pharmacy, the old man who always had a kind word for everyone who walked through his door, who knew the best remedies for every ailment. His ever-present reading glasses were shattered beside him, his body sprawled awkwardly in the middle of the street. The pool of blood around his head looked too dark, too thick to be real, as though it had been there forever, marking the place where the world had stopped.

Ethan pulled his thoughts away from the bleak scene, swallowing hard. His stomach twisted in protest, bile rising in his throat, but he couldn't afford to break down, not now. Not when Leo was beside him, looking to him for guidance. His baby brother's eyes were wide, filled with confusion and fear, but he remained silent. Leo never spoke when they passed the bodies; he never asked about the blood or the strange stillness of the world around them. He simply walked beside Ethan, the two of them moving through this nightmare together.

"We'll find Mom and Dad," Ethan had told Leo earlier, his voice unsteady but resolute. It was a lie, a promise he was sure he could not keep. But he couldn't abandon that promise, not now, not when Leo still believed it was possible. So, he kept walking, placing one foot in front of the other, even as the weight of the world pressed down on his chest.

It wasn't just the bodies or the ruins that haunted him. It was the knowledge that this was their world now, their reality. A place where life had been extinguished so swiftly that it felt surreal, like a nightmare from which they couldn't wake. And yet here they were, Ethan and Leo, left to survive in the ashes of everything they had known.

But Leo believed him, and that had to be enough.

2.3: Three Days Before the Collapse

One week earlier, the sirens had started at dawn. The shrill, wailing sound pierced through Ethan's dreams, pulling him from sleep with an unsettling urgency. He was still trying to understand what was happening when he felt rough hands shaking him awake. His father's voice, hoarse and strained, whispered urgently in his ear, "Get Leo. Now."

The panic in his father's tone jolted Ethan into full awareness. He scrambled out of bed, disoriented, his heart already pounding with a primal fear he couldn't quite place. As his father's face came into view in the dim light of the room, his usually calm expression was tight with worry. "Ethan, you have to get Leo and hide," he said again, gripping his son's shoulders hard enough to leave a mark.

Outside, the world was in turmoil. The street beyond their windows, once a familiar scene of neighbors going about their daily routines, had transformed into a chaotic war zone. The sky was dark despite the approaching dawn, but the street was alive with flickering lights and chaos. A mob surged through the road, their faces twisted with panic and rage, their movements frantic and erratic. People shouted at one another, their voices hoarse from fear, their actions wild and unpredictable. Torches flickered ominously in the hands of strangers, casting long, contorted shadows that danced violently against the walls. Makeshift weapons, anything they could find, glinted in the dim light: crowbars, broken bottles, rusted pipes, and shards of glass, all wielded with a savagery that seemed both calculated and senseless.

"They're burning the clinics!" someone screamed, their voice filled with hysteria that made Ethan's blood run cold. "Burn it all!" The words struck Ethan like a blow to the chest. He didn't need to ask which clinics they were talking about; he already knew. His mother, Dr. Lena Mercer, worked at one of GeneCorp's Fertility Solutions. Once, the name had carried a sense of purpose and promise, representing a place where cutting-edge science met a desperate need. But now, that name ignited fury.

His mother had been proud of her work, so proud. "We're giving people hope," she had told him one evening, holding up vials of amber liquid. The labels were crisp and sharp beneath the sterile glow of the lab lights: Precision Hormone Therapy. Design Your Legacy. Those words had been etched into his mind, part of a world that had once seemed solid and controlled.

But that was before. Before the first Accelerates were born. Before the virus had slipped free from the controlled environment of the lab. Before, the fury of human creation and ambition had turned into a monstrous legacy. Before the riots tore through the cities, transforming streets into battlegrounds and homes into ruins. Ethan's stomach turned to ice as the realization hit him.

His mother was still at the clinic. She didn't come home last night. She was caught in the chaos that was tearing the city apart, a part of the very events that had triggered the rage in the streets. His chest tightened as his father shoved a hastily packed backpack into his arms. It contained canned beans, a flashlight, matches, first aid kit, energy bars, a water canteen, duct tape and Dad's old hunting knife, bare essentials for survival.

Survival.

Ethan's fingers gripped the straps, but his mind was already racing. "But Mom is still at the…" His father's eyes fixed on his with a hard intensity. "Go," he said, the single word sharp and final, leaving no room for argument. Ethan hesitated for only a moment before his father's voice broke through again, brittle with something unspoken. "Take your brother to the safe room. Don't come out until morning."

Ethan nodded, swallowing the lump in his throat. He didn't want to leave his mother. He didn't want to abandon her to the chaos outside, but he had no choice. There was no time to waste. His father's command felt like a knife slicing through his chest, but he turned without another word, bolting out of the room and running toward Leo.

He ran faster than he had ever run before, his heart pounding with fear, for his baby brother, for his mother, for a world that was slowly breaking apart around them.

2.4: Where the Wild Things Are Not

The safe room was little more than a reinforced closet beneath the stairs, hastily lined with steel plates after the first wave of riots. It was meant to protect them, or so they had been told. Now, however, standing in the suffocating silence of the cramped space, it felt more like a tomb, a place to hide, to wait, and to pretend the world outside didn't exist. The air inside was dense, stale, and far too thin. Every breath felt like it was drawn through a straw, each inhaling a struggle against the oppressive weight of the room's four walls. The faint scent of dust and old paint lingered in the air, a reminder of the years of neglect that had gone into creating this makeshift shelter. Time seemed to move slower here, each second stretching out in the quiet, punctuated only by the soft, rhythmic sound of Ethan's breathing and Leo's sleepy murmurs.

Leo, tightly swaddled in a blanket, blinked up at Ethan with wide, drowsy eyes that still held the untainted innocence and sweetness of childhood, a sweetness that seemed to belong to another world, a world that no longer existed. "Eth? Story?" he asked, his voice small and fragile, like the last ember of a fire on a frosty night. Ethan's heart clenched as he thought of the terror lurking beyond the safe room's walls, knowing that the world he had known was slipping further away, leaving only remnants of his former life. But Leo didn't understand. He couldn't. He was just a child. Ethan wanted to shield him from the nightmare outside, to make it all go away, but the only way he could offer any comfort was through stories, stories that felt hollow now, distant from the shattered reality they were trapped in.

Ethan's hands trembled as he reached for a well-worn book, its cover soft from countless readings, the edges frayed from too many nights of being flipped through. Where the Wild Things Are, Leo's favorite. He had read it to him a thousand times, his voice always steady, always filled with warmth. But tonight, as he flipped through the pages, his hands were anything but steady. They shook under the weight of fear, loss, and the uncertainty that held onto tightly every corner of the room. The flashlight flickered in his grasp, casting eerie shadows on the walls as he skimmed the text. He skipped chunks of the story, his mind too distracted to focus, his voice unsteady as he tried to read the familiar words, though his ears weren't really listening.

He listened intently to the world beyond the door.

The sounds were unmistakable, loud, sharp, and violent. He heard the shattering of glass, the distinct crash of windows being broken, followed by a single, echoing gunshot that sent a jolt of panic through Ethan's chest. It was too close. Far too close. His breath caught in his throat as he strained to hear more. The steady thrum of his heartbeat drowned out everything, but then, through the muffled chaos, he heard her voice, his mother's voice.

"Please, they're just children!" she screamed, her tone shrill with terror, her words desperate. Ethan's stomach twisted. Her voice, filled with fear, was the last thing he ever wanted to hear.

Then there was a crash, a terrible, sickening sound, followed by a scream so raw and filled with agony that it seemed to tear through Ethan's very soul. He froze, his body stiffening as the blood drained from his face. His mind scrambled, unable to process the meaning, the finality, of that sound. And then, after what felt like an eternity, there was nothing. No shouting. No cries. No more noise from beyond the door.

Silence.

The world outside had ceased to exist. All that remained was the stillness of the safe room, the sound of Leo's soft breathing, and the weight of Ethan's unspoken thoughts pressing down on him like an unshakable burden.

2.5: Only Memories and Each Other Remained

When Ethan finally crept out at dawn, the apartment was unrecognizable. The once-cozy living room, with its familiar creases in the sofa and the comfort of family gatherings, had been reduced to something uninhabitable, gutted by violence and despair. The fabric of the couch was torn open, its innards spilling out like entrails, remnants of a life that once felt safe. Soft, white stuffing mixed with bloodstains, the scene grotesque in its starkness. Family photos that had once captured fleeting moments of happiness, smiles during birthdays, vacations, and milestones, now lay shattered on the floor. The glass from the frames glittered in the pale morning light, their jagged edges reflecting a broken world, a reminder of what once was.

The air reeked of smoke and the sharp tang of blood. The familiar smell of dinner, of home, was gone, replaced by the stench of destruction. Ethan's pulse quickened as his eyes darted around, trying to process the scene and grasp what had happened. It didn't make sense. This was where they had lived, shared quiet evenings and laughter. Now, it was a haunted shell, each corner whispering tales of violence and loss.

Next to the kitchen entrance, on the floor, half-hidden beneath a bloodstained rug, lay two bodies. Their limbs were twisted unnaturally, their faces frozen in the aftermath of violence, eyes wide in disbelief, mouths open in screams that would never be heard. The harsh reality hit Ethan like a punch to the gut. They were gone. His parents were gone. And the emptiness they left in their wake was suffocating. He barely registered the tears that welled in his eyes, the sting of grief cutting through him like a blade. This was it. The end of everything he had ever known.

Leo tugged at his sleeve, his tiny hand soft and uncertain. His small voice carried a confused note that stabbed Ethan's heart.

"Mommy napping?" Leo asked, his innocent eyes wide as he surveyed the destruction, unable to comprehend the full extent of their loss. Ethan's chest tightened, and the words caught in his throat. He wanted to tell Leo everything would be okay, that Mommy was just resting. But he couldn't. He couldn't lie to him like that.

The gas stove hissed from the kitchen, a ghost of normalcy. Before the chaos. Before the world was torn apart. Once, the sound of breakfast cooking made the apartment feel like home. Now, it served as a cruel reminder of what they had lost.

Ethan's heart pounded as he grabbed his backpack, its weight suddenly unbearable. The cold, harsh reality of survival was settling in. He had to protect Leo. He had to get them out. Gripping Leo's arm, he pulled him toward the door, his mind racing while his body moved on instinct.

They burst into the open air, and the world outside was a jarring contrast to the chaos they had just left behind. Everything felt wrong. The streets were eerily quiet, devoid of birds, people, even traffic, only a distant murmur hinting at something darker. Their house stood behind them like a fragile shell, silhouetted against the darkening sky, a memory now. Home. Yet the comfort it once provided was gone in an instant.

Then, the world tore apart.

A violent explosion shattered the silence. The air ignited with heat, and the ground trembled beneath their feet as a searing wave of sound and fire engulfed everything. Ethan's body jolted in shock. He instinctively pulled Leo closer, shielding him from the onslaught. The house shuddered, its foundation groaning as if it, too, were succumbing to the inevitable. Then, with a deafening roar, it collapsed in on itself, flames consuming everything in their path.

Ethan's breath caught in his throat as he stared at the devastation. The place that had once been their home, their sanctuary, was now reduced to rubble and ash. There was nothing left, no safe place to hold onto. Only smoke curled skyward, mournful, silent, into the cold dark ahead.

They had nothing now, no past, no home, no parents. All that remained were memories, each other, and an uncertain, unforgiving road stretched out before them.

Chapter 3: The Brothers

3.1: You're Lying

"Ethan, look!" Leo's voice was hoarse and laden with exhaustion, but a thread of hope ran through it as he pointed toward the flickering neon sign in the distance, Greenway Grocery. The sign, once bright and welcoming, now looked as if it had suffered the same decay as everything else around it. Some letters were shattered, their broken pieces dangling precariously, threatening to fall at any moment. The remaining letters struggled to glow, their brightness dulled by grime and the corrosive touch of time. Despite the ruin, the storefront still stood. The windows were boarded up, yet the building remained firm, like a battered relic from a long past. It was a sign of life in a world that in a shortest time had forgotten what it meant to truly live. For a fleeting moment, hope surged within Ethan. A miracle.

"We'll rest here," Ethan said, his voice rough with exhaustion, though determination shone through. He was already prying at a loose board, his fingers numb from days of travel and fear. The wood groaned in protest as he wrenched it free. The gap between the boards was small, but Ethan squeezed through, his body aching with every movement. He heard Leo's soft grunt as the boy followed, his smaller frame slipping through with ease. Outside, the world pressed in, threatening to crush them. But here, in this small, darkened corner of the world, they could breathe.

***

The inside of the store was not much better. The air was thick, musty, and suffocating. A faint scent of stale antiseptic lingered in the corners, clashing with the mildew and rot that had taken hold. The store's atmosphere felt oppressive, as if it too had succumbed to the slow decay of the world outside. The shelves, once filled with the comforts of everyday life, now stood empty and bare. It was difficult to even discern what had once been there. Everything seemed abandoned and forgotten.

Behind the counter, a body slumped against the shelves, its face barely recognizable. The figure's coat had blackened and curled at the edges, scorched by the fire that had claimed its life. What remained of its fingers clutched a pistol. The face, what was left of it, was charred and unrecognizable, the skin burned away in the fire that had failed to consume the rest of the body. The eyes were wide, unseeing, as if frozen in the terror of their last moments. The chilling, emotionless horror of the scene struck Ethan like a punch to the gut. The store, once full of life and comfort, had become a graveyard. Leo stiffened beside him, his voice barely above a whisper. "Is that...?"

"Don't look," Ethan said sharply, his heart racing. He grabbed Leo's wrist and pulled him toward the back of the store. They passed overturned shelves, spilled bottles, and cans scattered haphazardly across the floor. Ethan's pulse thudded in his ears, and his mind struggled to process what he had just seen. This was the world now, death and decay stretching cold fingers into every corner of their once-normal lives.

They reached the children's food aisle, but it was stripped bare. The shelves had been looted long ago, and nothing remained of the items that might have offered some comfort to Leo. However, behind a fallen display, Ethan spotted something unexpected, a small jar of vitamin gummies. It was dusty and long past its expiration date, but it was still sealed. Ethan fumbled with the lid, twisting it off and shaking a few gummies into Leo's palm. He didn't care that they were expired; they were food, they meant survival. Leo devoured them quickly, crunching down hard, his jaw working fast like a rodent gnawing on scraps.

The silence in the store was suffocating. For a few moments, Ethan allowed himself to believe they might be safe here, so that they could rest and recover. But then, Leo's soft voice broke the stillness.

"Eth? Are Mom and Dad mad at us?" The question was innocent, but it hit Ethan like a blow to the chest. His stomach lurched, and his throat tightened. He wanted to say something, to reassure Leo that everything would be okay, that Mom and Dad were just waiting for them somewhere safe. But he couldn't lie anymore.

"Yes," Ethan whispered, his voice rough. "For keeping you alive."

Leo stopped chewing. His face, pale and worn from exhaustion, seemed to grow darker in the dim light, as if his innocence was slipping away, piece by piece. He looked up at Ethan, his eyes unreadable, and when he spoke again, his voice was eerily steady, as though he had already processed what was happening and understood more than his age should allow.

"You're lying."

Ethan's breath caught in his throat. The words felt like a slap. Leo's gaze pierced through him, too knowing, too wise. Ethan's grip on the flashlight loosened, and it slipped from his fingers, hitting the floor with a dull clatter. The flashlight rolled, its beam slicing jagged shadows across the walls.

"Leo, you..." Ethan began, but the words caught, stuck on the raw edge of a truth he didn't want to face.

"I saw them," Leo continued, his voice small but steady. "Under the rug."

Ethan's body froze. His mind raced, a cold chill creeping through his veins as he processed what Leo had said. The flashlight flickered, casting long shadows that stretched and pulled at the very fabric of the room. His eyes searched Leo's face, trying to find any sign of a lie, but there was none.

Before he could respond, a crash from the front of the store shattered the silence, a loud, unmistakable noise. Someone was inside. Ethan's heart leaped into his throat, and his body tensed, ready to react, but for a moment, he couldn't move.

3.2: We Smell Your Genes

The sound of footsteps echoed through the store, drawing closer. Ethan's thoughts spun wildly as he tried to formulate a plan, but time was running out. They had to move. His breath caught as he shoved Leo behind a shelf, his heart pounding. He pressed a trembling finger to his lips, eyes wide with panic.

"Don't breathe. Don't move."

His whisper barely rose over the roar of blood in his ears. Leo's innocent eyes stared up at him, his small form huddled against the cold shelf, trembling with fear that matched Ethan's. But Leo didn't question him. He simply nodded, his small body frozen in place, mirroring the silence that hung in the air.

Footsteps echoed, light yet deliberate, as though the person walking knew exactly where they were going. The click of shoes on tile sent icy fingers crawling down Ethan's spine. It wasn't the rhythm of an ordinary person; it was lighter, too purposeful, too predatory. The sound crept closer, each step a slow drumbeat of dread.

Then, it came.

A giggle rang out, high-pitched and lilting, a sound that had no place in this world. It echoed, sharp and cruel, bouncing off the walls in the darkness. Too sweet. Too innocent. Like a nursery rhyme twisted into something terrible.

"Come out, come out," the voice sang, sugar-laced and shrill, like a child playing a game of hide and seek. "We smell your defective genes."

The words slithered into Ethan's ears, sharp and taunting, their sweetness hiding the venom beneath. The voice was too familiar. Too wrong. A sound no child should ever make, especially not one who should've been playing with dolls or building sandcastles, untouched by the world's horrors.

Ethan felt his pulse slam against his ribs, his body tense with instinctual fear. Not them. Please, not them. His eyes darted toward the aisles, searching for an escape, but the store was a maze of shadows and broken shelves. There was no way out.

Only hiding.

He had seen them before, glimpsed through cracked blinds, wandering the ruined streets amid smoke and fire. The Accelerates, children, but not really. They aged at a terrifying pace, their bodies and minds developing faster than nature ever intended. Though only forty days old, they possessed the intellect and sharpness of adults, calculating, cold, and dangerous. They spoke in clipped, adult-like tones, their cobalt-blue eyes glimmering with knowledge far beyond their years. Man, or virus made monsters cloaked in the guise of childhood. But never had they been this close.

Three figures appeared at the end of the aisle, their silhouettes stark against the dim light. At the front stood the leader, a girl who couldn't have been older than six in appearance, yet everything about her screamed unnatural. Her angelic face was framed by golden curls matted with blood, eerily still. Her unsettling cobalt-blue eyes, unnaturally large like the sky on a stormy day, seemed to look through him, as if she could see into his very soul.

Her dress was a tattered princess gown, its once-beautiful fabric now torn and dirty, the tulle skirt streaked with soot and grime. It clung to her small frame like the last vestige of something that had once been pure, a relic of innocence lost. A tiara sat crookedly on her head, one ear exposed, its gold dulled by the dirt of the streets. She resembled a child in a dress-up costume, but there was nothing innocent about her. Nothing at all.

Two boys stood beside her. They were equally unnatural. Young, yes, but their eyes held the same eerie intelligence and calculated malice. They moved as one, each step echoing with the same predatory rhythm as their leader. Ethan's breath caught in his throat as he pressed his back against the cold shelf, trying to make himself as invisible as possible, his mind racing for any way out of this nightmare.

The girl in the princess dress smiled; a sharp, knowing grin that made Ethan's stomach churn. "We can hear your heartbeats," she cooed, her voice sweet yet laced with something darker. Her stormy cobalt-blue eyes swept over the aisles, pausing just a moment too long on Ethan's hiding place. He held his breath, praying she wouldn't see them, hoping they might be overlooked. But there was no hiding from them. Not anymore. Not in this world.

The silence stretched. Then the girl spoke again, her tone shifting as though she'd grown bored with the game. "Come out, come out, wherever you are." Her voice had become a command, one that allowed no argument and offered no chance of escape. The smile didn't leave her face, but something darker flickered in her gaze, making Ethan's blood run cold. The Accelerates weren't just after survival; they were hunting for sport. And they never missed their prey.

The two boys flanked the girl like predators. Their faces were angelic, but their eyes, those piercing, unnaturally large cobalt-blue eyes, betrayed the truth. They glowed faintly in the darkness, reflecting the beam of Ethan's flashlight with an eerie, feline gleam that sent a chill crawling up his spine. Their golden curls, matted with dirt and grime, bounced as they moved in perfect synchronization with their leader. Their lips curled into twisted grins, revealing sharp, too-white teeth. They were nothing like the children they appeared to be. They were monsters, born of man's science, twisted by the virus, and the hunger in their eyes was unmistakable.

The girl, the leader, tilted her head slightly, fixing her intense gaze on Leo. She stepped toward him, and Ethan's heart clenched. Her voice was sickly sweet as she cooed, each word dripping with unsettling precision.

"Subject A-9," she purred, her tone almost musical. "Defect: delayed viral assimilation. Estimated expiration: ten days."

Her lips curled into a mockingly sympathetic smile, but there was no compassion in her eyes. She licked her lips slowly, savoring the moment like a predator assessing its prey. Then, as if Leo's fate were too trivial for further thought, her gaze shifted, like a snake locking onto its next meal.

"But the other one..." Her eyes slid to Ethan, and the smile on her face darkened, transforming into something far more dangerous, something predatory. "...is pure. Unaltered. Rare."

The words carried a venomous promise, a chilling admission that the girl understood just how valuable Ethan was in their twisted new world. The boys, still lingering at her side like eager hounds, snarled in unison. Their fingers flexed like claws, and their small faces contorted with hunger, an insatiable desire that went beyond mere survival. It was a hunger rooted in possession and domination.

Ethan's heart raced as he gripped the nearest object, a thick metal scale bar. With one swift motion, he yanked it off the shelf and raised it defensively. The weight of the bar in his hand felt comforting, a small but significant symbol of resistance.

"Stay back!" he commanded, his voice shaky but firm.

The girl's laughter pierced the air, sharp and discordant, like glass shattering under pressure. It grated on Ethan's nerves, making his skin crawl.

"Primitive," she murmured, almost pitying him. She gazed at him the way one might regard a curious animal, something to be studied, something to be toyed with. "Your survival probability is 2.7%."

Her words struck like a slap, an unflinching dose of reality. He had known they were dangerous, but hearing her state the odds so clinically made the threat feel even more insurmountable.

Then, without warning, she moved. Faster than thought, faster than anything he could have anticipated. Her small hand shot forward, fingers like iron, quicker than any child should have been capable of. Before Ethan could react, her grip clamped down on his wrist. The pain was blinding. She twisted his arm at an unnatural angle, and his wrist snapped with a sickening pop. The sound made him gasp as the pain radiated up his arm like fire.

Ethan staggered backward, unable to stifle the cry that tore from his throat. The metal bar slipped from his hand, clattering to the ground as he gasped for air, his arm now hanging limply at his side. The world spun. Through the haze of pain, he saw her face, still, calm, amused. There was no urgency in her movements, no trace of rage or fear. She wasn't a child. She was a machine, an inhuman entity designed to calculate and dominate.

Ethan's legs wobbled as he struggled to regain balance, his mind frantically scanning for a way out. But she didn't give him a chance. She stepped forward again, this time without the mocking grin. Her expression was focused, lethal. Her eyes darkened with something deeper than hunger, something far more terrifying.

The two boys behind her twitched like jackals, eyes gleaming with anticipation, mouths twisted into fierce grins. They didn't need words; they were content to watch their leader destroy.

Ethan's vision blurred. His heart hammered against his ribs. There was nowhere to go. Agony surged through his body, a blinding wave that exploded in his chest and spread like wildfire, consuming every nerve ending. His breath came in ragged, jagged gasps. His world tilted. He collapsed with a scream, the intensity of the pain threatening to shred him from inside out.

His wrist, dislocated or shattered, throbbed with an unrelenting ache, as if his bones were being crushed from within. He clenched his teeth to hold back another scream, but the agony broke through.

Then Leo's voice rang out, raw, primal, heart-wrenching.

The sound made Ethan's heart stutter.

Leo wailed, the cry ripping through the air, vibrating with a frequency Ethan didn't understand. It wasn't just a scream, was emotion turned to sound. A force of grief and terror so immense that it shook the very foundation of the world. For a split second, everything stopped.

Time staggered.

Ethan could feel the earth tremble beneath them.

The Accelerates recoiled as if struck. Their heads snapped back. Their hands flew to their ears. Their angelic faces twisted with something Ethan had never seen on them before: fear. Genuine, visceral fear.

Their eyes, normally cold, calculating, now flashed with confusion and panic. They staggered, movements clumsy and hesitant. The precision, the poise, they were unraveling.

The girl, the leader, shouted something incomprehensible. Her voice cracked in a rare break of composure. "Anomaly!" she shrieked.

"Terminate! Termin..."

But Leo's cry didn't stop.

It rose, louder, fiercer resonating with the air itself. The very walls of the store trembled. The floor trembled. The ceiling trembled. It was as though the sound pulled at the fabric of reality, unraveling it thread by thread.

Ethan felt the air grow thick, oppressive, bending under the weight of the sound. His chest tightened. His ears rang. The atmosphere warped around them, twisted and reshaped by Leo's will.

The pain in Ethan's body remained, but perhaps for the first time since their existence, the Accelerates looked unsure.

And that, somehow, was everything.

And then it happened.

With a violent eruption of sound, the store's remaining windows exploded outward. Shards of glass rained down, scattering through the air in a deadly spray, but they didn't seem to matter. The walls trembled, cracks spreading like veins of lightning, racing in jagged patterns across the surfaces. The shelves, once sturdy and still, buckled under the chaos, warping inward as if caught in the aftershock of some invisible, unstoppable force. The entire store quaked under the pressure; the thick air with a tension so heavy it made it hard to breathe.

The Accelerates, once so confident and assured in their superiority, screeched in agony. Their movements became frantic and erratic, their bodies convulsing and twitching as if Leo's cry were tearing them apart from the inside. Ethan couldn't fully comprehend what was happening, but the result was unmistakable: they were unraveling. Their unnatural strength and calculated precision collapsed under the weight of something they could neither understand nor control.

Then, just as suddenly, the sound of Leo's cry reached its peak. The three figures, once so terrifying, so relentless, seemed to fold in on themselves, their bodies spasming as if being pulled into the vortex of their own undoing. And then, like shadows caught in the wind, they vanished into the night. Their howls were swallowed by the darkness, their presence erased from the world, as if they had never existed at all.

The silence that followed was deafening.

3.3: You Saved Us

Ethan lay on the floor, panting, his breath ragged and shallow. His chest heaved with the aftershocks of pain, and though his wrist throbbed, the sensation now felt distant and muted beneath the weight of disbelief. The terror that had stiffened his limbs slowly ebbed, leaving him hollow and numb. Around him, the store resembled a war zone: shelves collapsed, aisles overturned, the air thick with dust and tension. And yet, for the first time in what felt like forever, the nightmare was over.

He turned his head slowly, eyes searching through the haze.

Leo stood trembling in the middle of the store; his fists clenched tightly at his sides. His small chest rose and fell into shallow, frantic gasps. His eyes were wide, and the terror from moments ago still clung to him like smoke. Streaks of tears cut through the grime on his cheeks, the evidence of fear and desperation etched onto his face. He looked lost. His small frame swayed slightly, as though the weight of what had just happened had unmoored him. His lips quivered. "Did I... hurt them?" he asked, voice barely above a whisper, as if he was afraid of the answer.

Ethan pushed through the pain in his arm, forcing himself upright. He ignored the searing ache in his wrist, the stiffness in his limbs, focusing only on the boy who now stood trembling before him. He reached out and pulled Leo close, wrapping one arm around him in a shaky embrace. He held on tight, trying to offer comfort he himself was still searching for.

His voice came out hoarse but steady. "No, Leo," he said, firm despite the weight of the truth pressing on his chest. "You saved us."

Leo's small body shook against him, but slowly, the tension began to drain from his limbs. His breathing, though still shallow, grew less frantic.

Around them, the store, once a battleground of chaos and violence, now lay still. Even the air seemed to hold its breath.

The nightmare was over.

For now.

3.4: Are We Monsters?

They huddled together in the store's break room as night slowly descended, enveloping the city in an eerie silence. The world outside seemed to hold its breath, and as the last light of day faded, it left behind only a suffocating darkness.

The room they had taken shelter in was cramped and musty, reeked of stale coffee and mildew. Forgotten lunches, ghosted conversations, time itself, everything lingered like the past had never left. The air felt thick enough to drown in. Every creak of the walls, every distant groan of the wind was a reminder: the world was broken, and so were they.

Ethan sat against the wall beneath the flickering flashlight. The cold edge of a metal shelf bit into his neck. He barely noticed. Pain pulsed through his wrist, fractured or worse, but it was background noise compared to the chaos in his head. The scream still echoed there.

Leo's scream.

It hadn't been just fear. It had changed the air, cracked it open like a thunderclap. The Accelerates had writhed, shrieked, and scattered like animals. Not out of confusion, out of fear. Real, human fear.

What had come out of Leo wasn't natural. Not a reflex. Not a sound. It was power. And it terrified Ethan more than anything that had come after.

He reached into his backpack, fingers shaking, uncooperative, and pulled out a roll of duct tape and a school ruler, both relics from a time that felt centuries away. With clenched teeth and grit, he made a splint, wrapping his wrist tight. The pain lanced through him like fire, but he welcomed it. It reminded him he was still human. Still fighting.

But Leo's scream? That wasn't human. Or was it?

A voice broke the silence.

"Eth?"

Soft. Barely there. But Ethan heard it like a gunshot.

He looked over.

Leo was curled beneath an old coat, his knees tucked tight against his chest. His wide eyes stared up at Ethan, eyes filled with something ancient. Fear. Confusion. Awareness.

Ethan's heart stuttered.

He crawled closer, reaching out. Leo flinched but didn't move away. His skin was ice cold. The flashlight flickered again, warping their shadows across the room like monsters on the wall.

Ethan saw it now, clearly. The light inside Leo was dimming. The innocence was still there, but it was fighting to survive. And Ethan, he was supposed to protect it. Protect him.

"I'm here," he said, forcing steadiness into his voice. "We're safe. We're together."

Leo didn't answer. Just blinked slowly, searching.

Then, the words came.

"Are we monsters?"

They landed like a blade.

Ethan opened his mouth. Nothing came out. No should have been instant. But it caught in his throat, tangled in the same doubt he'd been choking on since the outbreak began.

Leo stared at him, waiting.

"Are we?" he asked again, quieter.

Ethan looked at him, really looked, and saw a boy too young to understand the weight of survival yet carrying it all the same. A child shaped by fear, and something else creeping in beneath the surface.

Finally, Ethan found his voice.

"No," he said, barely more than a breath. It sounded wrong. Thin. Fragile.

"But the sick kids..." Leo whispered. "They're like me. Faster."

The words pierced deeper than any accusation. They weren't just facts, they were truth. Leo was different now. His body moved faster. His brain processed faster. He wasn't evolving. He was accelerating.

Just like them.

Ethan's stomach turned.

But Leo still reached for him in the dark. Still curled up like a child. He still needed bedtime stories and whispered reassurances. That had to mean something. That had to mean he was still Leo.

Right?

"Leo," Ethan said, the emotion catching in his chest, "You're my brother. That's what matters."

He tightened his grip on Leo's shoulder, needing to believe it. Needing Leo to believe it.

But Leo looked away.

His silence wasn't empty, it was loaded. With understanding. With something Ethan wasn't ready to face.

And for the first time, Ethan realized the truth he'd been running from:

It wasn't just the world that had changed.

It was them.

3.5: Mandatory Testing

Suddenly, a new sound shattered the heavy silence, the distant thud of something mechanical, rhythmic, and relentless. Ethan's heart leapt in his chest, and his stomach dropped. For a moment, he couldn't breathe.

Helicopters.

The sound was unmistakable. The distant thunder grew steadily louder, and his pulse quickened as he scanned the horizon through the break room's window, thoughts racing. What if it was a rescue? What if they were finally saved? What if this was the end of the nightmare? His breath caught as the noise escalated, echoing below.

"Stay here," he ordered Leo, though his voice cracked with unspoken fear. He turned and rushed toward the ladder that led to the rooftop access. His body screamed in protest, but he couldn't wait, not now. He had to see. He had to understand.

The rooftop was a desolate landscape, littered with rusted satellite dishes, twisted metal arms reaching into the smoke-choked sky like skeletal fingers. The city below was a ruin: burned-out buildings, shattered windows, dark, silent streets. But it wasn't the destruction that caught his attention.

It was the horizon.

Searchlights. Bright, unyielding beams pierced the night sky like knives, slicing through the murk. They swept across the rubble below, illuminating the wreckage.

Then he saw it.

A military convoy, an extensive line of trucks moving slowly through the decimated streets like a mechanical serpent. The heavy vehicles hummed with power, their massive tires crushing debris as they rolled forward. In the distance, machine-gun fire crackled, echoing through the night, followed by the shrill shrieks of the Accelerates. One by one, they fell as the convoy advanced, relentless, and unfeeling.

Ethan's breath caught in his throat. His heart thundered. A military rescue. Could it be? Was this what they had been waiting for? The cavalry had arrived.

But then, his eyes caught the symbol on the sides of the trucks, etched in sharp contrast. It seared itself into his mind.

A serpent coiled around a double helix.

GeneCorp.

The word hit him like a slap. The realization crashed over him like a wave of ice water. The very company that had brought them to this point, the one that had unleashed the virus, was now controlling the military force storming the city. This wasn't salvation. It was control. Containment.

The nightmare was far from over.

A crackle broke the silence, harsh and mechanical. A voice boomed from a megaphone, cold and unyielding:

"Remaining uninfected citizens, report for mandatory testing. Resistance is futile."

The words echoed through the night air, their icy finality hanging like a death sentence. Ethan flinched, breath caught in his throat. A spotlight slashed across the rooftop, its blinding beam searing through the dark. He dropped to the ground, body pressed low against the cold metal roof.

"Testing."

The word churned in his gut like acid.

The government, GeneCorp, the military, they didn't want to save Leo. They didn't care about survival. They wanted to study him. Dissect him. They would reduce Leo to nothing more than a lab specimen to unravel the flaws in the Accelerate program, to understand what had made Leo, and perhaps Ethan, different.

Ethan's throat tightened. The thought of Leo, his baby brother, strapped to a table, torn apart in the name of science, twisted something deep in him. Leo was still a child. He didn't deserve this.

Terror surged in Ethan's chest as the painful truth settled like lead in his bones.

They would never let Leo live.

They wouldn't care if he was Ethan's little brother. That he was just a baby. To them, he was data. A mistake. A thing to be studied.

Ethan bolted for the ladder, descending into the store below. His decision had been made.

They would run.

He would not let them take Leo.

They would vanish into the shadows, slip through cracks, disappear into the places no one dared to look.

They would survive. Together.

3.6: Somewhere They Can't Find Us

Back in the break room, the low hum of the fluorescent light above felt deafening. Leo was still asleep, twitching in the makeshift bed Ethan had crafted from torn blankets and a battered old chair. His little legs jerked involuntarily, yet another growth spurt, another cruel reminder that time was slipping away faster than they could outrun it. Ethan's jaw tightened, fighting the surge of helplessness threatening to overwhelm him. Leo, his baby brother, was changing too quickly. His body aged at an unnatural rate, his mind racing ahead of his age. And Ethan... Ethan was running out of time.

His breath hitched as he looked down at Leo, still so small, his angelic face peaceful in sleep. But that peace wouldn't last. Every day, Leo became something more; something harder to protect. The innocence was fading, and with it, Ethan's ability to keep him safe.

"Time to go," Ethan whispered, the words barely more than a breath. His voice cracked, thick with emotion, as he turned toward the backpack on the floor. He slung it over his uninjured shoulder, feeling the weight settle against him, the weight of their lives, their survival, all resting on the fragile straps that held their meager belongings.

Leo stirred. His eyes fluttered open, his voice small and rough, reached Ethan's ears. "Where?"

Ethan paused, glancing toward the rooftop. Searchlights still pierced the darkness, their beams sweeping across the skyline like sharp, jagged knives. The military was out there, scouring the city. He couldn't let them find them, not now. Not ever.

"Somewhere they can't find us," Ethan said, his voice steady with resolve, though his heart thudded heavy with dread. Somewhere out there, there had to be a place where they could be safe, where they could keep running, keep hiding, away from a world that hunted them like animals.

Leo nodded, a small frown creasing his brow as he tried to understand. He didn't ask more questions. He was exceptionally intelligent for his age and deeply aware of the danger they faced. With shaky hands, Leo pushed himself to his feet, still half-asleep but obedient as ever.

They slipped out the back door, the cool night air rushing against their skin as they vanished into the alley. Shadows engulfed them, hiding them from the outside world. The darkness was both shield and prison, offering no comfort, only the stark reality of their flight.

Ethan hesitated for a moment, glancing back at the store. A knot twisted in his stomach, a weight pressing against his chest. The burned body in the half-destroyed coat still lay behind the counter, its face frozen in an eternal grimace. Even now, Ethan felt as if it were watching them leave, trying to warn them, trying to say something they could never quite grasp. But he couldn't afford to linger. They had to move forward. They had to survive.

Somewhere, a clock ticked.

It had been forty days since the first Accelerate was born, forty days since the world changed in ways no one could have imagined.

Forty days to the end.

And yet, a flicker of hope remained, fragile, but alive.

Ethan was determined not to let it die. Not now.

Not when his baby brother's life depended on it.

Chapter 4: The End Is by Children

4.1: Design Your Legacy

The sun spilled across the city like an open wound, rust-colored light bleeding through haze and decay. It stretched shadows long and thin, draping the ruins in hues of copper and fire.

Ethan adjusted the straps of his backpack, its weight a constant reminder of how little they had left: three protein bars, a half-empty canteen, and a first-aid kit scavenged from a fire station that had already been picked clean.

Not enough. Never enough.

Beside him, Leo trudged forward, his small fingers clutching the torn sleeve of Ethan's jacket as if anchoring himself to something real. At just one year old, Leo's body was already betraying him. His limbs stretched unnaturally, his too-long legs straining against fabric that had fit just days ago. His sneakers, already split at the toes, left faint imprints in the ash-covered pavement. Growth spurts came in violent, silent bursts, skin stretched, bones creaked beneath a blueprint his body never had.

The virus had accelerated everything, except for sustenance. Leo's metabolism devoured calories like a furnace, leaving him hollow-eyed, his small frame trembling with exhaustion.

"Eth... hungry," he murmured, his voice soft and fragile in its childlike need, yet carrying something sharper beneath the surface, something older.

Ethan glanced down, his stomach twisting at the sight of Leo's sunken cheeks and trembling lips.

"We'll find food soon," Ethan promised, though the words tasted like dust in his mouth.

The city lay picked clean. Grocery stores lay gutted, their aisles littered with shattered glass and abandoned shelves. Pharmacies had been looted, there weren't even any bandages left, only the lingering smell of antiseptic and blood. The few buildings that remained untouched bore GeneCorp's quarantine symbols, red X-s slashed across their doors like warnings in a dead language.

They turned down an alley choked with debris, an overturned dumpster and the skeleton of a bicycle picked clean to its frame.

Leo suddenly stopped.

A poster peeled away from the brick wall, its edges curled with grime. On the paper, a baby smiled with an angelic face, golden curly hair, and eyes of an unnatural, crystalline blue. Beneath the image, the words gleamed in faded gold:

DESIGN YOUR LEGACY.

GENECORP PRECISION HORMONE THERAPY, GUARANTEED POTENTIAL & FUTURE.

However, someone had defaced it. A thick, black X slashed across the baby's face, smearing the features into obscurity.

Leo stared at the poster, tilting his head. "Is that... what I am?"

Ethan felt his throat tighten.

No. No, you are Leo. You are my brother. You are not them.

Yet the truth weighed heavily in his chest, like an anchor dragging him down into darkness. He forced himself to speak.

"No. You're just Leo. My baby brother."

The truth and the lie hung between them, thin as a breath, ready to shatter at the slightest touch.

***

Days earlier, huddled in the cramped safe room beneath the stairs, Leo had begun to convulse. His small body twisted, limbs jerking against the threadbare blanket as if battling something unseen. Then came the sound, deep, unnatural. Bone stretching. Ligaments tearing and knitting back together. A sickening symphony of growth.

"Make it stop!" Leo screamed, his voice hoarse with pain. His tiny fingers clawed at his skin, as if he thought he could peel the transformation away. Tears streamed down his face, pooling in the dim light of the flashlight flickering between them.

Their father knelt beside him, hands trembling as he stroked Leo's damp forehead. His voice, meant to be soothing, only intensified Ethan's fear.

"It's the hormones, my angel boy," he whispered. "They're... optimizing you."

Optimizing.

The word twisted in Ethan's stomach, leaving a bitter, uncomfortable feeling. It made Leo sound like a machine, a project, something to be improved, adjusted, perfected.

But Leo wasn't an experiment. He was a child.

And he was suffering.

4.2: The Princess and the Pipe Wrench

A gust of wind slithered through the empty streets, carrying the rancid stench of rot. Ethan gagged, pulling his shirt over his nose as his stomach twisted in discomfort.

Leo, oddly unconcerned, pointed ahead. A flickering neon sign buzzed feebly in the dim light, Joe's Diner. The windows were shattered, jagged glass framing the entrance, but inside, the booths remained eerily untouched. The cracked vinyl seats gaped open, their stuffing spilling out like overripe fruit.

"There," Ethan said, forcing optimism into his voice. "Maybe they left something behind."

The diner's door hung crookedly on its hinges, swaying with each breath of wind. The air inside buzzed with flies, a droning chorus of decay. A pie, its crust mottled with mold, lay on the counter, swarmed by insects.

Leo darted forward, spotting a crumpled chip bag beneath one of the tables. He lunged for it.

Ethan grabbed his wrist, his grip tight. "Not yet," he warned. "Let me check first to see if it's spoiled."

Leo pulled free, his voice breaking with frustration. "But I'm hungry!"

His outburst echoed through the silence.

Somewhere deep within the diner, a glass shattered.

Both boys froze.

A giggle echoed through the shadows, high-pitched, melodic, and unsettling.

Ethan's breath hitched. It was too close. He shoved Leo behind him, his fingers wrapping around the hunting knife in his pocket. The blade, dull from overuse, felt flimsy and useless.

Then, they emerged.

Three grotesque parodies of innocent, childish figures slipped out of the kitchen, moving with unnatural grace. The leader, the girl in a tattered princess dress, licked her lips.

The two boys twitched like jackals, their limbs coiled with feral energy. Their eyes glowed faintly, pupils dilated into black voids.

The girl's gaze landed on Leo. Her lips curled into a smile. "Subject A-9," she sang, tilting her head. "Defective strain. Viral assimilation delayed by... let's see..." She tapped her temple in mock concentration. "Insufficient hormone saturation."

Then she turned to Ethan, her grin widening to reveal teeth sharpened to needle-like points.

"But you..." her gaze lingered on him. "...pure. Unaltered. Delicious."

The boys hissed, saliva dripping from their lips.

Ethan's grip tightened on the knife. "Stay back."

The girl giggled. The sound was like splintering glass. "Probability of successful defense now: 2.3%. Adjusted for... this."

She flicked her wrist.

One of the boys lunged, swinging a rusted pipe wrench. Ethan dodged, but the metal grazed his shoulder, fabric tearing, skin splitting.

Pain flared hot.

"Run!" Ethan barked, shoving Leo toward the exit.

But the second boy was already there, blocking the door, lips peeled back in a snarl.

Then Leo screamed.

A raw, primal sound, the kind that split the air like a thunderclap.

The Accelerates froze. Their perfect faces contorted in agony. The girl staggered, nose bleeding.

"Anomaly!" she shrieked. "Terminate!"

Leo's scream intensified.

The windows exploded, glass hung suspended for a heartbeat, then crashed down like a rain of daggers.

The Accelerates reeled. The boys clutched their heads, howling. The girl snarled through gritted teeth:

"Retreat! Recalibrate!"

Then, they fled, their laughter trailing behind them like a curse. Silence settled over the wreckage, thick and suffocating. Only Leo's ragged breathing broke the stillness.

Ethan crouched, glass crunching beneath his boots. His shoulder throbbed, warm blood seeping through his shirt in slow rivulets. He swallowed the pain. "You okay?" His voice rasped.

Leo nodded, his small frame trembling. Ethan hesitated. Not because he didn't know the answer, but because he did.

"Did I... hurt them?"

Ethan exhaled, ruffling his brother's hair with a hand that wouldn't stop shaking. "You saved us again."

But in the pit of his stomach, something twisted.

What are you becoming?

Outside, the city moaned, distant screams pulsing through the streets like a dying heartbeat. Overhead, the rhythmic thrum of a helicopter shattered the quiet, its spotlight skimming the rooftops, a mechanical eye searching, scanning.

GeneCorp's insignia gleamed on its underbelly: a serpent devouring its own tail.

Ethan stiffened. "We need to move."

Leo hesitated, his gaze snagging on a shard of shattered glass glittered with menace. He stared at his reflection, and his pupils flickered, briefly expanding and contracting.

"Eth... I don't feel good."

Ethan's chest tightened. "Leo..."

4.3: It's in My Bones

The highway stretched like a decaying leviathan's spine, cracked asphalt lined with abandoned wrecks. Ethan's stolen sedan lurched through the maze of rusted metal, the engine wheezing in rhythm with Leo's labored breaths. The golden-hour light spilled across the sky, illuminating the skeletons of semi-trucks and SUVs, their windows shattered and webbed with cracks that caught the sun like jagged teeth. The air reeked of gasoline and rot, a nose-curling cocktail of decayed upholstery and bloated roadkill.

Leo slumped in the passenger seat, having just devoured a bag of chips from Joe's Diner. His small fingers followed the spiral of a fractal rash up his arm. The veins beneath pulsed violet, as if a bioluminescent poison seeped into his marrow. "It's in my bones, Eth," he whispered, his voice fraying at the edges. A cough wracked his body, wet and resonant, leaving flecks of black bile on his sleeve.

Ethan's knuckles turned white on the steering wheel. "We'll figure it out."

The lie tasted like battery acid.

Ahead, the Silver Pines Mall sign swayed on rusted chains, its neon letters dim and lifeless.

The sedan shuddered to a halt. Ethan stepped out into a silence so profound he could hear the tick-tick of cooling metal. His boots crunched over glass shards that glittered like ice in the fading light. The scent here was sharper, burnt rubber mingled with the tang of old wine.

4.4: Shadows in the Mall

The Silver Pines Mall had once been a cathedral of consumerism, its polished floors gleaming under fluorescent lights and its air thick with the scent of cinnamon pretzels and perfume samples. Now, it was a carcass picked clean by time and desperation. Ethan crouched behind the jagged remnants of a jewelry counter, his back pressed to cold marble as he tried to ignore the stench of decay seeping into his nostrils. Somewhere in the maze of collapsed storefronts, water dripped in a steady, mocking rhythm.

Drip... drip... drip.

A countdown to nowhere.

His brother stirred against his chest. Leo, one year old but already the size of a five-year-old, squirmed in the sling Ethan had fashioned from a torn curtain. The boy's cobalt-blue eyes flickered open, glassy with fever. "Eth...?" he rasped, his voice too deep and too raw for a child.

"Shhh," Ethan whispered, adjusting the sling. Leo's skin burned through the fabric, a furnace Ethan couldn't quench. He pulled the canteen from his backpack, the last of their water, and pressed it to Leo's cracked lips. "Small sips. Slowly."

Leo obeyed, his small hands trembling as they gripped the bottle. Ethan's gaze drifted to the mall's skeletal escalators, frozen mid-collapse. Vines clawed through shattered skylights. Sunlight filtering weakly onto a landscape of toppled kiosks and mannequins with hollowed-out eyes. He wondered, not for the first time, if the mannequins were the lucky ones.

He reached for his journal, its leather cover frayed and stained. The entries had started as a record of dates, rations, and mile markers, but now they were a lifeline. A way to tether himself to the boy he had been before the world ended.

Day 16. No signs of the Accelerates today. Leo ate half a can of beans. His hands keep growing. I found a first-aid kit in the old pharmacy, but the antiseptic is gone.

A metallic clang echoed from the food court. Ethan froze, his pen slipping from his fingers. Leo stiffened, his breath hitching.

"Stay quiet," Ethan mouthed, easing the backpack off his shoulders. He grabbed the fire poker he had scavenged from one of the stores, its rusty tip sharpened to a jagged point.

The clang came again, closer now. Ethan's pulse throbbed in his ears as he peered over the counter. Shadows slithered between the escalators, too swift, too fluid to be human.

Accelerates.

"Eth... scared," Leo whimpered, his fingers digging into Ethan's arm.

"I know," Ethan said, forcing his voice to stay steady. "But we're going to be okay. Remember the plan?"

Leo nodded, his lower lip quivering. "Run. Don't look back."

"That's right." Ethan tightened his grip on the fire poker. *God, he's too young for this.*

A high-pitched laugh echoed through the air, bouncing off the mall's carcass like a bullet. Ethan's stomach lurched. *They're hunting.*

He risked another glance. Three figures emerged from the shadows, their limbs elongated and their movements a grotesque parody of childhood.

Run. Don't look back.

They bolted into the mall's eastern wing, where Spencer's Gifts had become a cavern filled with melted lava lamps and scattered toys. Ethan's lungs burned. Leo's hot breath seared his neck. A display of novelty shot glasses exploded as an Accelerate lunged, its claws swiping the air just inches from Ethan's heel.

"USE IT, LEO!"

The scream tore from Leo's throat, a primal, seismic wail that shattered every remaining window in a fifty-foot radius. Glasses fell like shrapnel. The Accelerates recoiled, blood streaming from their ears. Ethan didn't stop. He barreled into a supply closet, slammed the door, and drove the fire poker through the handle.

Darkness enveloped them. Leo slid down Ethan's back, chest heaving.

4.5: Tell Me About the Rabbits

"Did... did I do good?"

"You did great," Ethan choked out as he fumbled for his flashlight. The beam flickered to life, illuminating shelves of janitorial supplies and Leo's fever-flushed, angelic face.

He was getting worse.

Ethan pressed a hand to the boy's forehead, then yanked it back. "Jesus, Leo, you're burning up."

"I'm sorry," Leo mumbled, curling into a ball.

"Don't apologize." Ethan rummaged through his pack for the last ibuprofen, crushed it into their dwindling water, and held the bottle to Leo's lips. "Drink. Now."

The boy gagged but managed to swallow. Ethan's hands shook as he unzipped Leo's oversized hoodie, a Salvation Army find from what felt like another lifetime. Angry red veins spiderwebbed across the child's chest, pulsing faintly.

The virus. Accelerating.

He'd first noticed the veins two weeks ago, tiny threads under Leo's collarbone. Now they spanned his ribcage, a roadmap to some terrible destination. Ethan's vision blurred.

***

On Leo's first birthday, when he began to accelerate in his development, they took him to the hospital. Ethan managed to smuggle a chocolate cupcake into Leo's sterile hospital room, the sweet scent of sugar mingling with the harsh smell of antiseptics. Their mother smiled weakly as Leo blew out the lone candle.

"Make a wish," she whispered, her voice thin with exhaustion.

Leo closed his eyes, a grin spreading across his face. "I want to be an astronaut!"

Ethan ruffled his hair, his voice warm with hope despite the grim surroundings. "You'll need a bigger cupcake."

Leo coughed, a wet, rattling sound that snapped Ethan back to reality. The boy's eyelids fluttered. "Story?"

"Again?" Ethan forced a smile. "Which one?"

"Rabbits."

Ethan sighed. Of course. The only book they had managed to salvage from a burned bookstore was a battered copy of *"Of Mice and Men."* Leo had latched onto it like a lifeline, demanding the same passage every night.

"Alright." Ethan leaned against the wall, with Leo's head resting in his lap. "Tell me about the rabbits, George…"

As he recited Lennie's plea, his flashlight caught something glinting under a shelf: a discarded Polaroid camera. Ethan reached for it, numb curiosity overriding his survival instincts. The first photo showed a family posing by Santa's Village, all toothy grins, and reindeer antlers. The next featured a teenager flipping off the lens, a Cinnabon in hand.

They were real people.

Leo's breathing evened out. Ethan set the camera aside, his throat tight. Outside, the shrieks of the Accelerates had faded. For now.

He opened his journal, the pen trembling in his grip.

Day 16 (continued). We're in the east wing supply closet. Leo's fever is at 103. Ethan.

He tucked the journal away, clicked off the flashlight, and prayed for dawn.

The supply closet's darkness was absolute, a burial shroud pressing against Ethan's eyes. Leo's fever radiated through the sling, his shallow breaths synchronizing with the drip of water somewhere in the mall's carcass. Drip. Drip. Drip. Drip… drip… drip.

Ethan counted them, a morbid lullaby, until the boy stirred.

"Eth...?" Leo's voice was like a dry leaf crumbling.

"I'm here." Ethan flicked on his flashlight, its beam cutting through the dust motes. The closet walls were lined with rusted mop buckets and empty bleach bottles. Leo's eyes gleamed in the light, his face gaunt, the veins beneath his skin pulsing faintly.

"Thirsty," Leo croaked.

Ethan shook his water bottle, a single swallow sloshed at the bottom. "You have to wait. Dawn's close. I'll scavenge then."

Leo's lower lip trembled, but he nodded. Too obedient, Ethan thought bitterly. He shouldn't have to be.

He pulled out his journal, its pages warped from rain and sweat.

Day 17. Still in the mall. Leo's temperature hit 104 last night. I found Polaroid proof that people existed, I guess. Accelerates are hunting. They know we're here.

4.6: It's Time to Scream Again

A skittering noise clawed at the door.

Both boys froze.

"Eth..."

"Shhh."

Ethan turned off the flashlight. The skittering intensified, nails on metal, a wet snuffling. Leo's fingers dug into Ethan's arm.

They're back.

The door shuddered. Ethan gripped the fire poker, its rusted edge digging into his palm. One strike. Aim for the eyes.

But the noise stopped.

Silence for a moment, but then: "Fresh meat," sang a voice, singsong and shrill.

Leo whimpered.

Ethan's mind raced. The supply closet had no exits, and they had no weapons but the fire poker. Think. Think.

His flashlight beam caught a ventilation grate near the ceiling.

"New plan," he whispered, hoisting Leo onto his back. "We climb."

The shelves wobbled as Ethan scaled them, Leo clinging like a koala. The grate groaned when he yanked it free, a tight squeeze, but possible.

"Go," Ethan urged, shoving Leo into the duct.

"No! Together..."

The door exploded inward.

The leader girl in a princess dress and tilted tiara stood in the threshold, her blonde hair matted with gore, her pupils swollen to amber pits. She grinned, revealing teeth filed to points.

"Found you," she hissed.

Ethan lunged, driving the poker into her shoulder. She howled, but the two Accelerates swarmed behind her, twin girls with ashen skin and broken-glass laughter.

"RUN, LEO!"

The boy scrambled deeper into the duct. Ethan swung the poker in a wild arc, catching one twin in the jaw. Bone crunched. The other lunged, claws raking Ethan's thigh.

"Eth!" Leo's scream echoed through the vents.

"GO!"

Ethan kicked the second twin into a shelf, chemicals exploding in a toxic cloud. He dove into the duct, slicing his hands on jagged metal as he wriggled after Leo.

The Accelerates' screams pursued them, distorted by the tinny tunnels.

The duct opened into the mall's defunct theater, its screen torn, seats gutted for kindling. Ethan collapsed onto the sticky floor, blood soaking his jeans. Leo crouched beside him, tears cutting through the grime on his face.

"Y-You're hurt."

"Just a scratch." The lie tasted like copper in his mouth.

Ethan ripped his sleeve, creating a makeshift tourniquet. The wound was deep and angry. Infected? He pushed the thought away.

"We need to move," he said, staggering upright. "Blood leaves a trail."

Leo froze. "Eth... look."

A trail of crimson droplets led to the exit.

"Shit."

The boy pointed to the ceiling. "Up there."

A catwalk spanned the theater, leading to a projection booth. Ethan hesitated; heights made his stomach lurch, but the snarls of the Accelerates echoed closer.

They began to climb. Dust-caked reels littered the floor. Leo found a half-eaten candy bar in a drawer, melted, but still edible. Ethan let him devour it.

"Why are they so fast?" Leo asked, licking chocolate from his fingers.

"GeneCorp rewired their brains," Ethan said.

"Am I... like them?" Leo asked.

Ethan's chest tightened. Leo's veins were visibly pulsing now, a red web creeping toward his heart.

"No," he said firmly. "You're Leo."

The boy frowned. "But I'm changing."

Before Ethan could answer, glass shattered below.

The Accelerates swarmed the theater, five, six, a dozen. The girl in the princess dress led them, her shoulder mangled, eyes blazing.

"Little piggies," she crooned, scaling the seats. "Come out, come out."

Ethan barricaded the booth door with a film reel rack. "It's time to scream again, buddy."

Leo turned pale. "But last time... I could hardly breathe afterward."

"I know," Ethan said, gripping his shoulders. "But it's the only way."

Tears streamed down Leo's cheeks. "I'm scared."

"Me too."

The first Accelerate violently punched the door.

Leo's scream was a living thing, a sonic tsunami that ripped the booth's door off its hinges, shattered the remaining screen, and sent the catwalk swaying like a ship in a storm. Accelerates crumpled, clutching their ears, blood streaming from nostrils.

Ethan's vision blurred, his eardrums screaming. He grabbed Leo, now limp and gray, and stumbled onto the catwalk.

It snapped. They fell ten feet into a pile of moldy curtains. Ethan twisted his ankle, a surge of white-hot pain shooting up his leg. Leo lay motionless beside him.

"No, no, no..." Ethan pressed two fingers to the boy's throat. He felt a pulse, weak, but there.

The Accelerates struggled below, disoriented but not dead. They're adapting.

Ethan pulled Leo into the mall's atrium, navigating past a dry fountain littered with skeletons. Sunrise streamed through the broken skylights, casting a golden hue on the decay around them.

"Almost there," he breathed, though he had no idea where "there" was.

Suddenly, a hand gripped his ankle.

The remaining one of the Accelerated twins grinned up at him, her jaw unhinged like a snake's. "Got you."

Ethan kicked. Missed. She lunged for Leo.

A slingshot glass ball to the skull dropped her.

Ethan gaped. A girl stood over the twitching Accelerate, a slingshot in hand. No older than twelve, her auburn hair braided with razor wire.

"You're welcome," she said.

Behind her, a girl in her late teens emerged from the shadows, gaunt, hooded, a jagged scar peeking from her sleeve.

"Move. Faster." the teen said. "Or die."

4.7: The Sisters

The cinder block fell with a wet crunch, silencing the snarling Accelerate. Ethan stared at the girl with the slingshot, Mia, her auburn braids glinting in the dawn light.

Behind her, her older sister Clara stepped forward, her hood pulled low, a crowbar dangling from her scarred hand.

"You're welcome," Mia repeated, slinging her weapon over a shoulder patched with duct tape. "Now run. More are coming."

Ethan scooped up Leo, the boy's skin alarmingly cold. "Who the hell are you?" he demanded.

Clara's gaze flicked to Leo. "We're people who don't want to die today. Move," she said firmly.

They fled through the mall, which had become a graveyard of shattered storefronts and rusted escalator skeletons. Ethan's ankle throbbed with every step, but he bit back the pain. Leo stirred weakly, his breath coming in shallow rasps.

Mia led them to a hidden service stairwell, its door barricaded with shopping carts. "Home sweet home," she said, kicking aside a pile of empty soup cans.

The stairwell reeked of mildew and urine, but it was defensible. Clara wedged the door shut with her crowbar while Mia lit a candle, illuminating the graffiti-scarred walls and a nest of moth-eaten blankets.

Ethan laid Leo down, pressing a hand to his forehead. He was still burning up with a fever.

Mia's sharp gaze landed on Leo. "What's wrong with him?" she asked.

Ethan's muscles tensed. "Nothing," he replied defensively.

Clara stepped forward, each movement heavy and labored. Her eyes flicked to Ethan's injured leg, taking in the jagged tear in his shirt and the slow trickle of blood.

"You're immune, aren't you?" she murmured. "Accelerate saliva is toxic. You'd be changing by now."

Ethan stiffened. He looked down at his leg, the bleeding had already slowed. A spark of something, fear, disbelief, hope, rippled through him. Immune?

Clara barely acknowledged his reaction. "We're heading north," she said, her voice tight. "Supposedly, there's a GeneCorp bunker in Redwood Valley."

Ethan narrowed his eyes. "Supposedly?"

Clara's smile was thin and brittle. "We're all gambling now."

Mia rummaged through a dented toolbox, tossing Ethan a roll of gauze. "Wrap that leg, you're dripping."

Ethan hesitated, glancing at Clara. "Why help us?"

Clara leaned against the wall, her face partially hidden in shadow. "You're the first survivors we've seen in days. I figured you might know something."

"Like what?" Ethan asked.

"A cure. A safe zone. Anything."

Ethan snorted. "There's no cure. Just running."

Leo coughed, the sound wet and rattling. Mia knelt beside him, pressing a canteen to his lips. "He's got accelerated aging, doesn't he? Like the others."

"He's not like them," Ethan said, low and tight.

But the truth was starting to fray. Leo hadn't just screamed, he'd shattered steel, minds, glass. And if Ethan were being honest with himself, he was even afraid to touch him now.

"He will be," Clara said. "Unless you let us help."

"Help how?"

Mia pulled a map-book from her pack, its edges worn. "We've been tracking GeneCorp convoys. They're holed up in Bunker 7 at Redwood Line junction. Rumor has it they've got a cure."

"Bullshit," Ethan replied. "GeneCorp started this."

Clara's jaw tightened. "They also have resources. Medicine. Security."

Leo's hand twitched, grasping at nothing. "Eth... hurts."

Ethan's resolve cracked. "What's your plan?"

"We need to move, as fast and carefully as we can," Clara said, her voice low but firm. "But first, we need to rest. After that, we'll scavenge for supplies, food, and water for the journey."

Chapter 5: Hunt in the Mall

5.1: Who's Ava?

By morning, the decision had been made. At Mia's insistence, they raided the mall's pharmacy at dusk. Shadows clung to the empty remains of shelves and counters, the air thick with the mixed scents of bleach and stale perfume. The heavy gloom outside painted the cracked windows with a sickly orange hue, remnants of distant fires. Inside, each footstep came with the brittle crunch of shattered glass, echoing through the silence like distant whispers.

Ethan moved carefully, his injured leg stiff but determined, with Leo strapped securely to his back in a makeshift sling. The toddler's weight bore down on him, yet the child remained unnervingly still, no cries, no murmurs, only wide, watchful eyes that glinted faintly under dim fluorescent lights sputtering like dying stars. Clara scouted ahead, her crowbar gripped tightly, knuckles white with tension. She moved like a shadow, scanning dark corners with her narrowed eyes.

Mia led the way, her small frame tense, shoulders hunched with the weight of resolve. Her slingshot dangled at her side, fingers brushing the leather pouch like a talisman. Every so often, she paused to listen, tilting her head. But there was only the steady drip of water from a fractured pipe, a sound that reverberated through the skeletal remains of the once-bustling mall.

"Stay close," she whispered, her voice barely audible. Her breath fogged in the stale air. "Could be Accelerates at hunt."

Ethan nodded, her words sending an icy shiver down his spine. He adjusted his grip on the fire pick, its cold steel offering meager comfort against the gnawing dread. They passed rows of toppled shelves, their contents strewn and looted. Expired boxes of cough syrup and empty pill bottles littered the cracked linoleum, evidence of desperate hands. Ahead, the pharmacy loomed, a hollow shell, its security gate twisted and torn open.

Mia knelt beside a broken cabinet, prying it open as shards of glass bit into her gloves. Loose pill bottles scattered like marbles, labels smeared with dust and grime. The shelves had long been ransacked, but a few stubborn remnants clung to cracked wood. She pocketed what she could, antibiotics, painkillers, gauze.

"Painkillers," Mia muttered, slipping blister packs into her backpack. "Antibiotics. Bandages." The straps of her worn pack creaked under the growing weight. Every movement was careful and deliberate. Ethan hovered nearby, shifting his weight uneasily.

The pungent aroma of antiseptic mixed with the cloying stench of something long dead. Ethan barely registered Mia's words. His gaze lingered on faded posters lining the cracked walls, smiling faces advertising flu shots and allergy relief, echoes of a world that no longer existed. The fluorescent lights flickered overhead, buzzing like dying insects.

The air inside the pharmacy was thick and stagnant, heavy with mildew and the sharp tang of spilled chemicals. Shattered glass crunched under their boots with each step. Overturned shelves loomed like broken ribs, skeletal remains jutting into the dimness. The only sound was the echo of dripping water, a steady reminder of the building's slow decay.

Leo shifted, his small hands clutching the fabric of Ethan's jacket. His breathing was labored, each exhale rattling in his chest. Ethan could feel the heat radiating from Leo's body; the fever was rising again. They needed supplies, fast.

Clara signaled from ahead, her silhouette outlined against the pale moonlight filtering through a shattered skylight. The once-pristine pharmacy was now a mausoleum, its rows of shelves reduced to jagged ruins. Ethan caught up to her, careful to avoid the glass shards littering the floor. He hated how vulnerable they were. Every dark corner felt like a trap, every rustling shadow a threat.

"Anything?" Ethan asked, his voice hushed.

"Bandages. Some antiseptic. Not much else," Clara replied, her jaw tight. "Looks like we're late."

"We're always late," Mia muttered bitterly. She slammed the cabinet shut, the metallic clang echoing through the store. The sound made Ethan flinch; any noise was dangerous.

"Careful," Clara hissed, shooting her a glare.

But Mia's frustration was justified. This was their fifth pharmacy in two weeks, and each time, the shelves had been stripped bare. Every step further from safety felt like another gambling they could no longer afford to lose.

"Eth... who's Ava?" The voice was soft, yet it sliced through the air like a blade. Ethan stiffened. Mia froze, her hands pausing mid-motion.

Clara halted as well. The crowbar lowered slightly, but her jaw clenched, the muscles in her neck tightened. Shadows danced across her face, twisting her expression into something unreadable.

"No one," she snapped, the word flung like a knife. Her voice echoed faintly through the ruined aisles.

Mia's brow furrowed. She crouched beside a pile of scattered pill bottles, the unease in her chest growing heavier. "You never mentioned Ava."

"Drop it." Clara's tone was flat, but the weight behind it left no room for argument. She turned away, shoving a half-empty bottle of aspirin into her bag as if the conversation had never happened.

Ethan shifted uncomfortably, his arms tightening protectively around Leo. The makeshift sling dug into his shoulders, but he hardly noticed. The child's eyes, wide and unsettlingly perceptive, remained fixed on Clara. There was something in his gaze, a quiet insistence that pressed against the cracks in Clara's composure.

The tension clung to the air like smoke. Even the distant hum of the city seemed muted, as if the world itself were holding its breath.

But before anyone could speak, a sound shattered the uneasy stillness.

5.2: Not an Accelerate

"We're not alone," Clara whispered.

A crash. Metal on tile. A sudden creak echoed from the back of the store. Ethan's heart slammed against his ribs. Clara froze, crowbar raised, her eyes locked on the darkness beyond the broken shelves. The echo bounced through the hollow pharmacy, making Mia's pulse race. She shot a glance toward the cosmetics aisle, where shelves had collapsed in a tangled heap of plastic and glass. Shattered bottles spilled their contents across the floor, the air thickening with the sickly-sweet scent of forgotten perfumes.

Mia's fingers curled around the handle of her slingshot, the glass ammunition clinking softly in her pocket. Ethan adjusted Leo's sling, his arms tightening protectively around his brother. They waited, breathless. In the silence, the shadows seemed to shift, and then, a low growl cut through the air.

Clara's grip on the crowbar tightened. "We're not alone."

"What if it's just the wind?" Ethan asked, but his words lacked conviction.

Mia shook her head. "No wind makes that sound."

From the shadows, a faint scuffling noise emerged, a rhythmic scrape followed by silence. The hair on Ethan's arms stood on end.

Clara stepped forward, narrowing her eyes. "Stay behind me."

The crowbar gleamed under the flickering emergency lights as she edged closer to the source of the noise. Every footstep was deliberate, the soft crunch of debris beneath her boots the only sound. Mia followed, her heart pounding, the weight of her slingshot reassuring against her side.

Another sound broke the stillness: a low, wet gurgle that twisted through the air like a whisper of something unnatural. A distant scraping followed a dragging shuffle, something heavy. Shapes twisted beyond the dim light, shadows bleeding into one another. The fluorescent bulbs overhead flickered, sputtering weakly before plunging them further into darkness.

"Mia, stay close," Ethan murmured, his voice low. He adjusted Leo's weight; the child's fragile breathing felt hot against his neck. Every step forward was cautious, his boots skimming the shattered glass to avoid the crunch that could betray their position.

Clara crept along the aisle, her crowbar trembling slightly in her grip. The gutted remains of the pharmacy loomed around them, shelves bare, and counters overturned. Faint traces of old perfume and antiseptic lingered in the air, but beneath it was a metallic tang, a hint of something worse.

Then it came again. The scrape. Closer.

A guttural rasp echoed through the silence, dry and uneven. Mia's knuckles whitened around her slingshot; the weapon felt absurdly small in the vast darkness. Her eyes darted, catching glimpses of twisted reflections in the shards of mirror-strewn tile.

"What is that?" she whispered, her voice trembling.

"Not an Accelerate," Clara answered, though the certainty in her voice faltered. "Too slow."

The words had barely escaped her lips when a shape staggered into view, a figure that might once have been a man emerged from the shadows. His body sagged unnaturally, skin marred with dark veins that pulsed beneath a slick sheen of sweat. His movements were jerky and incomplete. Tattered clothing clung to his frame, stained dark with filth. One arm hung limp, while the other dragged a metal pipe that scraped mercilessly against the floor. His face was obscured beneath a curtain of matted hair.

Mia swallowed hard, fighting the bile rising in her throat.

The man's head jerked toward the sound. A groan gurgled from his cracked lips. His milky, unfocused gaze swept across the shadows. The bulbous veins in his neck pulsed erratically, as if something unnatural stirred beneath the surface. Then, without warning, he lurched forward.

Clara's eyes flashed with urgency. She raised a hand, fingers curled in a silent command. "Back room, move."

Mia didn't hesitate. She clenched the straps of her backpack, feeling the weight of the looted medicine pressing against her spine. Ethan shifted Leo, the boy's fragile frame trembling against his chest. Without a word, they moved swiftly, silent as ghosts.

The door loomed ahead, its chipped paint peeling away like dead skin. Clara shoved it open, the creak of the hinges echoing through the dark. The air inside was thick with mildew, the stench clinging to the walls like a sickness. They slipped in, and Clara wasted no time, she jammed the crowbar beneath the handle, the metal groaning as it wedged tight.

"That won't hold forever," Mia whispered, her voice barely audible.

"It doesn't need to," Clara replied, her eyes scanning the room. A sliver of moonlight filtered through a broken vent above, illuminating rusted shelves lined with empty crates and discarded plastic wrappers. The floor was sticky with remnants of spilled chemicals, the scent acidic and bitter.

Ethan's voice trembled as he whispered barely audible, "What was that?"

Clara didn't answer. Her breath was shallow, and her ear was pressed firmly against the door. The rotted wood felt cold against her skin. She strained to hear, but the scraping had stopped. Only the uneasy hum of distant electricity remained, crackling like restless insects. The silence was much worse. Whatever was out there, it was waiting.

5.3: Five Minutes

Ethan lowered Leo to the ground, his hands shaking as he checked the boy's pulse. Leo's eyes fluttered, his cobalt-blue irises clouded with exhaustion. "He's burning up," Ethan muttered, the words catching in his throat.

"Ava..." Leo murmured in his fever, the name trembling through the stale air. It wasn't a question; it was a ghost, spoken aloud.

Clara stiffened. The sound of that name twisted through her like barbed wire, tightening and cutting. She didn't look at Leo. Instead, she watched the sliver of light beneath the door, waiting for the shadows to shift. But nothing moved.

"You said she was no one," Leo continued, his voice low and almost accusatory.

"And I meant it." Clara's tone was sharp, but the undercurrent of dread betrayed her. The name lingered, thickening the air between them. She could feel Leo's stare, searching and demanding.

Ethan tightened his arms protectively around Leo, the boy's slow, steady breathing being the only comfort he had. The child stirred slightly, his face pressed against Ethan's shoulder. Leo's small hand clutched at the torn fabric of Ethan's shirt, his fingers twitching with restless dreams.

Mia rummaged through her bag, the clinking of pill bottles the only sound. She found a small packet of fever reducers, her fingers fumbling as she tore it open. "Here. Crush it if he can't swallow it."

"We shouldn't stay here," Ethan said softly. "If it comes back..."

Clara nodded. She understood the risk. Every second they remained there was another invitation for whatever waited beyond the door. But fear tangled her thoughts. She still heard the echo of that distant scrape, the monstrous weight behind it. She'd seen the twisted reflections in shards of glass, too many limbs, too many wrong angles. She didn't want to face what came next.

"We'll wait five minutes," she decided. "Then we move."

Mia exhaled sharply but didn't argue. Her fingers toyed with her slingshot, the rubber stretched taut between her knuckles. Her father had taught her how to aim and strike cleanly, but even with glass ammunition bearings lining her pockets, she knew a slingshot was no match for what prowled the shadows now.

Clara's mind wandered despite her effort to focus. Ava. The name clung to her like a brand she couldn't scrub away. She thought of the day she first whispered it, the softness that once accompanied it, a name spoken with hope, not fear. But that was before. Before the screams. Before the world unraveled.

She remained at the door, her ear pressed against the splintered wood. The moaning had ceased, replaced by a rhythmic scrape. Something dragged itself across the tiles, slow and deliberate. The shadows beneath the doorframe quivered.

"It's still out there," she murmured.

Mia's heart pounded. She could almost feel the thing on the other side, lingering, listening.

"We'll wait," Clara said, her voice resolute. "It'll move on."

Ethan cradled Leo, gently coaxing the medicine past his cracked lips. The boy whimpered but obeyed, his frail body curling into his brother's arms. Mia hugged her knees to her chest, the weight of the moment crushing. She wanted to scream, to run, but even the air felt suffocating.

Minutes passed, though they felt like hours. The scraping finally grew distant, swallowed by the stillness of the ruined mall. Clara didn't move until she was certain. Only then did she lower the crowbar, her arms trembling and slicking with sweat.

"We keep going," she said softly. "But we're not alone."

No one argued. They rose in silence, their shadows flickering against the stained walls. The pharmacy had been gambling. And though they had gained supplies, the cost was a reminder, survival demanded more than courage. It demanded everything.

A soft groan came from beyond the door, distant and lingering. This time, it wasn't just a scrape. It coiled low, heavy, like a predator stretching awake.

Ethan's eyes darted to Clara, his face pale. "It's not gone."

Clara swallowed, forcing down the knot in her throat. "No, it's not."

Outside, the darkness remained patient, and somewhere unseen, something was waiting.

"It is time. Get ready," Clara whispered, gripping the door handle tightly.

Ethan adjusted the makeshift sling on his back, securing Leo against him. The child stirred, his tiny hands clutching Ethan's jacket. Mia hoisted her backpack, the straps digging into her shoulders. Her fingers brushed against the slingshot tucked into her side pocket, the glass ball ammunition clinking softly.

Clara didn't wait for further reassurance. She slammed the door open, crowbar in hand, and charged forward. They sprinted. Mia's feet pounded against the tile, adrenaline surging through her veins. Ethan followed, his breath ragged, each step jarring. Leo whimpered softly, his small form tense against his brother's back.

The twisted remains of the mall blurred past them, toppled mannequins, shattered displays, and gaping storefronts. Shelves lay like fallen towers, their contents scattered. The air was thick with the acrid scent of mildew and old chemicals. Clara navigated through the maze of debris with ruthless precision, her gaze flicking between the shadows.

Behind them, the creature stirred. A rhythmic clank echoed through the hollow space, metal against tile. It dragged something, the sound a dreadful pulse in the air. Ethan dared not look back, but he felt it: the weight of its presence. The guttural groans that followed were no longer alone; others had begun to stir.

"Keep going!" Clara barked, her voice sharp and unwavering.

A flicker of movement flashed from the side, a pair of eyes gleamed in the dark. Mia's heart lurched. She yanked her slingshot free, trembling hands fitting a glass ball into the cradle. But before she could aim, the figure scuttled away, limbs bent unnaturally, swallowed by shadow.

The emergency exit loomed ahead, a jagged frame of twisted metal. The once-red door, now blackened and rusted, stood partially open. Beyond it, the night awaited, cold and uncertain. Clara didn't hesitate. She slammed her shoulder into the door, the rusted hinges screeching in protest as the gap widened just enough.

"Go!" she commanded.

Mia stumbled through first, gasping as the chilly night air struck her lungs. The sky, veiled by thick clouds, cast the parking lot in shades of gray. Weeds curled through cracked asphalt. Ethan followed, legs shaking beneath him. Leo clung tightly to his brother, frightened whimper muffled against his shoulder.

Clara was the last to leave. She spun just as the creature's twisted form emerged from the shadows. Pale, sinewy limbs dragged it forward, hollow eyes gleaming ominously. The stench of decay rolled from its sagging mouth. But the door groaned shut, sealing the horror inside. Clara jammed a broken metal pipe through the handles to bar it.

They stumbled away from the mall's skeletal frame. The groaning chorus behind them faded, muffled by thick walls. For now, they had escaped.

But the echoes lingered, a reminder of horrors lurking in the dark.

Mia doubled over, hands on her knees, lungs burning. "We made it," she gasped, though relief felt distant.

Ethan sagged against a rusted lamppost, arms trembling as he lowered Leo to the ground. The child's wide eyes remained fixed on the door, as if expecting it to burst open at any moment.

Clara kept her gaze locked on the mall. "Not for long," she murmured. "We need to keep moving."

Mia nodded, feeling the weight of glass ammunition pressing against her hip. They'd survived the night. But survival meant nothing without motion. Tomorrow's threats loomed.

The Accelerates were still out there, and so was the past Clara refused to speak of, the name that haunted the shadows.

Ava.

But for now, the darkness held no answers. Only silence.

And somewhere beyond it, the road awaited.

In the silence, even the shadows seemed to breathe. The world hadn't ended, but something in them had.

5.4: The End Is by Children

They regrouped in an abandoned office building a few blocks away, where the shelves had toppled, scattering their contents like fallen feathers. Pages, yellowed and torn, drifted beneath their footsteps as they settled into the dim space. The acrid scent of burnt paper lingered, mixing with the stale air of a place long forgotten.

Mia cracked open a can of peaches, the faint hiss breaking the heavy silence. Her hands were steady as she divided the syrupy slices onto scraps of foil. "We had a farm," she murmured, her voice flat.

"The Accelerates burned it. They don't just kill..." Her jaw tightened. "They play."

Leo nibbled at his peach, his legs jittering beneath him. The sticky sweetness clung to his fingers. "Why?"

Across from him, Clara barely shifted. Her eyes remained distant and hollow. "The virus amplifies aggression," she said, not looking up.

"They're programmed to... cull the weak."

Leo stiffened, the word clawing at him. "Programmed?"

Clara's gaze finally met his, her expression unreadable.

"GeneCorp's drugs had a built-in contingency. If the virus mutated, it would trigger a behavioral modifier. Survival of the fittest, taken literally."

Mia's foot slammed against the floorboards, the sharp noise breaking the silence. "They're monsters."

Leo flinched. Ethan's hand settled firmly on his brother's shoulder. "Not all of them."

Outside, the distant thrum of a helicopter grew louder, its searchlights slicing through the dust-choked air. The rhythmic beat of the blades echoed like a war drum. Clara's eyes fluttered shut as she breathed steadily. "We need to go. Now."

***

They moved in tight formation through the crumbling streets. Hollowed-out cars lined the curbs, their windows shattered, their skeletal frames long abandoned. The air was thick with the scent of rust and decay. Only their footsteps broke the silence, accompanied by the wind whispering through twisted metal.

It wasn't long before they descended into the subway tunnels. The air grew colder, stale and damp. Faint remnants of graffiti adorned the cracked concrete walls, desperate messages left behind by those who had hoped for salvation:

SAVE US.

GOD HAS LEFT.

THE END IS BY CHILDREN.

The flickering remnants of battery-operated lanterns cast weak halos of light. Water dripped from above, and the distant echo of something skittering through the dark sent a chill down Ethan's spine.

Leo stumbled, his breath coming in short, shallow gasps, beads of sweat forming along his hairline. "Eth... my chest hurts."

Ethan dropped to one knee, his hands trembling as he pressed his palm to Leo's ribs. His heart was hammering, erratic, too fast. Panic twisted Ethan's stomach.

Clara knelt beside them, her fingers brushing over Leo's forehead. The heat radiating from him was unmistakable. Her frown deepened. "It's a fever. His body's fighting the virus."

"He's not infected!" Ethan hissed, the words escaping before he could stop them.

Clara's gaze softened, reflecting a painful truth in her eyes. "Aren't we all?" she whispered.

The tunnel shuddered, and loose debris fell from the cracked ceiling. A distant screech echoed through the darkness, the unmistakable sound of the Accelerates closing in.

Mia gripped her slingshot, the metal smooth and cool in her hands. Her muscles tensed, ready for action. "Move. Now."

The subway tunnel engulfed them, its vast darkness illuminated only by the flickering beam of Ethan's dying flashlight. The air was thick and stale, heavy with decay and dampness. Their footsteps crunched over shattered glass and rodent bones, the noise swallowed by the oppressive silence. Shadows shifted around them, twisting into fleeting shapes that seemed to watch their every move.

Leo's ragged breaths echoed off the graffiti-covered walls, where ominous warnings were smeared in black and red:

CHILDREN ARE THE END.

THEY'RE IN THE AIR.

Ethan forced himself to look ahead, his pulse quickening. The meaning of those words clawed at the edges of his mind, but he pushed it down. They had to keep moving.

Clara leaned heavily against Mia, her infected arm slick with oozing yellow fluid that glowed faintly in the gloom, pulsing like something alive beneath her skin. Each step she took was labored, the infection gnawing at her strength, yet she pressed on, determination etched into the lines of her face.

"How much farther?" Mia whispered, her voice barely audible. She tightened her grip on the crowbar, the metal cool and familiar. Her short, auburn hair clung to her forehead, sweat streaking the grime on her pale face.

"Not too much until the Redwood Line junction," Clara murmured, her voice strained. "If the maps are correct..."

Ethan glanced back at Leo, who was struggling. His little brother clutched his ribs, his long limbs trembling. The flashlight beam illuminated the sheen of sweat on Leo's pale face, his eyes deep hollows of exhaustion. Ethan's breath caught as he noticed how tight the skin was stretched over the shifting framework of bones beneath.

He ages a year every week. The thought burned in Ethan's stomach, twisting it with anxiety. He couldn't stop wondering what would happen if Leo caught up to him, when the accelerated growth outpaced his fragile body.

A scurrying sound broke the silence as a rat, its fur matted and eyes gleaming, darted across the tunnel floor. Leo flinched, curling into himself.

"Eth, I'm cold," he said, voice small and trembling. The words hit Ethan harder than the frigid air ever could.

Without hesitation, Ethan pulled out Leo's jacket from backpack and draped it over Leo's thin shoulders. The fabric hung awkwardly on his brother, sleeves barely brushing his wrists. It was unsettling, just yesterday, it would have fit.

Mia snorted softly, though without a trace of humor.

Clara let out a wet, rattling cough, her legs buckling. She braced herself against the wall, breath coming in ragged gasps. Mia stepped forward to steady her, but Clara shook her head, forcing herself upright.

"Save your energy," Clara muttered, voice thin. "You're going to need it."

The tunnel stretched endlessly ahead, darkness humming with distant, unseen threats. Ethan adjusted the flashlight; its beam flickered weakly. The light barely kissed the walls now, leaving most of the path in shadow. But they had no choice.

With Clara's labored breathing and Leo's trembling steps, they pressed on. One mile down. Then two. Every heartbeat, every shuffled step brought them closer to the junction, and whatever waited beyond.

***

Seven months ago, the sisters' farm looked like something from a postcard. Rolling wheat fields swayed gently beneath a golden sky, and the air was thick with the scent of sun-warmed earth and the steady hum of cicadas. A soft breeze danced through the crops, bending them into waves of gold that shimmered under the late afternoon sun.

Clara, three months pregnant, stood by the old tractor with its hood propped open, her sun hat pushed back to reveal beads of sweat glistening on her forehead. The scent of synthetic motor oil clung to her hands, black smudges tracing the lines of her palms. She frowned in concentration, twisting a wrench with deliberate care. The engine sputtered in protest, but Clara only shook her head and kept working. Even with a baby growing inside her, she refused to slow down.

Across the field, Mia's laughter rang out, clear and carefree. Her bare feet kicked dust as she chased a pair of butterflies that flitted just out of reach. Every so often, she paused to crouch low, cupping her hands in hopes of catching a grasshopper. The hem of her faded sundress fluttered as she leapt through the tall grass, her joy as boundless as the sky above.

From the shade of the wide farmhouse porch, their parents watched with quiet smiles. The wooden rocking chairs creaked softly as they sipped lemonade from frosted glasses, condensation pooling on the rims and dripping onto the porch boards. They spoke in low, thoughtful tones, their words laced with the anticipation of becoming grandparents. Clara had caught fragments of the conversation earlier, promises of bedtime stories, handmade quilts, and lessons passed down through generations.

A mockingbird trilled from the nearby oak tree, harmonizing with the distant whirr of cicadas. In that moment, the world felt simple and whole. There were no whispers of outbreaks, no shadows of fear, only the sunlit promise of a future and the laughter of sisters echoing across the golden fields.

5.6: Mama, Don't Run Again

The tunnel shuddered. A low, grating rumble slithered through the earth, sending dust cascading from the cracked ceiling. Loose chunks of debris tumbled from the shadows, the air thick with the sour tang of disturbed mold. It felt like a collapse, or something worse.

"We need to rest," Ethan said, his voice low. He glanced at Leo's trembling legs; the boy could barely stand. Sweat slicked his pale face, and every shallow breath rattled in his chest.

"Rest is death," Mia muttered, her knuckles white around the crowbar. Yet Clara nodded, already sagging against a pillar, her breath thin and uneven. The dirty bandage on her arm had slipped, revealing veins blackened like cracked marble. The infection was relentless, creeping higher.

Mia knelt beside her, her steady hands betraying fear flickering in her eyes. "You promised we'd stick together."

Clara's fingers brushed her sister's cheek, cool and trembling. "I still am."

Ethan rummaged through his pack and pulled out their last protein bar. Mia's eyes flicked to it, her expression unreadable.

Wordlessly, she took it and split it into four perfect quarters, each piece exact. Leo devoured his share in two bites, hunger overriding restraint. His wide eyes darted to Ethan's untouched portion.

"Aren't you hungry?" Leo's voice was barely above a whisper.

"Not really," Ethan lied, forcing a half-hearted smirk. The act came too easily.

Clara watched him, fever-bright and unblinking. "You need strength," she murmured. "For him."

Ethan broke off a small bite, grimacing as he forced it down. The rest he slipped into Leo's hand. The boy hesitated, then accepted it with a silent nod.

The screech came without warning, a high, ululating wail that sliced through the dark. It echoed off the walls, twisting and warping. Ethan's blood ran cold. Then came the light, a thin beam cutting through the tunnel's gloom, bobbing with each step. The deliberate click of polished shoes followed, unnervingly calm.

"Hide," Clara breathed.

They scrambled behind a mound of broken concrete. Mia crouched low, her crowbar clutched tightly. Ethan held Leo against his chest, feeling the rapid thud of the boy's heartbeat. Leo didn't dare move; even his trembling stilled.

Three figures emerged from the shadows, their silhouettes starkly illuminated by the light from a cracked phone screen. They were the Accelerates. Their bodies twitched unnaturally, with muscles bulging beneath their tattered clothing. One of them dragged a crowbar along the wall, the metallic scrape breaking the silence.

The tallest of the three grinned, his teeth too white and too perfect. "Fresh ones," he crooned, his voice lilting with twisted delight. The others sniffed the air, their eyes flicking through the dark like hungry wolves.

Ethan's pulse thundered in his ears. Clara's hand curled into a fist, her nails digging into her palm. They had no choice but to wait, hoping the darkness would keep them safe.

But the Accelerates were patient. And the tunnel walls carried every whisper, every heartbeat. The hunt had begun.

At the center, the girl in the tattered princess dress tapped at the device, tiara askew, golden ringlets stiff with grease and blood. She giggled as she scrolled, the shattered remains of once an innocent beauty clinging to her like a mockery.

"Subject A-9 was observed nearby. It was malfunctioning, but still valuable."

Leo stiffened at the mention of A-9. The weight of those two syllables crashed down on him, feeling suffocating.

From the horror in the Accelerate girl's voice, Clara felt her blood freeze in her veins.

Ava.

The second Accelerate, a cherubic-faced boy in a bloodstained lab coat, licked his lips, a glint of hunger in his wild gaze.

"I want his liver," he purred. "They say defectives taste sweeter."

"Focus," snapped the third, adjusting tiny, round goggles that gleamed beneath the fractured light. "The bounty's alive only. GeneCorp wants him intact."

Ethan's stomach twisted. Bounty. Leo wasn't just hunted; he was currency.

A sickening realization washed over him. They were no longer human. Whatever remnants of humanity they had once possessed had long since withered, leaving only the twisted puppetry of the virus.

The cherub boy went still, nostrils flaring like an animal catching a scent.

"Do you smell... weakness?"

The flashlight beam sliced through the darkness toward their hiding spot, and the tunnel walls felt as though they were closing in. Ethan's hand tightened around Leo's, every muscle screaming to run. But Clara moved first.

With a guttural cry born of pain, she burst from the shadows, her voice trembling with fury and grief. She hurled a jagged rock with a shaking hand, her words dripping with venom.

"Leave him alone, Ava!"

The phone shattered on impact, glass shards scattering like dying embers. Darkness swallowed the tunnel.

For a moment, it felt as if time itself held its breath. The Accelerates froze, and a haunting stillness consumed everything.

Then Clara's voice pierced the silence.

"Run!"

Chaos erupted. Mia yanked Leo forward while Ethan seized Clara, dragging her away. Their footsteps pounded through the tunnel, blind and desperate. The walls pulsed with shadows, their jagged graffiti screaming silent warnings.

Behind them, the Accelerates howled, a chorus of feral hunger and twisted laughter. Then Ava's voice rang out: high, singsong, laced with venomous nostalgia.

"Oh, Mammy. Sweet Mama, I miss you. Where have you been all this time? You left me alone. I miss you so much. Please come back, Mama. Don't run away again."

Her laugh slithered through the dark, a cracked, cynical echo that clawed at Clara's resolve. Tears welled, but she forced herself forward, feet pounding the filthy floor. She couldn't stop. Not now.

Even as the echoes faded, Ava's words lingered, ghostly whispers, cruel reminders of what had been lost, and what still hunted them.

Clara's ragged breath mingled with the stench of mildew as she pushed through the narrow service passage. The grimy walls pressed close, and the fluorescent glow of the maintenance lights flickered with a sickly hum.

The pounding came seconds later, heavy fists against the rusted door like a war drum. Each strike sent vibrations skittering across the floor, stirring up dust from decades past.

"Open," the cherub boy sang, syrupy and taunting, his voice muffled by metal. "Or we'll optimize your bones."

Leo's cry split the air, a sharp wail that twisted into something unnatural. It echoed off the walls, warping into a shriek that set Clara's teeth on edge. Then, silence. The pounding ceased.

Ava's cynical laughter followed, lilting and childlike, yet stripped of all innocence.

"Anomaly confirmed," she giggled, her voice brimming with glee. "The board will reward us. Mama, do you hear me? Come with me, Mama."

Her voice clung like toxic fog. Then came the rhythmic scrape of retreating footsteps. Silence wrapped around them once more, suffocating.

Leo slumped, knees buckling. A thin trail of blood trickled from his nose. Ethan caught him, panic in his eyes as he wiped the crimson smear away with trembling fingers.

"You're okay," Ethan murmured, voice shaking. "You're okay. I've got you."

Clara leaned against the wall, feeling the infection creep further up her arm. Her veins had darkened and twisted, pulsing with a sickly heat. She stifled a groan, the echo of Ava's laughter still twisting in her mind.

"They'll be back," she rasped. "With reinforcements."

Mia kicked the toolbox. Bolts clattered like bones across the floor. The noise echoed like the last remnants of defiance.

"We're trapped!"

Clara fumbled with the crumpled map in her pocket, the paper damp with sweat. Her trembling finger traced a jagged red line, smudged and torn.

"There's an exit... here," she murmured. "Old sewers. The line connects to the drainage tunnels."

Ethan frowned. "The sewers are flooded. They could collapse."

"Better than being processed," Clara shot back, her voice brittle.

Leo stirred weakly in Ethan's arms, his eyelids fluttering. "Eth... my head hurts."

5.7: Do the Thing

Ethan cupped the back of Leo's head, heart lurching at the warmth of the boy's fevered skin. He stroked his brother's damp hair, willing away the fear curling in his chest.

"Rest. I've got you," he said soothingly.

Mia stood rigid, her knuckles bone-white around the crowbar. The usual hardened glare in her eyes softened, though something raw remained beneath the surface.

"How do you keep going?" she asked, voice cracking. "After... everything?"

Ethan glanced down at Leo, the boy's frail frame trembling with each labored breath. He tightened his grip and brushed his thumb over his brother's brow. The answer came without hesitation.

"Same reason you do."

The sewer reeked of rot and chemicals, the air thick with the sour tang of decay. Knee-deep water sloshed around their legs, each step sending ripples through the stagnant filth. Mia gagged, one hand clamped over her mouth and the other gripping her crowbar. The walls were slick with moisture, crusted with black grime that dripped in sluggish rivulets. Overhead, rusted pipes lined the tunnel, groaning with the occasional gurgle of unseen sludge.

Clara stumbled. Her skin had taken on a sickly pallor, gray as grave dirt. Her breath rasped in shallow gasps, and her infected arm hung limp at her side. The veins beneath her skin pulsed with a dark, unnatural hue, creeping like ink through her bloodstream.

"Keep moving," she slurred, her voice brittle.

"You first," Mia snapped, though worry flickered behind her scowl. Before Clara could respond, her legs buckled, and she crumpled into Ethan's arms. He recoiled slightly at the heat radiating from her fevered skin.

Suddenly, the tunnel shuddered. A low groan, resembling the death throes of some monstrous beast, echoed through the darkness. Ethan barely had time to process the sound before a deafening roar filled the air. A surge of black water exploded down the passage, sweeping everything in its path. It hit them like a battering ram, waist-high, reeking of sewage and rot, and moving fast.

"Leo!" Ethan's voice rose in the pitch as he lifted his brother above the waterline, fingers gripping Leo's drenched jacket. The current tore at them, dragging debris, splintered wood, twisted metal, and the bloated carcass of a rat the size of a cat.

"Climb! Now!" Ethan shouted, shoving Leo toward a rusty service ladder bolted to the wall. Leo scrambled, his fingers clutching the cold metal, but then he faltered.

"It's blocked!" Leo's voice broke with panic. Above him, the ceiling had partially collapsed, choking the ladder with concrete and twisted rebar. There was no way up.

Clara's flashlight quivered as she swung the beam in search of another escape. The pale light skimmed over the walls, then caught the glint of a grated air vent just above the rising water.

"There!" she pointed, her voice ragged. "The vent!"

Ethan didn't hesitate. "I'll boost you!" He bent low, interlacing his fingers. Clara stumbled forward, her infected arm dragging at her side. She planted her good hand on Ethan's shoulder, grimacing as he heaved her upward. Her nails scraped against the rusted grate, but the metal barely budged.

"It's... stuck!"

"Leo!" Ethan's eyes locked onto his brother, desperation sharpening his voice. "Do the thing!"

Leo's lips trembled, fear clouding his wide eyes. But then he opened his mouth, and a piercing, unnatural scream erupted, reverberating through the tunnel. The sound struck the vent with such force that it shattered the corroded hinges. The grate clattered away, exposing the narrow shaft beyond.

"Go!" Mia urged, pushing Leo forward as her hands trembled. "Crawl. Don't look back!"

The water surged up to their chests, biting with an icy cold. Clara hesitated, her body shaking with exhaustion.

"Leave me," she gasped.

"Not happening," Ethan growled, wrapping an arm around her waist. With one final push, he propelled her toward Mia, who caught her with all her strength, struggling against the current that threatened to pull Clara away.

"Pull her up!" Ethan shouted, his voice cracking. Mia didn't hesitate; she braced herself against the vent, muscles straining as she heaved Clara into the shaft.

The water surged higher, lapping at Ethan's shoulders, while debris slammed against his legs. But as Clara disappeared into the dark vent, he finally grasped the edge and pulled himself up, his body trembling from the effort.

The tunnel let out a deep groan as a violent tremor shook its walls. When the surge reached its peak, a final, deafening crack echoed through the space, causing the ceiling to collapse. Stone and metal fell into the flood, sending a shockwave rippling through the water.

Ethan pulled himself into the vent just as the floodwater engulfed the space below. The roar of destruction pursued them, but the tunnel's darkness swallowed the sound completely.

They crawled in silence, the narrow metal shaft trembling beneath them. Behind them, the sewer lay in ruins. But for now, they had escaped.

The vent expelled them onto a rain-soaked street, the storm howling as if the sky itself were being torn apart. Sheets of water lashed their faces, and the concrete felt slick beneath their trembling limbs. Leo was the first to collapse, retching the foul, stagnant water from the sewers, his small frame wracked with spasms. Ethan dropped beside him, his hand steady on his brother's back as he murmured reassurances that neither of them fully believed.

Clara rolled onto her back, her chest heaving. The thin fabric of her shirt clung to her, soaked through and revealing the darkened veins creeping up her arm. The infection pulsed beneath her skin, black and grotesque reminder of how little time she had left. Every movement sent a new wave of pain slicing through her body.

Mia crouched nearby, her rain-matted hair plastered to her face. Concern lined her features, mingled with frustration.

"You're getting worse," Mia said, her voice barely audible above the wind.

"Noted," Clara replied, her raspy voice a feeble attempt at humor.

Ethan forced his gaze forward. In the far distance, GeneCorp's bunker loomed like a shadowy monolith, its cold floodlights slicing through the downpour, stark and mechanical, a fortress.

"We're close," he said, though the words felt hollow. "Two miles, max."

What he didn't know was that two miles would stretch into a pilgrimage, measured in aching days.

Leo tugged at Ethan's sleeve, his voice barely above a whisper.

"What if they don't let us in?"

"They will." Ethan lifted Leo onto unsteady feet, attempting to mask the gnawing uncertainty. "We've got a living weapon, remember?"

Leo's laughter was brittle, a ghost of mirth swallowed by fear.

As they trudged through the flooded streets, Clara lagged behind. Every step felt heavier. Mia matched her pace, her voice softening with rare tenderness.

"You should've told them."

Clara's smirk flickered, her eyes already elsewhere. "Told them what? That I'm a time bomb? They've got enough nightmares to deal with."

Mia's fingers found Clara's, their hands entwined with quiet desperation. "You don't get to die quietly."

Clara squeezed back, a faint trace of a smile flickering through her pain. "Wasn't planning on it."

Ahead, Ethan glanced over his shoulder, his eyes narrowing with suspicion. But the storm swallowed whatever question lingered on his lips. The bunker's lights gleamed through the rain, beckoning them forward, a promise of salvation or the bitter taste of betrayal.

Part II

Chapter 6: Love is the Last Rebellion

6.1: Between Sister and Daughter

The rain slowed to a gentle drizzle, filling the air with the scent of wet asphalt and decay. As the storm finally eased, the world seemed to hold its breath, each drop of rain like a tiny, slow-motion heartbeat against the silence. They stumbled into an abandoned bookstore, its windows boarded up, but the door hung ajar, as if the building itself had given up. The smell of mildew and decaying paper overwhelmed them, sour, and stagnant. Inside, the air hung thick, almost unbreathable, suffocating under the weight of forgotten stories and broken dreams.

Mia kicked aside a toppled shelf with a grunt, sending a cascade of dog-eared paperback romances skittering across the floor. The books scattered in all directions like abandoned memories, their pages yellowed and brittle, their covers desperately clinging to what little color remained. "Home sweet home," Mia muttered under her breath, her voice flat and emotionless, a hollow echo of her former self. Sarcasm was her armor, a way to shield herself from the raw emotions that threatened to tear her apart.

Clara, moving deliberately, leaned against a fallen shelf, seeking any comfort it could provide. The rough wood pressed into her back, but she barely felt it. Her infected arm, concealed beneath the torn fabric of a filthy lab coat, appeared emaciated against the bulk of the garment. Black veins crept across her skin, crawling up her shoulder like ink bleeding through parchment. The infection throbbed just beneath the surface, serving as a constant reminder of what was to come. Every breath dragged through her lungs like shards of glass, cutting her from the inside. But it wasn't the pain that drained her strength. It was the growing realization that the others already knew her truth.

Ava.

Clara caught the shared, unspoken understanding in their eyes, a quiet grief that hung in the air. Mia's gaze lingered too long on Clara's arm, her jaw tightening whenever Clara shifted beneath her coat.

Ethan, though stoic, could barely bring himself to meet her gaze. And Leo, poor Leo, kept his head down, desperately clinging to the shredded remnants of hope. They all knew what was happening. But even worse than the infection coursing through Clara's veins was the haunting image burned into her mind, her baby girl, no longer innocent, no longer a baby. Ava had been twisted by the virus, driven by something far more monstrous.

Clara had long dreaded the day she might see her daughter again. She knew the world was cruel, that the virus could turn even the most innocent into nightmares. But whispers had reached her, rumors of a girl clad in the tattered remnants of a princess dress, her golden curls matted with dirt and blood, and a tiara askew on her small head. A girl who giggled with delight as others screamed. A hunter.

The child was gone. GeneCorp had seen to that. Whatever twisted experiment they had unleashed had stolen Ava from her, leaving behind only a vessel of malice and torment. The thought was unbearable. Clara's hands trembled, her nails digging into her palms as if physical pain could pull her away from the memories.

She caught Mia watching her again. The younger girl's face was guarded, but her concern was evident. Clara wanted to shield her sister from the horrors that loomed just beyond the shadows, but how could she? How could she protect Mia when the thing she feared most wore the face of the daughter she had dreamed of cradling to sleep.

The air in the abandoned bookstore was thick with mildew and the rot of forgotten paper. Shelves remained toppled; their contents scattered like fallen leaves. Mia's movements were tense as she rifled through the debris, searching for anything useful. Clara envied her determination, but even Mia couldn't mask the heavy weight, pressing down on them all.

"She's going to come," Clara thought bitterly.

But the truth was more damning. Clara knew she wouldn't be able to face Ava alone, and if it came to choosing between her sister and her daughter, the decision was unbearable. Horror gripped her heart, gnawing through the fever of the infection. Mia was all she had left, the last fragment of family in a world that had already devoured so much.

Clara's jaw clenched, her resolve trembling under the weight of impossible choices. She would stand and fight, but whether it was for Mia or for Ava, she didn't know.

As Mia rifled through the wreckage of the bookstore's coffee shop counter, her hands moved with practiced speed and precision, but her eyes told another story. Beneath the flicker of determination was a void, a hollow space carved out by endless exhaustion and despair. She wasn't just scavenging for food or supplies; she was searching for something to keep going, anything that might provide a reason to push forward. Yet Clara couldn't shake the feeling that Mia had already given up hope, just as she had.

6.2: Can I Keep It?

Ethan gently lowered Leo onto a threadbare couch, its cushions swollen and misshapen, oozing foam like something half-dead. The boy's small fingers instinctively curled around a dusty teddy bear wedged between the armrests; its once-soft fur was now matted and grimy, a remnant of a life long gone. Leo's eyes were wide and empty, clouded by fever, yet he clutched the toy as if it were the last piece of normalcy left in a world that had forgotten what it meant to be whole.

"Can I keep it?" Leo's voice was weak, but the question was desperate, tinged with something unspoken, almost like a plea.

Ethan's throat tightened at the words, and for a moment, he felt the full weight of the world crash down on him. Leo hadn't asked for a toy at all, he never had time to ask. He hadn't asked for anything beyond food, water, a place to rest, and a story to be read. But now, with the remnants of innocence slipping away from him, the child was seeking something to hold onto, a memory, a fragment of the world he once hoped to know.

"Sure, buddy," Ethan said, his voice cracking under the strain of holding it all together. The words felt hollow as they left his lips, but he couldn't bring himself to say anything else. "You can keep it."

Leo nodded, clenching the teddy bear tighter against his chest. His breath hitched as his tiny fingers grasped at the fabric, and his body trembled with fever and exhaustion.

Once, Leo had made it dance across the couch to make Mia laugh. Now, it sat limp in his arms, no games left. Ethan looked down at him, heart breaking for the little boy who had once been full of life and laughter. Now, all that remained was a fragile echo of the child who had loved stories and believed in good things and simple joys. Those days were gone, and with them, so much of Leo's spirit had faded. In their place, there was nothing but a hunger to survive, to keep moving, to keep fighting, no matter how little strength remained.

Clara's eyes followed Ethan's movements, observing the tenderness he showed toward Leo. A pang of something, perhaps regret, washed over her, though she wasn't entirely sure. Bitterness churned inside her, thick and heavy, as she turned her gaze back to the dimly lit room, almost as if she could hide from the truth there. But she couldn't hide from it, not anymore. None of them could.

Ethan wiped the rainwater from Leo's feverish brow, his fingers trembling against the boy's damp skin. Leo's shallow breaths hitched, his chest rising and falling in an uneven rhythm. He sprawled unnaturally across the moth-eaten couch, its faded fabric torn and oozing tufts of yellowed stuffing. Outside, the storm raged on, water dripping steadily from the cracked ceiling. The boy's jeans, already too short, revealed ankles streaked with angry red stretch marks.

Ethan knelt beside him, peeling back the boy's torn sock to inspect his swollen ankle, the bone visibly protruding beneath pale, overstretched skin.

"Another growth spurt?" Ethan's voice was low, though the worry in it rang clear.

Leo nodded weakly; his face drawn. "It feels like my bones are stretching. Like something's pulling me apart."

Ethan swallowed the lump in his throat. He reached for the battered canteen, the metal cool in his shaking hands. Carefully, he pressed it to Leo's cracked lips. "Slow sips. Don't gulp it."

Leo obeyed, his trembling fingers curling around Ethan's wrist for balance. Each swallow hurt, the muscles in his throat working sluggishly. When he finally pulled away, a faint whimper escaped him. Ethan brushed a damp lock of hair from the boy's face, fighting the hopelessness gnawing at his gut.

Across the room, Mia stood with her arms crossed, an expression of concern etched on her face. Dark shadows clung beneath her eyes, unmistakable evidence of restless nights and worry that had taken its toll. "He's getting worse," she said flatly, her voice barely above a whisper.

"He's adapting," Ethan retorted, the words stiff and bitter. Yet, even as he spoke, the lie felt sour on his tongue.

Clara's voice, brittle and worn, broke the tense silence. "You need protein. Ethan, check the storage room."

He turned to her and noticed her pale skin and the sweat beading on her brow despite the chill in the air. The infection was spreading. The veins around her shoulder were darker now, twisting in jagged patterns beneath her thin shirt. Each breath she took seemed to rattle, and though she tried to mask it, the effort was evident.

"You look worse than he does," Ethan said, his concern slipping through his stoic facade.

Clara, though weakened, managed to smirk. "And you look like a drowned rat." Her words were strained, but the dry humor lingered. "Move."

Reluctantly, Ethan pushed himself to his feet and walked toward the splintered door leading to the back. Shadows enveloped him as the dim remnants of daylight barely penetrated beyond the threshold.

6.3: The Sunflower Field

Clara sank onto the edge of the dilapidated coach, each movement slow and deliberate. Pain flared with every shift, sharp and searing, as if icicles were threading through her bones. The infection had burrowed deep, its cold tendrils woven into her core, sending shivers through her fevered skin that mocked the memory of summer warmth.

Yet the physical agony paled beside the ache in her chest, a crushing, breath-stealing despair.

It was heavier than her limbs, more enduring than the fever, and it threatened to pull her under with each passing second.

Her breaths came shallow, lips dry and cracked.

She curled slightly, instinctively guarding the part of herself where the fragile dreams of motherhood once lived.

She had imagined Ava's touch, her laughter, her warmth.

But those dreams had never taken shape outside the womb.

The pressure behind Clara's eyes sharpened with each blink, and for a fleeting second, she wished she could forget.

Forget the world.

Forget herself.

Across from her, Leo sat in silence, clutching the tattered teddy bear he'd salvaged from the wreckage.

Its fur was matted, its seams frayed, its button eyes dull, a ghost of what it once had been.

Like everything else.

The silence between them wasn't empty.

It pulsed, electric, alive with unspoken truths.

Leo's eyes, too old for someone his size, studied her.

Eyes that held a knowing that no child should bear.

He was only one year old in time, but the experimental growth acceleration had aged his body and mind into something uncanny.

He saw things no one else did.

And he remembered.

"You're sick," he said, voice soft but leaden.

Clara met his gaze. Her composure wavered, control fraying at the seams. "Aren't we all?" she said, bitterness leaking through. She tried to smile, but it withered before it could rise.

Leo's grip on the bear tightened. "No," he whispered. "You smell like the bad kids. Did Ava do this to you?"

The words struck her like a hammer. Clara froze. She had heard those words before, passed from one trembling mouth to another. "Bad kids." It was a phrase steeped in terror. In corruption. In warning. Children who had been altered beyond recognition, vessels for infection, for loss. Her throat tightened. Her heart pounded. The phrase carried not just fear but condemnation, as if her transformation was a sin.

Leo's expression didn't change. He wasn't cruel. Just honest. "You're not bad yet."

Clara's chest constricted. Not yet. But soon.

"What do you mean?" she asked. Her voice trembled. "How do you know about Ava? I never told you about her. Not when we met. Not ever. But in the mall... you said her name. You asked about her."

Leo stroked the worn fabric of the bear with one finger. His eyes drifted toward something invisible, as if the air itself carried memories he could read. "She comes to me when I sleep," he murmured. "We stand in a sunflower field. She doesn't talk. We just look at each other."

Clara's vision swam. Her blood surged in her ears, drowning out the sound of the rain. The pain in her arm burned hotter, radiating through her chest like fire. She thought of the place she used to retreat when she was pregnant, a field, a breeze, sunflowers swaying under a sky full of light. Ava had never seen that world. She never could.

"She's beautiful there," Leo said. "Like a princess of all angels."

Clara flinched. That word, princess, unraveled something loose inside her. Ava had been imagined that way: bold, kind, fierce, sword in hand. Not a girl trapped in a tower, but one who charged the gates.

"When you found us in the mall," Leo continued, "that night she said your name. She cried."

Clara felt the walls of her heart collapse. Her mind recoiled from the image yet clung to it. The sound of her name comes from Ava's lips. The tears.

"What happened then?"

Leo blinked slowly. "She left. But sometimes I don't want her to." Leo, with his hauntingly mature perspective, seemed to embody the cruel logic of their fractured existence. His recollections of the sunflower field, a place of imagined beauty and fleeting peace, in his sleep offered a temporary escape from the horrors that defined their reality.

Clara clenched her jaw. The pain in her infected arm surged again. Her fingers curled, then flexed. "She didn't choose this," she whispered. "She didn't ask for any of it. It was Mark's fault. Mine too. We let GenCorp touch her."

Leo watched her without blinking. "And yet she became one. She's not like you dreamed. She's one of them now."

Clara reeled. The words sank deep, anchoring themselves in her spine. "She's still mine."

Leo tilted his head. "Is she?" he asked. "Would she say the same about you?"

The room shrank. The words dug under Clara's skin like glass. Not cruel. Just true. She turned her face to the window, tears spilling freely now. The storm outside blurred her reflection, but she could still see it: a face hollowed by pain, a stranger. A mother who had never been.

As the storm outside intensified, so too did the turmoil within Clara's heart. The room, with its peeling walls and remnants of a forgotten past, became a silent witness to her inner conflict, a struggle between the desire to hold on and the crushing weight of inevitable loss.

She brushed at the wetness on her cheeks, her fingers trembling. "I'm not giving up on her," she whispered. "I can't."

Leo said nothing.

Minutes passed. Or seconds. The clock had stopped ticking long ago. Leo's small hands clutched the remnants of an innocence lost to time, remaining still for a moment before he answered in a voice that was both resigned and resolute.

"We keep hoping."

Clara turned back to him. He was so small, still clutching the bear to his chest like a shield. But there was nothing small about his presence. He spoke like someone who had seen beginnings and endings and lived through them.

"Even if she's gone from here, I believe that somewhere, beyond all this pain, there's a place where she is still the beautiful Ava I remember."

Clara nodded, slowly. The ache in her body dulled, but the ache in her heart was a chasm. Still, Leo's words carved out space within her sorrow for something else: a breath, a possibility.

She stood, legs shaking beneath her. She crossed the room in silence, stood at the broken window. Rain traced chaotic lines down the glass like veins. Beyond the glass, the world sagged, bled, and waited.

"I won't let my dreams of her fade," she said. Her voice was low but firm. "I won't forget the girl I believed she could be."

Behind her, Leo pulled the bear tighter. He didn't speak, but the silence between them softened. He understood.

Clara turned from the window. Her limbs were heavy, but her spine was straight. Her chest ached, but her breath came easier.

"I will bring her back," she said. Not as a plea. As a vow.

Outside, the storm eased, the rain thinning into mist. Beyond the glass, the horizon blushed with the first fragile hint of morning.

But inside her, something stronger awakened.

Not peace.

Conviction.

Even if Ava never returned to her arms, even if she had become something unrecognizable, Clara would hold the line. She would endure the pain, the silence, the slow burn of infection. She would not let the world erase her child. Or herself. Not without a fight.

Love, in this world, wasn't comfort. It was a rebellion.

It was the last weapon she had.

For Clara, the struggle was not merely to hold onto memories of the past but to forge a future in which the bond between a mother and her daughter, though scarred by sorrow, could one day be mended. With every trembling step she took away from the window and toward an unknown horizon, she carried with her the fierce conviction that love was the greatest defiance against the cruel forces that sought to tear them apart.

And she would wield it to the end.

As the day slowly broke over the horizon, bathing the world in pale, tentative light, Clara, and Leo sat together in the quiet aftermath of the storm, their hearts heavy yet unyielding. In that fragile moment of clarity, amidst the soft whispers of a new day, the promise of redemption flickered, a silent, enduring vow that even in the face of overwhelming loss, hope would always be worth the fight.

Clara's chest ached with the dual torment of physical pain and the heavy weight of grief.

The infection pulsed through her veins, creating a slow, cruel rhythm that matched the murmur of the storm outside.

Each heartbeat throbbed like a reminder of her failing body, while memories of loss and shattered dreams filled her mind with unbearable sorrow.

Yet, even as the pain threatened to consume her, she refused to let fear dictate her every move.

"Get some rest," she murmured to Leo, her voice soft yet resolute.

With a tenderness born of deep love and desperation, she gently brushed a cool, trembling hand across his fevered forehead.

For a brief, fragile moment, his eyes, full of unspoken questions and ancient sadness, met hers, sharing in the silent communion of their suffering.

Then, as if in quiet resignation to the harshness of their reality, he curled into the ruined couch and clutched the bear tighter, seeking solace in its worn familiarity.

Time moved slowly in that small, broken bookstore, a dilapidated refuge where every breath seemed measured by the relentless drip of water and the persistent hum of failing machinery.

The storm outside raged on, its distant thunder a grim reminder of the chaos that lay beyond their fragile sanctuary. Wind clawed at the broken shutters, carrying the scent of ozone and ash.

Each droplet of rain echoed in the cavernous space, acting as a metronome to the rhythm of their despair.

In this twilight of neglect and ruin, hope was a rare commodity, but it was hope that bound these wounded souls together.

6.4: The Sunflower Watched

Amid this turmoil, Ethan reappeared.

His arrival was heralded by the clatter of his heavy steps on the warped wooden floor.

He carried with him a dented can of peaches and a well-worn first-aid kit, both symbols of the scant resources they had scavenged from the remnants of a world that had long since crumbled.

His forced grin did little to mask the shadows beneath his eyes, shadows that spoke of burdens too heavy for any one person to bear.

"Jackpot. Sort of," he said with a wry attempt at humor, though the hollowness in his tone betrayed the depth of his sorrow.

Mia, ever the pragmatist even in the darkest of times, stepped forward with a determined glint in her eye.

With practiced ease, she pulled out her cherished Swiss Army Knife, a tool that had seen more battles than most could imagine, and pried the can open. The metal lid screamed in protest, a discordant note that momentarily sliced through the ambient symphony of rain and machinery.

As the lid came off, a sickly-sweet scent of preserved fruit wafted through the damp air, a smell that evoked memories of simpler, long-forgotten days. It clashed with the metallic tang of rust and the musty rot of soaked pages nearby.

"Clara gets the first sip," Mia declared, her tone a curious blend of authority and tenderness, as if giving a small gift in the midst of their collective suffering.

Clara hesitated, her voice raspy as she murmured, "I'm fine." But the infection clawed relentlessly at her lungs, making each breath a grueling battle against an invisible enemy that sought to drain every ounce of her vitality. Mia's gaze sharpened, her eyes narrowing with a mix of compassion and urgency. "Drink," she said softly, her tone low and insistent, as if the simple act of drinking could momentarily banish the relentless pain gnawing at Clara's insides.

Reluctantly, Clara accepted the can from Mia's outstretched hand.

Her trembling fingers wrapped around the cold metal as she took a slice of fruit.

The thick, syrupy liquid, a bittersweet concoction of sustenance and sorrow, burned as it slid down her raw throat.

For a fleeting moment, the pain receded into the background, replaced by a numb, almost dreamlike reprieve.

Wiping her mouth with the back of her hand, she managed to make a weak, rueful smirk.

"Happy now?" she asked, her voice a fragile mix of bitterness and the faintest whisper of hope.

Mia's lips curled into a wry, almost mocking smile, a small, defiant gesture in the face of overwhelming despair.

"Ecstatic," she replied, though the weight of their shared sorrow tempered the echo of her words.

In the silence that followed, the storm outside continued its relentless assault, and the creaks of the crumbling building whispered of decay and forgotten promises.

Every sound was a reminder that time was slipping away, that each moment was a battle against both physical deterioration and the corrosive effects of grief.

In that battered refuge, every small act, every shared bite, every tentative touch, became a defiant stand against the relentless march of time and decay.

The room, scarred by neglect and the ravages of an unseen enemy, held a fragile hope that lingered in the shadows.

This hope was born of necessity, forged in the crucible of loss and survival, and sustained by the unbreakable bonds between those who refused to let go.

Amid the oppressive gloom, each shared moment was a rebellion, a silent, stubborn insistence that life, however broken, was still worth living.

As the storm continued its relentless fury outside, the quartet, Ethan, Leo, Mia, and Clara, sat together in the dim light, their faces etched with lines of pain and determination.

Ethan, ever the quiet anchor, held his younger brother close, his arms a fortress against a world that had lost all mercy.

The weight of responsibility sat heavily on his shoulders, but he bore it with stoic grace.

Leo, despite his age, exuded solemn wisdom far beyond his small stature.

His eyes, reflecting ancient sadness, held secrets of a world lost to madness and despair.

He understood the unspoken language of suffering, a language that resonated in every whispered sigh and tearful glance.

Mia's practical nature served as a steady counterpoint to the raw emotional turmoil that flickered across Clara's features.

Together, they formed an unlikely constellation of hope in a universe that had long since forgotten the meaning of that word.

In the oppressive quiet of that ruined bookstore, every moment was savored as if it were a fragile gift.

The persistent drip of rain through the cracked roof became a metronome for their shared existence, each droplet a reminder of both the passage of time and the enduring solitude they all faced.

Yet, in that solitude, there was also a strange intimacy, a connection that transcended words and bridged the gap between despair and hope.

The battered walls around them bore silent witness to their struggles; each peeling layer and fractured beam echoed the resilience of those who dared to dream in the face of relentless darkness.

Clara's thoughts wandered as she watched the rain trace intricate patterns on the broken windowpane. The droplets mingled with the grime and faded memories of better days, forming a tapestry of sorrow and longing. In her mind, she recalled a time when the world had been filled with light, a time when laughter and love were not luxuries but natural parts of everyday life. That world, now reduced to fragments of memory, seemed both impossibly distant and achingly near.

Every heartbeat, every shallow breath reminded her of all that had been lost and all that still might be saved.

Ethan's gaze often lingered on Clara, the pain in her eyes mirrored in his own. He didn't speak often, but his presence alone was an ointment. He moved through their fragile world like a shadow, mending broken things, gathering what little food they had, wrapping blankets around the others at night. His quiet devotion was a language of its own, one Clara had come to understand. She took strength from it, even when her own body began to betray her. The infection, this relentless adversary, continued its slow assault on Clara's body, a cruel rhythm that matched the mournful cadence of the storm outside.

Yet even as the pain intensified, she found herself drawing strength from the very act of defiance. Each sip of the syrupy liquid was a small victory, a momentary respite from the relentless agony that threatened to consume her.

With every gulp, she felt a spark of resolve kindle within her, a fragile flame that refused to be extinguished by the harsh winds of fate.

Mia, ever vigilant and steadfast, kept a watchful eye over them all. Her practical nature was tempered by an underlying compassion, a recognition that even in the darkest of times, small acts of kindness could make the difference between surrender and survival.

"We have to keep going," she murmured, her voice barely rising above the gentle hum of machinery and the distant rumble of thunder.

"Each moment we hold onto, each breath we take together, is a defiant stand against the oblivion that seeks to claim us."

Her words hung in the air, mingling with the sound of rain and the soft murmur of shared grief. In that battered sanctuary, the four of them understood that the struggle was far from over. The chaos of the outside world might rage on, its thunderous voice echoing through ruined streets and shattered dreams, but here, in this fragile haven, they had found a moment of stillness, a space where hope could be nurtured, however delicately.

Leo's quiet presence was a constant source of solace.

Even as he clutched his beloved teddy bear, his eyes shone with a wisdom that defied his tender age.

It was as if he carried the memory of a thousand lost souls, a quiet testament to the enduring human spirit.

When the storm finally began to subside, its fury giving way to a melancholy drizzle, the world outside seemed to hold its breath.

In the silence, a single sunflower pushed through a crack in the concrete just beyond the window. Its golden head tilted not toward the sky, but toward the room, toward them. A witness. A promise.

6.5: Hope in Dust Geometry

Leo lay curled on the tattered couch. His small body trembled. His fingers moved in slow arcs through the dust. Swirls and spirals took shape, quiet and strange. Dust shimmered in the dim light. It danced on invisible currents, as if alive. Fractals unfolded before him. Patterns inside patterns. Hypnotic. Almost sentient.

They mirrored something in him. Beautiful. Broken. Endless. Every movement of his hand was swift yet deliberate, the gestures carrying an unnerving exactness that revealed a soul caught in the liminal space between awe and terror.

In the doorway, Clara stood silently, a figure framed by the muted twilight. Her eyes were fixed on him. Wide. Distant. Worried. There was an unspoken gravity in her gaze, a profound unease twisting like a coiled serpent in the pit of her stomach. "You see them too, don't you?" she murmured, her voice barely more than a tremulous whisper. The words, laden with both anxiety and "The numbers," she added softly, each syllable steeped in dread as if they carried the weight of an inescapable fate.

At that moment, Leo's trance shattered. His eyes snapped wide open in a sudden burst of revelation, and the old teddy bear he had cradled, a relic of a far more innocent past, tumbled from his grasp. It landed on the creaking wooden floor with a soft, almost mournful thud, its plush form a silent casualty of his inner turmoil. "They're loud," he finally breathed, the simple words carrying a haunting mix of terror and fascination. For Leo, the numbers were no longer just inert symbols; they had become a roaring, overwhelming cacophony, a relentless barrage of sound that shattered the fragile quiet of his mind and echoed deep within his soul.

Clara's heart ached as she recognized the familiar, dreadful signs of GeneCorp's dark experiments. In Leo's uncontrollable cascade of accelerated cognition, the frantic bursts of mental calculation that now betrayed his innocence, she saw the unmistakable fingerprints of brutal, inhuman intervention. "GeneCorp's drugs rewired you," she said softly, her tone heavy with sorrow and regret. "The virus... it's trying to finish what they started." Her words, weighed down by despair, spoke of ruthless manipulation; an insidious force that sought to erase what little remained of their humanity, replacing it with a cold, calculated precision born of cruelty of science.

From the far corner of the room, Ethan emerged from the shadows, his presence commanding yet filled with quiet desperation. His hand tightened around a battered first-aid kit, his knuckles blanching as the mention of the virus ignited something raw and unyielding within him. "What do you know about the virus?" he demanded, his voice a low, guttural growl that mixed anger with vulnerability. The air tightened. Every heartbeat reminded them: more pain was coming.

In that decaying space, every speck of dust and every flicker of a dying shadow silently testified to a story of betrayal and transformation. The interplay of light and darkness, fragile order clashing with unyielding chaos, mirrored the internal struggle brewing within each of them. Their battered souls fought desperately to cling to the remnants of their humanity in a world ruthlessly reshaped by the cruelty of science. For a fleeting moment, the boundaries between memory and destiny blurred, revealing a harsh truth: nothing, not even the soft glow of hope, would ever be the same again.

The room, with its peeling wallpaper and creaking floorboards, resembled an ancient crypt where secrets lay buried beneath layers of despair and dust. Each shadow whispered forgotten tales of lost innocence and broken promises, while the dim light filtered through grimy windows, casting spectral images that danced in rhythm with Leo's tortured movements. The air reeked of sorrow. Each breath felt like a countdown.

Clara's thoughts spiraled back to memories of a life before GeneCorp's insidious influence, a time when the world was vibrant with possibility, when laughter filled sunlit rooms, and dreams felt as tangible as morning dew. But that innocence had been stripped away, replaced by an unrelenting onslaught of scientific aberration and human frailty. The very numbers Leo now conjured with his trembling fingers served as constant reminders of a stolen childhood, of a mind hijacked by forces beyond comprehension. They hummed a tune of despair. A lullaby no one could forget.

The scent of rust hit her, sudden, metallic, biting. It jarred her from the spiral.

Within the fragile confines of the room, Clara's soul trembled with both fierce resolve and aching sorrow. She watched Leo, his eyes lost in the hypnotic dance of numbers, and felt the weight of a collective burden pressing down on her heart. It was a burden shared by all who had suffered under GeneCorp's merciless experiments, seeping into every crack of the crumbling walls, every whisper of the freezing wind. Her mind was a battlefield of memories and fears, where the ghosts of what once was waged a ceaseless war against the specter of what might yet be.

Ethan's voice broke through her reverie with its unwavering certainty, a promise of escape from the clutches of despair. "We have to keep moving," he insisted, his tone a mix of determination and urgent resignation. "We'll find shelter, somewhere safe, maybe the bunker, and then, somehow, we'll put an end to this madness." His words, although filled with a spark of hope, were tinged with the bitter knowledge of the battles yet to come. They represented a promise that defied the suffocating darkness, asserting that even in the depths of their collective suffering, the human spirit could still rise and fight.

Yet Clara knew that hope was a fragile, ephemeral thing, a delicate flicker in an all-encompassing darkness. The virus, a relentless and insidious adversary, crept silently through Leo's and her veins, eroding their strength with every beat of their hearts. It was a constant, unseen predator lurking within, threatening to unravel the very fabric of their being. Still, despite the growing terror and despair, they could not afford to succumb. Not yet. Not when the future of them all hung precariously in the balance.

As the minutes stretched into what felt like an eternity, the interplay of light and dark deepened, casting the room into a surreal chiaroscuro of emotion and memory. Every creak of the floor and every sigh of the wind resonated with the quiet desperation of souls who had known only pain and loss. Leo's face, partially illuminated by the waning light, revealed the torment of a mind in constant battle, each fleeting glimpse offering a window into a reality where beauty and terror coexisted in a delicate, tragic balance.

Clara's eyes, shimmering with unshed tears, remained locked on Leo, her heart aching with the unbearable truth of what he had become. In their silent communion of shared suffering, she saw not just the shattered remnants of a young boy's innocence but also the enduring spark of a life that, despite all odds, still yearned for redemption. The swirling numbers and the relentless dance of geometry in the dust served as a testament to the transformative power of pain, a language written in the secret code of despair and hope.

As the spectral light of dusk surrendered to the encroaching darkness of night, the fragile assembly of survivors was suspended in a moment of profound introspection. The room, humming with memory and distant echoes, became a kind of sanctuary.

In that solemn space, every heartbeat was a silent pledge to defy the relentless tide of despair and resist the monstrous transformation that GeneCorp's experiments threatened to impose. For Clara, Leo, Ethan, and Mia, the path ahead was uncertain, fraught with perils both seen and unseen. Yet within that uncertainty lay a single, enduring truth: even as the numbers continued their endless, haunting dance in the dust, their indomitable spirits could never be completely silenced.

As the night deepened and the cold whispered through the shattered windows, Clara gathered her strength. With a determined glance at Leo, whose troubled eyes still flickered with the ghost of a long-lost childhood, and a shared, unspoken understanding with Ethan and the others, she resolved to hold onto that fragile ember of hope. It was a hope that, despite the relentless advance of darkness, whispered promises of a new dawn. The battle for their souls was far from over, and every tremulous finger tracing patterns in the dust became a silent vow to reclaim the world they had once known.

In that bittersweet symphony of fading light and encroaching shadows, the survivors braced themselves for the uncertain journey ahead. With every step, they carried the memory of what had been lost and the quiet determination to fight for what might yet be saved. The numbers would continue to haunt Leo's mind, echoing the painful legacy of GeneCorp's experiments, but in their shared struggle, there was also the spark of redemption, a defiant reminder that even in a world marred by cruelty, their hearts could still dare to dream.

As the spectral twilight gave way to the chill of night, the quiet room became a crucible of transformation. In the interplay of dust, light, and whispered promises, the survivors stood together, bound by a collective will to defy fate. Their fragile hope, like the delicate patterns Leo traced in the dust, stood as a testament to the enduring power of their humanity, a power that, despite the relentless cacophony of despair, would one day echo in a brighter, kinder dawn.

Clara's gaze met Leo's, a haunted look flickering in her eyes as if the weight of countless memories pressed upon her soul. "Enough to wish I didn't," she whispered, her voice a fragile murmur against the relentless howl of the wind outside. She tugged the coat tighter around her slender frame, its fabric doing little to ward off the biting cold that had long since seeped into her bones. Every thread of that coat held the remnants of better days, now marred by secrets too painful to forget.

In the dim light of the makeshift shelter, a crumbling room filled with echoes of past lives, Leo's fingers resumed their restless, almost ritualistic motion. They moved deftly over the dust that lay thick upon every surface, leaving behind ephemeral trails that formed equations and intricate fractals. These numbers, spiraling across the mildewed floor like ghostly echoes, were not merely symbols but living reminders of the insidious knowledge that GeneCorp had forced upon him. Every curve whispered what was taken from him. His past. His peace.

The numbers would keep coming, and yet they would move on.

6.6: We'll Make the Numbers Stop

At dawn, the world outside was a muted canvas of grays and broken light when Mia's boot nudged Ethan awake. "I found something," she announced, her tone low and edged with urgency. The fragile remnants of sleep clung to Ethan as he blinked against the dim morning light filtering through a narrow crack in the boarded-up windows. The air inside the bookstore's decrepit coffee shop was heavy with dust and memories, the ghost of better times barely noticeable amid decay.

Mia stood near the counter, her face streaked with dirt and sorrow, yet set in grim determination. Behind her, hidden in the shadows of crumbling shelves and the detritus of a once-bustling establishment, a secret alcove had been uncovered. Nestled in this forgotten corner lay a battered hand-crank radio.

Its edges were rusted, and a thick layer of grime covered its surface, as if trying to hide its purpose. With slow deliberation, Mia turned the dial, coaxing the ancient device to life. A disjointed static filled the silence, the hissing sound punctuating the oppressive quiet that had become their constant companion.

Gradually, the garbled hiss transformed into something more deliberate, the static twisting into an almost coherent pattern. Then, as if emerging from a long-forgotten channel, a voice, thin, mechanical, and devoid of warmth, broke through the noise: "To remaining survivors... GeneCorp's Redwood Valley facility offers sanctuary. Immunity guaranteed."

The words hung like a cruel joke, hope veined with venom. Ethan's jaw tightened, his mind racing with dark possibilities and bitter memories of loss. "It's a trap," he growled, his voice trembling with a mixture of anger and resignation.

Mia's eyes, however, remained sharply focused as she countered, "Or our only chance. We can't stay here forever." The harsh reality of their existence had forced them into corners with no exit but one, and hope, even if tainted, was a luxury they could ill afford to dismiss.

As if summoned by the conversation, Leo stirred from his slumber on a splintered couch. His small, fragile form appeared almost spectral in the waning light as he rubbed the sleep from his eyes. His voice, barely more than a whisper, broke the silence: "What's 'sanctuary'?" The innocence in his tone, juxtaposed with the weight of ancient experiences in his eyes, evoked a poignant vulnerability that tugged at every heart present.

Ethan swallowed hard, forcing steadiness into his voice as he replied, "A place where bad things can't find us." Though his words were meant to offer reassurance, he knew in his bones that the promise was a lie, a desperate fabrication to kindle hope in a boy who needed it, even if that hope was as fragile as gossamer.

Rainwater dripped steadily through the cracked roof, a metronome marking time in their forsaken refuge.

Then, cutting sharply through the familiar white noise, the radio sputtered, and a new voice emerged. This one was not the sterile monotone of the official broadcast; it was smooth, sweet, and disturbingly familiar in its terrible wrongness.

"Little A-9... we see you."

In that instant, Leo stiffened, his small frame shuddering as if struck by an invisible force. The color drained from his delicate face, and his trembling hands instinctively tightened around the old teddy bear clutched close to his chest.

"Come home," the voice purred, dripping with a sickly, almost maternal affection. "We'll make the numbers stop, the pain, the noise, the memories. All of it."

Without a moment's hesitation, Mia sprang into action. In one fluid, determined motion, she seized a heavy crowbar from beside the counter and brought it crashing down upon the radio. The device exploded in a shower of sparks and shattered metal. The crowbar's crack reverberated through the hollow space, drowning out the ghostly broadcast. For a brief heartbeat, silence reigned, yet the haunting words seemed to linger in the air, staining every corner of the room with their dark promise.

"They're tracking him," Mia spat, her chest rising and falling with the weight of unshed fear and determination. Her eyes flickered with a mix of anger and resolve as she surveyed the room, with every shadow standing as a silent witness to their predicament.

Ethan, his heart pounding in a rhythm of defiance and dread, spun toward Leo. Gripping the boy's thin shoulders, he declared, "You're not going back. I'll burn the world first." His tone was fierce, a promise to protect, no matter how dire the threat might be. But deep inside, a gnawing terror whispered that his words might be nothing more than a desperate lie.

Leo's eyes shimmered with unshed tears, and his small, tremulous voice broke the fragile silence. "What if they make it stop? I don't want to be a monster." His words, soaked with innocence and pain, revealed the burden of his inner torment, an unspoken plea for redemption and normalcy in a world twisted by cruelty.

At that moment, Clara, though weakened by the infection coursing through her veins, moved toward the boy. The virus had hollowed her body, but not her spirit, it still glowed, stubborn and tender. Lowering herself gently to Leo's side, she brushed a damp curl from his forehead with tender care. "You're not a monster," she whispered, her voice soft and laden with the bittersweet truth of a mother's love. "You're just... stuck." Her words, though simple, held a lifetime of sorrow and unwavering support.

Leo clutched her hand, his small fingers interlocking with hers as he sought solace in the only comfort he still knew. The static from the radio had faded into a ghostly memory, yet its presence lingered like a specter, a reminder of a malevolence that sought to reclaim them. Ethan's stomach churned as the memory of that seductive, sinister voice gnawed at his resolve, a dark promise threatening to shatter the fragile hope they clung to.

They knew that their physical safety in the bookstore was only temporary. In the battered remains of the coffee shop, now a makeshift refuge amid the ruins of a collapsed world, they had to act quickly. With grim determination, they gathered the shattered remnants of the radio, burying them beneath a pile of torn paperbacks and splintered wood. It was an attempt to hide the evidence of the insidious message, to cast it into oblivion so that its lingering echo might not fracture their already tenuous hope.

As the first slivers of sunlight began to pierce through the thick, storm-laden clouds outside, Ethan met Mia's gaze. In that silent exchange, the determination in her eyes mirrored his own, shared resolve to confront the darkness head-on. "We move at sundown," he said, his voice low yet brimming with resolute determination. "GeneCorp wants us to come. Then let's give them a reason to regret it."

The declaration hung in the air, heavy with both promise and peril. Outside, the storm raged with a ferocity that belied the fragile calm of their refuge. Each gust of wind, each distant rumble of thunder, was a stark reminder of the chaos that lay beyond the crumbling walls of their sanctuary, a chaos that threatened to engulf them all if they did not muster the strength to stand together.

The ruined bookstore's coffee shop, with its broken windows and battered furniture, had become an unlikely haven for these weary souls. Here, amidst decay and debris, they found moments of tenderness and fleeting solace, a shared meal, a gentle caress, the whispered exchange of dreams and fears. Every act of care, no matter how small, was a rebellion against the relentless march of despair. It was a testament to their unyielding spirit, a defiant refusal to surrender to the darkness that sought to claim their souls.

Mia's practical resolve and Ethan's protective fierceness were counterbalanced by Leo's quiet vulnerability and the enduring warmth of Clara's love. Together, they formed a fragile family, a small beacon of light amid the all-consuming shadows of a shattered world. Even as the infection gnawed at their bodies and the bitter winds of fate swept through the remains of their once-safe haven, they clung to each other with a desperate hope that tomorrow might bring a chance for redemption.

On that solemn morning, as the sun began its slow ascent and the storm's fury gradually abated, the group prepared for the journey ahead. The promise of GeneCorp's Redwood Valley facility, with its seductive offer of sanctuary and guaranteed immunity, was a siren call, one that could either lead them to salvation or plunge them deeper into the abyss of their own nightmares. Yet the prospect of remaining in the confines of their crumbling refuge was no longer an option. They had witnessed too much loss, suffered too many betrayals, and endured too much heartache to let fear dictate their every move.

Clara held Leo's hand, her fingers warm despite the fever. Whatever waited beyond the storm, they would meet it together. They were united by resolve. Carried by hope.

6.7: Beneath the Bruises, a Vow

The shattered radio sat like a corpse buried under books and paper in the corner, silent now but still pulsing with the memory of voices that had nearly torn them apart.

Without hesitation, Mia grabbed a heavy broom handle and threw it at Ethan. "Let's learn. Teach each other," she said, her voice filled with determination. The wooden shaft, worn smooth from years of use and countless struggles, now symbolized their readiness to fight, not just for survival, but for the hope of reclaiming the little humanity they had left.

Ethan raised an eyebrow, weighing the broom handle's balance and the ghost of violence carved into its grain. "To fight?" he asked, a hesitant challenge in his tone.

"To survive," Mia corrected, her voice as unwavering as the determination on her face. Without a moment's pause, she lunged forward, her movements fluid and precise, unleashing a burst of pent-up energy upon the silent bookstore.

The clash of wood against wood resonated sharply as Ethan barely managed to deflect Mia's forceful blow. The crack of wood on wood stirred something primal, defiance reborn. Their sparring session began in earnest, no rules, no hesitation, just the raw, unfiltered language of survival. Each movement became a lesson in resilience and strategy, a desperate ballet of force and finesse.

Mia's strikes grew fiercer with each passing moment. Her footwork was a blur as she moved with the grace of a shadow, relentless and determined. Every swing of her arm and every calculated jab served as a reminder that in a world stripped of certainty, the only refuge lay in the art of combat. Ethan, though less experienced, responded with equal determination. He parried her blows, stumbled but quickly found his footing, and struck back. His movements were a testament to the unyielding will that had carried him through endless nights of terror.

"Keep your elbows in," Mia said sharply, her voice cutting through the rhythm of their exchange. She dodged a swift jab, her eyes gleaming with the keen focus of a seasoned fighter.

"You're leaving yourself exposed."

Ethan adjusted his stance, allowing his body to learn quickly from each encounter and the lessons taught through pain and effort. Mia, her hair stuck to her face with sweat and determination, was already on the move again, a relentless force that refused to give in.

From the worn couch, Leo's enthusiastic claps punctuated the intensity of the sparring session. His wide-eyed admiration and unfiltered excitement broke through the tense atmosphere of the store, momentarily softening the harsh edges of their struggle. Clutching his dirty teddy bear like a talisman, he declared with a joyful lilt, "Mia is winning!" His laughter, pure and unburdened by the world's weight, filled the room with a spark of hope.

"Traitor," Ethan grunted, narrowly avoiding a sweeping strike that would have sent him sprawling. His tone, half-jest, and half-serious reproach highlighted the competitive spirit that was as inherent to him as the pain he endured.

They continued sparring until their breaths came in ragged gasps and the muscles in Ethan's arms burned from the exertion of their duel. The wooden broom handle, now a symbol of their shared struggle, became an extension of their will to survive. Eventually, Mia stepped back, resting the broom handle against her shoulder with a satisfied yet exhausted smile. "Not bad," she admitted, though her grin bore the awareness that there was still much to learn. "But you've got a long way to go."

Later, as they settled in a quiet corner of the battered bookstore, the atmosphere softened into a fragile calm. Mia carefully cleaned and bandaged a scrape on Ethan's arm, her fingers moving with the precision of someone who had healed far too many wounds. Her brow furrowed, not just in focus, but in something unspoken.

"Why would you take him this far?" she asked quietly, almost to herself. "After what happened with your parents... and what they say about kids like him, why risk it?"

The question struck Ethan like a physical blow. He flinched, his mind replaying the chaotic memories of that long-ago night, the frantic shouts, the guttural growls, the metallic scent of blood in the air. Above all, it was the memory of Leo's small hand trembling in his, the helplessness in the child's eyes, which cut the deepest. "He's my baby brother," Ethan replied simply, his voice steady but burdened with unspoken promises and lingering regrets.

Mia's gaze hardened as she absorbed his words, her expression etched with both understanding and stern resolve.

"That doesn't mean you owe him your life," she stated bluntly, a reminder that the bonds of family, while unbreakable, do not always guarantee safety from the harshness of the world.

Across the room, Leo had resumed his quiet vigil, tracing delicate patterns in the dust with his tiny fingers. Circles and triangles, twisting into intricate fractals, flowed seamlessly from his touch. His expression was distant, as though lost in an inner world of equations and memories far beyond immediate chaos. Ethan watched him, a silent witness to the fragile brilliance that flickered beneath the boy's delicate frame. "Yeah," Ethan murmured softly, the conviction settling in his chest like a solemn oath. "It does. I am my baby brother's keeper. He's the last piece I have of my parents."

Mia shook her head slowly, a mixture of regret and understanding passing over her features. Though her own scars, both seen and unseen, were a testament to the brutal world they inhabited, a part of her still clung to the belief that the bonds they fought to preserve might one day be their salvation. The world had stripped them of so much, yet amidst the decay and despair, there remained something worth fighting for: the remnants of trust, love, and the unyielding spirit.

In the fading light, as the sun dipped lower and cast long shadows across the crumbling floor, Clara emerged. Though the infection had drained much of the color from her face, leaving dark veins like scars upon her pale skin, there was a serenity in her eyes. It spoke of a quiet understanding that belied the turmoil within. She gracefully shifted her weight, moving with a tender balance of strength and vulnerability, and drew near to Leo. Gently, she brushed a damp curl from his forehead, her touch tender and soothing, laced with a mother's unconditional love, a balm for wounds too deep for physical healing.

As dusk settled over the battered bookstore, the quartet gathered their thoughts and pieced together a semblance of hope amid the ruins. The weathered broom handle, the lessons learned through sweat and blood, and the quiet determination reflected in their shared glances wove together a tapestry of survival. Each spar, every word spoken during their training, was a lesson in resilience, a promise that even in the face of relentless hardship, they would continue to learn, adapt, and fight.

In the fading light, as shadows lengthened into the encroaching night, Ethan's voice broke the silence with quiet resolve. "We move at sun dawn," he declared, his tone low but unwavering. "We have lessons to learn and truths to uncover." His words echoed off the peeling walls, a solemn vow against a world determined to crush hope.

Together, they prepared for the challenges ahead, a journey where every step was fraught with danger and every breath a battle against decay. In the battered bookstore, beneath Leo's gaze, they found quiet strength. They understood that the road ahead would be long and perilous, but as long as they stood united and continued to teach one another, learning from every scar and every triumph, there was a chance, fragile, shimmering chance, that tomorrow might be better than today.

In that hush, among bruises and quiet confessions, they sparked a quiet rebellion against despair. In every bruise and every soft word, they reclaimed belief in unity. And in the dim quiet, bruised, and breathless, they made a silent vow: to rise again and move on, together.

Chapter 7: Her Miracle, Her Monster

7.1: The Numbers and the Lullaby

Ethan jolted awake to a piercing, anguished scream that shattered the fragile silence of the night. The sound was raw and unrelenting, tearing through his dreams and sending a jolt of terror straight to his heart. He opened his eyes in the dim light, where a weak glow filtered through the cracked, boarded-up windows, casting shadows of despair around the room.

Across the room, on an old, moth-eaten couch that had seen better days, Leo convulsed violently. His small, fragile body writhed as if caught in the grip of invisible, malevolent forces. Sweat poured down his forehead in rivulets, and his tiny fists clenched so tightly that his knuckles turned ghostly white. "Make it stop! Make it stop!" he cried out, his voice trembling with desperate terror. Each cry shattered the quiet that had become their daily companion.

Mia stood frozen near the doorway, her hands trembling uncontrollably. The crowbar she had wielded moments before now hung uselessly at her side, its weight forgotten in the face of an overwhelming emotion. Despite the strength she had shown in countless battles for survival, this moment left her feeling helpless stripping away her resolve.

Without a moment to lose, Ethan lunged to Leo's side. In one fluid, desperate motion, he pinned the trembling boy's shoulders against the worn, threadbare cushions of the couch. "Leo! Wake up!" he shouted, his voice rough with the fear of another loss. Yet, even as Ethan's words crashed into the room, Leo continued his frantic, uncontrolled movements. His thin limbs thrashed with surprising power, and his small heels pounded against the couch as if trying to break free from invisible shackles.

Then, in a moment that felt like it froze time for Ethan, Leo's eyes snapped open. They were no longer the warm, curious pools of a child but instead dilated and black as ink, the whites of his eyes nearly disappearing under an unnatural, otherworldly sheen. "They're in my head, Eth," Leo whimpered, his voice breaking into tortured sobs as if he were caught between worlds. "The numbers." His words spilled out in a frantic rush, each syllable a desperate plea for escape from an invisible horror.

Ethan's pulse pounded like a war drum in his ears as he demanded, "What numbers?" The urgency in his voice was laced with both determination and dread, a man's attempt to unravel a mystery that threatened to tear his fragile world apart.

Leo's small hands shot up to his temples, clawing desperately as his nails dug into his tender scalp. "Countdowns. Equations. They're too loud. I don't understand!" The words came in a whisper, thick with fear that echoed through the ruined room.

In the background, Clara stepped back slowly from the dim recesses of the battered storefront. Her face was etched with worry and exhaustion, and her labored breathing filled the silent pauses between the chaos, a heavy cadence that spoke of battles fought both within and without. She clutched her infected arm to her chest, as though trying to shield herself from the virus that had left its indelible mark on her body. "Is he... is he turning?" she asked, her voice cracking under the weight of fear. "Like the Accelerates?" The question hung in the air, its implications more terrifying than any scream.

Ethan's voice, though laced with determination, trembled as he replied, "He's not them." But even as he spoke, his heart pounded with the knowledge that his assurance was built on a foundation of fear. He could feel the boy's tremors under his touch, violent convulsions that echoed through his own bones, a reminder of the contagion that had altered their lives beyond repair.

Leo's sobs, raw and primal, twisted into sharp, panicked gasps. In the depths of his terror, he continued, "They want me to be smart. They said I'm special. But I just want to go home." His voice, small and filled with anguish, carried the weight of a destiny he never chose, a destiny dictated by a mysterious, malevolent force that sought to transform him into something other than himself.

Ethan's throat tightened, his heart aching as he drew the trembling boy closer. Wrapping his arms around Leo with desperate urgency, he pressed him against his chest, hoping that the warmth of his embrace could stave off the darkness creeping into the boy's mind. In a moment of instinctive tenderness, a lullaby, the one their mother used to sing, slipped from Ethan's cracked lips. It was a low, broken hum, each note trembling with grief and fierce love. The melody, though fractured by grief, served as a lifeline, a fragile tether to a past where hope had not yet been swallowed by despair.

As Ethan hummed, his hand gently caressed the damp, tangled hair on Leo's head. The frantic thrashing began to slow, as if the familiar tune acted as a balm for the raging storm inside the boy's mind. His sobs softened into whimpers, the monstrous cacophony of numbers and equations receding like a tide under the steady pull of a soothing melody.

Mia, ever the vigilant guardian, hovered nearby. Her face was a mask of conflicting emotions, fear intermingled with sorrow, frustration shadowed by tenderness. "We can't keep pretending he's okay," she murmured, her voice barely audible above the faint hum of Ethan's lullaby. The words, heavy with the truth they could not deny, cut through the lingering silence like shattered glass.

Ethan said nothing in reply. His jaw tightened as he pulled Leo even closer, feeling the fragile boy's body melting into his embrace. He sensed every tremor, every ragged breath, as if they were his own. In that moment, Ethan knew that answers would have to come later. Tonight, he would be the shield between Leo and the darkness, a barrier against a threat that had already scarred them all.

In a low, trembling voice, Leo whispered, "I'm sorry. I didn't mean to scare you." The apology, heavy with regret, was laced with the innocence of a child forced to bear burdens far beyond his one-year-old self.

"It's okay. I'm here," Ethan replied, his voice thick with the unspoken promise of protection and love. His words served as both a comfort and a vow, a pledge that, no matter what horrors might come, he would not let the relentless assault of the virus, or the insidious machinations of GeneCorp, take Leo away.

Outside, the storm raged on, its fury a relentless reminder of the chaos that lay just beyond their fragile haven. Rain battered the boarded windows, each droplet a percussion in nature's symphony of sorrow. The wind howled through broken gaps, carrying with it the acrid scent of distant fires and lost hopes. In that dismal cacophony, the reality was stark: the virus had already left its mark, not just on Clara and Leo, but on every soul within the crumbling walls of their refuge. And somewhere, in the labyrinthine corridors of power, GeneCorp watched, its unseen eyes cold and calculating.

Ethan held the boy tighter still, each heartbeat a desperate plea for relief. He continued to hum the fractured lullaby, clinging to it as if it could repel the relentless numbers threatening to overrun Leo's mind. The soothing tune became a fragile shield against an enemy that could not be seen, a quiet defiance in the face of an overwhelming and invisible force.

As the minutes stretched into an eternity, the storm's roar outside melded with the soft cadence of Ethan's lullaby. Every sound in the room, the gentle rustle of clothing, the distant drip of water, the steady, rhythmic pulse of Leo's sobs, wove together into a tapestry of grief and determination. A moment caught between terror and fragile hope.

Mia's eyes, glistening with unshed tears, flickered between Ethan and Leo. She knew no amount of love or tender song could erase the scars of the virus. Yet, in that shared vulnerability, there was also a flicker of resilience, a stubborn spark that refused to be extinguished by despair. "We have to fight this," she whispered, her words trembling on her lips. "No matter what it takes."

In that quiet, heart-wrenching space, they sat together, each, a pillar of raw emotion and fragile strength. Ethan's arms remained wrapped protectively around Leo, whose once-innocent eyes now held a haunted depth. The numbers that tormented him, a maddening cascade of equations and countdowns, had not vanished entirely, but for now, they were held at bay by the power of memory and love. The broken lullaby was a lifeline to a time untouched by pain.

Clara stood at the periphery, watching with a sorrowful detachment. Dark veins snaked across her pale skin, a visible testament to her battle with infection. Though her body was weak, her spirit flickered with quiet resolve. Unable to join in the physical embrace of protection, her eyes conveyed a deep and abiding understanding. In that silent connection, every heartbeat and trembling breath symbolized the human capacity to endure, even when hope felt as fleeting as a whisper in the wind.

Ethan clung to a mother's lullaby, to the feel of her hand. Those memories became his light in the dark. As he hummed, the sound wavered yet persisted, a fragile melody battling against the dissonant clamor of unseen horrors. He prayed the tune would hold the numbers at bay, if only for one more night.

In that long, agonizing night, the storm outside and the torment within converged into a raw, unfiltered moment of a tale woven from the quiet grace of brotherly devotion. The air was thick with the scent of rain and the bitter tang of fear, while the soft, broken hum of the lullaby mingled with the sobs and gasps of a child fighting for his very soul. Every detail, the way Leo's fingers curled into desperate fists, the steady rhythm of Ethan's heartbeat against his chest, and the sorrowful resilience in Mia's eyes, spoke of a fragile family bound together by love that was both fierce and desperate.

As the night deepened and the storm's fury began to wane into a mournful whisper, Ethan held Leo even tighter, his arms a steadfast shield against a world gone mad. In the silence that followed, punctuated only by the soft echoes of their shared pain, he vowed silently to himself that no matter what lay ahead, he would continue to fight for his baby brother, for the remnants of hope, and for the promise of a new day, one where the numbers would become nothing more than a haunting memory of a past that no longer defined them.

In that moment, as the remnants of the lullaby faded into the night and the first hints of dawn began to paint the horizon with a pale light, Ethan's resolve crystallized into an unyielding promise. The virus had scarred them all, a mark a constant reminder of fate's relentless cruelty a constant reminder of fate's cruelty, and somewhere out there, GeneCorp's cold gaze still lingered. Yet, in the tender, desperate embrace shared in that battered room, there was a spark, a defiant spark of love and resilience that whispered of tomorrow. It was enough. For one more night, at least, the numbers would stay at bay, and hope, however fragile, would continue to endure.

As reluctant dawn crept in, Ethan's humming steadied, joining the sounds of a new day. In the hush between dark and light, he vowed the world wouldn't break them. Together, they'd forge ahead, lit by the embers of brotherly love, resilience, and the quiet song of their hearts.

7.2: Of Monsters and Mothers

The attack occurred before dawn. Suddenly. Unexpected.

A figure stepped from the shadows of the shattered doorway, the dim glow of a stolen GeneCorp tablet illuminating her gaunt face. Then, two more figures appeared, their bodies twisted and unnatural. Each movement was jerky yet deliberate.

The Accelerates.

But Clara's eyes were fixed on the leader, the smallest of the three, the girl draped in the tattered remains of a once-pink princess dress. The satin fabric clung to her slender frame, smeared with dirt, and dried blood. Her blonde hair, once golden and soft, now hung in brittle, tangled strands. The surgeon's scalpel was held delicately between her slender fingers, its blade gleaming in the dimming light.

"Subject A-9," she purred, her grin spreading unnaturally wide. "You have been upgraded." Clara's stomach twisted uneasily.

"Go!" she shouted, pushing Mia toward the back exit, her voice filled with urgency. But the girl's gaze shifted. Ava. Clara's daughter. Her baby.

A dark, twisted chuckle escaped the girl's lips, a sound far too mature and knowing. She tilted her head, her eyes consumed with dark gleaming malice.

"Oh, Mammy," Ava crooned, each word laced with venom. "Is she my Auntie Mia? Well, hello, Auntie." The sarcastic warmth in her voice sent a cold shiver down Clara's spine.

Slowly, Ava began to approach, her bare feet dragging over the broken glass without a hint of discomfort. Each step was slow, deliberate, like a predator savoring the decisive moments before the pounce.

"Ava, please," Clara's voice cracked, trembling with desperation. Tears filled her eyes as she clutched a crowbar in one hand and a heavy book in the other, makeshift weapons that felt useless against what Ava had become. "Leave us alone."

Ava smiled wider, but the darkness in her eyes remained. "Mammy," she cooed, "it's a family reunion. Did I tell you how it ended for Daddy?"

Clara's chest tightened as the words pierced her like a knife.

"You didn't have to watch him beg," Ava said, her voice filled with a chilling amusement. "But I did."

A ragged sob escaped Clara's lips. Just as she was about to respond, the moment broke apart.

Leo's scream erupted into the air. A piercing, ear-splitting blast that echoed through the walls. The sheer intensity of it caused the tablet in Ava's hands to crash to the floor, its glow flickering and then dying. The Accelerates staggered, clutching their heads in pain, their own shrieks blending with the haunting wail.

"Ethan!" Clara gasped.

Ethan lunged for Leo, wrapping his arms around the trembling boy. "Move!" he barked, pulling Leo toward the exit.

But Clara hesitated. Her legs buckled beneath her as the infection gnawed at her strength. The veins on her arm throbbed, black tendrils twisting beneath the torn fabric of her coat. She gritted her teeth and clutched the crowbar tighter.

"Mammy," Ava growled, her voice no longer sweet, only hollow. "You won't make it far."

Mia grabbed Clara's arm, her grip fierce. "Don't you dare quit!"

Clara's breath came in ragged gasps as she locked eyes with her daughter, seeing a twisted reflection of the child she once wished to have. Pain mixed with defiance as she pushed away the suffocating fear.

"Wouldn't dream of it," she rasped.

With one final, fleeting glance at Ava, Clara stumbled after Mia and Ethan, vanishing into the darkened night. The echoes of the past clung to her like a shadow, but for now, they were still alive.

7.3: Until I Can't

They fled to a derelict church, its steeple cracked like a broken bone jutting into the sky. Rain pattered through holes in the roof onto warped floorboards. The air was damp, thick with the scent of mildew and rotting pews. Shattered stained glass scattered slivers of color across the cracked walls and floor.

Clara collapsed into one of the pews, trembling, her arm sagging. The infection's blackened veins crept higher beneath her torn sleeve, twisting like dark roots beneath her pale skin. She tried to steady her breath, but each gasp came shallow and ragged, sweat dampened her forehead.

Mia lunged forward, her eyes wide with panic. "It's worsening, isn't it? Why didn't you..."

"Because you'd do the same!" Clara snapped, swatting Mia's hands away. Her voice trembled with strain, but her glare was fierce. "We don't have time for your hero complex."

Mia opened her mouth, then closed it again. Anger waged war with fear in her expression, but before she could respond, Ethan stepped between them. "Come on, Clara. Please. Stay with us." His voice trembled, but it cut through the fragile silence like a thread pulled taut.

Clara blinked, her resolve wavering. For a moment, the weight of the infection felt unbearable. Pain throbbed through her, reminding her of how little time she had left. Still, she met Ethan's gaze, stubborn defiance flickering in her bloodshot eyes. "I'll try. But it may only be for a few days."

"Then we make them count," Ethan replied softly.

Leo curled closer against Ethan's side, clutching his battered teddy bear. The boy's legs dangled limply, too thin and frail. His wide, uncertain eyes gleamed in the dim light. "Will you turn into a monster?" His voice was small, barely a whisper, yet the question echoed through the empty church.

Clara flinched, then looked straight at Leo. "I was already one," she said, but this time her voice didn't carry resignation, it carried warning.

The words hung heavily in the air, their weight undeniable. Mia flinched but didn't argue. They all knew what Clara meant: what she had done to survive and how the infection threatened to amplify those actions.

"You're not a monster, Clara." Leo knelt and reached for her hands.

She looked away, unable to meet his gaze. But she didn't pull her hand away. The infection throbbed beneath her skin, an echo of what waited ahead.

Mia paced near the altar, her jaw clenched. "We can find medicine. Or maybe even GeneCorp's facility at Redwood Valley. The radio..."

"The voice on the radio..." Clara paused, eyes narrowing, "it was Ava's. Not her voice exactly, but the cadence, the rhythm. She's learning. Copying. And it wasn't just a lure... it was a challenge."

"But we keep moving. We stay unpredictable. If Ava wants Leo, she's going to have to come for me first."

Ethan nodded, though the determination in his eyes couldn't mask the dread he felt. Leo's fingers tightened around his bear as the storm outside howled like the monsters they all feared.

For now, the church held its fragile peace, but dawn would come, bringing with it the fight for another day.

Later, Clara pressed the crumpled map into Mia's hands. The corners of the paper were worn from extensive use. Redwood Valley was circled in thick, dark ink, its edges marked with hasty, frantic notes: Avoid checkpoints. GeneCorp lies. Trust no one. The urgency in the scribbled words was almost palpable, a silent warning passed down from someone who understood the deadly game they were all playing.

Mia's fingers trembled as she traced the words, her eyes scanning the map with an intensity bordering on desperation. A single tear slid down her cheek, splashing onto the paper and blurring the ink just enough to make it seem like the road ahead was slipping out of reach.

"You're coming with us," Mia whispered, her words heavy with a mix of plea and command. Her voice buckled under the burden of it.

Clara didn't respond at first. Her eyes, exhausted and hollow, were fixed on the map, but her gaze drifted to a place the map couldn't reach, into a place where the future seemed uncertain, a place she wasn't sure she would survive. The silence stretched between them, thick with unspoken truths, until Clara's voice broke it, soft but final. "I can't."

The response hit Mia harder than she expected. Tears began to gather at the edges of her eyes, but she didn't let them fall. She blinked them away, trying to swallow the lump that had formed in her throat. She had come so far to find her sister again; she wouldn't lose her now.

Clara's hand, cold and faintly trembling, rested against the map one last time before she let it go. "I can't... leave him, Ava," she whispered, barely able to get the words out. She didn't have to say it. Leo, the only one left to carry their fragile hope. She could see him in the distance, standing beside Ava, though Ava had long since vanished. Or had she? His body a delicate mix of growth and weakness. His small frame stretched too fast for his body to bear. Yet, despite it all, he clung to life as if it was all he had. The infection was already working its cruel magic on Clara's mind, blurring the line between memory and nightmare.

At dawn, they set out, their footsteps muffled by the heavy fog that hung low over the earth, giving the world around them an eerie, otherworldly feel. The sky above was a dull, oppressive gray, reflecting the hopelessness that settled in Clara's chest. She lagged behind, her steps uneven and dragging, as though the weight of her body was too much to bear. Her infected arm dragged like a dead branch. But it wasn't the worst of what she carried.

Mia, ever watchful, matched her stride. Their shoulders brushed occasionally, and each time it happened, it felt like a small reassurance that they hadn't yet fallen apart. Neither of them spoke much; the silence between words grew heavier with every step. Yet there was an unspoken bond between them that was understood.

"Remember the sunflowers?" Mia asked, breaking the stillness.

Clara's lips twitched into something resembling a smile, tinged with bitterness. "You trampled half the crop."

Mia laughed softly, the sound almost bitter as it caught in her throat. "You yelled at me for an hour."

Clara's laugh was rough and hoarse, but there was a glint of fondness in it, even if it was fleeting. "Worth it," she coughed, her chest constricting painfully.

Ahead, Ethan moved with his usual quiet determination, hoisting Leo onto his back. The boy's legs dangled, too long for his jeans, and his tiny body seemed even more fragile with each passing day. It was a constant battle between growth and survival, one that he seemed to be losing.

"Keep him alive," Clara said. That was all that mattered. Even if it cost her everything else.

Mia tightened her grip on Clara's hand and gave a small nod, though her face was set in a grim line. "You come first," Mia whispered, even though they both knew it was a lie. They walked into sacrifice. It didn't wait. It traveled with them.

7.4: The Sky is Sad

Clara's breath fogged up the cracked windshield as Ethan drove the stolen ambulance through the skeletal remains of the city. The streets were eerily silent, broken only by the low rumble of the engine and the occasional groan of a building's frame settling in the breeze. Clara struggled to keep her head upright; her fever had spiked overnight, turning her skin a sickly shade of gray. Her once-vibrant complexion was now ashen, drained of life, and the black veins from Ava's bite crept up her neck and across her collarbone like twisted roots, spreading further with every passing hour. The pain gnawed at her from the inside, making each breath feel like an effort and each heartbeat feel like a betrayal.

Mia crouched beside her, the weight of her sister's decline pressing heavily on her. She was carefully rewrapping the oozing wound, her hands trembling as she tore strips from her own shirt, once a soft sunflower yellow, now faded to the color of rust, frayed, stained, and worn thin. As she pressed the fabric against Clara's skin, trying to stop the bleeding and contain the infection, nothing seemed to help. Her face was a picture of quiet desperation, her eyes filled with fear, a fear mirrored in the trembling of her hands.

"You're going to be fine," Mia muttered, her voice brittle and barely a whisper over the hum of the engine. The words were meant to be reassuring, but they lacked any weight of truth. "We just need to find antibiotics. I swear we will."

Clara let out a rasping laugh, which quickly turned into a wet, rattling cough that shook her frail body. She wiped her mouth with the back of her hand and gave her sister a tired, nearly bitter smile. "Liar," she managed, her voice hoarse and broken. She didn't need antibiotics. The infection was spreading faster than they could reach any supplies, and she knew the truth, even if Mia refused to acknowledge it.

In the back seat, Leo pressed his face against the cold window, his small breath fogging up the glass as he stared at the world outside with wide, innocent eyes. He tilted his head, his gaze caught on something in the sky. "Why's the sky green?" he asked, his voice small, filled with a curiosity that seemed too innocent for the world they were living in.

Ethan's eyes flicked to the horizon, where a thick haze hung, a disturbing cloud of smoke and chemical fallout from the bombed GeneCorp labs. The greenish tint in the sky wasn't the light of dawn; it was the toxic residue of a world that had already collapsed. Ethan gritted his teeth, trying to maintain his focus on the road while ignoring the tightness in his chest, the choking sensation that had been building for days. There were no answers left for him, no quick fixes for the world in which they were trapped.

"Pollution," Ethan muttered, his voice flat and mechanical, as if saying it could convince him that was all it was. He struggled to explain to Leo, or anyone else, what had really happened to the sky, the air, and the world they once knew. There were no words that could undo what had been done.

"No," Leo whispered, his voice trembling with a deeper, more profound emotion than the question he had posed. "It is sad. The sky is sad."

The weight of his words pressed down on the small cabin of the ambulance. Mia shot a desperate glance at Ethan, her eyes pleading, silently asking him to make things better, to fix the unfixable. But Ethan didn't have the answers anymore; he had no solutions left. All he had was the road ahead, empty, uncertain, and fraught with dangers they could not outrun. Deep inside, he feared that much like the sky, they were all too far gone to be saved.

7.5: The Sunflowers Still Turn

As they entered the abandoned hospital, the sound of footsteps echoed through the hollow halls. The sterile walls, once pristine, now bore the marks of neglect, broken tiles, peeling paint, and shattered windows letting in only the faintest sliver of daylight. The air was thick with the lingering stench of disinfectants, mingled with the musty scent of decay. In the corner, a faint sputter from the emergency generator stuttered through the silence, casting flickering, sickly light from the overhead fluorescents. These lights sputtered erratically, their glow creating jagged, distorted shadows across the broken floor, giving the space an almost unnatural, ghostly quality.

Mia pushed a gurney into one of the supply closets, her heart pounding with a mix of desperation and hope. The shelves inside were stripped bare, the remnants of medical supplies long scavenged by others. As her eyes scanned the empty shelves, she froze when she spotted something glimmering faintly in the dim light. In the corner sat a single vial, seemingly abandoned or forgotten. The label read "Experimental Antiviral -

Prototype 9X." Mia's breath hitched, and her hand shot out to grab it, the cool glass sending a shiver through her fingertips.

"Jackpot," Mia whispered, her voice barely audible over the hum of the generator as she held the vial up to the flickering light, inspecting its contents.

Clara's voice, sharp and immediate, cut through the silence. "That's a death sentence." Her words were cold, as hard as ice. She strode toward Mia, her face etched with pain and regret. "GeneCorp experimented with Accelerates. Melted their brains."

Mia tightened her grip around the vial, her pulse quickening as her emotions surged. "You're not them!" she snapped, her voice rising with the raw frustration that had been building for days. Her sister's hesitation and refusal to see hope in the darkness were wearing her thin.

"Aren't I?" Clara shot back, her voice bitter and laced with cynicism. She reached up, peeling back the sleeve of her jacket with a sudden, forceful motion. Beneath, her skin had begun to wither, a sickly patch of necrotic flesh creeping up her arm. The bite mark, the source of her torment, pulsed faintly, as though something inside her was alive, breathing, but not quite human. It throbbed in time with her heartbeat, a reminder of how little time she had left.

Ethan stood silently by the doorframe, arms crossed and his gaze calculating as he observed the tension between the sisters. His mind was already analyzing the situation, weighing the risks. "We will vote," he said quietly, though his tone lacked the conviction it had once held. "All in favor of..."

"No votes." Clara's interruption was loud and firm, like a hammer. Her voice was steely and unwavering. "My body. My decision."

Mia's eyes widened, a storm of anger and hurt rising within her. Without waiting for anything more, she turned on her heel and stormed out of the room. Her boots thudded heavily against the cracked tiles as she made her way down the hall, the sound of her fury echoing through the empty space.

***

One year earlier, things had been quite different. Clara had taught Mia how to drive the tractor under the warm, fading light of dusk. Clara's hands had steadied Mia's trembling ones on the wheel, her voice light with humor and reassurance. "Don't panic if it jerks," she had said, her hair damp with sweat as the sun caught the strands, dipping behind the horizon.

They had harvested the sunflowers together, their laughter mingling with the soft rustle of the flowers in the wind. Their parents' voices had echoed in the background, filled with joy and the simple contentment that came from a life built on love and hard work. But that night, when Mia had found Clara alone in the barn, her back turned and her shoulders shaking, everything had changed. Clara had clutched a pamphlet tightly in her hands, her breath ragged as she turned to Mia.

"Mark and I... we're taking the GeneCorp deal," Clara had said, her voice filled with both excitement and fear. Her eyes had been wide, but there was something else in them too, hunger, a hope for something better. "We're going to give our baby everything that we never had."

Mia had felt coldness settle in her chest, but she had shrugged, trying to mask the unease that gripped her. "Maybe he or she will be super smart," she had said, forcing a smile that didn't reflect her true feelings. Deep down, she sensed that nothing would ever be the same again.

***

By dawn, Clara's right eye had clouded over, the pupil consumed by the black void of infection, swallowed by darkness from within. Her skin was ashen, pale, and clammy beneath the dim light. She lay still, her once-fiery spirit now subdued, her breath shallow and rasping through the stagnant air. Her gaze, unfocused and vacant, was fixed on the cracks in the ceiling above her, fractures in the plaster that seemed to mirror the splintered edges of her soul.

When her voice finally came, it was flat and distant, as though she were speaking from another world entirely. "It is rewriting me. The virus. I can feel it... prioritizing."

Mia's hand clutched Clara's, her fingers trembling with fear but also with fierce determination. "Fight it," she whispered, her voice breaking with emotion. Every part of her screamed for her sister to hold on, to not succumb to whatever poison had taken hold of her.

Clara's lips twisted into a hollow smile, one that didn't reach her eyes, and she let out a short, brittle laugh. "Can't. It's smarter." She turned her head slowly, almost mechanically, her eyes eventually landing on Ethan, who stood silently at the edge of the room, his face a mask of helplessness. Clara's expression softened just a little as she spoke her next words with terrible certainty. "Redwood Valley's a lie. The bunker's a lab. They'll dissect Leo."

Ethan's body went rigid, a chill creeping down his spine. His pulse quickened. He pictured Leo curled asleep with his bear, and the image shattered him. "How do you know?" His voice was tight, barely a whisper, as if he couldn't fully process what Clara had just said. The thought of them doing anything to Leo, his little brother, the one thing he had left, was too much to bear.

"The Accelerates," Clara breathed, each word coming out ragged. "They're not random. GeneCorp is using them to... herd survivors. Test subjects."

Mia felt a wave of nausea rise in her chest. She had known something was wrong with the world, something insidious, but hearing Clara confirm it, hearing it so matter-of-factly from the sister she had trusted above all others, sent a cold, icy panic through her veins.

Leo, who had been perched at the edge of the gurney, his wide, confused eyes locked on Clara's face, spoke up in his small, innocent voice. "What is 'dissect'?"

Mia and Ethan exchanged a glance, a brief, silent understanding passing between them. They both wished they could shield Leo from all the darkness and pain, but they couldn't. They had no words to explain what that word meant, no way to protect him from the twisted truth of the world they were living in. "Nothing," they both said in unison, their voices breathless, a lie that hung heavy in the air between them.

Clara's breath hitched again, more ragged this time, as if the strain of speaking was too much for her. "Mia... the farm. The sunflowers. Remember how they always turned to the light..."

7.6: *You Were Supposed to Be My Miracle*

A crash echoed from the lobby, loud and jarring, cutting Clara off mid-sentence. The unmistakable sound of footsteps followed, heavy and deliberate, accompanied by the shrill, manic laughter of the Accelerates.

They had found them.

Ethan's instincts kicked in before his mind could even catch up. He shot to his feet, heart pounding in his chest, and bolted toward the door. He slammed an IV pole against the doorframe, quickly securing a makeshift barricade as the first Accelerated child, his face twisted with a grotesque smile, collided with the door. The boy was gripping a hammer in one hand, a broken toy soldier in the other. His giggles rang out, high-pitched and unsettling, as he taunted from the other side of the door. "Come out, A-9! We will make it quick!"

Mia's mind raced, but she knew there was no time to hesitate. She thrust a fire axe into Leo's trembling hands, her voice urgent yet steady. "Swing at anything that isn't us." She met his wide and frightened eyes and tried to reassure him, even though the fear gnawing at her insides threatened to consume her.

Clara struggled to push herself upright, her voice hoarse from the effort. "Distract them. I'll draw them off," she said.

"Like hell," Mia snarled, stepping in front of Leo with her protective instincts flaring. "You're not doing this."

"I'm dead either way!" Clara's voice cracked, raw with emotion, her face flushed from the effort to stay conscious. "Let me mean something."

The door splintered suddenly as the Accelerates began to break through, a deafening noise that sent a tremor through the room. The fight for survival was no longer a question of if, but when. They were running out of time.

Clara lunged before anyone could stop her. A desperate, wild motion born of both rage and surrender. She shoved Mia aside with such sudden, unrelenting force that Mia collided with the wall, the impact stealing the breath from her lungs. The air thickened with the urgency of the moment. There was no time to think. No time to react. The Accelerates descended upon Clara like a swarm of twisted, remorseless predators, their scalpels gleaming in the dim light, flashing with deadly precision.

But Clara didn't scream. Instead, she laughed, an awful, guttural sound that tore through the air like a raw, animalistic cry. It was so deeply unsettling that it seemed to freeze the monsters for a heartbeat, giving Clara just enough time to confront her worst nightmare head-on.

"Mammy, mammy, come, come to me. I missed you so much," came the voice, high-pitched and eerie, a mockery of the sweet tone a child might use. Ava, Clara's baby daughter, stood before her in the tattered remnants of a princess dress, the garb of innocence now stained with the horrors she had become. Her head tilted slightly to the side, as if she were a curious animal observing Clara's response. "Mama," Ava continued, her voice dripping with false sweetness, before her expression twisted into something darker, something monstrous.

The smile faded from Ava's face, replaced by a look of cold, horrifying rage. Her cobalt-blue eyes were now black, empty voids of malice, twisted by the dark force that had claimed her. She screamed with an unnatural voice, a guttural, terrifying sound that echoed in the stillness of the room. "Mama, I am going to eliminate you and everyone you love."

Clara's bloodshot eyes met Ava's, and a cruel laugh bubbled from her throat, harsh and bitter. She spat blood onto the floor at her feet, her voice low but filled with terrifying finality.

"You were supposed to be my miracle..."

With a ferocious scream, Clara swung the metal bedpan with all the force she could muster. The sickening crack of Ava's skull reverberated through the air. For an agonizing second, Clara watched as Ava's body crumpled to the floor, her eyes wide and unblinking. And then, in the briefest, most heart-wrenching instant, Clara saw it, the shift. Ava's eyes, once cold and monstrous, softened. They no longer reflected the grotesque cruelty of an Accelerate but were suddenly those of a child, vulnerable, innocent.

The transformation was Ava's final gift, or her cruelest trap. Clara couldn't tell. As Clara's breath caught in her throat, Ava's lifeless body hit the floor with a dull thud.

Clara collapsed over Ava, her body shaking, her hands trembling as she cradled the lifeless form. She held Ava as if she were a baby again, hoping to somehow shield her from all the violence and pain of the world. The irony of it struck Clara, this was the moment she had longed for but could never truly have: a mother trying to protect her daughter, even in death, from the horrors that had consumed them both.

But there was no time left for mourning. The Accelerates moved in without hesitation, their speed deadly as they pounced on Clara and Ava's lifeless bodies. They slashed and tore at Clara, sinking their teeth into her flesh, biting, and stabbing as if the dead had not been enough.

Clara's body, still trembling, struggled beneath them. But it was a losing battle. She was beyond saving now. Ava, her daughter, was gone, and so was any semblance of hope. Clara's body was no longer just a protector; she was a broken shell, a hollow echo of what she had once been.

And then, amid the chaos and the violence, the quietest, most painful truth settled in. Two lives were lost on that cold floor, one who had given birth but never had the chance to experience motherhood, and the other who had been born into a world that never allowed her to live as a child. The weight of that grief was unbearable, suffocating, as the lifeless bodies of mother and daughter lay forgotten, the cruel world continuing to churn around them.

As life drained from her, Clara's final thought wasn't of vengeance or fear, but the bitter truth: neither she nor Ethan had ever truly lived.

The memory of Clara's stand fused into their bones, like a scar that would never heal. Ethan grabbed Mia and Leo, his hands trembling but resolute, and pulled them toward the stairwell, each step heavy with the weight of what they had left behind. Clara's screams echoed in their ears, the raw, agonizing sound of a mother caught in the throes of something monstrous.

"Clara!" Mia cried out, her voice raw with desperation, but Ethan's grip tightened, unyielding, as he urged them forward. His breath was shallow, his chest tightening with every step, but there was no time to grieve. No time to hesitate. The decision had already been made, they couldn't go back. Not now.

They didn't look back.

7.7: Inheritance of Fire

The world outside seemed to be on fire as they stumbled into the parking garage, a suffocating haze of smoke curling up from the flames consuming the city below. The air was thick and heavy, the acrid scent of burning rubble mingling with the metallic tang of blood. Mia's head spun, the chaos of the world crashing down around her. Her heart felt like it was being crushed with every beat, yet she forced herself to keep moving. Adrenaline was the only thing driving her now.

She slumped against a concrete pillar, breath ragged as she pressed her shaking hands to her face, only to realize they were slick with Clara's blood. The cold, sticky substance soaked into her skin, a grotesque reminder of what they'd left behind. Her eyes stared blankly, guilt pressing in from all sides.

"I left her," Mia whispered, the words barely escaping her lips. They felt like acid, burning her throat as the reality sank in.

Ethan stood just a few steps away, his face gaunt, eyes distant. He, too, felt broken, but he couldn't afford to show it, not now, not when there was still something worth fighting for. He had to be strong for Mia, for Leo, and even for Clara, despite her absence. "She chose," he said, his voice cracking under the weight of that truth. Yet the words felt empty, devoid of meaning. Clara had chosen to stay behind, to face whatever hell awaited her. It was a decision he couldn't understand, but it was hers. They couldn't change it now.

Leo tugged at Mia's sleeve, his small, trembling hand pulling her attention away from the guilt threatening to swallow her whole. "Clara said... sunflowers," he whispered, voice soft and unsteady, eyes wide with confusion and fear.

Mia's head snapped up, struggling to process his words, to grasp anything that might make sense of what had happened. "What?" she asked, her voice hoarse, as if just speaking might tear her apart.

"In the car," Leo continued, his words tumbling out in a frantic rush. "She whispered... 'sunflowers' before she... before..." His sentence trailed off, his unspoken words hung in the air like a shadow.

Mia's heart clenched as the word "sunflowers" echoed in her mind. A memory flashed before the world fractured, before the nightmare swallowed them whole. Sunflowers had always grounded her, a symbol of life, of hope. It was the last thing Clara had said, the final piece of solace Mia could cling to.

Her gaze hardened, her face shifting into a grim mask. This wasn't over. It couldn't be. They couldn't simply walk away from what Clara had fought for, from everything they had lost. "We finish this," Mia declared, her voice low and fierce with determination. "For her."

The words were a promise she couldn't break. She didn't know how they'd manage, or what was even left to fight for in this shattered world. But they had to keep going, for Clara, for Leo, for the memory of everything they had once been.

Later that night, darkness enveloped the parking garage, swallowing the world whole. The only light came from the flickering flames below, casting long, twisted shadows across the concrete walls. Mia lay half-sleep, her mind racing with echoes of the day, images of Clara's last moments replaying again and again. Just as exhaustion began to pull her under, the shrill, gut-wrenching sound of Leo's scream pierced the night.

Ethan and Mia jolted awake, hearts racing as cries shattered the silence. Mia scrambled to her feet, her body aching, and rushed to Leo's side. Ethan was holding him as he was curled into a ball on the cold concrete, his small hands clutching his chest as if something inside him were trying to claw its way out. His screams were jagged, desperate, filled with a raw pain Mia couldn't comprehend.

"Leo, baby, what's wrong?" she whispered, her voice trembling as she knelt and pulled him into her arms.

But Leo didn't respond. His cobalt-blue eyes were wide, filled with terror and confusion looking at her, his body shaking uncontrollably. His cries grew more frantic, more pained by the second. And then Mia saw it, the unmistakable signs of infection creeping across her hand. Dark veins, thin and twisted, began to form beneath her pale, trembling flesh.

A chilling realization washed over her, and her heart sank. Clara's blood earlier on her hands infected her. The infection was spreading. It was only a matter of time before it consumed her, just as it had consumed Clara. Ethan's eyes in horror gaze on her arm.

And this time, there would be no saving either of them.

It was inside her.

The infection wasn't just in Leo.

Twisting, rising like smoke beneath the skin.

Dark veins.

Her hand. Her arm.

She wiped the sweat from her brow, then froze.

Ethan looked at her, not in fear for himself, but as if something inside her terrified him.

"I saw it... in my dream," Leo sobbed. "It's in you. The black veins. Like Clara."

Chapter 8: Wait for Me at the Turn

8.1: Choke Point

The highway stretched before them like a serpent's spine, cracked, jagged, littered with the skeletons of abandoned cars. Twisted metal and shattered glass glimmered in the harsh afternoon sun, creating a graveyard of motionless vehicles. Rusted hulks loomed like monuments to a world that had crumbled, their empty cabins whispering stories of those who never made it. The stench of scorched rubber and decay hung in the air, mingling with the distant, sulfuric bite of smoldering cities.

Ethan's knuckles whitened around the battered steering wheel as the pickup truck's engine sputtered, swerving around a crater filled with stagnant, oily rainwater. Each pothole jolted through his bones, the truck's rusted shocks groaning in protest. The gas gauge hovered dangerously close to empty, yet Ethan's foot stayed firm on the accelerator. Stopping wasn't an option.

In the passenger seat, Mia slumped against the door, her forehead pressed to the hot glass. Sweat slid down her temples, merging with the grime streaking her face. Her infected arm was tightly wrapped in a makeshift sling, a GeneCorp flag twisted into a crude bandage. The coiled serpent encircling a corrupted DNA helix emblazoned on the fabric seemed to sear against her skin, a grim reminder of the corporation's twisted grip. The black veins creeping beneath her pale skin pulsed slowly, like a serpent slithering just under the surface.

Leo's voice floated up from the truck bed, barely louder than the rushing wind.

"Ethan? How much farther?"

Ethan glanced at the boy in the cracked rearview mirror. Leo was little more than a bundle beneath a fraying tarp, his knees were curled to his chest, and his trembling fingers gripped what remained of Mr. Bubbles, the once-plush bear now threadbare and eyeless. Only a loose, crooked smile remained, stitched in defiance of all that had been lost.

"Soon," Ethan muttered, though the word tasted like ash. He tightened his grip on the wheel, unwilling to meet Mia's gaze. The map, Clara's map, was spread across her lap, its creased surface stained with dirt and blood. The red circle around Redwood Valley stood out, bold and certain, even as the inked edges blurred from Mia's trembling hands.

"Soon?" Mia's voice was dry and brittle, cracked from dehydration and grief. She shifted, wincing as the infected veins on her arm throbbed. "You said that hours ago. We're running on fumes."

Ethan's jaw clenched.

"We keep moving."

Mia opened her mouth to argue, but the words died on her tongue. Instead, she stared at the empty horizon, where jagged silhouettes of toppled billboards stood like skeletal sentinels. One, barely legible, still boasted GeneCorp's smiling promises: *A Brighter Future Through Innovation.* The paint had cracked and faded, but the mocking words lingered.

"Redwood Valley," Mia whispered. "Clara believed it was safe."

"Clara believed a lot of things," Ethan replied, his voice void of malice, only exhaustion and guilt.

The memory of Clara's last stand clawed at his mind, the ferocity in her eyes, how she had thrown herself into the fray without hesitation. Her screams still echoed. He swallowed hard, trying to force the image away. There was no time for ghosts.

"What if it's not safe?" Leo's voice was barely above a whisper, but it cut through the stagnant air like a blade.

Ethan didn't answer. He didn't have to.

The truck rattled on, coughing clouds of black smoke as the skeletal cityscape gave way to an open highway once more. The sun dipped lower, casting long shadows that danced like phantoms across the broken road. Still, the red circle on the map burned brightly in their minds, a promise, a threat, and a hope clinging by a thread.

Mia ransacked the truck's interior, her fingers scraping through layers of dust and scattered debris. Under the seat, she pulled out a dented can of energy drink, its label faded and peeling. She shook it slightly, hearing the faint swish of liquid inside. Then, in the glove compartment, her hand brushed against cold metal. She froze and carefully drew out a small pistol, its black frame dulled with grime.

"Ethan, look," she called, her voice low and tense.

Ethan's eyes flicked from the cracked road ahead to the gun in her hands. "Are there any bullets?"

Mia dug deeper, her heart pounding. Beneath a stack of yellowed receipts and crumpled papers, she found a half-full box of ammunition. She held it up; the paper carton was damp and warped, but the brass casings inside gleamed.

"Load it," Ethan said without hesitation. "It'll come in handy."

The truck rattled over a pothole, jolting Mia as she clicked the magazine into place. She cracked open the energy drink; the hiss of escaping carbonation was a jarring contrast to the growing tension. The sugary scent mingled with the stale, metallic air.

"We're being followed," she muttered, the can trembling in her hand.

Ethan's gaze snapped to the rearview mirror. In the distance, plumes of dust curled into the air. Two motorcycles emerged through the haze, their riders' black silhouettes against the glaring sky. They weaved through the debris-strewn road with practiced ease.

Accelerates.

Ethan's jaw clenched. "They're closing in."

The road ahead narrowed, the cracked asphalt funneling into a canyon lined with jagged rocks and sun-bleached boulders. It was the perfect choke point, an ambush site. His hands tightened on the steering wheel.

"This is where they want us," he growled. "Hold on."

Mia's fingers traced the grooves of the pistol's grip. She loaded the weapon with a smooth click; its weight was both reassuring and terrifying. Her voice remained steady, though her pulse raced. "They'll try to flank us."

The first motorcycle surged forward, its rider barely more than a boy, his cherubic face twisted in gleeful malice. In his hand, a Molotov cocktail ignited, flames dancing at the neck of the glass bottle. With a triumphant howl, he hurled it at the truck.

The bottle shattered on impact. Fire erupted across the hood, licking the windshield. The acrid smoke stung Mia's eyes. Ethan slammed the brakes, tires screeching as the truck fishtailed. Metal groaned in protest.

Before Mia could react, the second Accelerate made his move. A boy, no older than ten, his face obscured by cracked swimming goggles, leapt into the truck bed with terrifying speed. Leo's scream pierced the air, a primal sound that cut through the chaos.

The Accelerate recoiled, clutching his ears, blood trickling from his nose. But his partner wasn't deterred. A rock flew past and cracked the windshield.

Mia raised the pistol, hands trembling as she took aim at the boy in the truck bed. But the Accelerate moved like smoke, darting behind the rusted tailgate. Her shot rang out, the bullet striking the canyon wall, causing a burst of stone and dust.

"Go!" Mia shouted, her voice hoarse. "We're sitting ducks!"

Ethan slammed the gas pedal. The tires screeched as gravel flew up behind them, and the truck shot forward. The canyon walls blurred past, jagged cliffs looming on either side. The roar of motorcycles echoed behind them, a sharp reminder they weren't alone.

Leo huddled beneath the tarp, his small body trembling. He clutched his scorched teddy bear, Mr. Bubbles, tightly to his chest. Tears streaked his dirt-smudged cheeks, and his wide and frightened eyes never left the cracked windshield.

"Mia," Ethan said, glancing back. "We won't outrun them."

Ethan's jaw set, his eyes burning with resolve.

"Then we'll make them regret following us."

8.2: The Gas Station

They staggered into the ghost town, their shadows stretching long under the fading light. The welcome sign stood crooked at the town's edge, riddled with bullet holes: Pleasant Creek. Population 402. Someone had crudely scrawled a "0" over the last number, the paint dripping like blood. The only sound was the whisper of wind through shattered windows and the distant creak of something unseen swaying in the breeze.

The truck coughed once, sputtered, then wheezed into silence. Ethan slammed his fist against the dashboard, his jaw tightening. They had pushed it as far as it would go. Now, they were on foot.

Mia kicked open the passenger door, the rusted hinges groaning in protest. Her eyes scanned the storefronts, gutted, looted, their signs dangling by a screw. A diner sat on the corner, its windows shattered, and booths coated in dust.

Further down, a grocery store stood dark, its metal security gate twisted like a ribcage.

"We need fuel. And food," she muttered, adjusting the pistol at her hip. There was no room for hesitation.

Leo stumbled out of the truck, nearly collapsing as his legs gave out beneath him. "Eth..." His voice was barely a whisper. "I can't... feel my toes."

Ethan caught Leo before he hit the cracked pavement, dropping to his knees. With quick, desperate hands, he unlaced Leo's shoes and pulled them off. His breath caught. Leo's feet were grotesque, swollen, veined in dark blue under waxy skin. The boy's small toes curled inward, as if they were wilting. His body was failing, shutting down from exhaustion, hunger... perhaps something worse.

For a moment, Mia's hands froze. Her thoughts screamed, but her face remained stone.

Mia tossed Ethan a canteen. "Hydration first," she said flatly, though there was an edge to her voice, a tightness she couldn't hide. She knew what those veins signified. They all did.

Ethan pressed the canteen to Leo's lips, forcing small sips of stale water into his mouth. "We'll find a place to rest," he murmured, though he didn't know if he was speaking to Leo or to himself.

Mia turned sharply, scanning the street again as her mind shifted into survival mode. "We need to split up. Ethan, you find fuel. If we can get the truck running, we won't have to spend the night here." She glanced at Leo's trembling form, then back to Ethan. "I'll look for food and any medicine I can find."

Ethan hesitated. "Splitting up..."

"We don't have a choice."

Their eyes met, and a silent understanding passed between them, wordless but resolute.

With that, they moved. Mia turned in the opposite direction, gripping her pistol tightly as she disappeared into the ruins of Pleasant Creek, her figure swallowed by the dying town. Somewhere deeper in the ruins, something shifted. A whisper. A scrape. Maybe just the wind, or maybe not.

Ethan hoisted Leo onto his back and headed toward the skeletal remains of a gas station, its rusted pumps standing like grave markers.

The gas station stood hollow, its windows shattered, and shelves stripped bare. The pumps stood like rusted monuments to a time before the world fell apart. Ethan's footsteps crunched over broken glass as he approached them, the stale air thick with the stench of old gasoline and mildew. He twisted the nozzle of the nearest pump, but the hollow clunk of dry machinery answered him: empty, just like the others.

"Damn it," he growled under his breath, rubbing the grime from his hands onto his jeans.

But then, tucked behind the station, he spotted a flicker of hope. A rusted tanker truck loomed like a forgotten beast, its faded logo barely visible beneath years of dust and corrosion. The cylindrical tank caught the dying sunlight, its metal skin reflecting a faint orange glow. Ethan's heart thudded with cautious optimism. If the fuel inside was still viable, they might have a chance.

"Stay here," Ethan ordered, though his voice was gentler than before. He moved toward the tanker, its ladder creaking beneath his weight as he climbed to the top. The hatch was sealed tight, but with a grunt and a twist, it gave way. A wave of putrid air hit him like a physical blow. The scent of stale diesel and metallic rot clawed at his throat. He gagged, stumbled, but forced himself forward.

"We'll siphon it," he rasped, pushing the words past the bile rising in his throat.

Leo slumped against the tanker's wheel well, nearly swallowed by the dim light. He clutched Mr. Bubbles, the tattered teddy bear hanging limply in his arms. "What does 'siphon' mean?" His voice was soft, trembling under the weight of exhaustion.

Ethan forced a grin he didn't feel, the corners of his mouth twitching upward. "It's a magic trick," he said, though the bitterness in his voice betrayed his true feelings. "You take from something that's full and give it to something that's empty."

"Like... a glass of water?"

"Exactly. But this water could burn a hole through your skin."

Ethan pulled a piece of rubber tubing from the truck's emergency kit, its cracked surface barely holding together. With grim determination, he inserted one end into the tanker's hatch and lowered the other toward a rubber bucket. Then, taking a deep breath, he began to siphon.

The metallic sting of diesel filled his mouth at once. He gagged, spitting violently onto the asphalt. His throat burned, and his eyes watered. Despite the discomfort, the fuel continued to flow. A thin, black stream dripped into the rubber bucket, saturating the air with the scent of oil.

He coughed, wiping his mouth with the back of his hand. "See? Magic."

Leo didn't smile.

Then it came, a sound that made Ethan's stomach clench. A sharp, unnatural giggle. It echoed through the empty lot, twisting the silence into something far more sinister.

Ethan froze, instinctively reaching for the tire wrench. He scanned the shadows, his pulse quickening.

From behind a rusted dumpster, a figure emerged, small, wiry, and unnervingly still. The boy couldn't have been older than twelve, but there was something about the precision of his movements that made him seem ancient. His face was smudged with dirt, and he wore an unsettlingly wide grin, revealing his bared teeth. In his hands, a small drone controller gleamed, its screen flickering with data.

"Subject A-9," the boy taunted, his voice singsong and dripping with mockery. "You're trending on GeneCorp's bounty board."

Leo whimpered, clutching Mr. Bubbles tighter.

Ethan gripped the wrench tighter. He stepped in front of Leo instinctively, positioning himself as a human shield. The boy with the drone barely blinked, his unsettling smirk lingering. He tilted his head, a gleam of twisted amusement in his eyes. The controller in his hands pulsed with blinking lights, and the low hum of the drone vibrated in the thick, stagnant air. Its mechanical limbs twitched, and the camera lens narrowed like a predator's eye.

"Get lost," Ethan growled, his voice low and commanding.

The boy grinned wider, his finger dancing dangerously over a crimson button. "Why would I? The board loves real-time updates. They're watching, you know." He nodded toward the hovering drone. "Smile."

The machine buzzed closer, its lens focusing on Leo. Each bead of sweat and every streak of grime were recorded, cataloged, and transmitted. Somewhere, analysts would already be dissecting Leo's scream frame by frame, cataloguing stress patterns, spike waves, decay curves. Somewhere far away, in a sterile GeneCorp control room, the executives would be watching, studying, and enjoying.

"Subject A-9," the boy exclaimed, relishing the words. "And his anomaly."

Leo whimpered again, Mr. Bubbles clutched to his chest. His small frame shook with fear, and Ethan could sense the panic radiating from him. The sight twisted something deep within Ethan, rage mingled with fear. But just as he opened his mouth to speak, the air around them fractured.

Leo's scream erupted raw, shattering wail that pierced the silence. The sound didn't just echo; it reverberated. The drone's camera flickered erratically as its circuits shorted. It spiraled mid-air, spinning wildly before crashing onto the cracked asphalt with a sickening crunch. Fragments of plastic and twisted metal scattered across the ground, resembling the aftermath of a detonated bomb.

The Accelerate staggered, clutching his head as blood trickled from his ears. He gasped, eyes wide with confusion and pain, his cocky grin erased. Still, he didn't fall. He swayed like a broken marionette, something inhuman keeping him upright. As if he'd been built to withstand the impossible.

"Fascinating," the boy rasped, voice trembling. "Your anomaly is weakening." He blinked slowly, crimson rivulets from his ears smearing down his pale neck. "It won't last. They never do."

Ethan didn't wait. The boy's words twisted through his mind, but the moment for hesitation had passed. The cold steel of the tire wrench felt solid in his grasp. With a burst of fury, he swung it. The wrench connected with a sickening crack, the impact reverberating through his arms.

The Accelerate collapsed, his body folding like a rag doll. Silence followed. No twitching. No laughter. Just Ethan's ragged breathing.

He hovered over the lifeless figure, chest heaving. For a moment, he waited, for the boy to twitch, to grin, to whisper some final, twisted remark. But there was nothing. Relief didn't come, just the gnawing void.

Ethan turned. His gaze landed on Leo. Tears clung to Leo's wide eyes; his hands still clutched the torn bear. Ethan dropped the wrench with a hollow clang, his arms trembling. He opened his mouth, but no words came.

Relief? Disgust? He couldn't tell. It all swirled together.

"Let's go," Ethan rasped at last, his voice barely above a whisper. Without a word, Leo nodded. His small hand slipped into Ethan's, a little trembling, but steady. The road waited ahead. Behind them, GeneCorp's shadow stretched long. The broken drone still twitched faintly in the dust.

8.3: No Escape This Time

Mia stepped into the pharmacy, the door creaking on rusted hinges. The smell of decay hung heavily in the air, thick, suffocating. The shelves were nearly empty, their contents long scavenged, save for a single vial of morphine tucked behind a shattered glass display. She quickly closed her fingers around it, a small victory, but a necessary one.

Pain pulsed from the infected hand, radiating through her arm. The black veins had crept higher overnight, now coiling around her neck like a noose, a grotesque map of her body's betrayal. She clenched her jaw. Not yet. She wasn't dead yet.

As she stepped into the alley, movement flickered at the edge of her vision. A low growl sent a chill racing down her spine. Slowly, she turned.

A dog, if it could still be called that, stood before her.

Its ribs protruded beneath a patchwork of matted fur, its body trembling with hunger. Foam bubbled at the corners of its mouth, and its eyes, no longer the dull, lifeless gaze of a starving stray, glowed with something unnatural. Something was wrong.

The moment stretched thin.

Then, it lunged.

Mia fired without thinking. The crack of the gunshot split the air. The dog collapsed mid-leap, its body hitting the pavement in a twitching heap. Silence followed, thick, suffocating.

Then the echoes began.

Footsteps. Laughter.

Not just echoes, voices.

The sounds intensified.

They were close. Too close.

She held her breath. The laughter twisted into mocking singsongs. "Weakness detected," one of them crooned from the shadows, voice lilting and amused. Another giggled, the sound too high-pitched and unnatural.

Mia ran.

Boots pounding, pulse drumming, she ran. Ahead, the alleyway narrowed, funneling her directly toward the town square, a trap. They were herding her like prey. At the last moment, a shadow moved. A strong, unyielding hand latched onto her arm and yanked her sideways, pulling her into the darkness of a boarded-up diner. She nearly screamed, nearly fought back, until the familiar scents of sweat, gasoline, and blood flooded her senses.

Ethan.

Her chest rose and fell, shallow and fast. "Where's Leo?" she gasped, struggling to form the words.

"Safe," Ethan whispered, his voice taut and low. "For now."

Outside, laughter faded, replaced by slow, deliberate footsteps. Searching.

Mia pressed her back against the wall, her fingers tightening around the gun, her pulse racing as she met Ethan's gaze. They had only seconds, maybe less, before the Accelerates found them. This time, there would be no escape.

8.4: The Night in The Town's Church

They regrouped in the hollow shell of the town church. Moonlight poured through shattered stained glass, casting warped shapes on stone. The once-pristine pews lay overturned, splintered like broken bones. Dust and ash coated everything, muffling the sacred silence.

Leo lay on the cracked altar, curled beneath a moth-eaten blanket. His chest rose and fell in uneven, desperate gasps, each breath a battle he was losing. The boy's skin, once warm and golden, had turned an ashen gray. Sweat clung to his hairline, and his small hands gripped the remnants of Mr. Bubbles, the bear's torn fur damp beneath his trembling fingers.

Mia knelt by his side, the morphine catching the moonlight in her shaking hand. Not out of mercy. Not to save him. To feel something, before the numbness of what came next. The glass caught the dim light, glowing like something precious and forbidden. Her infected arm throbbed in time with her heartbeat, the black veins creeping higher, tendrils of the inevitable.

"For the pain," she whispered, her voice hollow. The words barely registered in her own ears.

Before she could move, Ethan's hand shot out, his fingers gripping her wrist tightly. The suddenness of it startled her, sending a jolt of panic through her chest.

"Don't," he said, his voice low and rough with fear. His dark, hollow eyes locked onto hers, pleading. "Mia, think."

She didn't pull away or argue. Instead, her gaze remained steady and unwavering, burning into his.

"It's not for him," she said, and for the first time, there was no sarcasm. No armor. Just the truth of someone who knew the end had already started.

Without waiting for another word, Mia drove the needle into her own arm. The sting was sharp but fleeting. The syringe emptied, and a wave of warmth spread through her veins. The relief was immediate, a dizzying release, like sinking into dark water. The pain dulled, the world softened. Even the constant ache of infection seemed distant now, a whisper beneath the roar of her pulse.

Ethan's breath caught in his throat. "You'll overdose," he said, fear making his voice tremble. "Mia, that's enough."

She shook her head, the haze of the substance already thickening around her. "Better than fading into something I'm not," she muttered. "I'll burn out clean."

But it wasn't just her fate she spoke of. She didn't need to say it, they both knew. Her eyes flicked to Leo, whose fragile frame barely stirred, his body betraying him. Ethan followed her gaze, and his face twisted in anguish.

"He's dying, Ethan," she whispered, her voice barely audible. "You know it."

Ethan's shoulders tensed, and he clenched his fists at his sides. The weight of her words crushed him. "I can't lose him too," he replied, his voice cracking with grief. "Not like Clara."

Mia swallowed hard. The memory of Clara's sacrifice, the blood, the screams, the laughter of the Accelerates, clung to them like a curse. The walls of the church seemed to echo with it.

Outside, the storm broke. Thunder rumbled low and threatening, shaking the ground. Rain cascaded in sheets, hammering against the shattered windows. The relentless drumming drowned out the distant taunts of the Accelerates, as though nature itself tried to silence the horrors surrounding them.

Ethan slumped against a broken pew, his head bowed. His fingers twisted in his hair as he fought against the tide of sorrow threatening to consume him. Mia remained where she was, the empty vial still clenched in her trembling hand. The morphine dulled her body, but not the ache in her soul.

Minutes passed, maybe hours, and neither of them spoke. The storm raged outside while Leo slept on, caught in the fragile space between life and death.

Finally, Mia murmured, her voice barely audible, "We need to finish this. For him. For Clara."

Ethan didn't respond, but the flicker in his eyes, a smoldering ember of determination, was an answer enough.

8.5: Wait for Me at the Turn

At dawn, the horizon was streaked with hues of gray and orange as the sun fought to rise through the thick haze. They discovered that the tanker's fuel was still usable, a small mercy in a world that rarely offered any. Ethan crouched beside the rusted truck, siphoning the fuel with careful precision. Each gurgle of gasoline into the rubber bucket counted down their borrowed moments.

Mia leaned against the hood of the car, her face pale and gaunt. The morphine dulled the pain, but not the storm in her eyes. Her pupils were wide, black with weight. She watched Ethan without truly seeing him, her thoughts a thousand miles away.

"Redwood Valley is a laboratory," she slurred, her voice thick and distant. "Clara said they will dissect him."

Ethan remained silent at first, twisting a bolt on the engine. His jaw was clenched, muscles twitching beneath his skin. The image of Leo strapped to a sterile table flashed in his mind, the boy's frail body torn apart in the name of science. GeneCorp never hid what they were. They labeled their atrocities as research, cloaked their greed in promises of progress.

"We've got no choice," Ethan said finally, the words bitter in his mouth.

Mia's fingers brushed against the edge of the hood, her nails leaving patterns in the fine layer of dust. "There's always a choice," she said.

Ethan felt a tightening in his chest. He wanted to argue, to tell her there had to be another way. But the road behind them had long since collapsed. They had no time left. Every second spent hesitating was another second Leo didn't have.

A distant hum broke the silence, growing louder. A pack of six figures emerged, their silhouettes twisting through the smoke, eyes glinting with feral hunger. They moved like shadows, predatory and precise, while their laughter echoed through the empty streets.

Mia pulled the truck keys from her pocket and tossed them to Ethan. The metal glinted in the dim light, a symbol of the decision neither of them wanted to make.

"Drive. Take Leo. Wait for me at the turn."

He caught the keys but didn't move. "You'll die," he said, concern evident in his voice.

"Yeah," Mia replied, a faint smile tugging at her cracked lips. "But not today."

Mia tightened her grip on the crowbar in her right hand and the Molotov cocktail in her left. The cool glass pressed against her palm, the fuel inside sloshing with potential. She stepped forward, the firelight from the tanker reflecting in her eyes.

"Hey, monsters!" she shouted, her voice piercing the early morning stillness. "Catch!"

She hurled the Molotov. The bottle spun through the air, and for a brief moment, it seemed the world held its breath. Then it shattered against the tanker, igniting in a flash of white-hot fury. The explosion roared like a wounded beast, a shockwave rippling through the town. Flames clawed at the sky, sending black smoke billowing upward like a funeral pyre.

The Accelerates staggered, momentarily blinded by the brightness. The fire's reflection flickered in their vacant cobalt-blue eyes, but even in their confusion, the hunger remained.

Mia didn't look back. She spun on her heel and ran, her boots pounding against the cracked asphalt. Her breath came in ragged gasps as adrenaline dulled the ache in her infected arm. Behind her, the fire raged, the smell of burning metal and scorched rubber thick in the air.

In the driver's seat, Ethan watched, his knuckles white against the steering wheel. The truck's engine roared to life, the vibration trembling beneath him. Leo's cries filled the cab, a raw and terrified sound that tore through Ethan like a blade.

"Mia!" Leo sobbed, twisting in his seat. "She's not coming!"

Ethan's hands shook. Every instinct screamed at him to turn back, to fight, to save her. But Mia's voice echoed in his mind, firm and resolute. "Wait for me at the turn."

He slammed his foot on the gas. The truck lurched forward, tires screeching against the cracked pavement. Flames licked at the shadows as the town shrank in the rearview mirror. Leo's sobs quieted to ragged breaths, his wide eyes fixed on the plumes of smoke that swallowed the sky.

Then, from the haze, Mia emerged. She sprinted from the inferno, her face streaked with soot, her eyes wild. Her body moved with the desperation of someone who knew every step could be her last.

"Drive!" she screamed.

Ethan didn't hesitate. He yanked the wheel, and the truck fishtailed as Mia leapt into the bed. The metal groaned beneath her weight, but she held fast, her fingers clutching the side. Behind them, the Accelerates gave chase, their silhouettes consumed by smoke and flame.

The road ahead twisted into the unknown, but the truck roared forward, defying the darkness that nipped at their heels. In that fleeting moment, they were not just survivors; they were something more.

Leo reached for Mia's soot-streaked hand through the rear window. She touched the glass. Just once.

They were family, and they were still alive.

Chapter 9: Bridge to the Dust

9.1: Where the Bridges Die

They drove through the night, the world beyond the truck shrouded in shifting shadows and restless winds. The highway stretched like a scar across the earth, cracked asphalt lit by the dim moon. The engine hummed wearily, each mile swallowed by the unknown.

By sunrise, they reached the end of the road. The bridge had collapsed long ago, its skeletal remains jutting out over the abyss like the ribcage of a long-dead beast. Beyond it, the river sprawled beneath the broken dawn, but it was no longer a river, it had become a festering wound upon the land.

The eastern sky bled crimson, its light filtering through the skeletal trees that lined the banks. Their twisted branches reached skyward like the desperate hands of beggars pleading for mercy. The air was thick with the stench of rot, stagnant and suffocating, as though the earth itself had given up and begun to decay. And the water, if it could still be called that, was something far worse.

A thick, oily black mass churned sluggishly below, a slow, bubbling expanse of poison and death. Rusted barges jutted from the sludge like forgotten tombstones, their hulls long since corroded by time and neglect. The skeletal remains of bridges reached out in futile desperation, their twisted steel beams tangled like broken limbs. Bloated bodies, human and animal, bobbed in the sludge, their faces long erased by the elements.

The stench was unbearable. Diesel, decay, and something worse, something sickly sweet, clung to the back of Ethan's throat, making every breath feel like inhaling death itself. He clenched his jaw, forcing down the nausea, his grip tightening on the truck's door handle as he scanned the desolation before him.

They had come so far. And for what?

Crouching in the shadow of the collapsed overpass, Ethan's eyes swept over the barren horizon. There was no movement, no sign of life, only the distant moan of the wind weaving through the ruins of a world that no longer belonged to them.

Beside him, Leo shivered, his small frame wracked with exhaustion and fear. He clutched Mr. Bubbles, his beloved teddy bear, now little more than a ragged bundle of stuffing and cloth. Leo's breaths were shallow, his lips dry and cracked, and beneath his fevered skin, a violet glow pulsed steadily, a cruel and constant reminder that the virus was winning.

Ethan's stomach twisted. How much longer did Leo have?

Mia leaned against the truck, her infected arm wrapped tightly in makeshift bandages. Her pupils blown wide from exhaustion and pain. She exhaled slowly, her breath visible in the chill of the morning air, her expression unreadable as she stared at the ruined world before them. This was supposed to be their way forward. Instead, it felt like the end of the road.

Then, without warning, a sound slithered into the air.

"Ring around the Rosie..."

The melody drifted, dissonant, hollow, carried by a phantom wind. It was the voice of a child, fragile and haunting yet warped, stretched thin by something unnatural. The melody coiled through the skeletal remains of the collapsed bridge, wrapping around them like a ghostly whisper from the grave.

Ethan's blood turned to ice.

From the mist, they emerged.

Eight figures moved like wraiths through the morning haze, their forms distorted by the shifting light. Their bodies twitched with unnatural precision, heads tilting at odd angles as if they were listening to something only they could hear. Their bare feet made no sound against the cracked pavement, and their movements were eerily fluid, like marionettes dangled from invisible strings.

The Accelerates.

The lead figure stepped forward, his head tilted in curiosity. When he spoke, his voice was clinical, devoid of emotion. "Subject A-9. Defect: delayed viral assimilation."

His words sliced through the morning stillness like a razor's edge. Ethan tensed, his grip tightening around the crowbar until his knuckles turned white. His heart pounded against his ribs, a primal beat of instinct and fear. He could feel Leo trembling behind him, the boy's small hands clutching the fabric of his jacket as though he could will himself into the safety of Ethan's shadow.

A strangled whimper escaped Leo's lips, and his entire body convulsed as if a freezing wind had passed through him. His wide, fever-bright eyes locked onto the advancing figures, and for a moment, his expression shifted, from fear to something else. Recognition.

"Ava?" he whispered, his voice barely more than a breath.

Mia snapped her head toward him, her eyes narrowing in alarm. "No!" she barked, yanking the pistol from her belt. Her hands were steady despite the rapid pulse hammering beneath her skin. "Someone's just parroting her words."

One of the Accelerates let out a rasping giggle, the sound skittering across the ruins like broken glass. Another cocked his head in amusement, repeating in a high-pitched singsong, "Ava? Ava?" before breaking into a fit of laughter.

Ethan didn't hesitate. "Leo, get in the truck," he ordered, his voice firm and commanding.

The boy hesitated for only a second before scrambling toward the vehicle, ducking into the cab just as Ethan planted himself in front of the door, his stance unyielding. He could feel the tension coiling in the air, thick as storm clouds ready to break.

Mia stood beside him, her pistol raised, gaze locked onto the figures as they drew closer. The silence stretched.

Then, with a shrill, unnatural shriek, the Accelerates lunged.

They moved as one.

Their howling screams ripped through the morning stillness, a piercing, discordant wail that sent a cold shudder down Ethan's spine. Their bodies twisted unnaturally as they sprinted forward, limbs moving with a disturbing, almost liquid fluidity, inhuman, relentless.

Mia fired.

The gunshot shattered the air, and the muzzle flash briefly illuminated the advancing figures. Yet they didn't stop or even flinch. If anything, the sound seemed to thrill them, their lips curling into wide, hungry grins as they closed the distance.

Ethan tightened his grip on the crowbar, planting his feet as he prepared for impact. Every muscle in his body tensed, and he could hear his heartbeat pounding in his ears like a war drum. Behind him, Leo was curled in the truck, his sharp breaths quick and shallow. The boy pressed his small hands over his ears, as if trying to block out the horror unfolding before them.

Then.

Two gunshots.

Loud. Precise.

Two of the Accelerates jerked violently, their bodies crumpling to the ground in limp, unnatural heaps. Blood pooled beneath them, dark and thick against the cracked asphalt.

Ethan barely had time to process what had happened before more shots rang out. The remaining Accelerates scattered, their shrieks warping into something almost animalistic as they vanished into the ruins, slipping like phantoms into the mist.

Silence fell.

9.2: Just Scared Kids

From beneath the ruins of the collapsed bridge, two figures emerged: a man in his late thirties and a woman in her late twenties. They stood with rifles still smoking in their hands. The woman wore a military uniform, while the man was dressed in a short-sleeved T-shirt and dark khaki cargo pants, held up by wide leather suspenders over his broad, athletic shoulders. Their movements were sharp and practiced, too controlled to belong to ordinary survivors. The man's grizzled face was lined with age, his eyes sharp behind smudged glasses. The woman, lean and sturdy, carried herself with the quiet authority of someone who had spent years commanding others.

Without hesitation, they fired a few more rounds into the shadows, ensuring the fleeing Accelerates wouldn't double back. Once satisfied, they slowly turned their attention to Ethan and Mia.

Ethan moved first, stepping in front of the truck door to shield Leo with his body. His knuckles whitened around the crowbar, his stance rigid. Mia, her breath steady, kept her pistol raised, tracking the approaching strangers with the barrel.

"Stop! Don't come any closer!" she barked, her voice sharp and unwavering.

The couple halted immediately, raising their hands in a deliberate display of peace. The woman, her sharp gaze assessing yet calm, spoke first.

"You don't need to be afraid," she said, her voice steady but kind. "I'm Lieutenant Aida Espinoza. This is my friend, Dr. George Jacobson."

Ethan and Mia exchanged a quick glance. The names meant nothing to them.

With slow, deliberate movements, the strangers placed their rifles against a fallen concrete column, stepping back from their weapons to show they had no immediate intention of using them.

Mia didn't lower her gun, and neither did Ethan relax his grip. Because in this world, trust wasn't just dangerous; it was a death sentence.

"Who are you?" Lieutenant Aida Espinoza asked, her voice calm and measured despite the weight of the moment. Her hands remained raised, palms open in a show of peace.

Silence settled like heavy fog. Neither Mia nor Ethan moved. They didn't lower their weapons or shift their stances. Their bodies remained taut, poised on the knife's edge between trust and survival. The morning air, thick with the stench of rot and oil from the river, felt suddenly suffocating.

Aida could see it in their eyes, the raw fear, the exhaustion, the slight tremble in their hands despite their firm grips on their weapons. These weren't soldiers or scavengers hardened by the wasteland; they were young kids and are running on instinct, on desperation.

Slowly, deliberately, Aida took a step back. Her boots crunched against the shattered concrete, but she kept her movements slow and controlled. She didn't dare break eye contact. Without turning her head, she spoke softly to Dr. George Jacobson, who stood rigid beside her.

"They're just scared kids," she murmured, her voice barely above a whisper. "Just move back slowly. No sudden movements."

Dr. Jacobson nodded slightly, understanding the urgency of her words. His hands, still raised, flexed as he mirrored her steps, retreating inch by inch. They remained in full view, their body language non-threatening and their postures careful.

Even as they approached their discarded rifles, they made no move to grab them. The tension in Mia's trigger finger didn't ease, and Ethan's grip on the crowbar remained ironclad.

Aida crouched, cautious not to startle them, and picked up both rifles, one in each hand, and lifted them high above her head, making it clear she wasn't aiming at anyone. The gesture was deliberate, an offering of trust in a world that had long since abandoned the concept.

Dr. Jacobson took another step back, keeping his hands raised as he moved toward the ruins of the collapsed bridge. His expression was unreadable, neither fearful nor aggressive, just the quiet patience of a man who had seen too much.

Mia's breath hitched, her heartbeat hammering against her ribs. She wanted to believe in them. She wanted to trust that there were still people who weren't out to kill them or worse. But trust was a luxury, and luxuries could get people killed.

Ethan wasn't taking any chances. He stood firm, acting as a silent barrier between Leo and the potential threat posed by the two figures.

Aida and Jacobson continued their slow retreat, the shadows of the bridge ruins consuming them step by step. They made no sudden moves and offered no further explanations, only quiet, measured steps until they finally vanished beneath the rubble, disappearing into the same darkness from which they had emerged just moments before.

The silence afterward was brutal.

Mia's arms ached from holding the pistol steady for so long, while Ethan's knuckles turned white around the crowbar. Neither of them lowered their weapons, not yet.

Frozen in place, Mia and Ethan held their breath, straining their ears for any sign of movement. The ruins surrounding them stood eerily silent, the only sound being the wind weaving through broken concrete and twisted steel. In the distance, the river gurgled, a slow decay that served as a constant reminder of how much the world had rotted.

9.3: The Long Way Around

It was only when they were certain the strangers had truly gone, vanished into the shadows beneath the collapsed bridge, that they finally exhaled. Even then, the tension in their bodies refused to ease.

Trust was a currency they couldn't afford to spend.

Mia cast one last glance toward the bridge before turning on her heel and climbing into the truck. Ethan followed, his grip on the crowbar still tight, as if expecting the strangers to reappear at any moment. The cabin felt colder than before, the weight of uncertainty pressing down on them like a thick fog.

Leo sat curled up in the back seat, his small hands clutching Mr. Bubbles, the stuffed teddy bear that had somehow survived this nightmare to comfort him. His pale fingers twisted the fabric, grip tight with unspoken fear. His breathing was uneven and shallow, each inhale a struggle, each exhale too quiet. The faint glow of his veins pulsed weakly beneath his skin, marking the presence of the virus threading through his body.

Mia swallowed hard and looked away.

For a long moment, none of them spoke. The silence was thick and suffocating. Outside, the world remained indifferent to their plight. The rising sun cast long shadows over the ruins, painting the landscape in hues of crimson and gold, beautiful in a haunting way.

Finally, Ethan shifted, breaking the quiet. "Do you think there's another bridge if we follow the river back?" His voice was low, edged with frustration. He hated feeling trapped, resented being forced into choices that led nowhere.

Mia had already unfolded Clara's map, its edges softened with wear and the ink faded in places. She traced her finger along the winding blue line that marked the river, searching for answers in the tangle of roads and forgotten landmarks.

"There's another bridge," she said at last, her tone measured and cautious. "About half a day's drive back, where the river narrows like a bottleneck, just after the ambush point where the Accelerates on motorcycles attacked, and right through the Pleasant Creek." She tapped the map, showing Ethan.

He frowned. "We passed it without noticing?" Regret and frustration laced his voice.

"We couldn't see it from the highway," Mia explained, her tone calm yet laced with exhaustion. "It's on a rural road, way off the main route." She hesitated, chewing on her bottom lip. "That bridge takes us far off course. There are no proper roads leading to the Bunker from that side. Once we cross, we'll have to go on foot."

Ethan let out a slow breath, rubbing a hand over his face. The exhaustion was catching up to him, dragging at his limbs and making every decision feel heavier than it should.

But what other choice did they have? If they wanted to survive and get Leo to the Bunker before it was too late, they had to keep moving, even if it meant taking the long way.

Ethan frowned, gripping the steering wheel to ground himself in the weight of the moment.

Mia sat beside him, her eyes still on the map, her voice quiet but steady. "It's longer," she said, almost to herself. "But it might be the only shot we've got."

There was no other choice. If Leo had a chance, they had to move. The thought settled over them like a heavy fog, thick and inescapable.

Mia let out a slow breath, resting her head against the seat.

"Even if we could cross from here, we'd still have to walk. We can't take the truck across; it's staying here."

Her words hung in the air, a quiet finality settling between them. The truck had been their shield, but no more. They would walk the rest.

Ethan turned his head and glanced at Leo in the backseat. The boy was curled up against the worn fabric, his small fingers still gripping Mr. Bubbles. Leo's breathing was shallow, each rise and fall of his chest too slow and too fragile. Mia reached out instinctively, adjusting the blanket over him. Ethan turned away. He couldn't watch him breathe like that, each rise and fall like a countdown. The faint violet glow beneath his skin pulsed weakly, a cruel reminder of the ticking clock they were racing against.

The virus was winning.

Ethan's jaw tightened. "How much further on foot?" he asked, his voice tight.

Mia studied the map again, her fingers ghosting over the lines. "A day, maybe two if the terrain slows us down. If we push hard, we could make it in less."

Ethan blew out a breath, his mind already calculating the supplies they had left and the risks that lay ahead. Every step on foot made them more vulnerable. The Accelerates could be anywhere, and so could bandits. The wilderness itself was no ally; it was an open grave waiting to claim them if they weren't careful.

Still, there was no alternative.

"Then we'll turn around and leave at first light," he said, his voice firm and resolute. "We'll drive as far as we can, then take what we can carry and move quickly."

Mia nodded, mentally cataloging their supplies. Food was low, gas for truck was low, water even lower, and they needed to ration the ammo carefully. Every ounce of weight they carried had to be essential.

She shifted her gaze to Leo, observing as his eyelids fluttered, caught between restless sleep and fevered consciousness. He was getting worse. The sight made her chest tighten with worry.

Turning back to Ethan, she said, "We have to hurry."

He didn't argue; he understood.

Outside, the wind carried a hush of forgotten promises through the ruins, carrying the scent of decay and damp earth. The world around them was still. Waiting.

They sat in silence, the weight of what lay ahead pressing down on them like an unseen force. Tomorrow, they will drive as far as the truck will take them. Tomorrow, the real journey will begin. Beyond the windshield, the mist was rising again.

9.4: The Kindness Gambit

Evening settled in, stretching long, eerie shadows across the cracked asphalt. The truck sat motionless in the middle of the desolate road, its metal frame absorbing the last warmth of the fading sun. Inside the cabin, silence hung thick, heavy with exhaustion and unspoken fears. Each person sat lost in their own thoughts, weighed down by the burdens of the road, the hunger gnawing at their insides, and the uncertainty of what lay ahead.

Earlier, Ethan had insisted they take turns keeping watch. Leo was too weak to defend himself, and they couldn't afford to let their guard down, not here, not now. With the light fading fast, he had suggested that Mia take the first shift while there was still some visibility. He would rest, gather his strength, and take over once night fell. She had agreed without argument, though the weariness in her eyes was evident. Leaning back in the passenger seat, she allowed herself a moment of stillness, her body aching from days on the run.

As the weight of exhaustion settled over her, Mia's eyelids fluttered. The gentle hum of the wind through the broken trees outside became a lullaby, coaxing her into sleep. Just a few minutes, she thought. Just enough to take the edge off. Her breathing slowed, muscles loosened, and darkness tugged at her.

Then,

"Hey, kids?"

The voice, unexpected and unfamiliar, cut through the stillness like a knife.

Mia snapped upright, her pulse hammering in her ears. Ethan's hand flew instinctively to his crowbar, his body rigid with alarm. Leo whimpered, clutching Mr. Bubbles tighter, his small body trembling. The air inside the cabin became suffocating, thick with tension, fear clamping around their chests like a vise.

Ethan's breath came in short, sharp bursts as his gaze darted to the windows. The truck's side mirrors reflected only the remnants of daylight bleeding into the horizon, but shadows danced along the edges of the ruins.

"Did you hear that?" Mia whispered, though she already knew the answer.

Ethan gave a tense nod, his grip tightening on the crowbar. Slowly and carefully, Mia reached for her pistol, her fingers curling around the cold metal as she scanned the landscape outside.

Then, they saw her.

Thirty yards from the truck, a figure stood with her hands raised, silhouetted against the dying light. Lieutenant Aida Espinoza. Even from this distance, they could see the cautious, non-threatening stance she had adopted. In each of her upturned hands dangled plastic bags, their contents shifting slightly.

They hadn't left. They had come back. But why?

Mia's gaze flickered toward the ruins where they had last seen the strangers disappear. Sure enough, Dr. George Jacobson was there, standing near a pile of collapsed concrete, his hands also raised, clutching plastic bags of his own.

Mia's stomach twisted. Gifts? A trap? Another cruel trick in a world that had taken too much.

Ethan swallowed hard, his grip firm on the crowbar.

The question wasn't just who these people were; it was what they wanted, and whether Ethan and Mia were willing to take the risk to find out.

They exchanged tense glances, their breaths shallow, their muscles coiled like tightly wound springs. Frantically, they scanned their surroundings through the grimy windows and side mirrors, their eyes darting across the decayed landscape. Every shifting shadow and every whisper of wind against the ruins sent a jolt of apprehension through them.

Ethan tightened his grip around the crowbar, amidst the rising panic. Mia, her hands steady despite the fear prickling at the edges of her mind, reached for her pistol. The worn grip felt familiar in her grasp, a small but reassuring piece of control in a world that had long since spiraled into chaos.

Lieutenant Aida Espinoza was still standing, her posture rigid but non-threatening, her arms raised in a deliberate gesture of peace. The golden hues of the dying sunlight cast long shadows behind her, stretching ominously across the fractured pavement. In both hands, she held plastic bags, their contents concealed but their presence oddly disarming.

What do they want? Ethan's instinct screamed at him to be cautious. In a world that had long bled kindness dry, no one offered it freely anymore. He scanned the ruins for any sign of an ambush, and his gaze landed on Dr. George Jacobson, standing near the crumbling remnants of the bridge, his stance mirroring Aida's. Both had their hands raised, gripping plastic bags, no weapons, no aggression, just an eerie stillness.

Ethan's jaw clenched. It could be a trap. They might be pretending, lulling them into a false sense of security before striking when their guard was down. He had seen it happen before and had learned the hard way that trust was a luxury few could afford.

Beside him, Mia inhaled sharply, her finger twitching slightly on the trigger as her eyes darted between the two figures. The tension was suffocating, stretching between them like an invisible wire ready to snap. In the back seat, Leo clutched Mr. Bubbles tightly against his chest, trembling as he peered over Ethan's shoulder. His wide, frightened cobalt-blue eyes locked onto the bags in Aida's hands, and his stomach let out a soft, involuntary growl.

Ethan heard it, so did Mia and, evidently, Aida. Her expression softened slightly, but she remained perfectly still. "Don't be afraid, kids," Aida called out, her voice firm but lacking malice. "We thought you might be hungry."

The words hung heavy in the air, unexpected and weighty. Mia's grip on her pistol faltered for just a moment. Ethan swallowed hard, uncertainty gnawing at him. Hunger clawed at their insides, an ever-present ache that never truly went away. But could they afford to believe in goodwill? Trust, in this world, was a dangerous thing. And yet, hunger gnawed at their insides, and Leo's quiet sobs reminded them of the merciless reality they faced.

Raising her hands a little higher, Aida added, "We have enough to share. No tricks. Just food."

Ethan's mind raced. This moment, this impossible moment, teetered on the edge of danger. Yet, for the first time in a long while, a sliver of something unfamiliar crept into his chest: hope.

Despite it, Ethan didn't loosen his grip on the crowbar. His knuckles were white, his fingers wrapped tightly around the metal until they ached. Mia kept her pistol steady, her breath shallow, her pulse hammering against her ribs. The world they had once known was gone, replaced by one where kindness often masked cruelty.

"Don't be afraid, kids," Aida repeated, her voice even and reassuring, but not pleading. She was careful not to push. "We thought you might be hungry. We have enough supplies for ourselves, and we're willing to share some food with you."

The word "food" struck like a spark in the dead silence, igniting something in Leo. From the back seat, his frail voice broke through the thick tension. "Ethan... I'm hungry," he whimpered. His small fingers clutched Mr. Bubbles even tighter, the fabric worn and fraying from constant comfort-seeking. His big cobalt-blue eyes, hollowed by exhaustion, locked onto the plastic bags in Aida's hands.

Ethan's jaw clenched. Damn it. He had been trying to keep Leo from speaking, to keep them from appearing vulnerable. But the kid was starving, and no amount of fear could suppress the basic need for food.

Aida gave a small nod, sensing the shift. She carefully stepped back and placed the bags on the cracked pavement. Every movement was measured and deliberate, intended to avoid triggering panic. "Here, you can have this," she said softly, her voice akin to the soothing tone a parent might use with a frightened child. Then she took another slow step back, raising her hands once more to prove she meant no harm.

Dr. Jacobson, standing near the crumbling bridge, followed her lead. His hands remained raised, trembling slightly as he took careful steps forward. Despite his worn features and unkempt beard, there was something undeniably fatherly about him. His gaze flickered between Ethan and Mia, assessing them not with hostility but with quiet, knowing sympathy. He had seen their kind before, children forced to grow up too fast, hardened by loss, suspicious of everything and everyone.

The bags lay there, filled with something more valuable than gold in a dying world: food. Hope.

Without their rifles, the only weapons Aida and Jacobson carried were hunting knives strapped to their belts, their worn leather grips a stark reminder that even in a world stripped of civility, survival demanded steel. Yet, as they slowly lowered themselves onto the ground with hands still raised in a show of trust, Ethan and Mia remained wary.

This could be a trick.

Survival had taught them one undeniable truth, kindness could be just as dangerous as cruelty. A friendly smile could be the bait before an ambush. A soft voice could reel them into a trap. They had seen it before and barely escaped it.

Silence pressed down in the truck's cabin, thick with unspoken fears. Outside, the world was just as still, the remnants of the collapsed bridge standing like jagged bones against the dimming sky.

Then, that silence shattered.

"Eth, I'm hungry."

Leo's trembling voice cut through the silence like a gunshot. The fragile sound cut through the tension, echoing louder than it should have in the quiet.

Ethan's breath caught.

Leo's face, pale beneath streaks of dirt, twisted with something raw, something desperate. His fingers curled tighter around Mr. Bubbles. His wide, frightened cobalt-blue eyes glistened with unshed tears, and when they finally spilled over, they carved clean tracks down his grime-covered cheeks.

Ethan felt a tightening in his chest. Hunger was a familiar ache, a constant companion since the world had fallen apart. They'd learned to push it down, to ignore it. But Leo was still just a kid, his body too small and fragile to endure it the way they did.

Still, instinct screamed at Ethan to be cautious, to think, to wait. But how much longer could they wait?

Mia, rigid beside him, hadn't moved a muscle. Her fingers tightened around the pistol, her knuckles pale from the force of her grip. Her wounded hand trembled slightly, the pain barely contained behind her hardened expression.

They were both thinking the same thing: What were they supposed to do?

The bags lay untouched on the ground, just a few steps away, filled with promises of food, of relief. The scent of something warm and real wafted through the air, twisting Ethan's stomach painfully and reminding him how empty it had been for days, weeks.

But trusting in what lay within those bags was a risk they couldn't afford. Yet hunger was a force that disregarded caution. And Leo, Leo was starving.

Ethan's fingers twitched nervously around his crowbar. Mia exhaled slowly. Aida and Jacobson remained where they were, watching quietly with unreadable expressions, their patience evident.

The choice weighed heavily in the air.

Take the risk or let hunger win.

Finally, Mia made her move.

This wasn't a decision she made lightly. Every muscle in her body screamed for her to stay put, to keep the doors locked and the gun aimed. But the soft, broken plea from the backseat, "Please, Mia," had already made the choice for her.

Her wounded hand trembled as she reached for the door handle, the sting of torn flesh sending sharp jolts of pain up her arm. She clenched her jaw, grounding herself.

"Mia, don't," Ethan warned, his voice low and tense. He tightened his grip on the crowbar as he reached for her arm, silently pleading with her. But she had already made up her mind.

She didn't look at him or hesitate.

9.5: The Fires We Don't Deserve

Only when Mia was safely inside the truck, the bags of supplies clutched tightly in her lap, did she finally allow herself to exhale. The breath she'd been holding escaped in a long, shaky sigh. The tension in her chest, which had built during the exchange with the strangers, began to dissipate, but only slightly.

"Kids," Jacobson finally spoke, his deep voice carrying an unmistakable gentleness. "Start with the hot soup in the canteen." His words weren't just practical; they were filled with warmth that had been absent for too long. "I'm sure you haven't eaten properly in days. The soup will help your bodies adjust before you eat anything heavy." His tone was authoritative but tempered with genuine concern.

Mia and Ethan exchanged a look, uncertain. Was he speaking as a doctor, or was it something more, a father figure? In a world like this, where survival was a daily struggle, it was hard to tell, especially when kindness had become something dangerous.

Mia didn't say anything; there was nothing to say. She opened the bag and carefully pulled out the canteen. The warmth of it against her hands nearly made her want to cry. It felt almost foreign, comfort, kindness, a reminder of something they hadn't felt in far too long. She handed it to Ethan, who reached for it with practiced ease. His movements held a quiet tenderness, every gesture weighted with meaning.

"Here, Leo," Ethan murmured softly, his voice full of affection as he unscrewed the lid. "Drink it slowly. Don't rush."

Leo's eyes, once dull and listless, sparked with life at the sight of the canteen. His small face, covered in dirt and streaked with tears, softened as he reached for it with trembling hands. His fingers shook as he gripped the canteen, locking eyes with Ethan in silent understanding. Slowly, he brought it to his lips and drank. Each sip was measured and cautious, as if drinking could somehow return him to a version of himself he had nearly forgotten. He followed Ethan's advice, savoring the warmth that spread through his body, from his lips to his chest.

Ethan watched him, his eyes heavy with unspoken thoughts. Meanwhile, Mia, still sitting beside Ethan, turned her attention to the bags of supplies. She began sifting through the contents, her fingers brushing against assorted items, each one a reminder of the life they had once known. It felt almost surreal; these things seemed like treasures from a world long lost. Items she hadn't seen in what felt like days, maybe even weeks.

Chips with their bright packaging still intact, canned beans with faded but legible labels, crackers stacked neatly in their box as if they had just come off a grocery store shelf, and dried sausage tightly wrapped in wax paper. It all seemed so small, yet in this moment, it was everything. These items were luxuries now, feeling like treasures too precious to waste.

She took a deep breath, feeling the hunger gnawing at her gut, but she didn't dare indulge just yet. Watching Leo drink, seeing his small face brighten, made the food feel more important. It wasn't just survival, it was restoration.

As Leo finished the soup, Ethan reached for the bag again. He began pulling out the dried sausage, breaking off small pieces and handing them to Leo. Leo accepted them eagerly, his mouth moving quickly, but he still kept his pace slow, as though afraid to overindulge in the comfort this food offered.

Mia watched them, her own stomach aching with need. Her eyes flicked back to the strangers outside, to the gesture of peace they had offered. Could they trust them? Could anyone trust anyone anymore? She didn't know.

As she turned her focus back to the bags, a thought lingered in her mind: one step at a time. For now, they had food. They had warmth. And for the first time in what felt like forever, maybe, just maybe, they could stop merely surviving long enough to truly live.

She ran her fingers over the packaging repeatedly, her touch almost reverent, as if she couldn't quite believe what she was holding. These were items that, not long ago, were taken for granted, ordinary goods you'd find on a gas station shelf or in a corner store. Snacks, canned goods, dried meats, things people would grab absentmindedly without a second thought. Yet now, they were relics from another lifetime, remnants of a world that had collapsed, leaving behind only fragments of the normal life they once knew. For Mia, the act of touching the wrappers and holding these items felt like a connection to a past that seemed more distant with every passing day.

Aida and Jacobson remained in the same spot, their postures unchanged, but there was a subtle difference now. Their hands, once held high in a show of trust, rested quietly on their laps. The tension between them and the children had eased, even if only a little. The smiles that tugged at Aida's lips were fragile but genuine, a reflection of something long buried: compassion. Jacobson's eyes, too, shone with something Mia couldn't quite identify, was it hope, or perhaps relief? Whatever it was, it glimmered in the faint light now bathing the scene. Both of them watched intently, their gazes softening as they observed the children eating. There was something undeniably human about the moment, something that transcended the harshness of survival, a simple joy in witnessing others sustain themselves.

Leo, still too thin and frail, was the top priority. Mia and Ethan fed him with care, ensuring he regained some strength. His hands trembled as he reached for the food, but the hunger in his eyes was unmistakable, a hunger that had gnawed at him for days. Ethan kept a steady hand on the canteen, guiding it to Leo's lips, while Mia passed him the food, her movements slow, deliberate, and almost maternal. Each bite Leo took seemed to rekindle a spark of life in his tired eyes, a glimmer of something resembling comfort. As he finished, a quiet sigh of relief escaped Mia, and even Ethan's normally steely expression softened for a moment.

Once they were certain Leo was full and content for the first time in days, Ethan and Mia finally allowed themselves to eat. There was hesitation at first, a reluctance to take more than necessary, as if part of them feared the luxury of it, like it was too much to ask for or too much to deserve. But hunger was insistent. It clawed at them both, relentless, until they finally surrendered, pulling apart the crackers, tearing open the sausages, and savoring the long-lost flavors of food that wasn't just sustenance but something more, a reminder of normality, of simpler times. They ate quickly but without the usual desperation, taking small moments to look at each other and share a quiet, almost unspoken acknowledgment of the strange peace they had found, if only for a fleeting moment.

Once everyone had eaten, a sense of relief hung in the air like a delicate thread, fragile yet comforting. However, Mia's practical side quickly reasserted itself. She wiped her mouth and glanced at the remaining supplies. "We should save some of this for the road ahead," she suggested, her voice steady but edged with concern. She knew that whatever peace they had found here could be short-lived. The road would be long, and they couldn't afford to become complacent. There was a future to prepare for, and they couldn't waste any of the precious food they had managed to gather.

Her calm words resonated with Ethan. He nodded in agreement, the simple motion filled with an unspoken understanding of their precarious situation. He reached down and grabbed the backpack from the truck's floor, the worn fabric scraping against his fingers as he pulled it up. His hands moved quickly, almost instinctively, as he began to pack away the remaining food. Mia joined him, her fingers working deftly as they tucked away the chips, canned beans, crackers, and dried sausage, everything they had managed to gather. They worked with a sense of purpose, each item a small treasure in a world where food had become a rare commodity. The supplies felt fragile, their value immeasurable. Every ounce of food held the power to mean the difference between life and death on the road ahead.

For the first time in what seemed like ages, Leo looked content. His small hands still clutched the canteen, his fingers barely able to grasp it as he held it close, unwilling to let go of the comfort it offered. His belly, full for the first time in days, felt the gnawing hunger that had plagued him finally soothed. His face softened with a fleeting expression of peace, an emotion so scarce in their world. A faint smile tugged at his lips, and for a breath, the weight of survival eased. But even as joy blossomed in his eyes, the awareness lingered in the air, unspoken but undeniable: no one knew how long this comfort would last. The harsh reality of their world, where each day was a struggle for existence, was always just beneath the surface, waiting to reassert itself.

After the meal, Mia and Ethan felt an unexpected wave of fatigue wash over them, the warmth of the food settling in their bodies like a long-awaited embrace. For the first time in what felt like ages, their limbs didn't feel heavy. Leo, his face flushed with contentment, finished the soup quickly, his hunger finally satisfied. He handed the canteen to Mia with a small, shy smile, his hands still trembling slightly from the relief of having a full stomach. Ethan helped Mia replace the cap, the simple task a comforting reminder of the small, everyday rituals that still remained in this world.

"We should return this and thank them," Mia said quietly, her voice filled with gratitude as she looked at the canteen in her hand. Ethan nodded in agreement, his gaze thoughtful yet appreciative. The kindness of the strangers had touched something deep within him, a reminder that even amid their struggle, there was still humanity left in the world.

Mia rolled down the truck's window, her movements slow but deliberate. The frigid air felt refreshing against her skin as she leaned out and called out, her voice loud but full of sincerity. "Thank you so much!" she yelled, her heart swelling with genuine appreciation.

"Thank you very much," Ethan added, his tone warm. "This was a treat for us, especially for Leo. You've really helped us more than you know."

From the back seat, Leo's small voice piped up, filled with the unbridled sincerity of a child. "Thank you, Mrs. Soldier, and Mr. Doctor!" he called, his words ringing with joy. A smile tugged at the corners of his lips as he finished, and for a moment, the harsh reality of their situation seemed to fade away, replaced by the innocence of a simple, heartfelt thank you.

Then, from a distance, Aida's trembling voice, full of emotion, cut through the air. "You are more than welcome." Dr.

Jacobson's face broke into a wide smile as he looked toward the truck. Aida's voice softened further as she continued, "You're welcome to join us at our campfire. We have enough for all of us to last several days." Her words carried a warmth that eased the tension in the air, offering something rare and precious, hospitality. It was a simple offer, yet in the children's world, it meant more than Aida could know. The kindness she extended was like a balm to the rawness of their situation, a reminder that even in the harshest times, moments of compassion still had the power to heal.

She smiled, a soft and reassuring expression that made her appear less like a threat and more like someone who understood the delicate balance of survival. "We also have clean water," she added, her voice growing gentler. "You can wash up. It's been a long time, hasn't it?"

Dr. Jacobson, who had been quietly observing the exchange, nodded in agreement. His expression was one of compassion, his face weathered but kind. "And if either of you is injured, I can help," he added, his words carrying a sincerity that made Mia and Ethan pause. "You don't need to be afraid. We may be adults with big guns, but we've lost just as much as you have."

His voice, deep and steady, carried the weight of shared experience. The subtle truth behind his words struck a chord with Mia. She knew the pain of loss too well, the way it gnawed at your soul and shaped every decision and interaction. Jacobson wasn't just offering medical aid; he was offering something more: understanding and empathy. It was a gift, though they had no idea if they could accept it. The world they had been thrust into had taught them that kindness could be as dangerous as cruelty, but there was something in the way both Aida and Jacobson spoke that felt different, sincere, almost fatherly, as though they, too, understood the long road of hardship.

The invitation to join them by their campfire hung in the air, tantalizing in its simplicity. It was a choice that could lead them to safety or bring new risks. Yet, in that moment, it felt like a lifeline, offering warmth, nourishment, and something akin to a fleeting sense of normalcy.

The children in the truck remained silent. They neither accepted nor rejected the invitation from the peculiar yet kind-hearted strangers. The warmth of the meal still lingered in their stomachs, but their minds were a whirlwind of conflicting thoughts.

A thousand questions, both terrifying and tempting, raced through Ethan's and Mia's minds. What if they were murderers? If they were, they had plenty of chances to kill them earlier without feeding them first. What if this was a trap? But why go through the trouble of offering food and supplies just to lure them in? What if they were cannibals? That thought was the most chilling of all, one neither of them wanted to dwell on. But then again, cannibalism wasn't something that happened overnight after the world fell apart; it was a last resort, the ultimate step in losing or preserving one's humanity. Aida and Jacobson didn't seem like people who had taken that step. And yet, trust was a luxury they could not afford.

Mia and Ethan locked eyes, silently communicating their thoughts, asking, and answering the same unspoken questions. Their expressions shifted with uncertainty, fear, logic, doubt, and hope all battling within them. Every possibility, every risk, every small glimmer of safety fought for dominance in their minds.

Chapter 10: Bridge of Hope

10.1: For Tonight, You Are Safe

The children moved cautiously, their steps slow and deliberate, with fear lingering in every movement. Despite the warmth of the invitation, their instincts screamed at them to remain wary. The world had changed, and trust had become a currency far too costly to spend lightly.

Aida and Jacobson stood waiting, their postures open and their expressions gentle and welcoming. Neither of them reached for weapons nor made any sudden movements; instead, they simply stood there, offering something rare, patience.

As they closed the distance, Aida knelt to meet Leo at eye level. Her eyes, filled with longing and kindness, softened as her hand extended, trembling a hand, brushing his unruly curls with her calloused soldier's fingers. A tender smile graced her face, one that spoke of long-cherished memories and better days.

"And who are you?" she asked, her voice gentle, almost motherly.

Leo hesitated, clutching Mr. Bubbles closer to his chest, his small fingers digging into the worn fabric of his stuffed companion. He glanced at Ethan and Mia, as if seeking silent approval.

"Leo," he finally murmured, his voice barely above a whisper.

Aida nodded encouragingly.

"She's Mia," Leo continued, gaining a bit more confidence. He turned slightly toward his older brother. "And he's Ethan, my big brother." The last words carried a note of pride, a child's unwavering trust in his protector.

Aida's smile widened. With an ease that seemed second nature, she lifted Leo into her arms. The boy tensed at first, but the warmth of her embrace, so reminiscent of something he had almost forgotten, melted his resistance. Clinging to Mr. Bubbles, he allowed himself to rest against her shoulder as they began to walk.

Together, they moved toward the ruins of the bridge. The landscape around them was grim, a chilling reminder of the brutality they now faced. The river, once a lifeline, was tainted with death. Bodies, some of the monstrous Accelerates, others unfortunate people, lay strewn along the banks and in the water. The air reeked of decay and damp earth, yet amidst the carnage, something stood apart.

Fresh graves.

Five of them, each carefully covered with dirt, were marked only by the solemn presence of military helmets resting atop them. The sight made Ethan and Mia pause, their gazes heavy with understanding.

"This is Aida's squad," Jacobson explained, his voice low and respectful. "They fought to the end, but GeneCorp's security forces... and their drones... took them down."

A heavy silence settled over them. Aida's grip on Leo tightened just slightly, her jaw clenching as she looked toward the graves of her fallen comrades. For a brief moment, her welcoming warmth flickered, replaced by the weight of grief. Yet she didn't let it consume her. Inhaling deeply, she steadied herself before leading them forward.

The ruins of the bridge concealed something, a hidden entrance tucked away from prying eyes. Beneath the crumbled structure was an old maintenance room, once a place for repairs but now repurposed into a shelter. Its metal door remained miraculously intact, untouched by destruction.

Aida and Jacobson led the group through the gate into a world that, for now, promised safety. Inside, the space was unexpectedly cozy, a sharp contrast to the desolation outside.

It bore the remnants of a time when life had a sense of order, a maintenance bunker once used by bridge workers before the world crumbled. Now it served as sanctuary, pieced together from the wreckage of the past.

Iron chairs were scattered around a sturdy metal table, their surfaces scratched and worn with age. Against the far wall sat a battered old sofa, its stuffing spilling out from the seams, flanked by two armchairs that had seen better days. In one corner, a set of bunk beds held mismatched but clean sheets, a luxury in this world. Crates and metal chests were stacked along the walls; some held canned food, water bottles, and medical supplies, while others contained tools, spare clothes, and whatever else Aida and Jacobson had managed to scavenge.

A small but well-stocked armory was tucked away near the back, a grim necessity in a world where survival depended on firepower. Beyond it, a narrow hallway branched off, leading to additional storage rooms, a bathroom, and a shower, a rare luxury, remnants of a life that once was. At the very end, a small generator hummed softly, its steady rhythm a quiet testament to the fight against the darkness.

Dr. Jacobson turned to Leo, who was still cradled in Aida's arms. His voice was gentle yet reassuring. "Let me take a look at you," he said, crouching slightly to meet the boy's gaze. "Once I've examined you, I'll check on Mia and Ethan as well. After that, you can all clean up and get some rest."

Mia shifted uneasily, her instincts screaming at her to keep moving. "We have to leave. Can you hurry, please?"

Jacobson sighed, a mix of patience and concern softening his face. "My dear girl, it's getting late. With nightfall, dangers begin to rise. Let us take care of you tonight. You can leave in the morning if that's still your choice. But if you decide to stay, you're welcome here." Before he could continue, Aida interjected, her voice thick with emotion. "After everything we've endured, everything we've lost, having you here would give us a reason to keep going, a purpose to hold on to."

Her hands tightened around Leo, her eyes shimmering with unshed tears. But after a moment, she took a steady breath and gently placed Leo onto the iron table as if it were a hospital bed.

Jacobson set to work, his movements precise and practiced. He ran his hands gently over Leo's arms and legs, checking for injuries. He examined the boy's feet, listened to his heartbeat, and took his temperature. Throughout it all, he maintained a reassuring smile, offering comfort through the clinical routine.

"So, you're the famous Leo that everyone in this new world is after," he mused, his voice light and almost amused.

The air in the room shifted in an instant.

Ethan and Mia stiffened. In a heartbeat, Mia's hand went to her pistol despite her injured arm, while Ethan tightened his grip on his crowbar, his knuckles turning white. Their bodies tensed, ready to fight and protect.

Jacobson immediately noticed the change in their demeanor. The easy warmth on his face faded. "Oh, dear," he muttered, exhaling slowly as if realizing his mistake. "I see you didn't know."

Mia's eyes burned into him. "What do you mean, 'famous Leo'?" Ethan's voice was low and menacing.

Jacobson hesitated, glancing between them as he read their reactions carefully. He took a breath, steadying himself before speaking again.

"He's all over the radio waves. GeneCorp, the Accelerates, bounty hunters, desperate survivors, everyone is looking for the poor boy."

Ethan's jaw clenched. Mia's finger twitched near the trigger.

Jacobson held up his hands, signaling that he meant no harm. "I knew about him when I worked for GeneCorp. I was one of their scientists before I escaped." His voice carried the weight of an old burden, of truths too heavy to bear alone.

Silence filled the room, thick and oppressive.

Leo sat on the table, gripping Mr. Bubbles tightly. His small body was still and watchful; he didn't fully understand but knew enough to be afraid.

His eyes flicked to Ethan, confusion clouding his face. "Why am I famous?" he whispered, not fully understanding but feeling the fear it caused.

Aida looked at Jacobson, her expression grave. "Tell them," she urged softly.

Jacobson nodded. "I will. But first, let me finish checking Leo. Whatever I tell you next, I want you all to hear it with full bellies, clean faces, and the knowledge that you are safe, at least for tonight."

Mia and Ethan exchanged glances. Their wariness didn't fade, but something in Jacobson's voice gave them pause.

For now, they would listen. But trust? That was still far from certain.

Dr. Jacobson examined each of them with meticulous care, his trained hands moving with precision as he assessed their wounds and overall condition. He cleaned and dressed Mia's and Ethan's injuries with steady, practiced movements, ensuring that infection wouldn't take hold. The antiseptic sting was a small price for safety. Afterward, he handed each of them antibiotics and painkillers, making sure they took the proper doses.

Meanwhile, Aida turned her attention to Leo, carrying him with the tenderness of a mother as she led him to a small tub filled with warm, soapy water. Steam curled up, warming the dimly lit room with fleeting comfort. She gently lowered him into the bath, her hands careful and soothing as she scrubbed away the layers of dirt and grime that had settled on his delicate skin. Leo let out a soft sigh, sinking into the warmth, his small hands splashing the water as bubbles danced around him.

For a moment, he felt like a child again, innocent, happy, and free. Yet the harsh reality of his condition lay just beneath the surface. The virus inside him, which accelerated his growth, had taken more than just his childhood; it had stolen his future, pushing him forward at an unnatural pace. Still, in this moment, with Aida's gentle hands washing his hair and the warmth of the bath surrounding him, he allowed himself to simply enjoy the experience.

After the bath, Aida sifted through their collection of salvaged clothing, carefully selecting fresh outfits for each child. For Leo, she chose clothes that were two sizes too big: a pair of beige corduroy pants, a soft t-shirt, and a cozy hoodie. As she dressed him, she folded the sleeves of the hoodie and the cuffs of the pants, securing them with neat stitches using a needle and thread.

"If you grow too fast," she explained with a warm smile, "you can just tear the seams, and your clothes will grow with you."

Leo giggled at the thought, his bright eyes sparkling with amusement. "Like magic clothes?" he asked, clutching Mr. Bubbles to his chest.

"Exactly," Aida replied with a soft chuckle, brushing the damp curls from his forehead.

Once Leo was dressed, he admired his new boots, wiggling his toes inside them and delighting in their warmth and sturdiness. They weren't just clothes, they were a promise, a hope that he would continue to grow and have a chance of surviving.

Ethan and Mia emerged from the shower looking almost unrecognizable after taking turns to wash up. The dirt, blood, and exhaustion that had clung like second skin finally washed away, revealing their youthful yet battle-hardened faces. Their complexions, once dulled by grime and fatigue, now appeared brighter, and their features sharper, as if cleansing themselves had lifted a weight from their souls.

Dressed in fresh military cargo pants, sturdy combat boots polished to a near shine, and holsters secured firmly at their sides, they radiated newfound confidence. The rough fabric of their clothes felt strange against clean skin, a stark contrast to the ragged, bloodstained garments they had left behind. Ethan squared his shoulders slightly, his posture stronger and more assured. Mia ran a hand through her damp hair, adjusting the strap of her holster with quiet determination.

For the first time in what felt like an eternity, they were not just surviving, they were standing tall and ready. The world outside remained brutal and unforgiving, but for this moment, they had reclaimed a part of themselves. Even if it wouldn't last, it was enough to remind them of who they truly were.

10.2: What Was Done

Aida moved with practiced ease, setting out plates and utensils with a care that suggested she had done these many times before. She placed Leo's plate closest to hers and, with a gentle smile, positioned a small ammunition box on the chair beside her. To make it more comfortable, she folded a blanket over it to create Leo's seat.

Dr. Jacobson turned out to be not only a skilled doctor but also an excellent cook. Despite the limitations of their rations, he managed to create a meal that was nothing short of remarkable. Using sparse ingredients, concentrated food packs, canned goods, and preserved supplies, he assembled a feast that felt almost indulgent. The air filled with the comforting aroma of hot chicken soup, creamy mashed potatoes, and fluffy scrambled eggs. The scent of spaghetti in marinara mingled with warm, canned roast beef. Bowls of canned chili, tender peas, crisp black olives, and tangy pickles were placed around the table, transforming the dull, metallic setting into something resembling home.

The group settled around the table, finding a quiet comfort in each other's presence. Aida, as she always did before a meal, paused for a moment. She closed her eyes, inhaling deeply, and then gently touched the small silver cross hanging from her neck, resting just beside her worn dog tags. When she opened her eyes, she looked around at the weary but grateful faces before her and spoke in a soft yet unwavering voice.

"Let us enjoy each other's presence and what we have."

There was no need for further words. In a world that had taken so much and where every day there was a battle for survival, moments like this, sharing a meal and finding a brief respite from the chaos, were rare and precious. The children, who had been running on little more than fear and adrenaline, allowed themselves to indulge in the warmth of the food before them.

Leo, seated beside Aida on his makeshift chair, took small, careful bites, his tiny fingers wrapped around his spoon. His big cobalt-blue eyes glowed with something close to wonder, each taste a new discovery. He savored each spoonful of soup and each soft bite of eggs, as if afraid they might disappear if he ate too quickly. Every now and then, he let out a small, contented sigh, his body visibly relaxing in a way that was heartbreaking to witness. How long had it been since he had last felt safe enough to simply enjoy a meal?

Ethan and Mia ate steadily and efficiently, their training and experience evident in the way they consumed their food. However, there was a difference tonight. The tension that usually hung over their shoulders like a shadow seemed to ease, even if only slightly. The exhaustion etched into their faces softened. They were still survivors, still wary, but for the first time in what felt like an eternity, they allowed themselves to feel something approaching normal.

Yet, even as they ate, another hunger remained unfulfilled, the hunger for answers.

Once their stomachs were full, Ethan and Mia's gazes shifted to Jacobson. Silent but expectant, their expressions made it clear they had not forgotten his words from earlier. He had promised them answers, answers about Leo, about why people were after him.

Jacobson, sensing their eyes on him, set his fork down, exhaling as he wiped his hands with a cloth. His expression darkened under the weight of the past. He leaned back slightly, glancing toward Leo and then back at Ethan and Mia.

Finally, after a long pause, he spoke.

"Yes, I knew about Leo when I worked for GeneCorp. Actually, not at the time, but later, after they first treated him. I read about it in the paper. Living off the grid, the newspaper was my only way to keep up with events," he admitted, his voice quiet but firm. "I was one of their scientists... before I escaped. Before I defected." Dr. Jacobson took a slow sip of his tea, the warmth offering fleeting comfort against the memories threatening to surface. He exhaled heavily, his fingers tightening around the ceramic cup as if anchoring himself to the present.

"In the beginning," he started, his voice heavy with years of regret, "GeneCorp had good intentions. They were developing a revolutionary cancer treatment, one that could have saved millions of lives." He paused, his eyes shadowed by distant sorrow. "The genius behind it all was Dr. Anya Voss. She wasn't just brilliant, she was the only scientist capable of making the breakthrough they needed. Her discovery was a miracle. But miracles, in the wrong hands, become nightmares."

Reaching into the chest pocket of his shirt, he pulled out a worn wooden pipe. Though there hadn't been tobacco for a long time, he placed it between his lips, inhaling as if savoring the ghost of a habit long abandoned. After a moment, he exhaled slowly and continued, his voice thick with bitterness.

"One thing led to another. The executives and board members at GeneCorp, greedy, power-hungry opportunists, realized that Anya's research could be modified and repurposed. They saw something far more profitable than a cancer cure. They shifted their focus from saving lives to pursuing eternal youth."

He scoffed, shaking his head. "And from there, it only got worse. If they could manipulate cell regeneration, why not enhance fertility? Why not design children in the womb, manufactured to perfection, created to live longer, stronger, more youthful, and ultimately more compliant? They pushed further and further, blind to the consequences. And that... that led us here."

Jacobson fell silent for a moment, his gaze distant, as if watching the past unfold before him. Then, quieter, more somber, he spoke again. "Leo was the first."

Mia and Ethan stiffened, the weight of those words crashing over them. Jacobson nodded, confirming their unspoken fears. "He was the first patient to receive Dr. Voss's original treatment. The drug was meant to save him. And it did... in a way. It worked flawlessly on animals, 99.9% success rate. But the real question, one we never had the chance to answer, was whether it would work on humans without catastrophic side effects. The science was incomplete. We didn't know the risks. And then..." He trailed off, taking another deep, empty inhale from his pipe.

"Before Leo's treatment could be completed, before we could know for sure, the infertility hormone therapy backfired.

It mutated and became a virus." His expression darkened. "Seventy-two hours. That's all it took. In three days, the world collapsed."

A heavy silence settled over the room. Leo, blissfully unaware of the conversation, focused on his half-empty plate, but Ethan and Mia sat rigid, their hands clenched into fists. Jacobson met their eyes, his own filled with grim honesty. "GeneCorp was slipping further and further away from government oversight. They had the money and the power. They corrupted everything, the Senate, Congress, the executive cabinet, the courts. Every institution meant to protect people, they poisoned." He exhaled sharply, shaking his head.

"But it wasn't until a few years ago, when I was sent to Redwood Valley Bunker to work on the final stages of the infertility drug, that I again met Dr. Anya Voss."

Hearing "Redwood Valley" and "bunker" in the same sentence sent a jolt of tension through Ethan and Mia. Their eyes locked in an instant, exchanging an unspoken understanding. Redwood Valley carried weight, too much weight. It wasn't just a place; it was the past. It held answers they might not be ready to face.

If Jacobson noticed their reaction, he gave no sign. He remained lost in his recollections, his voice carrying the burden of a past steeped in regret.

Jacobson glanced at Aida, who had remained silent the entire time. Her face was unreadable, but her fingers trembled slightly as they gripped her dog tags.

Turning back to the children, his voice softened. "That was when I utterly understood what GeneCorp had done. And that was when I knew... I had to escape."

He shook his head, his expression filled with a mix of anger and sorrow. "Anya Voss was kept there like a hostage," he said. "She wasn't working anymore, not by choice. The GeneCorp board refused to let her leave, refused to allow her to continue any research that didn't serve their agenda. She was their property, locked away like a bird in a cage."

He ran a weary hand through his graying hair. "Other scientists continued the work, pushing forward with infertility and youth hormone treatments, but Anya knew. She understood the disaster that was coming, and she tried to stop it. She argued and fought, but GeneCorp didn't care. Profits mattered more than consequences."

Ethan tightened his grip on the table, his knuckles turning white. Mia swallowed hard, forcing down the storm of emotions rising inside her.

Jacobson let out a slow, exhausted sigh. "I realized it too," he admitted. "Fortunately, I saw it early enough to save myself. Unfortunately, I recognized it far too late to save everyone else."

For a moment, he simply stared at his empty plate, as if searching for answers he would never find. "The day president Dion was elected, I just... walked away," he finally said, his voice barely above a whisper. "I left and never went back. No warning, no goodbyes. I knew if I stayed, I'd either become complicit... or I'd die."

Mia exhaled slowly, her pulse quickening.

Jacobson's fingers fidgeted with the edge of his pipe, a nervous habit. "GeneCorp retaliated, of course. They didn't take kindly to defectors. They went after my elderly mother, my friends, even my ex-wife. I don't know what happened to them. I went dark after that, kept off their radar as best I could." His voice turned bitter. "But even in hiding, I tried. I wrote letters, made calls, reached out to people in power: scientists, senators, journalists. I begged them to listen, to act before it was too late."

He let out a sharp, humorless laugh. "But no one listened. No one ever listens until it's already too late."

10.3: The Silence of Belonging

A thick silence filled the room, settling over them like an oppressive fog.

Leo, curled up in one of the lower bunker beds, was lost in peaceful slumber, blissfully unaware of the world's horrors. But Ethan and Mia? They were wide awake. Because for them, the nightmare wasn't over; it was just beginning.

"At the last minute, the government sent me and my squad to find Dr. Jacobson," Aida broke the silence, her voice heavy with memory. "This room... this bunker... was one of his hideouts. But we were too late."

The dim light flickered, casting shadows over her weary face. She hesitated for a moment, gathering her thoughts before continuing. "When we arrived, GeneCorp's forces were already here, with security drones and armed patrols. It was as if they had been tracking us the entire time. And now, looking back, I realize... they had been." She took a slow, steadying breath. "Someone... someone from higher up was feeding them our troop movements. Someone betrayed us."

Her voice trembled, but she pressed on. "My squad never had a chance. We were ambushed from behind. At first, they pretended to assist us, to fight alongside us. But the moment we turned our backs, they opened fire. The bullets came fast, precise... merciless." She swallowed hard, the weight of that day pressing on her chest like a boulder. "My soldiers fought until the very end."

The room fell silent. Even the flames seemed to dim. The only sound was the soft, rhythmic breathing of Leo, still sleeping in the corner, blissfully unaware of the ghosts lingering in the air.

Jacobson was the first to break the silence. "So, Ethan, Mia... where are you heading in the morning?" His voice was steady and calm, as if trying to ground them in the present. "Tell us, so we can plan supplies for you." Then, after a brief pause, he added, "But the offer still stands, you can stay with us."

Ethan and Mia exchanged guarded glances. There was trust growing in this room, but still, trust was a dangerous thing. It could be used against you.

Jacobson had mentioned Redwood Valley, the very place they were headed. What if, the moment they revealed their destination, things changed? What if Jacobson and Aida had their own reasons for wanting to go there, or worse, for wanting to keep them from going?

The air between them felt charged, silent words passing through locked eyes. Ethan hesitated. Naming their destination meant exposing their entire plan. One word, and this fragile alliance could turn.

Finally, Mia took the lead.

"We need to be in Redwood Valley Bunker," she said, her voice firm but careful as she watched their reactions closely. She expected shock. She expected resistance. But neither Jacobson nor Aida flinched.

Ethan quickly followed up, his gaze unwavering. "For Leo."

Jacobson's eyes flickered toward the sleeping child, something deep and unreadable crossing his face.

Ethan sighed, running a hand through his clean hair before continuing. "Clara, Mia's sister, gave us the map. She said there are people in Redwood Valley who can help Leo."

"We didn't know the bridge was collapsed," Mia added, shaking her head. "We lost days trying to find a way across. Now, we have to backtrack half a day and take the rural roads on foot to the bunker." She gestured to their worn-out gear. "These clothes and the boots you gave us... they'll help us make the journey."

Jacobson and Aida were still staring at them, but their expressions were not filled with shock or concern. Instead, there was something warmer. They looked at Ethan and Mia with something like love. It was the kind of gaze one gives to family. To someone they lost, only to find again in the most unexpected way.

For a moment, there were no words, only silence. But not the kind born of grief or fear. This one was different: the silence of understanding.

Aida's eyes shimmered, not with tears but with something deeper, an aching, unspoken longing. Jacobson's shoulders, which had carried so much weight for so long, seemed to relax just a fraction.

The fire crackled, casting golden light through the room. For a brief, fragile moment, the world outside didn't exist. The ruins, the war, the betrayals, all of it faded into the background. They were just people. People who had lost too much. People who had found something unexpected in each other.

Jacobson finally exhaled, his lips pressing into a firm line before he spoke. "Redwood Valley," he murmured, as if testing the weight of the words on his tongue. Then he nodded. "We'll help you prepare."

Mia's eyes widened slightly, as if she hadn't quite expected this easy acceptance. "You're not... surprised?" she asked cautiously.

Jacobson let out a small, dry chuckle. "Surprised? No." His eyes darkened slightly. "Redwood Valley has always been at the center of this mess. It makes sense that your journey would lead you there."

Aida leaned forward slightly, her expression soft but serious. "We'll get you what you need, food, water, and extra ammo if we can spare it." Then, after a pause, she added, "But if you change your mind, if the road proves too dangerous... you can come back here. You have a place with us."

For the first time in a long time, Ethan and Mia felt something foreign creeping into their hearts, hope. It was dangerous to hope, but sometimes, in a broken world, it was the only thing left.

Mia glanced at Ethan, who nodded slightly. It wasn't much, but it was enough.

As they sat together in the warmth of the maintains room, a new kind of silence settled over them. Not the silence of grief. Not the silence of caution. But the silence of something almost like belonging.

And for now, that was enough.

10.4: *What He Took With Him*

For the first time in weeks, the children slept in real beds, wrapped in clean, fresh pajamas. As soon as their heads touched the pillows, exhaustion overtook them. There was no tossing or restless shifting, just deep, dreamless sleep, as if their small bodies finally allowed themselves to believe they were safe, even if only for the night.

Jacobson and Aida remained awake, seated in worn-out armchairs that had long since lost their stuffing. Time had torn and frayed the fabric. The dim glow of the lantern cast soft shadows around them, the flickering light making the maintenance room feel almost warm, a fragile illusion of normalcy in a world that had long forgotten what normal was.

Jacobson sat hunched over his old notebook, the pages thick with age, their edges curled from years of use. It was more than just a notebook; it was a sketchbook, a time capsule of the people he had met and the lives he had lost. In the flickering light, he carefully sketched Leo's peaceful sleeping face, the boy's small frame curled around his tattered stuffed bear. Leo looked so young and fragile, yet in sleep, he carried none of the burdens the waking world had placed upon him.

Jacobson had already drawn Ethan and Mia, capturing the sharpness in Ethan's wary gaze and the quiet determination in Mia's eyes. His book was filled with faces, his mother, old friends, Aida, and the soldiers of Aida's lost squad. Some he had drawn from memory, others from fleeting moments, but all remained vivid in his mind. His photographic memory had never faded; it was as sharp now as it had been when he was a teenager.

When Jacobson defected from GeneCorp's research program, he didn't leave empty-handed. He took with him all his research data, everything he had worked on and discovered. That was why GeneCorp was hunting him so relentlessly. He wasn't just another scientist; he was one of the leading virologists in the world. His expertise extended far beyond medicine; he was a brilliant researcher, a pioneer in biotechnology, and a man whose knowledge could either save humanity or doom it, depending on who wielded it.

But Jacobson was more than a virologist. He was an adventurer, a survivalist, and a relentless seeker of knowledge. By his mid-thirties, Jacobson was a multilingual biotechnologist and survivalist who had studied ecosystems across every continent, including the poles. His insatiable curiosity led him to move fluidly through cultures and landscapes alike.

Yet, despite his accomplishments, Jacobson had always been drawn to something far older and more powerful than science, nature itself. He spent most of his free time in the wilderness, living off the land, observing ecosystems, and trying to understand the fundamental laws that governed life. Even when traveling through foreign cities, he would carve out time to escape into nature, wandering through dense forests, scaling mountains, or trekking across deserts with nothing but his backpack, camera, magnifying glass, and sketchbook. He documented everything with a naturalist's rigor and a sketchbook's intimacy. In many ways, he was a Renaissance man trapped in the chaos of the end of the twenty-first century.

After defecting from GeneCorp, Jacobson vanished. He erased himself from the digital world, going completely off the grid. He never held onto any electronic device for more than ten minutes, just long enough to gather information before disappearing into the shadows once more. He mastered the art of staying hidden, slipping through society's cracks like a ghost.

In the cities, he sought refuge among the homeless, treating their wounds and providing them with medicine and care. In return, they helped him stay hidden, passing messages, offering shelter, and warning him of patrols and GeneCorp agents lurking nearby. They became his eyes and ears, his silent protectors in a world that had turned against him.

To stay ahead of his pursuers, Jacobson set up safe houses in abandoned buildings, underground tunnels, and forgotten maintenance rooms, places like the one he, Aida, and the children now occupied. Moving between these hideouts, he avoided main roads, traveling through backcountry trails and hitchhiking when necessary, always blending in and staying one step ahead.

Despite all he had seen and endured, Jacobson still cared, deeply, for people, for life, and for the future of the world. But no one had listened. The warnings he had given, the pleas he had made, had all gone ignored. The government had realized the truth too late.

As he had told Ethan and Mia, he had been lucky enough to save himself. Tragically, he had been unable to save everyone else.

When the virus became airborne, it spread like wildfire, infecting every newborn and every child up to the age of ten. It was merciless, altering their biology at an accelerated rate and forcing their bodies to grow rapidly while rewiring their minds. These children, once innocent, full of laughter and promise, became something else entirely. Their aggression surged uncontrollably, and their hunger transformed into a savage, insatiable need. They turned...

10.5: Graves in the Ash

Aida was a combat veteran, shaped by years of service. After completing her active duty, she was serving in the reserve when the virus outbreak plunged the world into chaos. Her husband, a retired captain and fellow combat veteran, had once fought on distant battlefields but returned home wounded, having lost his leg above the knee in one of the wars overseas. Despite his injuries, he built a new life as a high school math teacher in their small town, where they were raising their two young daughters, ages three and five.

When the world fell apart, Aida found herself cut off from her family. There were no messages, no news, only silence. Trapped beneath the collapsed bridge in the maintenance room with Jacobson, she clung to the desperate hope that they were still alive. Jacobson, however, carried a terrible secret, one he could not bring himself to share with her. The virus targeted children under the age of ten, accelerating their growth, mutating their bodies, and warping their minds into something monstrous. He knew that revealing the truth could crush her spirit, so he chose to withhold it, promising instead that once things settled, he would help her find her family. He wanted to give her hope, even if it was built on fragile ground.

Aida had already lost so much. Her squad, her brothers, and sisters in arms, had died trying to protect Jacobson, believing that his knowledge might hold the key to their salvation. They trusted GeneCorp security, who posed as allies but struck the moment backs were turned. It was an ambush. The betrayal was swift and brutal. However, Aida's squad did not go down without a fight. Although they were outnumbered and outgunned, they fought with everything they had, taking down the GeneCorp forces along with them. By the time the battle ended, the battlefield was littered with bodies, both friends and foes. Only the gravely wounded Aida and Jacobson survived.

The grief, combined with the intense pain from her injuries, was unbearable, a heavy weight pressing down on her chest. Jacobson cared for her with unwavering dedication. He stitched and dressed her wounds, fed her, and spent sleepless nights at her bedside in the maintenance room to ensure she survived the worst of it. Days passed, and when Aida could finally stand and walk without collapsing, she made her decision. Despite the pain and Jacobson's quiet protests, she refused to abandon her fallen comrades to decay in the open.

With unwavering determination, she set to work, digging their graves with her bare hands, one by one, honoring them in the only way she knew how. Jacobson, deeply moved beyond words, silently picked up another shovel and joined her. They worked side by side, their grief expressed in the rhythmic motion of digging, and their silence spoke volumes about the pain they shared.

In that moment of loss and sacrifice, during the quiet yet profound act of laying the dead to rest, something unspoken passed between them. A bond was forged, one that transcended mere survival. It was deeper than friendship, stronger than duty. It was the understanding of two souls bound by shared suffering and the desperate need to hold onto something, anything, in a world that had lost everything.

Since that day, they had relied on each other, fought side by side, and endured together. The world was now unrecognizable, filled with horrors neither of them could have imagined. Yet, they pressed on, moving through the ruins, scavenging, and surviving. Then, by some twist of fate, they found the children, Ethan, Mia, and little Leo.

It had been weeks since either of them had felt anything resembling hope. But when they looked at those three fragile lives, something shifted inside them. For the first time since the world had collapsed around them, they had something worth protecting, something that made all the pain, loss, and suffering worth enduring.

In a world that had turned into a waking nightmare, these children remained a fragile thread of humanity that was still unbroken. Against all odds, Aida and Jacobson were willing to fight for them.

10.6: The Last Stitch

Aida paused, her needle hovering just above the fabric. She shifted her gaze to Jacobson, observing him as he worked in quiet concentration. The lines of his sketch were smooth and deliberate, filled with the same care he had always dedicated to everything he did. For a moment, she simply watched him. Then, in a voice just above a whisper, she asked, "You never stop, do you?"

Jacobson didn't look up. He continued sketching, a faint smile tugging at the corner of his lips. "Some things... you have to keep alive, even if only on paper."

Aida tightened her grip around the bear, a flicker of sadness in her eyes. "Memories fade."

Jacobson paused for a moment before resuming his drawing. "Not if you hold on to them hard enough."

In the silence that followed, they both understood, they were clinging to whatever they had left.

"What do you think about their health?" Aida's voice was barely above a whisper, but in the heavy stillness of the maintenance room, it might as well have been a shout.

Jacobson paused mid-stroke, the pencil hovering just above the sketchbook. He exhaled deeply, setting the pencil down as he glanced over at the children. The flickering lantern cast soft shadows over their sleeping faces, Ethan's steady, deep breaths, Mia's barely perceptible rise and fall of her chest, and Leo curled tightly under blanket.

With the careful precision of a doctor, Jacobson answered in a hushed, solemn voice. "Ethan is immune. The virus won't touch him, it never could. His body simply rejects it."

Aida blinked, absorbing the news, but Jacobson wasn't finished. His voice lowered further, as if speaking the truth aloud would make it worse. "Leo has the same immunity in his system, but it's weak. His body fights, but not well enough. The virus is still inside him, changing him. And Mia..." He hesitated, his eyes darkening. "Mia has no immunity at all. It's killing her slowly."

Aida sucked in a sharp breath, her grip tightening around the half-mended bear in her hands.

Jacobson continued, his expression grim. "The virus is mutating inside both of them. It's not just attacking; it's altering their DNA, their blood, their nervous systems... it's reshaping them at a fundamental level." He looked down at his hands, those of a man who had spent his life trying to heal, only to witness so much destruction. "For Leo, it's worse. The virus is accelerating his growth, forcing his body to adapt in ways it was never meant to. His bones, muscles, ligaments, everything is being violently reshaped. His brain, his knowledge... it's all evolving at an unnatural speed. But no child should carry that much mind inside such a small, breaking body. Every day, the changes become more drastic. And with every passing moment, their chances of survival shrink."

Aida let out a shaky breath, blinking rapidly to keep the moisture in her eyes from spilling over. She hugged Mr. Bubbles tight, pressing the patched bear to her chest. For a long moment, she remained silent. Then, as silently as the tears came, she wiped them away, steeling herself.

"What if we go with them?"

Jacobson turned, brow furrowed.

Aida took a deep breath before continuing, her voice steadier now. "Think about it. I don't believe there's anything left for us here. In the past two days, have you seen a single GeneCorp helicopter? A drone? Their security forces? Even our own military?" She shook her head. "They're gone, Jacobson. All of them. The only threat left now is the Accelerates."

A heavy silence stretched between them.

Jacobson exhaled through his nose, glancing once more at the children. Could they really do it? Could they risk everything to help them reach Redwood Valley? Deep down, he already knew the answer.

Jacobson placed his pencil inside the sketchbook, closed it, and set it gently on the table. He exhaled deeply, leaning forward in the worn-out armchair. He pressed his hands to his tired eyes, trying to scrub away the weight of exhaustion. A heavy sigh escaped his lips.

"I don't know, Aida," he finally murmured, his voice rough with uncertainty. "What about your family? Your parents, your girls, your husband? We agreed that once things settled, we would look for them." He lifted his head, meeting her eyes in the dim light. "I can't ask you to walk away from that, not for me, not for these kids."

Aida held his gaze but didn't speak. Her hands clutched Mr. Bubbles tightly, her fingers running over the newly sewn bowtie she had just finished stitching onto the stuffed bear.

Jacobson rubbed his temples before continuing. "It's good that there aren't any helicopters, drones, or security forces in sight, but... what if they're just hiding?" His words hung in the air like a warning, a ghost of paranoia that had kept them alive for so long.

The lantern flickered, its glow dimming as the fuel ran low. Shadows stretched along the bunker walls, swallowing the two figures in darkness.

Minutes passed in silence. Then Jacobson sighed again, softer, resigned.

"But... I think you're right."

Aida's head snapped up.

Jacobson sat back, his expression unreadable. "The longer we wait, the slimmer the chances of finding your family." He hesitated only a moment before admitting, "You know I don't have anyone left. My mother passed..."

Part III

Chapter 11: Glowing Like Fireflies

11.1: One Hour Until Dawn

Ethan was the first to jolt awake, his heart pounding from the sudden clatter that echoed through the maintenance room. A moment later, Mia stirred, her eyes snapping open in confusion. A loud, metallic clatter, something heavy hitting concrete. Their survival instincts, sharpened by weeks of hardship, sent a rush of adrenaline through their veins before they could even process what had happened.

Blinking in the dim light, Ethan sat up, his breath uneven. He quickly scanned the room for danger and spotted the source almost immediately: an empty ammunition box lay overturned on the floor, having fallen from the chair where Aida had placed it the night before.

Near the exit, Jacobson stood frozen, gripping the edge of a large supply crate he had been shifting. He sighed when he noticed Ethan and Mia staring at him, their muscles still tense from the sudden awakening.

"Sorry, kids," Jacobson whispered, his voice low and apologetic. "That was unintentional."

Leo, still curled up in his bed, remained undisturbed, his small chest rising and falling in deep, peaceful sleep.

Ethan rubbed his eyes and swung his legs over the edge of the bunk, his bare feet touching the cold floor. "Are you going somewhere?" he asked, suspicion lacing his voice. His body remained rigid, instincts warning him to stay alert.

Jacobson turned to him with a broad, reassuring smile. "Yes," he replied. "We are. All of us."

Mia, now sitting up as well, exchanged a quick glance with Ethan, her expression mirroring his concern.

Ethan narrowed his eyes. "Where exactly are we going?" His voice was steady, but there was an unmistakable edge of unease.

Jacobson's smile remained, but he did not give a direct answer. Instead, his eyes glinted with a quiet mystery, as though he knew a secret they were not ready to hear. "Go back to sleep," he said gently. "Breakfast will be ready soon. You still have a good hour until dawn."

Neither Ethan nor Mia lay back down; sleep had already abandoned them. Instead, they watched silently from their bunks as Jacobson continued stacking boxes near the exit, methodically arranging them as if preparing for something significant.

Minutes passed, filled only with the rustling of supplies and the soft scratching of wood against concrete. Then, from outside, the deep, unmistakable roar of an engine cut through the quiet. The low, rumbling sound echoed down the maintenance room's corridor, growing louder as it approached the entrance.

Ethan and Mia tensed again, their fingers gripping the edges of their blankets. But Jacobson merely grinned. "Aha. Aida's here."

The moment her name was spoken, both Ethan and Mia felt their bodies relax, just a little. They didn't know what was happening, but at least they weren't alone.

Moments later, the heavy bunker door creaked open, and Aida stepped inside. Her presence, steady and unwavering, settled the unspoken tension lingering in the room. For the first time that morning, Ethan, and Mia released a breath they hadn't realized they were holding.

11.2: Still Fragile as Glass

At the breakfast table, Leo sat cross-legged on his chair, turning Mr. Bubbles over in his small hands and admiring the teddy bear's new button eyes and freshly sewn bowtie. A bright smile spread across his face as he traced the stitches with his fingers, marveling at the careful craftsmanship. Without warning, he scrambled off his chair and flung himself into Aida's arms.

"Thank you. Thank you so much," he whispered against her shoulder, his voice thick with gratitude.

Aida held him close, blinking back the tears welling in her eyes. She had spent most of the night repairing the worn-out bear, and seeing Leo this happy made it all worth it. Across the table, Jacobson quickly turned his face away, pretending to cough to hide the emotion threatening to overtake him.

Once the quiet moment settled, Aida and Jacobson exchanged a look and began to explain their plan.

At first, Ethan and Mia listened in silence, their expressions unreadable. However, an uneasy suspicion soon crept into their faces. Their minds raced with doubts, and dark thoughts clouded the fragile trust they had built. What if they didn't take us to the bridge? What if they took us somewhere else, another GeneCorp facility? What if this was a trap to hand over Leo, to dissect him like an experiment?

A flicker of fear passed between them, and instinctively, they recalled Clara's warning.

Aida and Jacobson were sharp enough to notice the shift, the way Ethan and Mia's shoulders tensed, the way their hands curled slightly, ready to react. For them, the trust was still fragile as glass.

Sensing their hesitation, Aida leaned forward, her voice calm and reassuring. "You don't have to ride with us in the armored truck," she said gently. "We'll fill your pickup with a full tank of gasoline, and we've packed enough supplies in the back to last you at least five days. You'll have everything you need."

She reached into her pocket and placed a small black device on the table. "Here's a long-range radio. Our designated channel will be seven. Every day at noon, turn it on. If we're within range, we'll talk. That way, you'll always know where we are."

Jacobson added, "We also packed extra warm clothes and boots for all three of you. And a stroller for Leo, it'll make walking through the rural roads easier. I reinforced it with an extra frame and fitted it with large wheels. It can handle rough terrain." He met their eyes. "I know those roads well. My last job was in that bunker."

Aida continued, her tone firm but kind. "You'll drive ahead of us, so we can keep an eye on you from a distance. Keep the radio on in the car." She hesitated for a moment before pulling out a handgun and handing it to Ethan. "Do you know how to use this?"

Ethan swallowed hard, gripping the weapon with both hands. "Yeah," he murmured. "Mia showed me how to use it."

Aida nodded approvingly and handed them their utility belts, complete with hunting knives and other essential tools. "I adjusted these while you were sleeping, but feel free to make any final changes to ensure they fit you better."

Jacobson cleared his throat, his voice growing softer and more personal. "Kids, we'll escort you to the start of the rural road. From there, you'll continue on foot. Once you're out of sight, Aida and I will head toward her family's farm, it's about a three-day drive from Redwood Valley." He hesitated, carefully choosing his words. "If we find them... we'll all come to the bunker. If we don't, we'll still come back to you."

His eyes softened, revealing a rare vulnerability in his voice. "Just keep the radio with you. Always. Please." This wasn't just a request; it was a plea.

11.3: The Sky Caught Fire

Ethan gripped the steering wheel tightly as he made a U-turn, his knuckles whitening from the pressure. Beside him, Mia sat rigid, her fingers nervously twisting the fabric of her jacket. In the back seat, Leo clutched Mr. Bubbles, his well-worn but now well-dressed teddy bear, a small source of comfort in an uncertain world. They were dressed in fresh, clean clothes, their stomachs full for the first time in what felt like forever. Yet, as the wheels rolled forward, carrying them into the unknown, an unspoken tension filled the air. The road ahead was unknowable.

The convoy of two vehicles moved steadily away from the collapsed bridge, their departure marked by the sound of gravel crunching beneath thick tires. Leading the way was the old pickup truck, its engine humming steadily under Ethan's control. Thirty yards behind, an armored vehicle followed, its heavy frame built for battle. Dr. Jacobson was behind the wheel, his sharp eyes constantly scanning the road ahead. In the gun turret above, Aida stood like a sentinel, clad in military fatigues, the Lieutenant stripes on her arm catching the sunlight as she moved.

Her head was on a swivel, never lingering too long in one direction. Through high-powered binoculars pressed to her eyes, she examined every ridge, every ruined structure, and every shadow that might conceal a threat. A heavy machine gun was mounted in the turret, fully loaded and ready to tear through anything that moved with hostile intent. Within arm's reach rested her sniper rifle, its polished barrel gleaming faintly in the morning light.

The convoy had been on the road for about an hour when a burst of static crackled through the radio on the pickup truck's dashboard. Ethan and Mia tensed immediately.

"Mia, Ethan," Aida's voice came through, calm but firm. "Do you see that black dot on your right side? It's about three hundred yards away and fifty yards up in the sky."

Both of them turned their heads, scanning the horizon.

"It's a GeneCorp drone," Aida continued from the turret. "Probably one of the last ones. Don't panic. Keep your pace."

Leo whimpered, fingers digging into Mr. Bubbles as he shrank. The ominous hum of the drone filled the air, growing louder by the second. Initially a small, nearly imperceptible shape, it quickly became clear, a mechanical predator with its unblinking electronic eye locked onto them.

Aida, her heart pounding steadily, rotated in the turret once more to ensure there were no additional drones lurking in the sky. Satisfied, she reached for her sniper rifle.

With practiced ease, she adjusted the scope, her breathing slowing as she settled into the familiar rhythm of the hunt. The crosshairs found their mark, and she exhaled, her finger tightening on the trigger.

The shot rang out.

A sharp, metallic crack echoed through the landscape.

Then another shot.

The drone shuddered midair, smoke trailing from its frame, then exploded as it fell.

The radio buzzed again.

"What happens next, don't be afraid. Ethan, keep steady. Stay calm." Aida's voice, though firm, carried a reassuring steadiness, as if she already knew what was coming.

The tension in the pickup eased slightly. Ethan relaxed his grip on the wheel, and Mia let out the breath she had been holding. Even Leo, though still frightened, looked up at the sky with a little less terror in his wide eyes.

Then Aida disappeared from view, ducking down into the turret for a few seconds. When she emerged again, she was holding something far more menacing than her sniper rifle, an RPG grenade launcher.

Ethan swallowed hard and exchanged a quick glance with Mia. If Aida was bringing that out, things were about to get much worse.

Then they heard it, a new sound. A deep, rhythmic thumping that sent vibrations through their chests. It was coming from the same direction as the fallen drone. Aida had been right; the drone had been a scout. Now, something bigger was coming.

Ethan's heart pounded as the shape of a helicopter emerged over the horizon. It wasn't like the others, no missiles, no mounted guns. This wasn't an assault chopper; it was a transport, capable of carrying at most four people. But that didn't mean it wasn't dangerous. GeneCorp wouldn't send a helicopter unless they had something, or someone, on board worth protecting, and whoever was inside wasn't coming for a friendly chat.

Aida braced herself, lifting the RPG onto her shoulder. Her grip steady, stance firm.

"Get ready," she muttered, narrowing her eyes as she calculated the helicopter's trajectory.

Ethan pressed his foot on the gas, pushing the pickup forward, desperate to put as much distance as possible between them and whatever was coming. Jacobson followed in the armored vehicle, maintaining formation.

Mia reached back, gripping Leo's hand tightly.

"Stay down," she whispered.

Leo nodded, burying his face into Mr. Bubbles, his small body trembling.

The helicopter roared closer, the wind from its spinning blades kicking dust and debris from the ruined road.

Aida inhaled deeply.

Then she fired.

The helicopter exploded midair, a shockwave ripping the sky before it crashed in flames.

Without wasting a second, Aida swiftly lowered the grenade launcher and grabbed her binoculars. Her movements were sharp and precise as she scanned the surroundings, her eyes darting across the landscape in search of any additional threats.

11.4: The Quiet Before the Song

The next three hours on the road were marked by a strange, deceptive calm. The sun hung high above the cracked horizon, casting long shadows across the ruined highway. Its golden rays reflected off the shattered windshields and rusted hoods of cars long abandoned. Ethan gripped the oversized steering wheel of the pickup truck with both hands, driving with surprising confidence and skill. He weaved between wreckage, potholes, and ditches with the finesse of someone far older than his fourteen years. Occasionally, his jaw clenched as he passed the burnt-out husk of a minivan or a flipped school bus, each serving as a grim monument to the chaos that had erupted weeks earlier.

Trailing thirty yards behind him was the armored vehicle, its matte black hull glinting under the sun. Inside, Dr. Jacobson sat at the wheel, alert but calm, while Aida manned the turret above. Through the narrow slit of her helmet, her eyes scanned the road constantly, rotating in smooth, controlled arcs. The rhythm of the road, the distant sound of wind brushing through brittle tree branches, and the rumble of tires over fractured pavement created a strange harmony, tense but oddly peaceful.

Both adults silently admired the boy leading them. For someone barely a teenager, Ethan handled the truck with practiced precision. Jacobson observed from behind, impressed. This was no ordinary child; he had been forced to become something more, just like all of them.

Pleasant Creek finally came into view. It was a quiet, ghostly sprawl of buildings warped by fire and neglect. Just days ago, Mia had thrown her Molotov cocktail into a swarm of Accelerates, igniting chaos. The remnants of that moment were still visible, blackened walls, scorched pavement, and the haunting echo of a battle barely survived.

Suddenly, the radio in Ethan's truck crackled, interrupting the silence. "We need to refill the trucks," came Jacobson's voice. "Might be good to stretch and eat something, too."

As they drove a few more blocks, they stopped outside the church where the children had taken shelter not long ago. The structure stood unchanged, its once-majestic stained-glass windows now jagged shards of colored glass, its wooden pews splintered like shattered ribs, and the entire sanctuary blanketed in a thin layer of ash and dust. Sunlight filtered through the broken panes, casting eerie, fractured rainbows across the floor.

As they stepped from their vehicles, Aida and Jacobson immediately moved to check on the children. But then, the air changed. A sound faint at first, then unmistakable, sliced through the stillness.

"Ring around the Rosie..."

Aida's heart clenched. The nursery rhyme, once harmless, was now a siren of death.

"Accelerates!" Aida whispered, her voice a mix of dread and instinct. "Quick! Everyone into the big truck! Hurry!" she shouted, grabbing Leo and sprinting for the armored vehicle. Her boots pounded against the pavement as the child's tiny arms clung to her.

Jacobson pushed Ethan toward the truck. "Go! Now!" He scooped Mia into his arms and dashed for the driver's seat.

Inside, Aida tucked Leo into the most secure corner, shielding him behind crates of ammunition and protective plating. She then climbed into the turret, positioning the heavy machine gun with practiced urgency. Her sniper rifle remained at her side, loaded and ready.

11.5: The Scream and the Silence

From every alley and every shadow, they emerged.
The Accelerates.
Dozens. Then hundreds.
The Accelerated children swarmed from every direction, feral, fast, furious. Once-cherubic faces had twisted into grotesque visages, skin stretched thin over mutated bone. Their lips peeled back over jagged teeth, eyes glowing an inhuman shade of blue, lifeless, yet brimming with rage. White foam dribbled from their mouths. Their bodies moved with jerky, unnatural speed, like puppets on invisible strings.

Jacobson slammed the armored vehicle's doors shut, locking them with reinforced bolts. He loaded his rifle and handed ammunition to Mia, who, despite her trembling hands, nodded and took her small handgun. Leo cowered in his corner, clutching Mr. Bubbles, his stuffed bear, trembling like a leaf caught in a storm.

Aida opened fire. The turret roared to life, cutting through the oncoming wave. Shells ejected in a glittering stream of brass, the gun spitting death and thunder. Bodies fell, but more kept coming.

"Jacobson, get the ammo ready!" she shouted. "Lock the doors and don't open them. Shoot through the slits!"

Jacobson fired from the side panel. Mia joined him, her hands steady as she took aim with each shot. But it wasn't enough; the sheer number of Accelerates was overwhelming.

Several of the Accelerates climbed onto the truck, pounding their fists and clawing at the reinforced windows. Aida, spinning in the turret, saw two of them already clambering onto the hood.

They were outnumbered.

Ethan turned to Leo, his eyes filled with desperation. He didn't need to speak, his expression said everything.

Leo met his brother's gaze. Although only a year old, Leo was trapped in a six-year-old's mutated body, yet he possessed the wisdom of someone much older. He understood the silent plea.

Without a word, Leo stood.

He took a shaky breath, held Mr. Bubbles to his chest, and opened his mouth. The scream that followed was inhuman.

A sound wave, high-pitched and otherworldly, burst from Leo's throat. The air around him shimmered like heat rising from asphalt. The truck trembled violently, its metal plating vibrating with the force of the blast.

Outside, the town of Pleasant Creek shook as if struck by an earthquake. Windows shattered for blocks. Walls cracked and buckled. The earth rippled.

The Accelerates were thrown backward in a tsunami of sonic force. Their screeches turned to agonized wails as they bled from their ears and eyes, their fragile minds shredded by the supernatural frequency.

Many collapsed instantly, their limbs twitching, faces frozen in expressions of sheer horror. Others fled, vanishing into alleys and ruins, their monstrous courage shattered by the scream of the one they were programmed to worship or destroy.

Inside the armored vehicle, all was still. Everyone clutched their heads, trying to block out the sound. Even Aida dropped into the turret, holding her ears, her breath ragged.

Then, silence.

Only Leo's heavy breathing remained, his body swaying, his legs giving way beneath him. Ethan caught him, pulling him into a tight embrace. The boy was pale, drained, but alive. Outside, nothing moved. Pleasant Creek was a graveyard once more.

Jacobson lowered his rifle, his hands trembling.

Aida slowly emerged from the turret, her eyes scanning the destruction. "They're gone..." she said, her voice low, disbelieving.

Mia clutched little Leo's hand, tears streaming silently down her cheeks.

Ethan held Leo close. "You did it," he whispered, his voice cracking. "You saved us."

But Leo didn't respond. His eyes were closed, and his small chest rose and fell with shallow breaths.

Jacobson knelt beside him, checking his pulse. "He's stable... but drained."

Aida stepped forward and placed a hand gently on Leo's forehead. Her eyes glistened with unspoken emotion.

He was their weapon. Their savior.

And still just a child.

11.6: Only the Armored Truck Left

Outside, the air was still, and smoke drifted lazily through the ruins. Pleasant Creek stood silent once again, bearing witness to another miracle... and yet another tragedy narrowly avoided.

The battle was over, for now. But Jacobson knew the war was far from finished.

Still in shock, Jacobson sat frozen in the driver's seat of the armored truck. His trembling hands gripped the wheel as he stared through the narrow slit of the reinforced windshield. Outside, barely thirty feet away, a battered and scorched pickup truck sat as a twisted shell of what had once been their lifeline. Smoke curled lazily from the hood, bullet holes riddled the sides, and shattered glass sparkled like broken stars across the asphalt.

He exhaled shakily and turned to the narrow side viewport. After a cautious glance, he cracked open the armored door just enough to slip through, his handgun already drawn. The silence following Leo's scream was eerie, no distant moans, no whispers of footsteps. But Jacobson knew better than to trust the quiet in a world like this.

"We need to salvage what we can from the pickup," he muttered grimly, half to himself and half to anyone listening. "I don't think it'll start again."

Ethan and Mia were already climbing out of the truck, their faces pale, eyes wide yet steady. They moved with the gravity of those forced into adulthood by fire and blood.

"Ethan, my boy, try to start it," Jacobson said softly, his voice hoarse.

Ethan nodded, slid into the scorched driver's seat of the pickup, and turned the key. The engine coughed, groaned, and died. He tried again. Nothing. Not even a spark.

"It's gone," Ethan said flatly, stepping out. "Completely shot."

Back in the armored truck, Aida cradled Leo in her arms, rocking him gently as she scanned the surroundings through the narrow slits in the vehicle's reinforced plating. Her fingers gripped the stock of her rifle, always at the ready. Leo's chest still rose and fell too quickly, the aftermath of his sonic scream, but his breathing was slowly beginning to settle.

Outside, Jacobson and the children began unloading the back of the pickup, sorting through what hadn't been destroyed. A few packs of supplies, a metal toolbox, a half-crushed case of water bottles. Then Jacobson spotted something beneath a torn tarp in the bed of the truck.

"Good. This has only one hole in it," he said, pulling out Leo's stroller. It was dented and singed, but the frame was intact. "Only the armored truck left," he added, more to gauge Ethan and Mia's reaction than anything else. There was hesitation in his voice, the unspoken question lingering in the air: Do you still trust us? After everything?

Mia looked at Ethan, and he returned her gaze. Their eyes locked, silent communication flowing between them. After everything, after the betrayal at the bridge, the massacre, the horror of the Accelerates, what else did they have, if not each other? And Aida and Jacobson, who had chosen to walk away from safety just to help them, protect them, and fight beside them. They weren't just allies; they were family now. In this world, blood didn't always mean kin.

Ethan didn't answer right away. His hands hovered for a moment, then closed around the stroller. He stepped forward, his voice quiet but resolute. "Where and how can I secure this on the truck?"

Jacobson's face cracked into a small, tired smile, not with joy, but with understanding. He gestured to the back hatch of the armored vehicle. "There's an anchor point just behind the second seat. Strap it down there. If we hit anything rough, we don't want it shifting."

Together, they moved quickly and silently, securing the supplies and stroller. Aida, now with Leo gently asleep on her lap, watched as the others worked. She saw the exhaustion in their movements, the trauma that hadn't yet settled. But there was also resolve, a quiet, burning will to survive.

Inside the church, shadows danced across the broken pews and jagged glass. The scent of smoke and blood still lingered faintly, a reminder of the recent horror. Yet outside, in the fading light of the day, something else hung in the air, a fragile sliver of hope.

"Let's move," Jacobson said once everything was secured. "We can't stay long. That scream... it may have cleared this area, but if anything's still out there, it heard us."

Aida nodded, gently laying Leo into the seat and strapping him in with motherly precision. Her hands lingered for a moment on his small, fragile body before she climbed into the turret, her eyes sharp once again.

Mia and Ethan climbed into the armored truck. Jacobson took the wheel. The engine roared to life, heavy and indomitable. As the sun began to dip beneath the horizon, casting long shadows across Pleasant Creek, the armored truck moved forward again, stronger in bond.

None of them spoke. There was only the rumble of tires, the hum of the engine, and the distant memory of a nursery rhyme turned nightmare. Yet as they left the ruins of the town behind, something like hope clung to the air, fragile, faint, but real.

11.7: Glowing Like Fireflies

The armored truck rumbled to a stop at the start of a long-abandoned rural road leading to the GeneCorp bunker, the site where Jacobson had defected years ago. The thick silence inside the vehicle was suffocating. No one had spoken since Leo's last scream, the echoes of which, a raw, terrifying power, still lingered in their bones, a constant reminder of what the child was capable of and the immense toll it had taken on him.

Jacobson turned sharply to Aida. His eyes carried the weight of a decision already made. Aida met his gaze and nodded, her voice calm yet firm. "Yes, Jacobson. You're right. We should take them as close to the bunker as we can." It was as if she had read his mind.

Encouraged by her agreement, Jacobson exhaled. "It's about two to three hours by car from here. On foot, it'll take more than a day, possibly two. I know this terrain well; I defected from here. There's a dense forest a mile or two from the bunker where we can hide and watch as the kids make their final approach."

Aida nodded with military precision. "Then we have a plan. Drive."

The truck groaned as Jacobson accelerated, pushing forward toward the terrain. The road was cracked and rough, lined with skeletal trees clawing at the twilight sky. The sun dipped below the horizon, casting long shadows across the harvested sunflower fields ahead. In the distance, the only sign of life was a small, pulsing red light flashing steadily in the darkness, the entrance to the GeneCorp bunker.

Jacobson pulled the truck to a stop beneath the cover of the trees. The moment the engine shut off, the world fell into an eerie stillness. Aida scanned the perimeter through her binoculars, her breath steady. Then, with a quick nod, she signaled for everyone to disembark.

Ethan and Mia climbed out, their movements hesitant, reluctant to leave the only protection they had left. Jacobson moved to the back, retrieving the stroller. With the gentleness of a father, he lifted Leo, his small body still frail from the exertion of his earlier scream, and placed him inside. The child barely stirred.

Aida crouched beside Leo and covered him with a warm blanket. Then, methodically, she peeled long strips of fluorescent tape, pressing them onto his chest and back, ensuring they'd glow in the dark. She marked the stroller too, its glow points forming a trail they could track.

"This will help us follow you in the dark through the binoculars," she murmured, securing the final strip.

Then she turned to Ethan and Mia, placing the same fluorescent markers on their backs and chests. The soft green glow was barely visible in the moonlight, but through the right lens, they'd stand out like fireflies in the night.

Satisfied, Aida exhaled and leaned back on her heels. She looked at them, not as soldiers, nor as burdens, but as children thrust into a world that had taken too much from them.

"I promise we will be back. Soon. Very soon. Once I find, or… bury, my family, we'll come for you," she said gently.

Leo's lip quivered, his small fingers clutching Aida's wrist. His big, tired eyes shimmered with unshed tears. "I hope you find them," he whispered, his voice cracking under the weight of his emotions.

Jacobson cleared his throat, the persistent cough a desperate attempt to mask his feelings. He turned away, as if looking elsewhere could stave off the lump in his throat.

"Just keep the radio with you. Always," he pleaded again, his voice softer than usual. "We won't move from here until you tell us you're safe."

The goodbye carried a weight, words couldn't express. The moment stretched, no one ready to shatter the fragile peace.

Leo, still nestled in his stroller with Mr. Bubbles pressed to his chest, suddenly threw his tiny arms around Aida's neck. His voice, barely a whisper, felt deafening in the quiet.

"Thank you, Mrs. Soldier. Thank you for everything, so, so, so much. I will never forget you. Never, ever."

Aida stiffened at the title, feeling it strike deep. Mrs. Soldier. She swallowed against the ache in her chest and pressed a firm kiss to his temple.

Jacobson coughed again, clearing his throat one last time. His hands clenched and unclenched at his sides, his face turned toward the darkness, but the moisture in his eyes betrayed him.

"It's time," he finally said, his voice rough.

Mia nodded, lifting the flashlight. Ethan, his hands steady, gripped the stroller handles. One final look, one last second of unspoken words, and then, slowly, they moved forward, disappearing into the harvested sunflower field.

Aida climbed back into the turret of the armored truck, pressing her night-vision binoculars to her eyes. Through the lens, the fluorescent patches glowed faintly, moving further and further away. Each step they took brought them closer to safety or danger, she wasn't sure which, but she was certain they were moving further away from her. Holding her breath, she tracked them through the darkness, unwilling to look away until they were safe.

Chapter 12: The Cure on the Tombstone

12.1: Speak the Name

The GeneCorp bunker loomed like a tombstone, its bone-white walls stark in the moonlight. The structure was massive, a relic of a time when safety was measured in feet of reinforced steel and layers of top-secret security protocols. Now, it stood as a fortress against an unforgiving world, its weathered surface marred by time, yet still exuding an air of unyielding authority.

A chain-link fence, topped with cruel spirals of barbed wire, encased the facility like a skeletal hand gripping its last possession. The GeneCorp logo, a stylized double helix entwined with a serpent, was emblazoned on the rusted steel gate, its once-pristine sheen dulled to a shadow of its former glory. It was a silent mockery of the corporation's promise of salvation, a grim reminder of the experiments that led to the world's downfall.

The children stood at the threshold, their journey culminating in whatever fate awaited them within those walls. Ethan came to a halt, gripping the stroller's handles with white-knuckled tension. Mia raised the flashlight, its narrow beam slicing through the gloom, illuminating the gate's weathered surface. The sight sent a shiver down her spine.

Leo, wide-eyed and silent, sat motionless in the stroller, his small fingers clenching Mr. Bubbles as if the worn-out teddy could shield him from whatever lurked beyond. His breathing was shallow but steady, the aftermath of his devastating sonic scream still weighing on his fragile body. The tape on his chest and back glowed faintly under the flashlight's beam, casting eerie, fragmented reflections onto the cold steel.

Ethan swallowed hard. "We're here," he murmured, his voice barely above a whisper. His gaze flickered from Leo to the impenetrable structure before them. The weight of the moment pressed heavily on his barely teenage shoulders.

Mia tightened her grip on the pistol in her hand, her thumb instinctively brushing the safety. The cold weight of the weapon was both reassuring and terrifying, a necessary evil in a world that had long abandoned innocence.

A soft mechanical whir broke the silence. Above the gate, a rusted security camera, its lens encrusted with dust and decay, jerked to life. The red light embedded in its center blinked once, then twice, a glowing eye assessing them from above. The speaker mounted next to it crackled with static before a distorted, undeniably human voice pierced the night.

"Identify yourselves."

The voice was female, sharp, and commanding, yet tinged with something else, a weariness, perhaps, or a caution born of too many betrayals.

Mia squared her shoulders and raised her chin. She forced steel into her voice. "Survivors," she called out, her words firm despite the knot of unease tightening in her stomach. "Clara Davtian sent us."

For a moment, silence reigned, stretching unbearably as the weight of their words settled over the bunker's gate. Then came the groan of metal, slow, agonizing, as the gate creaked open. The sound sent a shudder through Mia's spine, its screeching hinges a chilling prelude to whatever lay beyond.

Ethan exhaled slowly. He exchanged a glance with Mia, unspoken understanding passing between them. There was no turning back now. Clutching the stroller's handles with renewed determination, he took the first step forward into the unknown.

***

In the dense, moonlit woods, Aida crouched in the turret of the armored truck, her knuckles white as she gripped the night-vision binoculars. The cold metal pressed against her brow as she scanned the distant bunker.

"The gates are open," she whispered, her voice barely audible over the rustling wind.

Beside her, Jacobson stood rigid, his rifle clutched tightly against his chest, his breath held as if exhaling might shatter the fragile moment.

"They're moving through," Aida continued, her eyes locked on the glowing figures of the children as they disappeared beyond the threshold. The bunker swallowed them whole.

Jacobson exhaled slowly, a shaky breath of relief. But the tension lingered in his shoulders. Not completely.

"We wait," Aida murmured. "Until they tell us they're safe."

Only then, perhaps, could they finally let go.

12.2: *Where the Serum Burns*

The bunker's interior enveloped them like the belly of a long-forgotten beast, cold, silent, and faintly humming with the remnants of ancient science. As the gates clanged shut behind them, the outside world vanished, replaced by a chilling stillness that seeped into their bones.

The corridor stretched like a steel ribcage, lit by buzzing tubes flickering like dying insects. Each light cast elongated shadows that crawled across the cracked tile floor. Glass tanks lined the walls, most shattered, their contents long since dried or scavenged. The faded labels on the tanks peeled and gathered dust: SUBJECT A-1 through A-8.

Leo's wide eyes locked on the final tank, its broken glass glinting faintly, the label missing but the void unmistakable. The empty space where A-9 should have been sent a sharp chill down Ethan's spine. He didn't speak the name aloud, nor did Mia. The truth hung in the recycled air, a shadow too large to outrun.

They followed the faded signs, some smeared with fingerprints or blood, until they reached a rusted steel door marked "Control Hub." Inside, the room was cramped and humming with low electricity. Console lights blinked sporadically, and cables snaked across the floor like roots.

At the center stood a woman in her early sixties, Dr. Anya Voss. Her lab coat, once white, was stained at the cuffs with rings of coffee and something darker, something long dried. She looked up from a terminal, her face pale and drawn, but her eyes sharp as glass scalpel blades.

Behind her, a wall of monitors displayed desolate footage, abandoned labs overtaken by rust and decay, corridors choked with debris and silence. But one screen pulsed with movement. A single Accelerate paced like a caged animal, its sunken cobalt-blue eyes, parted mouth, and face pressed against the camera lens in a silent scream.

"You're immune," Dr. Voss said, her gaze locking on Ethan's unscarred hands. "Fascinating." Her eyes flicked briefly to Leo, who lay bundled in the stroller, pale, and shivering. "And Leo...?"

Mia and Ethan were stunned. How did she know? But they quickly realized, half the world was after Leo. Why wouldn't she know who he was?

"Dying," Ethan growled, stepping forward. "We didn't come here to be studied. Can you help him or not?"

Dr. Voss didn't flinch. She turned back to her console, her fingers dancing over the keys. A holographic projection burst into the air above her desk, Leo's DNA, rotating slowly like a glowing helix of fire. Entire strands pulsed in crimson, a visual representation of the virus tearing through his body.

"The virus is rewriting him," she said. "It's not just infecting him; it's transforming him. His cells are undergoing hyper-accelerated evolution. If we can suppress it, we might..."

"If?" Mia snapped, stepping beside Ethan, her voice sharp with fear. "Clara said you'd dissect him. That you'd cut him open the moment you saw him."

"Clara was a pessimist. Besides, GeneCorp, after today, after you shot down the drone and the helicopter, has effectively ceased to exist. I'm the last one left, and I never supported how they twisted my original research," Dr. Voss replied coolly, never looking away from the glowing projection. She then turned to Ethan and Mia, her expression unreadable.

"Now, you can tell Dr. Jacobson and his soldier companion that you're safe, and that the only remaining member of GeneCorp is his mentor, Dr. Anya Voss. I assume you have a way to contact them?"

***

Aida remained inside the gun turret of the armored truck, her night-vision binoculars fixed on the distant gates of the bunker, unwavering. The green glow of the lenses reflected in her eyes as she scanned for any flicker of movement. Suddenly, the radio crackled to life, startling Jacobson from his silent vigil.

Mia's voice came through the speakers, soft, steady, almost musical, like a lullaby in a world starved of comfort. "Aida, we're fine. We met Dr. Voss. She's the only one left from GeneCorp. The drone and helicopter we saw earlier today were the last of them. We'll stay here and wait for your return. Good luck."

Aida slowly lowered the binoculars from her face, exhaling deeply, as if releasing a burden too heavy to carry. She turned to Jacobson. "She said they're safe," she murmured.

Jacobson's face broke into a rare, genuine smile, worn and weathered, but real.

Moments later, the armored truck disappeared into the forest, swallowed by the unknown dark.

***

Dr. Voss glanced briefly at Leo's twisted, trembling hand before crossing the room. She moved with clinical calmness, as if she had performed this procedure a thousand times. At a nearby counter, she opened a drawer and took out a tray filled with vials and syringes.

"I need a blood sample," she said, her tone flat but urgent. "If I can isolate the mutated strain, I can synthesize a stabilizer, something to slow it down, or maybe even stop it."

For a moment, there was only silence, broken only by the soft hum of the monitors and the faint rasp of Leo's breathing.

***

Sometime before the world unraveled, in a moment that would haunt him forever, Ethan had held Leo's tiny hand as they sat together in a gleaming, overly bright GeneCorp laboratory. The room, bathed in sterile white light, somehow managed to feel almost cheerful, despite its clinical coldness. A friendly nurse, her face bright with a smile and decorated with a colorful array of stickers, gently explained the procedure to the anxious parents.

"This will make you strong," their mother had whispered, her voice soft and full of hope, a hope only a mother could summon in the face of uncertainty.

Leo, barely one year old with a charming gap-toothed grin, looked up at his mother with wide, trusting eyes that absorbed every word. His innocent curiosity shone through as he babbled, "Like Superman?" His voice trembled with wonder and unspoiled hope. For a fleeting moment, everything seemed perfect, a fragile cocoon of trust and love amid the sterile environment.

Ethan, lost in the memory of that precious time, remembered how he had focused solely on the warmth of Leo's small hand. He hadn't noticed the syringe's label then: Subject 9X, a detail that would later unravel their world. In that seemingly innocent moment, the seeds of a future marred by betrayal and loss were sown, and Ethan's heart, once full of naive hope, began to ache with a premonition of the darkness to come.

***

Dr. Voss led them down a long, sterile corridor to a surgical suite that reeked of antiseptic and cold metal. The harsh fluorescent lights cast erratic shadows on the walls. The room was clinical, unyielding, a place where hope and despair collided in a single, tense moment. Leo recoiled at the gleaming surgical table, its leather straps, and cold, unforgiving steel restraints. "Eth... don't," he whispered, his voice trembling as fear gripped him.

Ethan forced a reassuring smile, but inside, his heart pounded with dread. "It's okay," he lied, the words tasting like ash. He had promised no more lies, but in this shattered world, he had no choice. Dr. Voss moved with efficiency, drawing a syringe and slowly filling it with Leo's blood. The fluid filled the vial gradually, as though even it resisted its extraction.

"His cells are consuming themselves," Dr. Voss murmured, her voice steady but tinged with cold finality. Her eyes stayed locked on the vial's swirling substance. "The stabilizer might extend his life by weeks... or even months."

Ethan's voice sliced through the silence, sharp and urgent: "Or what?" His tone held desperate frustration, a plea for an answer that might heal the fractures in their world.

"Or nothing," Dr. Voss replied without looking up, injecting the serum into Leo's fragile neck. Instantly, Leo's body convulsed violently. His form racked with a primal scream that shattered the sterile stillness. His limbs jerked uncontrollably; his face contorted as the serum coursed through him. In that agonizing moment, his fused hand, a grotesque blend of metal and flesh, began to unravel, as though the very essence of his being was tearing itself apart.

Ethan lunged forward, pinning Leo down. Tears streamed down his face as he held the boy tightly. "Make it stop!" Leo cried, his voice cracking under the weight of his anguish. His cry was not that of a baby but a scream from the depths of despair, raw and unfiltered, echoing off the walls and reaching the souls of everyone who heard it.

Dr. Voss remained clinical: "It's working. The mutation is reversing." Yet her eyes betrayed a deep sadness, aware that their efforts might only delay the inevitable.

A tense silence settled, broken only by the staccato beeping of the cardiac monitor and the labored breathing of the suffering child. Ethan pulled Leo close, his heartbeat wild with fear. Mia's eyes, wide with silent terror, darted between Ethan and Dr. Voss, desperate for reassurance, any sign that salvation was still possible.

In that moment, as the clinical hum of machinery underscored the catastrophic transformation unfolding before them, every breath and every heartbeat became a plea, a desperate cry for a miracle in a world gone mad.

12.3: Only Days, At Most

While Leo slept soundly in his makeshift bed, Ethan and Mia ventured deeper into the bunker's lower levels. The passageways were cloaked in dim, oppressive light, and the air hummed with the hissing of malfunctioning hydraulics and the distant drone of long-forgotten machinery. Each footstep echoed, as if the bunker itself mourned a lost world, its walls scarred by neglect and decay. The corridors twisted like veins in a dying creature, leaving behind remnants of a once-advanced facility now silent in ruin.

As they moved further into the bunker's underbelly, they came across what seemed to be a cell block. Behind a thick pane of reinforced glass, a group of figures, children altered beyond recognition, watched them intently. Their eyes were cold and calculating, like shards of broken glass, tracking every movement with unnerving precision. These were not the feral children of the early days; they were older now, remnants of GeneCorp's first experiments. Their bodies, unnaturally preserved yet grotesquely mutated, spoke of a time when cruel and desperate science traded humanity for a twisted semblance of control.

Among them, one girl stood out. With auburn hair, reminiscent of Clara's, she pressed a trembling palm against the glass, seeking solace or connection. Her voice, hollow and mechanical, drifted across the barrier:

"Subject A-9's anomaly is unique. GeneCorp requires further study."

The words hit Ethan like cold shards, intensifying the dread that coiled within him. He recoiled, the image of their haunted eyes seared into his memory. These children were living test subjects, victims of a failed experiment, their minds twisted by the relentless virus. They were no longer innocent; they had become grotesque instruments of science, relics of a broken promise of eternal youth and enhanced life.

Before Ethan and Mia could fully process the disturbing scene, Dr. Voss stepped from the shadows. Her presence was sterile, detached, like the cold, white walls around them. She moved with the efficiency of someone numbed by too much. "GeneCorp tried to fix them," she said, her voice flat, emotionless. "But the virus... it adapts." Her words were clinical, as though describing a malfunctioning machine instead of lives in decay.

Mia's eyes filled with fury as she stepped forward. "You created them," she spat, her voice rising with raw intensity. "I saved them," Dr. Voss countered, gesturing toward a monitor where Leo's vitals flickered weakly, a silent testament to the virus's relentless assault on his fragile body. "Your brother's body is rejecting the serum. He has only days, at most."

The weight of those words struck Ethan like a physical blow. In that cold, dim corridor, the stakes were clear: their precious Leo, once a symbol of hope, was slipping away. His future was being written in dying cells and unfulfilled promises. The images of the mutated children, their eyes devoid of warmth, mixed with the hum of machinery, creating a dissonant symphony of despair.

Ethan's heart pounded as he exchanged a glance with Mia, a silent, desperate plea for answers in a world that no longer offered any. Each beat of his heart echoed the slow countdown of Leo's remaining days. The cavernous silence of the bunker pressed in on them, making every whispered word and labored breath a testament to their shared anguish.

Dr. Voss, her face as impassive as stone, continued in a monotone voice that revealed nothing of the turmoil she must have felt. "The virus is rewriting his DNA," she explained. "It's accelerating growth and mutating cells beyond recognition.

What was meant to be a cure has become a curse. While I can slow it down, I can't stop it completely."

Her words were a stark reminder of their inescapable reality, they were fighting a losing battle against an enemy that was both biological and inevitable. As Ethan and Mia absorbed the gravity of the situation, the memory of a simpler time, before the virus, before GeneCorp's cruel experiments, seemed to fade into the background.

All that remained was the harsh now, every moment borrowed.

In that moment of shared despair and determination, the cold reality of their situation crystallized. They had to hold onto whatever dwindling hope remained. Clinging to each other, their eyes locked in silent solidarity, they felt the eerie hum of the bunker's machinery merge with the heartbeat of a dying world. And somewhere in that relentless darkness, the fate of Ethan's baby brother and Mia's newly found little brother, and their own, hung in the balance, a fragile thread of life threatened by a force that refused to be undone.

12.4: Countdown to When I Stop

Leo's scream tore through the bunker like a signal flare in hell, shrieking through both air and mind. It felt as if the very structure of his bones had cracked under an invisible pressure, each fracture echoing with a resounding, agonized snap. His small frame convulsed as he cried out, "They're in my head, Eth! The numbers!" His voice, raw with terror and confusion, reverberated off the cold walls, filling the space with desperate urgency.

Ethan's heart pounded as he pulled Leo into a tight embrace, clinging desperately to his trembling little brother. He tried to soothe him, to hold him together, even as the sound of

Leo's distress threatened to tear him apart. "What numbers, Leo?" Ethan pleaded, his voice thick with fear and sorrow, searching for any explanation that might quell the torment in his brother's eyes.

Through the haze of panic, Leo managed to gasp, "Countdowns... to when she takes over," Leo whispered, eyes wide, voice trembling. "To when I stop being me." His words, heavy with the promise of an ending he feared, trailed off as his pupils dilated, the familiar blue of his eyes darkening into an encroaching void. "I don't want to stop," he whimpered, the raw emotion of his plea mingling with the quiet despair that had been building inside him.

At that moment, Dr. Voss appeared in the doorway, an imposing figure, as cold and clinical as the sterile room itself. In her hand, she held a syringe that glowed with an eerie blue light, its luminescence a stark contrast to the surrounding darkness. "Final option," she stated flatly, her tone devoid of any empathy. "A retrovirus. It will kill the mutation. Or him."

Ethan's eyes rested on the syringe, then on Leo's face, on his brother's agony, on his countdown. The weight was unbearable. Slowly, Ethan reached for his brother and, caressing Leo's cheek tenderly, whispered, "If I could take it for you, I would."

The gravity of every choice, every consequence, seemed to converge in that single, shining needle. "You don't know?" he asked, turning to Dr. Voss, his voice cracking with a mixture of disbelief and despair.

"Science has become guesswork," Dr. Voss replied, her voice as detached as if she were reading from a textbook rather than addressing a living, suffering child. Her eyes, cold and unyielding, offered no comfort, only a clinical inevitability that seemed to seal Leo's fate.

Then, as if summoning the last vestiges of his courage, Leo's small hand shot out with desperate resolve. With trembling fingers, he grasped the syringe, his eyes wide and haunted. "Do it," he whispered, his voice echoing the stark, painful truth that had taken root in his mind. It was a plea for relief, for an end to the relentless agony that was tearing him apart from the inside.

In that agonizing moment, time seemed to slow. Every heartbeat and every ragged breath resonated with the intensity of a final countdown. Ethan's heart shattered further as he realized that the cruel hands of fate were closing in on them. The retrovirus was a double-edged sword, it could provide a temporary reprieve by halting the mutation, but it also risked extinguishing the spark of life within his precious brother.

The sterile, flickering light of the room, the cold metal of the syringe, and the raw terror in Leo's eyes merged into an overwhelming moment of both despair and hope. In that instant, each second felt like agony and salvation, a fragile thread on which Leo's future, and perhaps all of theirs, hung in precarious balance.

The retrovirus surged, setting Leo ablaze from within. His body convulsed, limbs jerking uncontrollably while frothy blood began to form at the corners of his lips. In the dim, flickering light of the control room, Dr. Voss cursed under her breath, fingers flying over the control panel as alarms blared in a discordant chorus. "Cardiac arrest! I need..." she barked, panic and scientific detachment mixing in her voice.

Before she could finish, Ethan lunged forward, shoving her aside with raw desperation. "Leo! Stay with me!" he cried, his voice cracking with fear and determination. His plea echoed off the sterile walls, merging with the beeps of failing monitors and the mechanical whir of the retrovirus causing chaos.

Mia, unable to hold back her grief, broke into uncontrollable tears. Her infected hand trembled as she clutched Leo's fragile one, as if her touch alone could revive him. With her other hand, she cupped his disheveled hair, her whispered refrain, "Leo, Leo...," a broken mantra, a desperate plea to stave off the inevitable.

Then, in an instant that froze time, Leo let out a guttural, primal scream. It was so raw and otherworldly that it shattered the already failing lights, sending monitors into a chaotic frenzy. In that moment, the cells of the Accelerates, twisted remnants of human life, seemed to rupture in unison. Their collective agony filled the room, a macabre symphony of anguish. Nearby Accelerates collapsed, their cries and frantic clawing at their ears creating an atmosphere of unmitigated horror.

Amidst the chaos, Leo's gaze locked with Ethan's. There was something eerily calm in his eyes, a resigned acceptance that belied the turmoil within him. In a soft, almost imperceptible voice, Leo whispered, "I fixed it," a statement so detached from the pain surrounding him that it sent a chill down Ethan's spine. Then, as abruptly as it had started, the scream faded, and Leo fell silent, his body slumping into stillness.

He sounded not like a boy, but something else entirely, something that had glimpsed the edge of the world and chosen not to fall.

Dr. Voss's face drained of color as she checked the monitors. "He is... asleep," she said flatly, her voice lacking the urgency from moments before, as if reciting a grim fact rather than witnessing a miracle, or a tragedy.

Ethan cradled Leo's hand, light as fragile kindling, and a surge of fury and despair washed over him. "You're all monsters," he spat, his voice a mix of anguish and bitter rage directed at the unseen forces that had tormented his baby brother.

In the haunting silence that followed, every sound, the distant beeps, the failing machinery's heavy thud, and the quiet rhythm of Leo's shallow breaths served as a poignant reminder of their shattered world. The room, once filled with sterile hums of science and hope, now pulsed with the raw agony of loss and the desperate struggle to survive. Each of Leo's fragile heartbeats, every tear shed by Mia, and Ethan's anguished cry underscored a bitter truth: in this forsaken world, the line between human and monster had blurred beyond recognition.

12.4: Dormant Hope

The bunker's hydroponic garden stood as a sorrowful relic, a forgotten shrine to what once was, now overtaken by despair. Wilted lettuce leaves drooped from their stalks, their edges browned and brittle. Shriveling tomatoes lay scattered like discarded dreams, while herbs that once exuded fresh, vibrant aromas were now choked by the relentless encroachment of wild ivy. This garden, once a symbol of nourishment and renewal, now mirrored the desolation of a world long abandoned by hope.

Mia clawed through cracked dirt, eyes wild with grief, each motion a silent plea for something, anything alive. "There has to be something, seeds, spores, anything," she murmured, her voice raw with frustration and yearning. In the dim light filtering through the bunker's battered ceiling, every handful of soil was heavy with memory, the promise of a harvest, the hope of rebirth. Each clump of dirt felt like the potential start of a new beginning.

Ethan stood in the doorway, arms crossed, his gaze fixed on Mia with quiet, weary resignation. He had witnessed too much loss and too many wasted moments to indulge in hope without caution. "You're wasting calories," he remarked softly, his tone pragmatic, tinged with bitterness. Yet, his eyes betrayed a deeper worry, every ounce of energy spent in fruitless labor was energy they might need for survival.

Mia's eyes flashed with defiance as she tossed a clump of soil at him. "You're wasting time. Help me or shut up," she snapped, her voice trembling with urgency and raw determination. The accusation hung in the stale air, thick with decay and the hum of failing systems.

After a long, resigned sigh, Ethan stepped away from the doorway and joined Mia on the cold ground. The silence between them was broken only by the rustle of dead leaves skittering across the dirt and the distant mechanical hum of ancient machinery struggling to function in a dying world.

Leo drifted into view, pale and fragile, like a memory made flesh among the wreckage. Clutching Mr. Bubbles tightly to his chest, the little boy's eyes shimmered with a blend of wonder and quiet sorrow. Despite his weakened state, Leo managed a tentative smile and asked softly, "Are we farming?" His innocent words cut through the hardened tension.

"Trying," Mia muttered, not looking up from her task. Her tone held exhaustion, but beneath it pulsed unyielding hope. A stubborn refusal to let the world's cruelty extinguish even the smallest spark of life.

With utmost care, Leo reached down and poked at the cracked soil. His small fingers unearthed a shriveled carrot, its once-vibrant orange skin now mottled with patches of black. His eyes lit up with curiosity and childlike wonder as he held the limp vegetable in his tiny hands. "Can we plant this?" he asked, his voice soft but filled with the weight of hope only a child could possess.

Ethan frowned, glancing briefly at the withered carrot before shaking his head. "It's dead," he replied curtly, his tone a mix of sorrow and resignation, as if every dead seed were a reminder of all that had been lost.

But Leo, ever the beacon of stubborn innocence, cradled the carrot as if it were a fragile treasure. With tender care, he placed it beside Mr. Bubbles on the ground. "Maybe it just needs a friend," he murmured, his voice a blend of optimism and melancholy.

In that moment, the battered hydroponic garden became more than just a symbol of decay; it transformed into a silent testament to the fragility of hope in a ravaged world. Each wilted leaf, every shriveled tomato, and every choking vine of ivy spoke of lives cut short, and dreams left unfulfilled. Yet within the despair, there remained a stubborn ember, a spark of life that, if nurtured, might one day bloom again.

Ethan gazed down at Leo's earnest face, the tiny carrot cradled gently in his small hand and felt a surge of conflicting emotions, a deep sadness for all that had been lost, and a fierce, defiant hope that perhaps, against all odds, they could rebuild. Mia, wiping a smear of dirt from her determined eyes, scanned the desolate garden before turning to the children. Their shared silence was thick with unspoken promises: to keep fighting, to scavenge every trace of life from the ruins, and to hold onto the fragile hope that, even in the darkest times, renewal might be possible.

The cracked earth, the garden's remnants, the children's faces, each a stark reminder of their desperation. But even as the world around them crumbled, the simple act of planting, even a dead carrot, became an act of rebellion against fate. In that small, ruined garden beneath the bunker, hope was not dead; it lay dormant, waiting to sprout if only they dared to believe.

12.5: A Hum in the Hallow

The fluorescent lights in the bunker buzzed with a low, steady hum, casting a pallid glow over the sterile room. In the dim light, Ethan sat slouched in a worn swivel chair, his tired eyes reflecting the collapse of a world he no longer knew. The burden of responsibility and regret pressed heavily on him, every passing moment deepening his despair.

Across from him, Leo lay curled on a moth-eaten cot, his shallow breathing the only sound in the otherwise silent room. Ethan had wrapped a GeneCorp lab coat around him, a poor substitute for warmth, but the dark veins snaking up Leo's neck remained stark, a grotesque marker of the retrovirus consuming him.

At the observation window, Mia stood motionless, her palms pressed flat against the cracked glass. The hallway outside stretched into darkness, shadows shifting behind sealed doors. Through the fractured reflection, she saw the ghostly forms of the Accelerates, children twisted beyond recognition, flickering like phantoms against the desolate corridors. Dr. Voss's words echoed in the stale air: "No cure. No future. Humanity's final generation." That prophecy pressed down on them, squeezing life from every breath.

Mia broke the silence, her voice trembling. "We can wait for Aida and Dr. Jacobson to come back, look for others," she said, her words tentative with a fragile hope. "Clara mentioned survivors up north."

Ethan's voice cut through her optimism, low and resigned. "You heard Voss," he said, bitterness threading his words. "The virus is airborne. It infects every newborn until seven. Even if there's someone left, they're already doomed."

In that moment, Leo stirred, his eyes opening slowly. The once-vibrant blue had darkened, clouded by the encroaching virus. "Eth? I'm cold," he whispered, his fragile voice carrying the weight of both innocence and impending doom.

Ethan draped his jacket over Leo's shoulders, trying to ward off the cold threading into his bones. The sight of those dark veins, the grotesque reminder of the virus's relentless assault, made Ethan's blood run cold. It had been two days since the retrovirus had failed to contain the infection, two days since the seizures had begun.

Mia turned toward Ethan, her reflection fractured in the cracked window, like splinters of a past that refused to heal. "So, we just... wait?" Her voice was a mix of despair and defiance, questioning whether waiting was even an option anymore in a world so broken.

Ethan's reply was heavy, a bitter truth he couldn't deny. "We should ask Voss to check your infected arm and continue monitoring it." His words tasted like ash, every syllable a reminder of their grim reality, of the slow decay that had taken hold of them. Hope was a ghost, flickering just beyond belief.

In the small, desolate room, the trio sat in fragile silence, the hum of failing machinery and the quiet breaths of the dying child filling the space. Every moment felt suspended, a battle between holding on and letting go. As they gazed at the shadows beyond the window, they could almost hear echoes of a world full of promise, now reduced to memories, haunting and distant.

But within that silence, a spark of resilience flickered, an understanding that, even amidst the virus's relentless advance, they would fight, they would protect, and they would hope. In that fragile cocoon of humanity, every breath, every heartbeat, every whispered word was a defiant stand against the encroaching darkness.

Chapter 13: The Baby That Stole the Stars

13.1: When the Numbers Stop

That night, the bunker's air was thick with dread and despair. The fluorescent lights flickered erratically overhead, casting long, wavering shadows across the cold metal cot where Leo lay. Suddenly, his fever spiked. His small body convulsed violently, thrashing as if overwhelmed by an unseen storm. His tiny hands clawed at his chest, trying to expel the searing pain. "Make the numbers stop! Make them stop!" he cried, his voice raw with panic, a primal scream that echoed through the sterile, oppressive room.

Ethan, heart pounding, leaped into action. With strength born of desperation and love, he rushed to Leo's side, gripping his brother's shoulders and pinning him to the cot in a futile attempt to ground him. "What numbers, Leo? Tell me!" he demanded, his voice trembling with fear and hope, grasping for an explanation to halt the relentless virus consuming his brother.

Leo's eyes, once vibrant blue, now seemed hollow, darkness swallowing what remained of his soul. In a voice trembling with terror, Leo gasped, "Countdowns... to when I... go away." His words were heavy with resignation, a desperate admission of a fate he could not escape. "I don't want to go, Eth," he pleaded, his voice vulnerable, filled with a fear that no child should bear.

Mia, unable to hold back her tears any longer, hurried over. Her infected arm trembled as she retrieved a damp cloth and pressed it to Leo's burning forehead. Her own hands shook uncontrollably as she tried to comfort him. "Tell us about the numbers, Leo. Maybe we can fix them together. Please," she urged, her voice breaking with sorrow and desperate need for understanding. Each word clung desperately to hope.

For a long, excruciating moment, Leo's voice turned cold and mechanical. "Subject A-9's cellular decay is irreversible. Estimated viability: 33 hours," he stated, his tone devoid of warmth, as if the virus had stolen his humanity. The words struck Ethan like a physical blow, twisting horror deep in his gut. "That's not you, Leo. That's the virus talking," he insisted, his voice raw with disbelief and heartache.

Leo blinked slowly, the blue of his eyes flickering weakly through the consuming darkness. "But I'm scared," he whispered, his small voice barely audible over the hum of failing machinery in the background.

Mia, filled with desperate resolve, reached for Ethan's frayed notebook, a battered journal full of scribbled notes and fading hope. Her hands, stained with sorrow and sweat, opened it carefully and handed it to him. "Write it down. Everything he says. Maybe... maybe it matters," she implored, her words trembling with the weight of their shared agony.

Ethan took the notebook, his fingers brushing the worn paper as he began recording Leo's every word. The act felt like both ritual and prayer, an effort to give shape to the unspeakable. Outside, the bunker's walls hummed with the distant echo of a lost world, while inside, the raw emotion of that moment pulsed like a heartbeat on the verge of breaking.

In the dim, sterile space, the reality of their existence pressed down on them. Each word Leo spoke was a testament to the cruelty fate had dealt. A countdown to an inevitable end they weren't prepared to face. Ethan's chest heaved as he wrote, each number marking Leo's fading time.

The fluorescent lights above buzzed and flickered, each stutter a reminder of their unstable lives. Every sound, the scrape of a pen, the hum of failing systems, Leo's labored breaths, was magnified by the oppressive weight of despair. In that moment, hope and desperation intertwined, creating a bittersweet symphony of human frailty and unyielding love.

Ethan's eyes, filled with unshed tears, locked with Leo's. In that silent exchange, words were unnecessary. They shared a profound understanding that this moment, heavy with agony and impending loss, was a final stand against the encroaching darkness. Each heartbeat, every ragged whisper from Leo, was both a plea for help and a defiant proclamation that they would fight until the very end, no matter the cost, no matter the sorrow threatening to consume them.

13.2: The Day the Universe Wept

Leo's final hours were a fevered blur, his world fragmented, time and space collapsing into a haze of fragmented thoughts and relentless equations. His body, once full of energy, now lay frail and trembling beneath the virus consuming him. His eyes, once bright, had become dark pools of confusion, locked on the spiraling vortex of numbers that haunted him.

Curled in the dim corner of the bunker, Leo's fingers twitched as though trying to grasp invisible threads in the air. He scribbled frantically on the walls, leaving jagged charcoal marks, his movements frantic. "If I solve it... the numbers stop," he murmured, clinging to a solution that slipped further away with each passing moment.

Ethan stood there, gutted, and useless, his hands twitching with the need to do something, fix something, but there was nothing left to fix. His heart howled as he watched his baby brother, once laughter and light, now trembling wreckage, hollowed out by the thing eating him alive. His voice cracked as he asked, "What numbers, Leo?" Desperation colored his gaze, hunting for any answer that might halt the torment.

Leo's hands shook, the chalk slipping from his fingers like dust. His eyes, once full of life, were distant, unfocused. He spoke with the certainty of someone grasping at the remnants of a fading dream. "Everything," he whispered. The word hung between them, heavy with meaning but wrapped in confusion. His breath grew shallow, as if each word drained him further. "It's too big... too heavy..." His voice trailed off, filled with sorrow, embodying the weight of every burden he could no longer bear.

Ethan's hands trembled as he tried to steady Leo, but his brother was slipping away, beyond his reach. The cruel truth loomed, Leo was already lost, the virus tearing him apart from the inside. Yet, Ethan refused to let go. He couldn't.

Mia appeared in the doorway, her face pale, the weight of everything pressing on her. She hurried over, her hands finding their place alongside Ethan's as they gently lifted Leo from the floor. He felt impossibly light, too fragile in their arms as they carried him toward the rooftop access door.

Together, they forced the rusted door open, its groan echoing through the bunker's hollow silence. Outside, thick black smoke blanketed the sky, choking the air, casting everything in a dull, oppressive haze. The sun sagged low, bloated, and red, as if it, too, were dying. Its blood-tinged light cast an eerie glow, mirroring the desolation inside them.

Leo managed to lift his gaze to the sky. His voice was weak, but his words cut through the gloom like a blade. "Look, Eth," he whispered, his voice filled with a fragile wonder. "The sky's not sad anymore."

Ethan's heart tightened as he cradled Leo closer, holding him against the oppressive heat of the sun, but feeling only the warmth of his brother's fragile body. "It's beautiful," he whispered, his voice breaking, the grief overwhelming. It was all he could offer, a final gift, a simple truth wrapped in pain.

Leo's eyes fluttered, his breath shallow. "Ethan..." he whispered again, the name so soft, it felt like a prayer. "Tell me the astronaut story..."

The request froze Ethan's heart, so small, so innocent. The astronaut story, the one Ethan had told a hundred times, was Leo's favorite. A tale of adventure, a boy reaching for the stars, escaping the Earth's gravity to a place where nothing could hurt him. The idea of flying beyond the world's cruel grasp had always been Leo's dream.

Ethan swallowed, the pain in his throat unbearable, and began the story in a strained whisper. "Once, there was a boy who wanted to catch the stars..."

But Leo's hand slipped from his grasp, falling limp at his side. The story hung unfinished, suspended like a breath never taken.

Time held its breath.

The world froze as the boy who had dreamed of soaring among the stars lay still in Ethan's arms. The wind, once gentle, froze in its path. The sky, painted in hues of red and orange, seemed suspended, a cruel reminder of the life snuffed out far too soon. Ethan stood motionless, breathless, his heart shattering with the weight of Leo's absence.

Mia stood beside them, her eyes devoid of tears, there were none left. Her hand found Ethan's shoulder, but even her touch could not soothe the agony that tore through him. The words left unspoken loomed between them, a chasm that no comfort could bridge.

The silence stretched on, suffocating them, pressing down with unbearable weight. There were no more equations to solve, no more numbers to chase. Only the raw, unbearable pain of a world that had taken too much remained, leaving hollow spaces where dreams once lived.

In that moment, the sky, the wind, and the world seemed to hold their breath, mourning alongside them. Time ceased to matter. Only the absence of Leo remained, an aching void that would never be filled.

Then a sound shattered the silence, a piercing, otherworldly wail that didn't echo but detonated. It was a celestial scream, a blade cutting through the stillness. It wasn't made by man or machine; it was too vast, too mournful, too eternal. The air vibrated with it. The very atmosphere trembled as if the Earth itself had gasped. The bunker groaned beneath their feet, as if an ancient beast stirred in pain. Dust drifted lazily from the ceilings like ash after an explosion. In the distance, the already crumbled remnants of buildings cracked anew, their skeletal remains bowing to a force unseen and unnamed.

It felt as though the universe had wept.

Though no one said it aloud, every heart in the bunker knew: that sound was Leo's final echo, a dying star collapsing in on itself, a soul turning to light, then to nothing.

As suddenly as it had come, silence swallowed the world once more. But this silence wasn't the same, it wasn't the absence of voices or movement. This was deeper, more unsettling. A vacuum. An absolute void. No distant moans of Accelerates roaming the scorched wasteland. No claws scraping against reinforced steel. No groaning of mutated creatures hungry in the dark. Not even the hum of the failing generator dared break the stillness. Time itself seemed to have halted to mourn.

Inside the containment wing, the caged Accelerates, those cobalt-blue-eyed, once-human beings infected by the same twisted virus, froze, as if thunderstruck. Their usual writhing, snarling, and scratching ceased in unison. They turned slowly, blinking in confusion, no longer the feral predators they had become. Something ancient shifted inside them, beyond the reach of science or reason. Their monstrous breathing slowed, and their dilated eyes filled with tears.

One by one, they retreated into the corners of their cells like frightened children during a storm. Some dropped to the cold floor, trembling. Others sat upright, cross-legged, eyes downcast in reverence or regret. Silent tears tracked down bloodstained cheeks. No more guttural growls, no vicious screeches, only stillness. Grief.

It was as if Leo's death had triggered an unexplainable metamorphosis. The boy they had fought so hard to save had reached beyond death to touch something in them that still remembered love, pain, and humanity. The Accelerates no longer appeared as monsters. In that moment, they resembled broken cherubs, mourners shrouded in shadows, trembling amid the wreckage of their own ruin.

13.3: Echo of the Dying Star

After the wail, Ethan, Mia, and Dr. Voss stirred, barely regaining consciousness. For a moment, they thought they might have dreamed it. Their heads throbbed, their vision blurred, and their balance felt unsure. They looked around, dazed, as if surfacing from a shared hallucination, minds aching from something that defied all logic. Mia blinked hard, rubbing her face as if trying to scrub away the unreality. Ethan groaned as he pushed himself upright, feeling aches in places he hadn't noticed before. Dr. Voss swayed, bracing herself against the cold steel wall. Their voices emerged in soft whispers, slurred and uncertain.

"What was that?" Mia croaked.

No one had an answer.

When the weight of what had happened finally settled, when the stillness became unbearable, and the truth crept back in like a bitter wind, they gathered Leo's lifeless body in their arms.

They carried him through cold, sterile corridors, their footsteps echoing like thunder through the void he left behind. They passed empty labs, where shattered glass and faded monitors stood as mute witnesses to humanity's ambition and hubris. The overhead lights flickered sporadically, casting them in and out of shadows as they moved.

In the operating room, they gently laid Leo on the surgical table. His limbs hung limp, his lips slightly parted as though he were about to speak again. One hand remained curled tightly around Mr. Bubbles, the once-plush toy that Aida had lovingly repaired, now stained with tears.

Dr. Voss stood beside the table, her hands trembling as she reached for a half-burnt, soot-smudged surgical sheet. For a moment, she hesitated, her fingers hovering just above the boy's still chest. Her eyes brimmed with something ancient and heavy, guilt calcified over years of helplessness. She gently pulled the sheet over his body, leaving only his face exposed.

That face, peaceful now, free from the torment that had plagued him in his final hours, looked more like the baby boy in the photographs. The gold of his curls shimmered faintly under the harsh fluorescent lights. His cheeks were pale but soft. The pain was gone. The numbers were gone.

Mia and Ethan stood at the table, their shoulders touching. Neither had the strength to speak. Too exhausted to rage, too heartbroken to pretend they were still strong, they cried without restraint, silently, like the teenagers they still were, for the first time since the world had ended. Their silent sobs tore through the sterile room, raw, animalistic, born not just of sorrow but of grief made primal and absolute. They were the silent tears of children hidden too long from the light, tears from those who had carried too much, seen too much, and lost everything that once made the world feel safe.

Time crawled. The air thickened. Silence reclaimed the room like fog creeping over a field of graves.

Then Mia jolted.

She gasped sharply and grabbed Ethan's arm. "Ethan... my hand..."

Panic exploded in his chest. Dread pooled like ice water in his stomach. Not her too, he thought. Please, not her.

"What is it?" he demanded, already bracing for the worst.

Mia turned her wrist and extended her arm toward him. Her voice trembled, but not with fear. It was filled with wonder.

"Look," she whispered.

Ethan squinted. Her veins, those horrible, pulsing black lines that had been creeping up her arm toward her throat, were receding. Slowly, almost imperceptibly, they were retreating back toward the original wound. The tendrils of death uncoiled from her bloodstream, like smoke returning to a shattered bottle.

"Mia, the virus is receding," Dr. Voss said from behind them, her voice no longer detached and clinical, but stunned, almost reverent. She blinked hard and stepped forward, her hands no longer shaking. "We'll know more after I test your blood... but this... this is impossible."

Mia and Ethan exchanged a glance, their faces streaked with tears, disbelief etched into every line. They didn't know how to interpret it. Was it Leo? Had his death somehow shifted the makeup of the virus? Had he saved them after all?

That night, the three of them didn't really sleep. There was no rest, only the stillness that follows a storm, when nothing has yet been rebuilt, but everything has changed.

Ethan sat beside Leo's covered body, his fingers resting on the sheet near the boy's hand, as if proximity alone could hold onto the warmth that was already gone. He didn't speak; words felt useless.

Mia curled up on the operating room bench, clutching Mr. Bubbles to her chest, silent tears carving rivers down her cheeks. She kept glancing at her arm, afraid the black veins would return the moment she looked away.

Dr. Voss remained in her lab, analyzing Mia's blood under flickering lights, whispering prayers she hadn't spoken since childhood. Every cell she examined felt like a betrayal of science, and a gift from the divine.

No one dared speak of hope. Not yet.

They were the remnants now, survivors of a war they didn't understand, heirs to a world shattered by ambition and perhaps, just barely, restored by a child too fragile to endure... and too extraordinary to forget.

In the silence of the bunker, beside the boy who once dreamed of stars, humanity held its breath.

And they waited.

13.4: He Taught Us Beauty

At dawn, three children emerged from the misted veil of night like fragile apparitions, drawn together by fate, and something older than reason. Cold and unyielding, the bunker's perimeter cameras captured every movement as the children pressed their faces against the glass, their wide eyes reflecting a blend of wonder and sorrow. These were Accelerates, but not like those of old; their eyes, once wild with unrestrained madness, now shimmered with an eerie calm, as if they had learned to coexist with their affliction. Their postures, once predatory and unhinged, had softened into something more contemplative, even melancholic.

The eldest among them, a girl of about twelve with lustrous copper hair reminiscent of Mia's own, stepped forward. In her delicate hands, she held a sunflower whose petals glowed in an unnatural shade of gold, radiating a soft, almost ethereal light in the dim morning glow. Its vibrant hue pierced the gloom like a relic of beauty long thought extinct.

Inside the control room, Mia gripped Ethan's hand tightly, her knuckles whitening with tension as she watched the scene unfold on the surveillance feed. "They... they don't look sick at all," she whispered, her voice trembling with disbelief. Ethan leaned closer, zooming in on the screen until the images became crystal clear. On the monitors were three angelic faces, each radiating a sadness too deep for their age, their large eyes reflecting a silent, shared grief.

Before anyone could speak further, Dr. Voss appeared behind them, her presence slicing through the heavy silence like a scalpel through tissue. Her lab coat, stained and worn, still carried an air of resigned authority. "The virus is dying inside," she announced, her voice wavering with both sorrow and disbelief. "Leo's death was the cure." Her words echoed in the room, reverberating off the cold, metallic surfaces. For a moment, time seemed to slow, as if the universe itself mourned the loss of a life that once had held so much promise.

Ethan's gaze remained fixed on the sunflower, its petals glowing with a defiant shimmer, a symbol of life persisting in the face of relentless decay. "Let them in," he finally said, his tone resolute, as if that simple command could bridge the chasm between the past and a fragile new future.

At the bunker's threshold, the eldest girl, reluctant envoy of a changed species, watched as her companions stepped beside her. Her bright, unwavering eyes focused on the screen displaying Leo's genome, a complex array of numbers and letters pulsing rhythmically.

With unnerving calm, she declared, "We have come for the remains of Subject A-9." Her voice was measured and disturbingly detached as she continued, "His code must be preserved." The words fell like ice in the stillness of the room, carrying a weight that belied her youthful appearance.

"We have evolved," she continued with quiet certainty, though an unspoken weight hung behind her words, heavy with the burden of knowledge. "We no longer wish to destroy; we want to... remember." Her voice carried the sorrow of generations and the desperate hope for a future that might still be salvaged.

Mia's response was immediate, a sharp, bitter laugh that echoed through the room. "Nonsense. You killed Clara. You killed everyone." Her words, sharp with fury and heartbreak, accused the girl of a betrayal so deep it fractured language itself.

The girl's expression softened, a flicker of regret momentarily passing through her eyes. "That's how we were designed," she replied, her voice now tinged with something almost sorrowful. "The virus rewrites us. And now... we feel remorse." Her tone was haunting, mesmerizing, like someone describing the turning of the Earth or the ache of memory.

Dr. Voss stepped forward, her gaze narrowing into a steely glare. "What do you want?" she demanded, her question a challenge, a call for accountability in a world where nothing seemed to matter anymore.

"An exchange," the girl replied calmly, her words measured and controlled. "Our genetic archives in return for the anomaly of Subject A-9." Her voice lacked malice, yet it carried an unmistakable undercurrent of finality, as if the fate of countless lives hinged on this transaction.

Before anyone could react, Ethan's hunting knife flashed into view, pressed firmly against the girl's throat. His eyes burned with protective fury as he growled, "His name is Leo, not Subject A-9, and you will not touch him." The knife's edge glinted under the harsh fluorescent lights, a cold reminder of the violence that had become their daily reality.

The girl, unflinching and resolute, met his gaze with unnerving calm. "We have your mother's notes," she said, her voice quiet but insistent. "All the notes from the original hormonal experiments. Perhaps... the cure." Her words lingered in the air, fragile with hope, both terrifying and tempting.

Mia's face twisted with disbelief, her eyes wide as she whispered, "You're lying." In response, the girl slowly extended her palm. A soft blue light unfurled from a small device, casting a hologram of a DNA strand interwoven with the delicate helix of a sunflower. The ethereal light bathed her face in a gentle glow, and her voice dropped to a near-whisper. "We learned beauty... from him. From Leo."

In that charged moment, the room seemed to hold its breath. Every eye was fixed on the hologram, each person caught between the harsh reality of their shattered world and the fragile promise of something beyond destruction. The truth in the girl's words, combined with the weight of loss that hung in the air, created an atmosphere thick with both despair and hope.

Ethan's heart pounded in his chest as he struggled to process the revelation. Leo, whose life had become a battleground for conflicting destinies, now symbolized something far greater than a mere anomaly. He had become both a relic of innocence and a prototype of something new, an impossible contradiction too sacred to reduce to code.

As the hologram's soft light pulsed rhythmically, each beat resonated with the silent agony of those who had been lost. Ethan, Mia, and Dr. Voss were forced to face a brutal truth: the virus had not only reshaped lives, but it had also rewritten the very meaning of being human. In the cold, unyielding confines of the bunker, surrounded by the remnants of a once-bright future, they were all bound by a shared and painful reality, a truth that spoke of redemption, hope, and a destiny forever intertwined with the enigmatic, mournful soul of Leo.

As the sun began to rise, casting a pale, trembling light over their desolate sanctuary, they realized that, regardless of the cost, they would fight to preserve not only the legacy of Subject A-9 but also the very essence of what it meant to remember, to love, and to live in the face of overwhelming darkness.

13.5: The Words Remain

They buried Leo's writings, not his body. The Accelerates insisted, "The body decays. The words remain." In the heart of the ruined bunker, amidst shattered screens and faded posters of a once-hopeful future, Mia found a battered notebook tucked beneath Leo's bed. Its pages were scrawled with frantic equations, sketches of stars and rockets, and a single desperate line repeated like a mantra: *I don't want to go.* Each repetition was a plea, a raw cry against the darkness looming just beyond the margins of their fragile world.

Mia's fingers trembled as she traced the faded ink, trying to grasp the weight behind Leo's words. They spoke of dreams and fears intertwined, of a boy who once looked toward the heavens with wonder and curiosity. In that notebook, Leo became more than a victim of circumstance; he was a chronicler of loss and hope, a silent guardian whose thoughts were etched into fragile pages like a secret code meant for a future that might never come.

Across the dim light of the bunker's common room, the copper-haired girl from the Accelerate trio, the one who had carried the sunflower, studied the notebook. Her eyes were as sorrowful as the ruins beyond, her expression unreadable. "We will teach this to our future generations," she declared, her voice echoing in the still air, "if, of course, we have any." Her tone held a brittle hope, an echo of a promise to preserve what little humanity remained.

Dr. Voss, standing in the shadowed corner of the room, interjected with cold finality. "You cannot reproduce," she stated, her voice devoid of warmth. It cut through the tension like a blade. Then, with the detached calm that had become her trademark, she continued, "You will no longer grow. The virus will continue to change you until you exist with nothing but the memory of a single day. Even if you live forever, you will remain as you are now, living dolls with perfect faces like angels. Ethan and Mia's generation was the last. And so, my generation, with its selfishness, pride, vanity, and greed, has destroyed everything."

Her words lingered like a dirge, mourning a future destroyed by genetic ambition and corporate greed. The truth settled like ash over every heart in the bunker, a reminder that even beauty could be twisted into something monstrous. The girl with the notebook looked up from her reading and gazed out a broken window, where the dying light of day painted the crumbling walls in hues of red and orange. "The sunflower's pollen carries his anomaly," she murmured, her voice barely audible, as if confessing a secret to the wind. "We will see it. Let the wind decide."

Ethan's grip on Mia's hand tightened until his knuckles turned white, his heart pounding with a mix of defiance and despair. "No," he breathed, the word a weak protest against the inevitability Dr. Voss had described. But Mia, her eyes glistening and resolve etched firmly on her face, pulled her hand free. "Yes," she whispered, her voice steady, resonating with a determination born of loss and love.

They gathered the notebooks carefully, almost reverently, as if each page held the promise of Leo's memory, a beacon of hope that might still light their way through the darkness. Outside, the bunker's corridors echoed with the distant sounds of the crumbling world: the soft moan of wind through broken windows, the slow drip of water, and somewhere far away, the mechanical hum of a generator fighting against the cold.

In that moment, as they huddled together amidst the ruins, the weight of Leo's words and the bitter truths of their new existence pressed down on them. They had lost a brother, a beacon of innocent wonder, and in his absence, they were left with these fragments, a legacy of pain interwoven with glimmers of beauty. The notebook was not just paper and ink; it was Leo's voice, a lifeline to the past when hope had not yet been extinguished by the relentless march of the virus.

Mia could almost hear Leo's whisper echo through the bunker, urging them to remember the simple joys, the warmth of sun, the sound of laughter, and the faint promise of a tomorrow not yet stolen by grief. In every scrawled equation and hastily drawn rocket, there was a whisper: even in a world drowning in despair, hope could flicker again, if someone dared to believe.

As they read the pages, each word took on new meaning, creating a mosaic of memories and regrets. Dr. Voss's clinical detachment, Ethan's raw anguish, Mia's steady resolve, and the haunting echoes of Leo's repeated plea all melded into a testament to what had been lost and what might still be salvaged. It was a fragile covenant with the past, a promise that Leo's story would not vanish into oblivion.

The sun's dying rays filtered through the shattered glass, casting a golden light on the open notebook, as if nature itself were offering a blessing. In that soft glow, they made a silent vow: to preserve Leo's legacy, not as a mere casualty of a twisted experiment, but as a spark of resistance against a future that sought to erase everything they held dear. In the bunker's ruins, among shattered dreams and broken promises, Leo's words glowed like embers, quiet sparks of defiance, reminding them that even in ruin, there could still be beauty. Still be hope. Still be love.

13.6: The Baby Astronaut Who Stole the Stars

It was a bright, moonlit night, a night the world hadn't seen in a long time. The sky was free of ash, and no black clouds of soot hung above the earth. For once, the firmament stretched out pure and endless, as if the heavens themselves had finally exhaled.

The moon loomed large and luminous above the bunker, warm and kind, not cold or indifferent. It hung like an ancient guardian, a grandfather watching over Earth's children, puffing a celestial pipe, and smiling gently through a haze of stars.

It had been so long since the world had known a night like this.

The stars sparkled restlessly, flickering with unusual intensity, as though whispering excitedly among themselves. There was a palpable sense of anticipation in the air, as if the entire cosmos were holding its breath, waiting. Waiting for someone. For Leo.

They laid his body gently, delicately, reverently, into a small, pristine capsule. The casing, made of polished silver alloy, was lined with nano-weave memory foam to preserve his fragile form. It was a GeneCorp atmospheric drone, originally designed to withstand volatile storms for planetary surveys. It had never been meant for this, carrying the body of a baby boy trapped in a six-year-old's form, wrapped in a thermal shroud, clutching a worn-out teddy bear named Mr. Bubbles. The bear had once been brown, but now its matted fur was gray and threadbare, with patches sewn back together by Aida's trembling hands, her stitches crude but heartfelt.

Mia had painted the drone's outer shell by hand. Every brushstroke was slow, deliberate, filled with care. Bright golden sunflowers bloomed across the metallic hull, vivid against the dull gray, defiantly alive. Their petals curled toward the heavens, reaching for something brighter, something more. They were a tribute to Leo's favorite flower, a symbol of the hope he embodied.

Ethan had made his contribution as well. Scrawled in red paint along the side of the capsule, beneath the sunflower stems, were a series of numbers: RA 14h 39m 37s / Dec -60° 50 ' 02". These were the coordinates of Alpha Centauri, the closest star system, a direction, a destination, and a desperate hope that Leo might journey beyond the boundaries of this ruined planet to find a place untouched by war, plague, and human cruelty. Somewhere clean. Somewhere safe.

A gentle wind rustled through the grass near the bunker's edge, and in the distance, the real sound of crickets, not the synthetic mimicry of pre-programmed environments, sang softly beneath the pale moonlight. For the first time in human history, nature seemed to join in the farewell.

The Accelerate girl, still unnamed, her identity perhaps too complex for a single name, approached the control console. Her expression was unreadable: neither sad nor joyful, but something far older and more burdened. A solemn duty coursed through her as she extended one slender finger and pressed a button.

There was a mechanical whir, a high-pitched hiss, and then, lift.

The drone's engine activated silently, its propulsion almost imperceptible. Slowly, it began to rise.

Mia gasped. For a split second, she swore she saw condensation fog inside of the capsule's glass, like the breath of a sleeping child. The sunflower-painted hull caught the moonlight, glowing with ethereal brilliance as it ascended, higher and higher, through the thinning air, through the veil of clouds, toward the stars.

It pierced the sky, an arrow loosed toward forever.

Mia stood at the edge of the launchpad, her shoulders trembling, arms hanging limply by her sides. The moment the drone disappeared into the blanket of stars, her knees gave out, and she sank to the ground. Her sobs were quiet at first, choked and strangled, as if her throat had forgotten how to produce sound. But then they poured out of her in waves, raw, broken, childlike.

Her tears carved paths down cheeks once crusted with dirt and blood, softening what war had hardened. A girl who had learned to fight and survive in a world without light was now weeping like a child who had lost an adopted brother, an older sister, and her parents, not in battle, not to the virus, but to the heavens.

Ethan stood beside her, unmoving. His eyes were locked on the sky, searching for any last glimpse of the drone, though it had long since vanished. There was no noise, no vapor trail, just an empty sky echoing with silence.

His chest felt like a tomb, sealed and silent, echoing with things he would never say.

Inside, something had shattered, but it did not cry out. It did not weep. A glass shard of guilt lodged in his chest. He had held Leo's hand as it grew cold. He had felt the pulse fade away. He had whispered promises that were never fulfilled.

And Leo was gone.

The others stood in respectful silence behind them. Dr. Voss, her face carefully masking her scientific detachment, wiped a tear from the corner of her eye. Even the Accelerates, once nightmares in the shape of children, bowed their heads. The virus within them had dulled and retreated. Something about Leo's death had shifted its course. The madness had subsided, replaced by regret and, strangely, grief.

The girl with the copper hair stepped forward again, her gaze fixed on the stars above.

"Your brother," she said, her voice quiet and hollow, "was not meant to be born. But he lived anyway. He became more than code, more than anomaly, he became a spark against the dark. He became meaning."

She turned to Mia and Ethan, her expression not one of consolation but of awe.

"We do not understand it yet, but he taught us beauty and empathy. He gave us... a mirror."

Mia didn't respond; her head rested in her hands, her shoulders shaking. Her cries still clawed at the air. Ethan's fingers clenched into fists, his voice barely more than a rasp.

"He deserved to grow up."

The girl nodded once. "He will. In every one of us. In every petal of the sunflowers. In every strand of pollen. His anomaly doesn't spread through infection, but through memory."

A breeze swept across the launchpad, rustling, bending the grass, and lifting Mia's hair.

"Let the wind decide," the girl whispered.

Behind her, the other two Accelerate children placed small objects on the ground: a drawing, a broken circuit board, a marble. These were things they had taken and kept when they were still monsters, an offering to Leo's memory, whom they had once torn apart.

Dr. Voss approached slowly, her face stern but softened by emotion.

"This night," she said, "will be the last recorded day of our world as we knew it."

She looked toward the stars.

"And the first day of something new."

High above, the capsule silently entered the mesosphere, its trajectory gently shifting toward the orbital current that would slingshot it past Earth's decay. The onboard systems activated, recording data and preserving the child's body in perfect stasis. Mr. Bubbles, gripped in frozen fingers, stared blankly out of the viewing window as stars drifted by.

Somewhere, in that vast ocean of emptiness and brilliance, Leo had found his way home, the baby astronaut who stole the stars.

Chapter 14: Epilogue to the Age of Pisces

14.1: Twilight and Dawn

In the heart of the valley, an ocean of sunflowers stretched endlessly, their golden faces basking in the sun's warm embrace. Each bloom stood as a testament to resilience and hope. Amid this sea of yellow, a new species emerged, majestic stalks that towered above the rest, their bright yellow petals tinged with obsidian edges, as if night had gently kissed their rims. Their stems reached skyward, yearning to caress the heavens, embodying a silent prayer for ascension.

The children were the first to stumble upon these enchanting blossoms. Their laughter echoed through the valley as they wove the dark-edged sunflowers into intricate wreaths, adorning their heads like crowns, an intertwining of twilight and dawn. Their innocent fingers traced the velvety petals, marveling at the delicate contrast between light and dark, life and mystery.

At the valley's threshold, above the formidable gates of the bunker, a sign stood as a sentinel of change. Bold letters, set against a backdrop of stars rendered in vibrant hues of red, blue, and white, proclaimed a heartfelt message, a declaration, a promise, a vow to remember: "Welcome to Leoland."

14.2: The Names We Remember

"Who am I?" asked the blue-eyed, angel-faced boy, his voice soft yet trembling under the weight of unspoken questions. The air between them stilled. Though he appeared no older than ten, a closer look at his flawlessly symmetrical features and hauntingly large blue eyes revealed a sorrow far too deep for a child, a weary, timeworn soul trapped in the fragile frame of youth, shaped by loss, and burdened by memories no child should carry.

Dr. Voss looked up at him from her chair, the sun catching the silver threads in her hair. Her gaze held his without flinching, patient and unwavering, as if she had been waiting for that question for years. "Today," she said, her voice warm but husky with age, "you are Leo again." She smiled, a soft, wistful curve of her lips. "And your task for today is to push me in my wheelchair wherever I ask you to take me in Leoland."

The boy blinked slowly, as if testing the name in his mind, trying to wear it like an old coat rediscovered in a forgotten closet. "Leo," he repeated under his breath.

Dr. Voss sat swathed in a red blanket striped with faded blue, the fabric worn from use but clearly cherished. Her wheelchair creaked gently as she shifted, its aged frame as much a part of her now as her bones. She had long since made peace with its presence. What once represented limitation had become a vessel of resilience, proof that even broken bodies could carry unbroken spirits.

Her face bore the map of her years, lined with deep furrows of grief, hope, and hard-earned wisdom. Her silver hair, tucked neatly behind her ears, glowed like moonlight in the sun. She wore her lab coat loosely over a knit sweater, still scented faintly of antiseptic, a scent woven into her being like a memory. If one leaned closer, they would detect the faint perfume of herbal tea, lemongrass, chamomile, and something rarer, something ancient.

She was a woman who had once saved lives with steady hands and a fierce mind. The same hands that had sutured flesh, drawn blood, held dying patients, and penned formulas that changed the world, both for better and for worse. Her legacy was stitched into the very soil of the valley, into the children who now roamed freely where there had once been only quarantine and fear.

She reached out one hand, palm open to the boy. He took it.

For a moment, the valley hushed. A breeze stirred the sunflowers surrounding them, some golden and soft, others taller, strange, and new. Their petals fluttered like murmured blessings.

Some said the black-edged petals were Leo's breath, crystallized in pollen. Others believed the sunflowers turned not toward the sun, but toward the sound of laughter, especially the kind that was brief and unremembered. On quiet days, the valley whispered back, like tiny bells struck by invisible hands, echoing the names of children who had forgotten themselves but not each other.

Together, they moved forward, an old woman and a boy who was not quite a boy, two souls scarred by science, distraction, and time, pushing through the remnants of a broken world toward something that finally felt like healing.

14.3: After the Star Fell

Fifteen years ago, in the devastating aftermath of Leo's death, the world changed. Just hours after his passing, the virus that had ravaged the bloodstreams of the Accelerated children began to falter, its malevolent energy slowly fading away. Within days, the relentless plague that had once cast a shadow of dread over everyone vanished completely, leaving only memories of horror and loss. Leo, the anomaly whose brief life had been both a curse and a beacon of hope, ascended into the stars, his fate sealed in silence.

In that moment of bittersweet transcendence, Dr. Voss, a once-revered scientist whose work had been undermined by corporate greed, suggested that Ethan and Mia leave the safety of their bunker and flee north to Greenland. She offered them the keys to the last Amphibious Combat Vehicle, a relic from a bygone era of desperate survival, but they refused. They were done running. They declared they would wait until Aida and Jacobson returned, clinging to the hope of reuniting with their makeshift family.

And so, they stayed, Ethan, Mia, and the silence left in Leo's place.

Not to survive.

But to remember.

Three weeks after Leo's passing, Aida and Jacobson finally reappeared, like ghosts emerging from the ruins of a shattered world. Their return was bittersweet; both had foreseen the inevitable end, yet Leo's loss cut deeply into their souls. When they arrived, the sight of Mia's hand, miraculously healthy despite the devastation, sparked a fragile joy amidst the sorrow. They discovered that Aida's family farmhouse had been reduced to smoldering ashes, neighbors, gripped by fear of contagion from her little daughters, had burned it down while her family slept soundly.

Reunited, Dr. Jacobson and Dr. Voss, the former student and mentor, shared a quiet, unspoken relief in seeing each other again. Once more, Voss extended the offer of the Amphibious Combat Vehicle, proposing they move north. However, the four of them, Ethan, Mia, Aida, and Jacobson, chose to remain behind and care for the surviving children. Though the virus had dissipated, its lingering effects left the Accelerated children with a peculiar curse: they never aged beyond the point at which the virus left their bodies, and each morning, their memories would reset, leaving them with only a single day's recollection of their lives.

Yet, despite this cruel anomaly, the children awoke each day filled with unbridled joy. Their laughter, pure and unburdened by the weight of yesterday's sorrows, echoed through the bunker's corridors as they played in the hydroponic garden or among the sunlit fields of vibrant, defiant sunflowers that cloaked their refuge.

In that fragile sanctuary of survival, hope mingled with heartache. The promise of a new day shone like a beacon against the relentless march of time and memory loss. Although each sunrise brought the same challenge, living in the moment without quite remembering who they had been, the laughter of the children, the resilient spirit of the survivors, and the quiet determination of those left behind wove together a tapestry of defiance. Even as the scars of the past lingered, this small band of souls vowed to cherish every fleeting moment of love, remembrance, and hope, clinging to the belief that life, in all its fragility, was worth the fight.

14.4: The Ones Who Remembered

No one knew whose voice rang out first, a child's giggle, bright and irrepressible, spiraling up through the cracked concrete corridors of the bunker and scattering the shadows like startled birds. In that moment, it didn't matter what had come before, or what sorrow might return when the sun set again. For a little while, the only thing that existed was sunlight, dust motes, and the echo of joy.

One morning, a girl called Olivia, her name newly given, woke to the scent of lemon soap and soil. She didn't know where the scent came from, but it made her want to dance. She twirled through the hydroponic garden, arms outstretched, chasing motes of dust like fireflies. When Mia handed her a bowl of porridge, she whispered, "Thank you, Mama." The word startled them both, but for that day, it fit.

In the beginning, there were only nine children, six locked away in the cold, dark cells of the bunker, and three visitors who arrived in the wake of Leo's tragic death. Those first days blurred into a storm of fear and flickering hope. Ethan, Mia, Dr. Jacobson, and Aida roamed the desolate outskirts of ruined cities, searching for anything that could restore a semblance of life. As they wandered, they found more children, small, gaunt figures with eyes that shone with both hunger and a strange, stubborn delight. Each one was brought back to the bunker, carried like a secret promise.

Within those narrow walls, Ethan, Mia, Jacobson, Aida and Dr. Voss patched wounds, soothed fevers, and coaxed laughter from trauma. Mia and Aida washed and comforted the children with trembling hands, their own tears often falling silently into the bathwater. Sometimes a child would ask, "Why are you crying, Mama?" Or simply, "Thank you, Mama." In those moments, grief and gratitude mingled, binding the makeshift family closer.

So, the bunker transformed, piece by piece, from a vault of loss into a haven of memory. Each day began anew, every child reborn to their single day of selfhood, but the ones who loved them remembered everything.

In the soft glow of flickering fluorescent lights, the once sterile, oppressive space gradually morphed into a haphazard home, a place where hope felt as fragile as it was precious.

Over time, that ragtag group of children grew, evolving into a single, intertwined family. Their numbers grew to thirty-three, sixteen boys and seventeen girls, each orphaned by a world that forgot how to care. Every morning, a ritual began that was equal heartache and hope. The caretakers gathered the children in a central hall and, with a mixture of solemn duty and tender affection, assigned each child a name and daily tasks. At first, the names were chosen at random, and the chores were simple, desperate attempts to inject order into chaos. But as the days blurred into nights, and as each sunrise wiped away the previous day's memories, Dr. Jacobson meticulously developed a system. He affixed permanent name tags to each child's tattered shirt and kept a detailed journal of their talents, abilities, and small triumphs. Every morning, he would read aloud from that journal, a gentle, almost ritualistic reminder of who they were meant to be, even if their memories reset with each new dawn.

To these children, and to Ethan and Mia Dr. Jacobson and Aida had become parental figures in a world that had lost its families. Though Jacobson had never embraced traditional fatherhood, he found himself evolving into a steady, compassionate figure, a mentor whose stern exterior softened under Aida's nurturing warmth. For Ethan and Mia, who had known only the harsh lessons of survival, Dr. Voss became the grandmother they never had, a beacon of gentle strength amid the storm of loss and transformation. Though her research had been twisted by others, Dr. Voss carried no regret, only a quiet, unwavering commitment to mend what had been broken.

She remembered the first child she tried to save. Aran. Brown eyes. Liked toy trains. Dead within six days. His name was written in a leather-bound notebook she kept locked in a steel drawer, though she no longer needed to open it to see his face. Now, she whispered children's names to the sunflowers when no one was watching, planting their syllables like seeds. She hoped something holy would grow from what had been taken from her work.

Each day, the children's laughter echoed through the bunker like a fragile melody. They played in the hydroponic garden, where wilted lettuce and resilient sunflowers swayed together, a strange juxtaposition of decay and hope. In those moments, they discovered talents and abilities with surprising ease, and for a few blissful hours, they believed in the possibility of a future. However, by the next morning, all progress was wiped clean, and every child awoke as though it were the first day of their existence, a cruel twist that left them with only a single day's memory of who they once were.

In this turbulent, ever-reset world, Ethan, Mia, Jacobson, Aida, and Voss clung to one another. The daily ritual of naming and assigning tasks became an act of defiance against the erasure of their identities. Every time Dr. Jacobson read the names from his journal, it was as if he were resurrecting each child, affirming their existence in the face of an indifferent universe.

The bunker became a living archive of loss and hope, a place where every scraped knee, every burst of laughter, every tear shed stood as a testament to their resilience. Amidst the chaos, the bond between Ethan, Mia, Jacobson, Aida and Dr. Voss and the children grew unbreakable. They formed a family forged in the crucible of disaster, where the simple act of remembering one's name became a rebellion against oblivion.

Through every harsh sunrise and every dark, memoryless night, they endured. In the bunker, among the echoes of the past and the constant hum of survival, they discovered that hope could be rebuilt, even if it was measured in fleeting moments, in whispered names and laughter that defied the relentless passage of time. As the children played and Ethan, Mia, Jacobson, Aida, and Dr. Voss labored, they held onto the belief that each new day was a gift, a chance to rebuild a world where, despite everything, they could still remember who they truly were.

Now in their mid-twenties, Ethan and Mia had transformed into steadfast guardians of the poor children, watching over them with a fierce tenderness reminiscent of devoted siblings. The day the virus finally receded was etched into their souls, a day of raw, unfiltered emotion. As the once-feared malady dissolved into nothingness, the children emerged reborn. Their wide, unblemished eyes shone with brilliant clarity, and their angelic faces were alighted with pure laughter and unrestrained curiosity. In that moment, the monstrous, violent instincts that had once defined them as Accelerates were replaced by delicate innocence and fragile joy.

Ethan and Mia, who had borne the burden of loss and despair for so long, could not hold back their tears. The sight of these children, so untouched by the horrors of the past, ignited a profound, bittersweet hope within them. Every giggle and every small hand reaching out in wonder reminded them of what humanity had once been and what it could be again. The children, cleansed of the virus's shadow, embodied a rebirth of purity in a shattered world. For Ethan and Mia, it was a moment of catharsis, a promise that even after the darkest nights, dawn would come, bringing with it the potential for healing and renewal, a future built on the unyielding strength of hope and compassion.

14.5: *When the Earth Knew His Name*

In his early twenties, Ethan's heart began to change in ways he had never expected. What began as duty, protecting Mia, his closest friend and confidante, had become something deeper, almost sacred. He found himself looking at her with a tenderness that bordered on awe; his gaze lingered on her features with quiet affection, as if he were memorizing every line and curve for a future he could scarcely imagine. His protectiveness over her, once a reflex born of shared hardship, intensified into a fierce, all-consuming need. Mia, for her part, sensed this change. Part of her welcomed the closeness, a bond that could fill the void left by all they had lost, yet another part quivered with fear. In a world where she had already lost her parents, Clara, and even Leo, the thought of losing Ethan, the last person she held dear, filled her with an unspeakable dread.

The weight of her fear eventually became too much to carry alone. So, Mia turned to the one person who had always been a beacon of understanding: Doctor Voss, now known as Grandma Anya. In the quiet, dim light of the bunker's infirmary, Mia poured out her heart, her voice trembling as she recounted the terror of loss and the uncertainty of what the future might hold. Doctor Voss, a woman whose life had been marked by tragedy yet who still radiated resilient warmth, embraced Mia with compassion that made her feel truly seen. Each conversation with Grandma Anya was like a balm for Mia's aching soul, soothing her worries with a tenderness that sharply contrasted with the harshness of the world outside.

As time passed, Ethan's protective nature towards Mia and the children deepened even further. Life, as cruel as it had been, had also opened up new possibilities. Mia was now four months pregnant, a glimmer of life emerging amid the wreckage of their past. They had long ago decided on names, Clara for a girl, Leo for a boy. Yet, on a quiet afternoon in the bunker, Doctor Voss, with a knowing smile that expressed both sorrow and hope, delivered news that transformed their understanding of the future.

"You won't have to choose," she said gently, her voice filled with rare tenderness. "You'll have Clara and Leo. Twins." Her words landed like a quiet blessing, and for a moment, the burden of uncertainty lifted, replaced by cautious, flickering hope.

When the twins came, under a pink dawn and trembling sky, Ethan held Mia's hand as if anchoring her to the Earth. Clara came first, fists clenched, crying like the wind. Then Leo, silent... until a gasp escaped him. It sounded like pages turning.

Afterward, Ethan signed their names on torn paper and buried them beneath a sunflower. The next day, Leo's name had disappeared. "The earth already knows him," Mia whispered.

14.6: The Dawn Beyond the Reset

A year ago, a faint radio signal crackled in from Greenland, a message from another GeneCorp bunker where a small group of survivors had clung to life against all odds. Clara was right; there were survivors up north. Three families had emerged from that refuge, eleven adults and fifteen angel-faced children, arriving just two days prior. Their arrival, unexpected and miraculous, stood as a testament to the resilience of the human spirit, a beacon of light in dark times.

Leoland, as they called it, was alive with laughter. The once dreary bunker now resonated with rich, heartfelt echoes that spilled into the sunflower valley. The bunker, once dreary and silent, now echoed with laughter that spilled freely into the sunflower valley. It became a place where joy and strength coexisted, where the battered remnants of humanity found ways to smile despite grief and the march of time.

Ethan and Mia, once prisoners of their own despair, began to see new possibilities in the faces of the children who played in that hidden haven. The children, known as the Accelerated, experienced a daily reset of their memories and lived in an ephemeral existence. They now symbolized something more profound, a chance to rebuild, to start anew, and to reclaim a future that had been stolen from them. Every morning, as the children awoke with gleeful innocence and embraced each day as if it were their first, the caregivers found solace in the fragile rituals of naming, feeding, and comforting them. Each day was a small victory, a soft defiance against the tide of forgetting.

Yet, amid this tentative rebirth, the ghosts of the past still lingered. Mia's nights were haunted by memories of loss, and Ethan's eyes bore the weight of every tear shed for Leo, for Clara, and for the lives that had been extinguished in the wake of the virus. Still, even as they carried the deep scars of their former lives, they clung to the belief that every new dawn held the promise of renewal.

Dr. Voss, Dr. Jacobson, Aida, Ethan, Mia, and the families from north, all of these souls, battered yet defiant, formed a makeshift family in that underground sanctuary. Their days were filled with the labor of survival and the quiet determination to nurture the next generation. Every word, every kindness, every moment of shared laughter or tears became a quiet rebellion against the darkness that once swallowed them. They understood that rebuilding was not just about reclaiming physical space; it was about healing the shattered human spirit and finding beauty amid ruin.

As they gazed at the horizon, where the first light of dawn broke through the gloom, Ethan's thoughts often turned to the future, one where his children might grow up knowing not only the pain of loss but also the strength of love and the resilience of hope. It was a future they all longed for; a promise whispered in the quiet moments before sleep, a promise that even in the aftermath of devastation, life could and would endure.

In that hidden bunker, where memories reset each day and the past was as fragile as a whispered secret, the caregivers and their children forged a new beginning, a testament to the enduring power of hope, love, and the unyielding will to survive. And in that uncharted territory, they began, slowly, to heal.

Part IV

Prelude to the Age of Aquarius

In the deep, dark reaches of the Centaurus Constellation, where cosmic silence reigned and distant galaxies whispered secrets to the void, a brilliant star shone like a beacon. Its radiant light spilled across the abyss, gravity reaching out like an unseen hand, drawing in a small, weathered spacecraft. The ship, a muted gray vessel, was unexpectedly adorned with vibrant yellow sunflowers, a striking emblem of hope amid the cosmic desolation. It was as if nature had made a final, defiant stand in the face of endless space.

Hovering near the star, the spacecraft drifted slowly, inexorably drawn toward the luminous orb. On the surface of a nearby barren planetoid that orbited the star, four small figures, humanoid children, no older than five, gathered in a circle. They were clad in pristine white tunics, their garments flowing like spectral robes in the gentle cosmic breeze. Their expressions were solemn yet filled with childlike wonder, as if they sensed the arrival of this small ship was no accident, but destiny. With wide, open eyes, they watched in silent anticipation as the spacecraft descended toward them, cradled by the star's gravitational embrace.

The children, with angelic features and luminous eyes, embodied an unspoken promise of renewal in a universe that had long forgotten warmth. Each child was unique, a delicate variation on a celestial theme. One had pale, porcelain skin framed by a halo of golden, curly hair, his large blue eyes radiating crystalline innocence. Another boasted deep ebony skin that shimmered like polished onyx, with soulful black eyes and tight, midnight curls that gave him an air of enigmatic mystery. A third child had light golden skin, capturing the glow of the rising sun, complemented by warm brown eyes and softly curled hair framing his cherubic face. The fourth child had a rich copper-toned complexion with subtle olive undertones, his round face accentuated by gently wavy deep brown hair and striking olive eyes that sparkled with quiet determination.

Together, these children stood as living symbols of hope and resilience. Their diversity in appearance was a testament to the beauty of life's infinite variations, a tapestry of light and color promising that even in a desolate world, renewal and the gentle warmth of humanity could still blossom anew. Their small hands reached out tentatively, as if they could touch not just the craft, but the miracle it carried. In that moment, the harsh, cold vacuum of space seemed to pause, allowing a glimmer of life and beauty to flourish amid the ruins of cosmic desolation.

As the spacecraft drew nearer, its surface reflecting the star's dazzling light, the children's excitement mingled with quiet, almost reverent fear. Their hearts, pure and unburdened by adult sorrow, beat rapidly in anticipation. Each sunflower on the ship's hull glowed with an inner fire, a final burst of color in an otherwise monochromatic expanse. The scene presented a breathtaking juxtaposition of the cold, infinite void and the tender, fleeting spark of life.

In the silence of the cosmos, with only the hum of distant stellar winds breaking the quiet, the children's hopeful eyes shone like beacons. They were waiting, guardians of a new beginning, for the spacecraft to land. It was a sign that even in the vast emptiness of space, hope and beauty could still emerge. This moment represented a profound connection, where the natural world and the human spirit converged in the luminous embrace of a distant, brilliant star, a timeless testament to the enduring resilience of life, no matter how small and no matter how far from home.

The star's inner gates opened slowly, releasing a brilliant cascade of light, like liquid fire bursting across the darkness of space. From this celestial cascade emerged a small vessel, a fragile craft bearing the remnants of Leo, accompanied by four children whose faces shone with an almost divine purity. These children, possessing serene and otherworldly features, floated gracefully into the star's embrace. The vessel, scarred yet dignified, was gently guided into its designated shell, a chamber bathed in shimmering light that transformed its metal walls into an ethereal mosaic of colors.

Inside the softly illuminated chamber, the angelic children moved with deliberate grace. They approached a hovering keyboard glowing like stardust and energy, its mysterious symbols dancing across the keys in a language long forgotten by humankind. With tender precision, they began their work, their small fingers orchestrating a cosmic symphony as they recorded the annals of the past while simultaneously scripting the blueprint for the future. In that luminous sanctum, the symbols floated and converged, gradually assembling text that resonated with both ancient prophecy and hopeful promise:

"In the year 2100 of Our Lord on planet Earth, the human civilization of the Age of Pisces, originating in the year 1 with the miraculous birth of Our Lord's Son, came to an end. The new civilization of the Age of Aquarius on Earth began in the year of 2101 of Our Lord, marked by the passing of the Son of Man. May Our Lord bless the new beginnings of Man's children."

As these words appeared in the glowing light, the atmosphere was charged with a profound sense of transformation and destiny. The star's light bathed the scene in a celestial glow, and every pulse of energy seemed to resonate with echoes from centuries past. The angelic children, silent and focused, continued their work with an almost ritualistic fervor. Their eyes, deep and knowing, carried the weight of ancient secrets, and each keystroke balanced grief and hope.

The vessel, now securely encased, served not only as a resting place for Leo's remains but also as a guardian of a world undone by the weight of its own contradictions. The radiant message, inscribed in symbols older than time, stood as a testament to both the fall of one era and the rebirth of another, a declaration that from ruin, a new age would rise.

In that moment, the boundaries of time and memory blurred. The star's brilliant light mingled with the ethereal hum of the cosmic archive, and although the angelic children's voices were silent, they seemed to whisper promises of renewal. Every element of the scene, every flickering symbol, and every tender touch upon the glowing keys, spoke of an eternal cycle of destruction and rebirth. It was a solemn, bittersweet reminder that even as one era crumbled into dust, the seeds of the future were being sown in the radiant glow of a new dawn.

THE END

Table of Contents

If this book stayed with you, a quiet word shared with other readers helps it travel further.

About the Author

Tak Salmastyan writes speculative fiction that blurs the line between grief and transformation. A storyteller of emotional depth and visionary worlds, he explores what it means to survive the end of things, and to love anyway.

The Accelerates: Forty Days to Dust is his first novel.

More about him and his work as an artist can be found at: www.TakSalmastyan.com

Subscribe to my newsletter. Unsubscribe anytime.
For questions Email: drtaksalmastyan@gmail.com
www.TakSalmastyan.com

All Rights Reserved
Tak Salmastyan Art

www.ingramcontent.com/pod-product-compliance
Lightning Source LLC
Chambersburg PA
CBHW070440300726
48975CB00007B/1989